Hideaway

D0776443

ROCHELLE ALERS

NATIONAL BESTSELLING AUTHOR

A Hideaway Novel

Hideaway

ARABESQUE®

If you purchased this book without a cover you should be aware that this book is stolen property. It was reported as "unsold and destroyed" to the publisher, and neither the author nor the publisher has received any payment for this "stripped book."

Recycling programs
for this product may
not exist in your area.

HIDEAWAY

An Arabesque novel published by Kimani Press/October 2009

First published by BET Books in 1995.

ISBN-13: 978-0-373-83167-8

© 1995 by Rochelle Alers

All rights reserved. The reproduction, transmission or utilization of this work in whole or in part in any form by any electronic, mechanical or other means, now known or hereafter invented, including xerography, photocopying and recording, or in any information storage or retrieval system, is forbidden without written permission. For permission please contact Kimani Press, Editorial Office, 233 Broadway, New York, NY 10279 U.S.A.

This is a work of fiction. Names, characters, places and incidents are either the product of the author's imagination or are used fictitiously, and any resemblance to actual persons, living or dead, business establishments, events or locales is entirely coincidental.

® and TM are trademarks. Trademarks indicated with ® are registered in the United States Patent and Trademark Office, the Canadian Trade Marks Office and/or other countries.

www.kimanipress.com

Printed in U.S.A.

Dear Reader,

When *Hideaway* was first published in 1995, I couldn't have anticipated the overwhelming response to the story of Martin Cole and Parris Simmons, and the characters and stories that have followed. Since that first novel, the series has been a reader favorite. I'm constantly being asked when the next HIDEAWAY romance is coming out. Not surprisingly, I find myself returning to these characters and their stories over and over again.

I am currently hard at work on the fourteenth novel in the series, which will be released next year. And for those of you who are fans of the Coles and their extended family and friends, I hope you enjoy the first book as much as the others.

Yours in romance,

Rochelle Alers

HIDEAWAY SERIES

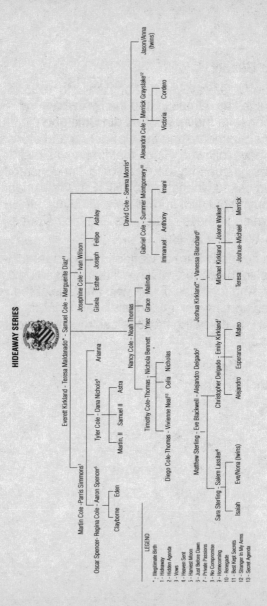

Everett Kirkland - Teresa Maldanado* - Samuel Cole - Marguerite Diaz[11]

Martin Cole -Parris Simmons[1]

Oscar Spencer- Regina Cole - Aaron Spencer[6]

Clayborne

Eden

Tyler Cole - Dana Nichols[5]

Arianna

Martin, II   Samuel II   Astra

Nancy Cole - Noah Thomas

Josephine Cole - Ivan Wilson

Gisela   Esther   Joseph   Felipe   Ashley

David Cole - Serena Morris[4]

Gabriel Cole - Summer Montgomery[10]

Immanuel   Anthony   Imani

Alexandra Cole - Merrick Grayslake[12]

Victoria   Cordero

Jason/Anna (twins)

Timothy Cole-Thomas - Nichola Bennett

Diego Cole-Thomas - Vivienne Neal[13]   Celia   Nicholas

Ynez   Grace   Malinda

Joshua Kirkland* - Vanessa Blanchard[3]

Christopher Delgado - Emily Kirkland[7]

Alejandro   Esperanza   Mateo

Michael Kirkland - Jolene Walker[8]

Teresa   Joshua-Michael   Merrick

Matthew Sterling - Eve Blackwell - Alejandro Delgado[9]

Sara Sterling - Salem Lassiter[2]

Isaiah   Eve/Nona (twins)

LEGEND

* – Illegitimate Birth
1 – Hideaway
2 – Hidden Agenda
3 – Vows
4 – Heaven Sent
5 – Harvest Moon
6 – Just Before Dawn
7 – Private Passions
8 – No Compromise
9 – Homecoming
10 – Renegade
11 – Best Kept Secrets
12 – Stranger In My Arms
13 – Secret Agenda

IN LOVING MEMORY OF MY
FLORIDA ANCESTORS...

The Jameses and the McLearys—
for their pride and determination

and

Marie Tuggle—
for her beauty and her strength

The wicked bring on themselves the suffering they try to cause good people.
—*Proverbs* 21:18

Prologue

"Yes, Joan?" Martin Cole asked when he heard his secretary's voice on the intercom.

"Mr. Kirkland is here to see you," Joan informed her boss in her usual competent manner, "and, Martin, I want to remind you that you have a luncheon appointment with your father at twelve-thirty."

Martin, rising to his feet, laid aside the file he had been studying. "Send Mr. Kirkland in. Then call my father and let him know I'll be late. Tell him to have a drink on me, but wait to order lunch."

A smile creased Martin's face the moment Joshua Kirkland stepped into his office. Joshua's deeply tanned skin, shimmering pale green eyes and grim expression went unnoticed as Martin spied the large envelope under his friend's arm. He extended his hand. "Welcome back. How did it go?"

Joshua shifted the envelope to shake Martin's hand. "Well enough, but I could use a drink right now."

Martin nodded although the last thing he wanted was to turn this meeting into a social drinking session. He'd been waiting two weeks for the information he was certain Joshua had gathered for him.

"Brandy or scotch?" Martin asked, moving over to a credenza

stocked with the finest imported wines and liqueurs. He glanced over his shoulder at the tall, slender man now seated on a leather chair beside his desk.

"Scotch, straight up," Joshua replied.

Martin poured a double shot of premium aged scotch into a glass, then prepared a splash of brandy for himself. His footsteps were muffled on the thick carpeting in the spacious sun-filled office which towered above West Palm Beach's populous and traffic. Florida was enjoying its warmest winter season in years.

Joshua took the glass, raising it in a salute before draining its contents quickly. He stared at the prisms of light in the multifaceted glass for several seconds. His transparent gaze shifted to Martin's arresting face, his stoic expression unchanged.

"Have your drink first, then take a look at this." He handed Martin the envelope.

Martin tossed off the brandy, grimacing as a burning sensation exploded in his chest. He ran a finger under the flap of the envelope, spilling its contents out on the desk.

The natural color drained from Martin's dark face, leaving it a sickly, sallow, yellowish shade. He closed his eyes, but the images on the black and white photographs littering his desk continued to attack him. He could see Parris Simmons's haunting face, and that of a young child. It had only taken a glance to know who the child was.

"I take it you didn't know about the child?"

Sagging weakly to a chair, hands gripping the armrests for support, Martin felt weak. How could he feel hot and cold at the same time?

"Martin? Are you all right?" came Joshua's voice when he didn't respond.

"Josh," Martin finally whispered. His voice came out ragged, weak. His hands were shaking, but there wasn't anything he could do to stop them as he picked up the photos.

"Where is she?"

"Parris lives in New York. Westchester County to be precise."

"Is she married?"

Joshua let out his breath slowly, noting the return of healthy color to Martin's face. "You asked me to locate Parris Simmons and I did."

Despite his shock, Martin smiled. Joshua Kirkland only did what he was ordered to do. No more, no less. There were times when he believed the man was a machine. In the seventeen years he had come to know him, he never saw an outward display of emotion. It was as if there was no room in Joshua's life for love, laughter, or even anger.

"Give me some more background information on the lady, Martin, and I'll let you know what I've come up with."

Martin leaned over and pushed a button on the intercom. "Joan, hold all my calls, and cancel my appointment with my father. I'm unavailable for the remainder of the afternoon."

"What about the Jeffries meeting?" the secretary questioned.

"Cancel it!" His tone had taken on the sharp edge Joan rarely heard. She did not argue with him.

Martin could not pull his gaze away from the photographs. Memories came rushing back to open wounds he'd allowed to heal with time. His head came up slowly, and he found Joshua watching him and waiting for him to speak. Martin didn't know how to begin to tell him about the woman who once held his fate within her hands, but decided he'd start at the beginning. That way it would be easier.

"I met Parris at an engagement dinner party ten years ago…"

PART ONE

Chapter 1

Martin Diaz Cole was thoroughly bored; bored with the people gathered in a private room at a Palm Beach restaurant, bored with the woman standing by his side and bored with her incessant nonsensical chatter.

"Will you please be a darling and get me another glass of white wine, Martin," the petite brunette crooned, her tiny hand thrusting an empty wineglass at him.

Ignoring her request and the outstretched glass, Martin's attention was momentarily diverted. His dark eyes were fixed on a woman who appeared to float into the room.

His gaze took in everything about her in one quick penetrating glance. This woman, this stranger, and a stranger she was because he knew every one of the guests Jon Grant and Brittany Alexander had invited to their engagement party.

She was tall, at least five-eight, and incredibly slender. The off-the-shoulder white dress ended several inches below her long shapely legs, clinging to and outlining the curve of her full breasts, narrow waist and slim hips.

Staring at her, Martin experienced an emotion he hadn't felt in years: lust. No, he thought, it was more like a craving. He saw something he wanted, and there weren't too many things he wanted that he did not get.

"Martin," the brunette wailed, her lovely features distorted in distress as she noted the direction of his attention.

"Excuse me, Sonia," he apologized softly, making his way across the room, leaving a pouting Sonia to find another fawning male to do her bidding. He watched as Brittany hugged the woman before pulling back and showing her the diamond ring on her finger.

His own hands were thrust into the pockets of his black linen slacks as he waited patiently for Brittany to notice him. Brittany glanced his way and he smiled at her.

Brittany tossed back a head of naturally waving ash-blond hair, gesturing. "Martin, please come meet a friend of mine. Parris and I were roommates at college. Parris Simmons, Martin Cole. Martin's Jon's best man," she said to Parris, not pausing to take a breath.

Stepping closer to Parris, Martin stared down at her upturned face. Her golden-brown skin was deeply tanned from the Florida summer sun and radiated a natural glow of good health which did not come from makeup. Her chemically-straightened dark shiny hair was styled in a flattering shag-cut feathering around her face and neck. Naturally arching eyebrows and thick long black lashes framed a pair of eyes that were a clear brown with just a hint of dark green in their mysterious depths. Her nose was short and rounded at the tip and her mouth was full, temptingly curved, and Martin found Parris to be the most beautiful woman he'd ever met.

Extending a slender hand, Parris gave him a tight smile. "It's nice meeting you, Martin."

It took several seconds before he reacted to her polite greeting. The low husky timbre of her voice was not what he had expected from her. The dulcet throaty tones were like a fog, cloaking and enveloping in a sensual web of raw seduction.

He grasped her hand, holding it firmly before releasing her fingers. "The pleasure is all mine," he replied, finding his own voice.

"You'll get a chance to talk to Parris later, Martin," Brittany promised. "I want to introduce her to Jon."

Martin nodded, staring at Parris as she walked away with Brittany. He spent the next twenty minutes chatting with some of the other guests until he garnered Brittany's attention again.

"I want you to seat me next to Parris," he said quietly.

Brittany's pale gray eyes widened with his request. "No, Martin."

"Why not?" he countered.

"She's not like that."

"Not like what, Brittany?"

She exhaled audibly. How could she explain to her fiancé's best friend that Parris Simmons was not like the women Martin Cole usually dated.

"She's different," she explained, a need to protect her friend surfacing. "She's not like the women you men pass around whenever you tire of her."

Martin's face darkened under his deeply browned olive complexion. Running a hand through the thick curling black hair falling to his shoulders, he glanced down at the highly polished toes of his imported slip-ons and smiled.

"I don't want to sleep with her Brittany," he replied softly. "I just want you to make certain we're seated together when we sit down to eat."

Brittany stared at the man whose devastatingly dimpled smile was hypnotic. She was always astounded by Martin's masculine beauty. His African-American-Cuban ancestry had afford him exquisite dark-brown coloring, large dark eyes, sweeping black eyebrows, high cheekbones, a thin delicate nose and a full sensual mouth which made him almost too beautiful for a man. He had it all—looks and money.

"You're not lying to me, are you?" she asked him.

Twin dimples creased the lean tanned cheeks of the man with the curly black hair and winning smile. "No."

She didn't understand him. Martin usually had women fighting one another for his attention. At twenty-nine he was one of the most sought-after bachelors along Florida's Gold Coast. Women usually chased Martin Diaz Cole, not the other way around.

"Okay," she conceded. "But if you try…"

"You worry too much," Martin interrupted. "I'll take good care of her."

He spent the remainder of the cocktail hour totally entranced by Parris Simmons. He watched her as she smiled and flirted with many of the single men who appeared as equally entranced as he. He ignored all that was going on around him, studying the woman who had cast a spell over him without her being aware of it.

Everyone filed into an adjoining room at the restaurant as waiters announced that seating was prearranged and directed each guest to their assigned table.

Parris searched her table, locating her name on a place card and a large dark-brown hand pulled out a chair for her. She glanced up to find Martin Cole standing beside her.

"Miss Simmons," he said, his mellifluent voice soft and caressing, as he offered to seat her.

"Thank you," she replied shyly, permitting him to seat her. He sat down next to her and she sucked in a lungful of air. Being in Martin's presence was like his walking into a room and using up all of the oxygen from the other occupants. He left her gasping and feeling lightheaded.

She had read about Martin and occasionally heard his name mentioned by several of the interior designers she worked with, but he had been just that—a name. This tall man looming over her by more than half a foot was intoxicating.

She remembered an article branding him as "the brash, young Rupert Murdoch of the Caribbean." He had acquired large tracts of land throughout the Caribbean the way Rupert Murdoch acquired newspapers and television networks.

Martin's business acumen had netted his family holdings untold wealth and power while the Cole name had become synonymous with the importation of tropical produce, private villas and vacation resorts throughout Central America and the Caribbean.

Business Week, Money and *Forbes* magazines had all reported the meteoric rise of the Cole influence in the world of Latin American finance. The articles noted that Martin had inherited his business expertise from his Cuban-born maternal grandfather who once owned the largest cigar-producing plantation in pre-revolutionary Cuba, and his own father. Samuel Claridge Cole was the great-great-great-grandson of African-American slaves, who after the Civil War went into business cultivating the crop that their disenfranchised ancestors grew and picked: cotton. The cotton crop gave way to peanuts and finally to soybeans.

After taking a surreptitious glance at Parris's profile, Martin stared at her ringless fingers. "Are you also into art?" he asked, initiating conversation. She arched a questioning eyebrow. "Brittany said the two of you were college roommates," he reminded her. If she went to college with Brittany, then that meant they were about the same age—twenty-two or twenty-three, he calculated quickly.

"No, I'm an interior decorator." Both she and Brittany had attended the Savannah College of Art and Design. Brittany majored in art history while she studied design.

"And I know what you do," she said, watching a flush darken his face.

He arched his sweeping black eyebrows. "And just what is it I do, Parris?" There was a slight rolling of the double r's in her name when he said it.

Her hazel-colored gaze was fixed on his mouth. "You're…" She hesitated, hoping to come up with an appropriate description of his business activities. Calling him a corporate raider or shark was a compliment.

He leaned closer. "I'm a what?"

"An oppressor of human beings," she said instead.

He laughed softly. "I'm a businessman, Parris. Everything I do is legal and ethical."

"You own plantations. Your companies make slaves of people because they're only paid pennies a day."

His large eyes widened until she could see their black depths. "The companies my family owns pay adequate wages."

"Slave wages?"

"It appears as if you've been misinformed, or perhaps you'd

like to subsidize their *pennies."* A hint of a smile touched his mobile mouth. "I think we should talk about this later, and…"

"I won't be around later," she cut in. "I'm only here for the dinner."

Martin felt his pulse quicken. "You don't live here?"

Parris almost laughed at his startled expression and she gave him what she called her best "kool-aid grin." It was apparent Martin Cole was used to having women at his beck and call.

"No." What she didn't tell him was that she didn't live in Palm Beach, but in neighboring West Palm Beach.

She turned her attention to the man on her right, giving him a sensual smile while Martin's dark eyes gleamed like glassy volcanic rock.

He listened to the haunting sound of her low voice as she conversed with the other man. He saw Brittany smile at him from another table across the room.

Brittany was surprised when he didn't return her smile but she did register frustration on his handsome face. It was apparent his charm had been lost on Parris. There was no way she could reveal to him that the last thing Parris wanted was to become involved with a man—even if that man was the enviable Martin Diaz Cole.

Several courses were served before Martin solicited Parris's attention again. He pointed to the full glass of wine at her place setting. "You don't drink." His query sounded more like a statement than a question.

She turned and stared at him. "Not very much."

"You should at least try it. It happens to be an excellent vintage."

"I'll pass on the wine tonight."

Leaning closer, he pressed his shoulder to hers, the fragrance of her scented body lingering in his nostrils. "Are you always this charming?" he whispered.

He registered her slight intake of breath and the rapidly beating pulse in her throat. He had gotten a response from her.

Parris bit down on her lower lip, praying the heat in her face would subside quickly. When was she going to stop punishing other men for her ex-husband? she thought suddenly. Perhaps she had been too hard on Martin.

Resting her chin on her hand, she offered him a warm, open smile. "You should see me when I really turn it on," she teased.

"Oh really?"

She nodded, lowering her lashes. "Really."

"That should be something to see." He hit his forehead with the heel of his hand. "I forgot. I'll never get the opportunity to see it because you're only here for the dinner."

She sobered quickly. She knew she wouldn't see Martin again until Brittany's wedding. Brittany and Jon were to be married on September twenty-eighth, and that was four weeks away.

"I'll see you at the wedding," she reminded him.

He studied her face thoughtfully for a moment. "I suppose I'll have to wait until *then,* won't I?"

Parris saw an open invitation smoldering in the depths of his eyes, and decided to ignore it. "Yes, Martin," she whispered.

His jaw tightened noticeably. He had to find out what it was about her that drew him to her.

Brittany was right. Parris was not like the women he usually dated. They were older and appeared much more worldly than the woman sitting next to him. And more likely than not they were the sisters, cousins, nieces, and a few of them, daughters of business associates.

"Is this your first time meeting Jon?" Martin asked.

"Yes, even though I feel as if I've known him as long as Brittany has. Brittany and I keep in touch by phone."

"Where do you live?"

"West Palm Beach."

"That's only…"

"I know," she cut in. "It's only a few miles away, but I don't have much time for visiting friends. My job takes me out of the state for at least twenty days each month."

And when she returned home it was to a furnished studio apartment. She sold her car because it sat in her landlady's garage for four months without her moving it. Now, whenever she needed to go somewhere she called a car service.

"What do you decorate?"

"Corporate offices. I select everything: desks, chairs, tables, lighting and accessories."

He registered the breathless quality of her voice and the excitement lighting up her eyes as she spoke. Like him, she enjoyed her career.

"Do you like the traveling?" he questioned.

"It depends on the place and the time of the year," she replied honestly. "Hawaii is always nice, as is Puerto Rico. Arizona and Nevada in the summer are always brutal, but staying in the best hotels with all of the amenities makes up for it."

Martin waited while a waiter removed their dishes before serving the next course. He was fascinated with Parris. She was different from the other women because she had talent to go along with her perfect face and body. It was the first time he discovered all three components in one woman.

"Take me, for instance," he said, resuming their conversation. "You seem to know about my line of business. How would you decorate an executive office for me?"

"It's not that easy." She gave him a warm smile. "Your executive style must harmonize with the image of your company while it lets you show your individuality. It must set you off but not dominate you, reflect you but not overpower you."

"How do you determine an office's personality?"

"I work from an executive's professional dossier."

"How do you feel about awards and personal photographs?"

"A profusion of family photographs may transmit too much intimacy; however a wall full of diplomas and awards signals insecurity to more people than it impresses."

Martin was impressed with Parris and her intelligence.

"How did you get your job?"

"I was recruited after I graduated. One of my professors worked for the architectural and design firm, so I suppose you can say that I had an in."

"Where do you see yourself in relation to the firm in another ten years?" It was a question he asked the many applicants who applied to ColeDiz for even fewer coveted positions in his family-owned company.

Parris reached for a water goblet and took a sip of water. She placed the goblet down beside the glass of wine. She knew where she wanted to be in ten years, and it was not in Florida.

"I'd like to live abroad. I want to decorate international offices, restored châteux, villas, and castles."

"I take it the company you work for has an overseas branch?"

She nodded the affirmative, giving him the name of the firm, and he whistled softly. Parris worked for the most prestigious architectural and design firm in the country.

"I think you'd better eat your filet mignon before the waiters serve the next course," she suggested in a low throaty tone.

She spent the next three-quarters of an hour exchanging pleasantries with both Martin and the man on her right. The silent, efficient waiters cleared the tables once again before coffee and dessert were offered. Cordials and liqueurs were passed around, and again she refused their offer.

She and the other guests sighed and murmured approval as Brittany opened boxes and cards. Most of the gifts were purchased from Nieman Marcus where Brittany was listed with their bridal registry.

Everyone's attention was directed to Martin after Brittany opened an envelope and read the printed card. He had offered to pay all of the expenses for Jon's and Brittany's honeymoon anywhere in the world.

Parris watched as Martin's expression never changed. He merely nodded his thanks, his dark eyes moving from Brittany's to Jon's smiling faces.

Glancing down at her watch, Parris noted the time. She had to leave. It was almost eight-thirty. The car service was scheduled to pick her up in ten minutes.

Placing her napkin on the table beside her plate, she whispered a "nice meeting you" to the dining partners flanking her and walked out of the room.

The restaurant's lobby overflowed with elegant men and women in formal dress. The precious stones hanging from scented pampered necks and wrists competed with the many shimmering lights on the massive overhead chandeliers.

Parris saw him before he saw her, but still she could not escape. Standing by the entrance to the restaurant was Owen Lawson, her ex-husband. There was no way she could get past him without him seeing her.

Then without warning, he turned away and she walked quickly through the door and out to the restaurant's parking lot.

Her heart pounded uncontrollably as she paced back and forth in the lot, smiling nervously at the young men who wore the short red bolero jackets of the valet parking staff.

Glancing down at her watch, Parris prayed silently for her driver to appear. She did not want a confrontation with Owen. Her trying to secure an annulment to their short-lived marriage had been too stressful and their last face-to-face confrontation too volatile to risk another encounter with him.

She felt the fingers snake around her upper arm before she heard the voice.

"Do you need a ride?"

"Don't scream, Parris," he warned. "And please don't make a scene."

She ignored the runaway pumping of her heart in her chest as she faced down Owen Lawson. "What the hell do you want?" she spat out.

"You still have a tongue that cuts like a whip." He managed a smile but it looked more like a sneer. "Roll it up, Parris."

"Let go of me."

"Not yet. Not until we talk."

She stared up at the man she thought she had loved beyond reason. The tall gaunt man with the most beautiful ebony-colored skin she had ever seen. The man whose intense dark eyes had

had the power to read her thoughts. The man she loved until she married him.

"There's nothing to talk about, Owen." She wanted to scream at him whatever they'd shared had died. There was truly nothing left to discuss.

Owen's dark eyes behind the lenses of his equally dark glasses swept over his ex-wife's face and body. She was more beautiful than when she left him. It was as if she had grown up in only a year.

"Just this last time, then I'll walk away from you and never bother you again. I promise."

"I'm waiting for my driver."

"I'll take you home," he insisted.

She tried pulling away from him. "We'll talk another time. I'll call you…"

Owen tightened his grip. "Let's go."

Parris winced at the punishing hold on her upper arm. This was an Owen she had never seen before. They had exchanged heated words, but he never attempted to hurt her.

"Don't fight with me," he hissed near her face, his gaze brimming with white-hot rage and resentment.

Owen glared at his beautiful wife. Parris Simmons had walked out on him. She left him while mockingly issuing a threat which continued to haunt his every moment of wakefulness, and it was only now that the threat attacked him even as he slept. He had tried to forget her but he couldn't. Parris was too indelibly imprinted on his brain to forget. She was a witch who had cursed him, and he wanted to be freed from her wicked spell.

He signaled a valet who rushed to bring his car to the front of the lot. The young man thanked the man in formal dress profusely while silently admiring the woman whom he held possessively to his side.

Owen settled Parris into his low-slung Miata, then walked around to the driver's side. He started up the car, switched on the headlights, then roared out of the parking lot. The setting sun was a large ball of orange fire as he drove toward the beach, unaware that a sleek black Jaguar purred quietly behind him, keeping a respectable distance.

Chapter 2

Owen pulled into a parking area less than three hundred feet from the ocean. He came around the car, extended his hand and helped Parris out.

They walked together in silence under the full moon, hand-in-hand, until the dampness of salt water seeped into their shoes. Owen glanced up and down the beach, smiling. There was no one else in sight.

He tightened his hold on Parris's hand, making her his prisoner. "You're not going to leave me again."

She fought against his cruel grip. "Wrong, Owen. Because I *left* you."

He pulled her to his chest. "Wrong, Parris. You're not going to leave me because I'm taking you with me."

She panicked as Owen dragged her toward the incoming tide. "Stop! You're mad!"

"If I'm mad it was you who made me mad, Parris Lawson. I wanted you and needed you so much that I went just a little crazy. But you never wanted me. You never loved me."

Sheer black fright swept through Parris when she realized Owen wanted to drown her. "No," she gasped, panting in terror.

"It's too late for pleading, Mrs. Lawson," he intoned. "It's too late for me. Too late for us."

Panic rioted within her and she fought him with every ounce of strength in her body. Her free hand pounded his face.

Owen cursed savagely under his breath and he knew he had to end the nightmare quickly. Half-carrying and half-dragging Parris, he pulled her into the water as angry waves swelled, breaking over his knees.

His sunglasses fell and he cursed louder when the lenses cracked under the heel of his shoe. He looked down into the blackness of the swirling water his grip on Parris slacking.

Her right hand swung again, connecting with his left eye. He howled in pain, heat and bright lights sending him to his knees. She went down with him while struggling vainly to escape.

He pulled her back with a jerk of her hair. His right arm swung up in a curve and came down once, his fist connecting with the left side of her face.

Parris heard the snap of bones, the searing fire, then blessed blackness.

Owen stared down at her motionless body, tears filling his eyes. He hadn't meant to hurt her. He loved her too much to hurt her. Picking Parris up gently, he rose to his feet and faced the Atlantic Ocean once again. Balancing her limp body, he cradled her to his chest.

"I love you, Parris. I love you," he murmured over and over as he walked out into the pounding waves.

The swirling dangerous undertow pulled him down and he dropped Parris. Struggling to regain his footing, he searched the water for his wife.

Whispering a small prayer of thanks, he caught the back of her dress and lifted her from what would have become a watery grave. He didn't want her to go without him. They would go together.

He lifted her higher as the waves assaulted his chest, ignoring the sting of salt water and the iciness beading his flesh. Soon both of them would be warm. Warm and asleep together.

Owen never heard the footsteps spewing sand, the raspy heavy breathing and the shouting over the roar of the waves. His gaze was fixed on the cold wet blackness beckoning him. But he did feel the numbing pain at the back of his neck which seemed to sever his spinal cord. He also felt the next blow which spun him around and closed an eye within seconds. The third blow fell, but it was lost on the unconscious man who sank down to the water in slow motion, relinquishing the woman in his arms to the ocean.

Martin swept Parris from the water and stumbled back to the sand. His fingers searched for a pulse. It throbbed weakly under his touch. She was alive.

Breathing easier for the first time since he stood on the beach watching the man carry Parris into the ocean, Martin stood up and raced back to the water. A cold knot formed in his stomach when he couldn't find the fallen body. He looked around frantically until his foot hit a solid form. Hooking his hands under Owen's shoulders, he lifted him easily over his own shoulder and retraced his steps back to the beach.

Owen lay on the sand, moaning and crying at the same time. He tried standing, but collapsed face-down. His whimpers sounded like those of an injured animal.

Martin ignored the man as he swept Parris up in his arms and carried her to his car. Her skin was cold—too cold. He had to take care of her.

Placing her unconscious body on the rear leather seats, he searched the trunk of the car and found a blanket. Quickly and methodically he wrapped the blanket around her body. She hadn't moved or made a sound. The Jaguar's dome light revealed the damage to her jaw, and Martin nearly lost his composure as he stared down at the quickly swelling mass of bruised flesh that had been a delicate cheek.

Reaching for his car phone, he dialed a number and smiled when he heard the break in the connection. His voice revealed none of his anxiety as he asked that Luis Lopez meet him at his house.

Parris felt the rocking motion and came awake. Glancing around, she saw the pale color of leather seats. She was in a car not the ocean. She was safe. Owen decided not to drown her.

Her breath came out in a ragged shudder as she tried sitting up. The motion intensified the fire along the left side of her face, and when she tried opening her mouth that side of her face seemed to collapse. Streaks of fire shot to her temple and she sank down to the seat, mewling like a kitten.

After what seemed like hours the car stopped. Parris was chilled to the bone and every time she clenched her jaw she experienced another spasm of pain.

The back door opened and she was lifted gently into a pair of strong arms. Closing her eyes, she reveled in the warm body cradling hers.

"How is she?" she heard a male voice ask.

"She's in pain, Luis. A great deal of pain."

Parris's eyes opened when she recognized the second voice. Her mouth couldn't form the words but her head screamed his name. Martin Cole had saved her life!

"Put her on a table," Dr. Luis Lopez ordered, as he unlocked the front door to Martin's town house.

Overhead lighting in the large modern kitchen highlighted the ravages of Martin's battle with the ocean to rescue the woman with the severely bruised face. His thick black hair was plastered to his scalp and coated with salt.

"Why don't you clean yourself up while I examine her," Luis suggested. "She'll be all right, Martin," he assured him when he didn't move.

It was with a great deal of reluctance that Martin left Parris to Luis's professional medical ministration. Walking up the staircase to his bedroom and into an adjoining bath, he removed his watersoaked shoes, socks, shirt and slacks, leaving them on the tiled floor. He headed for the shower stall and stood under the warm spray of the shower until he felt clean.

Flexing his right hand, he stared at his bruised knuckles. A violent shudder rippled through his body as he recalled the rage taking him beyond himself when he'd hit the man trying to drown Parris.

He had never assaulted another human being in all of his life, but he had experienced perverse pleasure in beating the man. At that moment he had wanted to kill him. Bracing his back against the cool tiles along the stall, he closed his eyes reliving the frightening scene.

He'd called himself the king of fools when he decided to follow Parris because she was not receptive to his advances, not knowing he would have to rescue her from a madman.

A wry smile softened his sensual mouth by the time he reached for a bottle of shampoo. He washed his hair, soaped and rinsed his body twice before he felt cleansed. The water washed away his guilt for injuring another person and it also redeemed him. He had saved a life.

Dressed in a pair of well-worn jeans, a white golf shirt and a pair of running shoes, Martin walked into the kitchen.

"How is she?" he asked, speaking in Spanish and hoping Parris didn't understand the language.

"She can't hear you," Luis said. "I've put her under."

Martin moved closer to the table, trying not to stare at Parris's face.

"You were right, Martin, her jaw is shattered. She should be in a hospital. Her jaw needs to be immobilized so the bones can heal properly."

"Can't you do it here?"

"Martin, I'm not a miracle worker. Your kitchen is not a mobile hospital."

He knew what he was asking Luis to do was not only unprofessional, but unethical. He had asked Luis to treat Parris at his home instead of at a hospital. But what Luis didn't know was that he couldn't risk exposing Parris to further danger. He didn't know who the man was who tried to kill her, and he had no way of knowing if there was someone else who wanted her dead.

"Luis, please. Put her face back together for me." There was a faint tremor in his voice.

Martin's voice was low, the words pleading, and for the first time since Luis Lopez had come to know Martin he recognized humility in the man. He didn't know who the woman was who lay on the table in the dining area, but he knew she had to be special.

Against his better judgment, Luis ordered, "Get a couple of sheets and spread one out on the countertop. I'll use the other one to cover her body." He mumbled under his breath about not operating under sterile conditions, but he mumbled to himself. Martin had left to do his bidding.

Parris woke the following afternoon and stared up at the nut-brown face belonging to a smiling figure dressed in a white uniform. She couldn't return the friendly smile so she nodded instead.

"Well, gal," the nurse said, "Ruby Johnson is going to take good care of you." She placed a cool hand on her forehead. "It looks like Dr. Lopez did a fine job of taking care of your jaw. A real fine job indeed." She smoothed down a lightweight blanket, folding it back to the foot of the large bed.

"You're real lucky, gal," Ruby continued. "You managed to get yourself one of the best surgeons in the state and one of the best-looking men on the planet for a fiancé."

Parris sat up but Ruby moved quickly, pushing her gently down to the pillows cradling her shoulders. "Stay put or you'll pull the IV out of your hand." Ruby's friendly smile faded. "You're not allowed out of bed. I'll let you know when you can get out."

Closing her eyes, Parris wanted to scream that she didn't have a fiancé.

"Mr. Cole said he would cook for you once Dr. Lopez orders the removal of the IV. But you know of course everything will have to be pureed and ingested through a straw. And you'll probably lose some weight before you're able to chew solid foods. Not that you can afford to lose an ounce. You're nothing but skin and bones already."

Ruby Johnson, with more than thirty-five years of experience as a hospital staff nurse, relished her second career in private duty nursing. She worked when she wanted to, was offered a choice of cases and the per diem rate of pay was excellent.

Parris listened and watched Ruby moving around the

bedroom. Turning her head slowly, she examined the space, her uninjured eye registering sliding doors leading to a balcony. She heard the distant roar of rushing water through the screen before realizing the increasing roar was within her own head.

She closed her eyes, suffering in silence as the dull throbbing pain in her face intensified. She needed something for the pain. Tears, she couldn't control, leaked from under her lids, over her cheeks and into her hairline. The pillow beneath her head was dotted with moisture when Martin walked into the room to look in on her.

"What's the matter, Parris?"

She opened her eyes and saw Martin by the bed. Her lower lip trembled uncontrollably as her chest rose and fell under the cover of a sheet.

His face loomed closer. "Are you in pain?" he asked perceptively. She nodded once. He disappeared. He reappeared almost as quickly with Ruby at his side.

Parris felt the sharp prick of the syringe in her hip, and within minutes everything around her disappeared.

She floated in and out of consciousness for the next twenty-four hours, feeling full even though she hadn't eaten, not remembering who came and went in the bedroom, nor the day or the time.

But the first face she saw when she woke up, clear-eyed and clear-headed, was Martin's. He sat on a chair beside the bed, reading a newspaper. She remembered him wearing a black silk shirt not a white T-shirt. She also remembered his long hair floating down around his shoulders not queued at the nape of his neck with an elastic band. His long hair seemed more appropriate for an artist or musician than a corporate executive. She moaned softly and Martin rose to his feet, smiling. He placed the newspaper on a side table.

"Welcome back."

How long have I been gone? she mused, trying valiantly to return his smile. Her jaw had been wired so tightly that it was almost impossible for her to part her lips.

Moving closer to the bed, Martin took her hand in his, examining the purpling bruises from the IV feedings. Luis had ordered removal of the IV earlier that morning. He wanted his patient ambulatory as quickly as possible.

"I suppose you're wondering what day it is?" he questioned, reading her mind. She nodded. "It's Monday."

Monday! How did she lose two days? Her eyes widened. She was supposed to be in Santa Fe.

Martin noted her agonized expression. "Is there someone you want me to call to let them know where you are?"

She nodded, trying to communicate. She pantomimed writing. He released her hand and opened a drawer to the table and withdrew a pad and pen.

Parris pulled her body up in a sitting position, supporting her back against two pillows. The sheet fell down to her waist, revealing an oversized T-shirt. She was certain the shirt was Martin's.

She took the pad and pen from him, writing, *Please call office and let them know that I had an accident.* Her head came up and she saw Martin watching her.

"Don't worry, Parris. I won't give them any details."

Closing her eyes briefly, she nodded.

"I recovered your purse," Martin informed her. "I took it off the front seat of Owen Lawson's car after..." He didn't finish the statement. What he didn't say was that he had taken it because he didn't want Parris linked to the police investigation which had ensued after the man's body was discovered early Sunday morning by an elderly man who strolled the beach every morning, rain or shine, since his retirement.

Local newspapers reported that the Palm Beach Police Department was baffled by the crime. It didn't appear to be a robbery because the victim's jewelry and money were not taken and the victim said he wasn't able to give the police a description of who had assaulted him.

Parris felt a fist of fear squeeze her chest at the mention of Owen's name. Martin knew who had tried to kill her.

She began to shake as the fearful images rushed back to attack her again. Gasping, she panted in terror. The pressure on her chest wouldn't allow her to breathe. The more she struggled the more frantic she became and she couldn't free herself. Then came the wet salty cold.

The pounding waves tossed her high up in the air before sending her crashing down to the ocean depths. Water rushed into her mouth and she coughed and coughed until her throat was raw and burning. She screamed and nothing came out.

She couldn't make a sound because someone had placed a hand over her mouth.

Owen! Owen was trying to kill her!

"Parris! It's okay, Parris. It's over, baby."

Martin held her, one hand making circular motions on her back, the other cradling her head and pressing her face to his shoulder.

"It's all right, darling," he crooned, attempting to comfort her. "No one is going to hurt you." She sniffed loudly, her fingernails biting into his shoulders. "I'm here, Parris. I'm here for you."

He felt as if someone had cut out a piece of his heart as she cried without making a sound, her tears soaking the front of shirt, her shoulders heaving uncontrollably.

Parris appeared calm until he mentioned Owen Lawson's name. What was his connection to her?

A look of determination settled across his features. He'd do what he should've done the moment he discovered who Parris's attacker was. At first he thought of Philip Trent. Philip was the most adept troubleshooter ColeDiz had hired, however, Martin changed his mind about utilizing the services of an employee. His association with Parris was too new, too personal. She was the first woman to spend more than two nights under his roof since he bought the town house six months ago.

He would hire a private investigator to check further into Owen Lawson's background.

Luis Lopez sat on the patio at Martin's house, admiring the fauna surrounding the property. Potted palms, cacti and yucca plants spanned the length of the patio, providing maximum privacy from neighboring residences.

Running a hand over his close-cut prematurely graying hair, he forced his attention back to what Martin was saying.

"I'm not a psychiatrist, but I've seen enough cases of post-traumatic-stress-disorder to tell you that Parris is receiving the best medical care available to her."

Martin visually examined the young doctor. Luis's eyes shone like copper pennies, crinkling attractively whenever he smiled, and he always had a ready smile for his patients as he offered words of comfort. A sprinkling of freckles across his nose and cheeks made him appear younger, offsetting the effects of his graying hair.

He and Luis had grown up together. They attended the same schools only separating when Luis attended Harvard Medical School while he stayed in Florida to earn a M.B.A. Luis had received offers to work for several large teaching hospitals in New York City and Boston, but he turned them down. Luis claimed he couldn't adjust to the long winters.

"Are you saying that she'll spend the rest of her life experiencing flashbacks?" He had confided to Luis the circumstances surrounding her injury.

"No, I'm not. She may have them for a while. What she needs is to feel safe, protected. Make her convalescence as comfortable and stress-free as possible because it's likely her face will heal a lot faster than her internal scars. She has to trust you, Martin. You saved her life."

I hope you're right, Luis, Martin told himself.

Chapter 3

Martin strolled into the plushly carpeted reception area at ColeDiz and smiled at the receptionist.

"Good morning, Grace."

"Good—good morning, Martin," she stuttered, glancing up at a large silver and brass clock on the wall to her right.

He arched a sweeping eyebrow at her before looking at the clock. It was ten o'clock.

Grace lowered her head, bright color creeping up her face and matching her shimmering red hair. She stared at Martin's retreating back, rising slightly to watch him as he made his way down the carpeted corridor to his office. She was still staring when one of the secretaries from the legal department walked into the reception area.

"What are you looking for?" she asked Grace.

"It's not what I'm looking for, but who I was looking at," Grace admitted.

The secretary registered Grace's dreamy expression. "Martin Cole," they whispered in unison, shaking their heads in wonderment.

"Mercy!" the secretary gasped.

"Hel-lo," Grace intoned.

* * *

Martin's personal secretary's solemn expression did not change as he greeted her cheerfully. Forty-two-year-old Joan Shaw was mature and competent. Highly skilled, she supervised the clerical staff and shielded her boss from any unnecessary distraction. Her dark eyes were intelligent, her dark skin smooth and unlined, and her no-nonsense business manner respected.

Martin made his way into his own office and hung his suit jacket in a closet artfully concealed along a wall of mirrored glass. This morning he did not take the time to admire the comfortable spaciousness of the room where he spent most of his time.

There were days when he worked in his office for twelve hours, conducting meetings over conference calls from three different times zones and eating dinner when most people were either sleeping or readying themselves to go to bed. He had accomplished in four years what most men who had worked at ColeDiz hadn't in twenty. He tripled the corporation's net profit.

His office was one of many in a suite taking up the entire eighth floor of a modern downtown West Palm Beach office building. He had taken over the day-to-day operation of ColeDiz yet he refused to occupy the executive wing along with vice-presidents, attorneys and financial officers whose solid oak doors with gleaming brass name plates identified them as the corporate elite.

His refusal to move his office angered his father but enhanced his standing with the support staff. He was always available and approachable.

Checking the telephone messages lined up like soldiers on his desk, Martin quickly prioritized their importance.

"What's this I hear about you coming in late this morning?" came a familiar voice through the intercom.

"Guilty as charged, Dad," he confessed after pressing a button on the small box.

"Is this a one-time offense or do you intend to join the other offenders who completely ignore the nine-to-five work schedule?" Samuel Cole was pedantic about punctuality.

"I don't know, Dad. It all depends on how I feel tomorrow morning," Martin teased.

"You can come in anytime you want tomorrow. Just don't be late for your flight to San José on Wednesday. You've been booked for a seven A.M. departure from Miami International."

Reaching over, he picked up the telephone receiver. "Get someone to cover for me."

An explosive expletive crackled through the instrument. "You have to go, Martin!"

"I don't have to go, *Father.*"

Samuel registered his son's firm refusal. It wasn't often that he and his oldest child opposed each other but whenever Martin referred to him as *Father* he knew any ensuing dialogue would not be amicable.

"What's up, Martin?"

How could he tell his father that he couldn't go to Costa Rica because of Parris; that he couldn't leave her; not now.

"I'm tired, Dad." His tone softened noticeably. "I'd like to stay home and sleep in my own bed for a change. Strange faces, strange beds and sometimes even stranger foods don't excite me anymore.

"I've bought a house that I haven't taken the time to decorate or enjoy. I've never taken advantage of the development's tennis court or swimming pool. I sat on my patio for the very first time yesterday afternoon. The first time in *six months,* Dad.

"The cleaning service comes twice a week to dust and vacuum rooms I never go into. And if I didn't enjoy cooking for myself I wouldn't need a kitchen. I'll turn thirty in another four months and I don't feel as if I've been living. I've been working and existing."

"But you go out, Martin. You see women," Samuel countered.

"That's just it. I've gone out with women, but there's never been a special woman. That one woman I'd like to see more than two times before I'm flying off on some corporate junket."

There was a pause before Samuel spoke again. "What's this conversation all about, Martin? Are you telling me that you want out of ColeDiz or that you've met someone?"

He wanted to say that he had met someone. Someone he would have for a while before he had to let her go. Someone he could come home to at night.

"I just want to curtail the traveling," he said instead.

Samuel registered the resignation in Martin's voice, and he also recognized the stubborn trait that was so much a part of his own personality.

"All right, son. I'll get someone to fill in for you."

Leaning back on his chair, Martin closed his eyes and smiled. "Thanks. And, Dad. I hope you're considering my suggestion to purchase a jet for ColeDiz. The money you'll save chartering private flights will pay for a Lear or an Astra in less than two years."

"What else do you recommend, Wonder Boy?"

Martin laughed. He had earned the sobriquet as an undergraduate student. A business course project gave each student a nonexistent stake of one thousand dollars to invest in the commodities market. Martin's investment had turned a sizable profit for him while many of the other students lost every cent.

Once word leaked out about his "sixth sense" in the market he was courted and pursued by investment firms he had never heard of or read about. He shied away from interviews, but granted one which set the stage for his image as a risk taker. He was quoted in his college newspaper saying, 'I'm going to have a piece of everything I want. Some of it may not work out, but I'm still going to have a piece of it anyway.'

"Communications, Dad."

Samuel snorted. "I'll leave that field for Ted Turner, Rupert Murdoch and that eyeglass-wearing boy who plays with computers…"

"Bill Gates."

"Yeah—he's the one."

The two men exchanged pleasantries then rang off. Even though his father disdained computers Martin was glad he had mentioned them. It was what he needed to communicate with Parris.

* * *

Martin knew the day had not gone well for Parris the moment he walked through his living room door and saw Ruby Johnson waiting for him.

"What's the matter, Mrs. Johnson?"

"She won't eat."

"She ate breakfast," he reminded Ruby.

"But she didn't eat lunch or dinner."

His brow creased with worry. She had to eat or…He refused to think of the consequences.

"Where is she?"

"Upstairs. She's been sitting out on the balcony." Ruby didn't get the chance to finish her statement as Martin raced by her and took the staircase to the upper level.

Martin slowed his pace as he walked into the bedroom Parris had occupied since he brought her to his home. Staring across the room, he saw her sitting out on the balcony on a chaise, sleeping. As he moved closer he realized she wasn't asleep but reading.

Standing at the doors, he stared through the mesh of the screen and wondered why Parris Simmons had come into his life. Why now? Why when he was experiencing only what he now recognized as apathy and boredom?

He had accepted challenges and had proven himself a winner. People in the world of business and finance recognized his face and many more knew his name. The mayor of West Palm Beach had given him a key to the city on behalf of the contributions ColeDiz had made to its citizens.

He had been told that he had it all: the family name, his family's fortune and the pick of any eligible woman for a wife.

He had it all and he had nothing. The name, money, clothes and the fame were merely window dressing because under the facade was a man who would give it all up for love.

It had taken Martin a long time to realize what had been missing in his life. He dated and respected women, offering them generous gifts for their birthdays or special holidays. But dating them had become a diversion. They filled up the empty blocks of time when he wasn't working on a ColeDiz deal.

Staring at Parris, he wondered if she too would be just a diversion, someone to pass the time with.

Sliding back the screen, he stepped out onto the balcony.

Parris closed the magazine. It was several seconds before she realized she was not alone. Martin stood, silently, watching her.

She stared mutely, her heart pounding. Even if she had been able to speak she still would've been momentarily speechless.

It was the first time she'd seen him dressed in a suit, and the expert cut of a navy blue, maroon pinstripe garment fit every line of his graceful body. The collar to his stark white shirt gleamed against his brown throat. He would look exquisite dressed completely in white, she thought. A solid maroon silk tie, matching pocket square, understated gold monogrammed cuff links and black leather wingtips completed his winning fashionable business attire.

"Good evening, Parris."

She inclined her head slightly, trying to slow down her heart as he walked over to her and took a rattan love seat with cushions matching the one on the chaise.

He examined her face, noting that some of the swelling had gone down and what had been deep purple bruises were changing to a yellowing-green. Luis had assured him her jaw would heal without scarring.

"Mrs. Johnson says that you won't eat."

Did Mrs. Johnson tell you that I couldn't eat after I caught a glimpse of my face in the mirror for the first time? Did she? Parris raged silently.

Martin saw her expression change. "Did something happen to make you not eat?" he asked perceptively.

Parris stared at him. She was amazed that he seemed able to read her thoughts. She nodded.

"What happened?"

Reaching for the pen and pad, she wrote down how she saw her face in the mirror and how she became sick.

Martin shifted from the love seat to sit at her feet on the chaise. He tried to ignore the length and smoothness of her long legs stretched out beside him. He tried not thinking of what lay beneath the cotton of the T-shirt concealing her nakedness from him.

He read what she had written, shaking his head. "No, Parris, you're not ugly. You're healing nicely. You'll be as beautiful as before." Closing her eyes, she nodded vigorously that she was.

Grasping her wrists gently, he pulled her to him and she lay half-on and half-off his lap. The heat from her bottom burned his thighs through the silk of her bikini underpants and the light-weight wool of his trousers. His body responded instantly.

"Parris. Parris, look at me." She opened her eyes and he smiled down at her, the heat from his body and the smell of his cologne intoxicating her.

"You are beautiful," he stated in a reverent tone. "You are the most beautiful woman I've ever seen in my life. I can say that because I've traveled all over the world and I've seen many, many beautiful women.

"Why do you think I followed you? Did you really think you could flirt with me then walk away?"

Her breasts rose and fell until the cotton fabric of the T-shirt as heat suffused her battered face. The pompous, arrogant idiot. *Flirt with you? Did you actually think I was flirting with you?* The humiliation and rage warred within her, and how she wished she could open her mouth and have the words spill out. Flirt with him indeed.

"Don't look so insulted," he continued, watching her stunned expression. "But I must admire your come-on. If purring and batting the lashes don't work, then insult the hell out of him. Right, Parris?" He tightened his loose grip on her delicate wrists when her fingers curved slightly.

He knew she hadn't flirted with him, but he'd say anything to get a response from her; he didn't want her to wallow in depression and stop eating.

Okay, she nodded. *If you, say I flirted with you, then I did,* she thought, showing him her clenched teeth. *Just let me go.*

He released her wrists and curved an arm around her waist. Exchanging positions, he settled her to sit between his outstretched legs.

Parris felt every nerve in her body quivering as Martin pressed his chest to her back. It was only now that she'd become aware of how he looked and felt. She knew he was tall, but didn't realize how well his tailored clothing concealed the bulk of his large body. The black silk shirt and linen slacks he wore the night of the engagement party had minimized the dimensions of his powerful physique.

She inhaled his cologne, trying to identify the ingredients. It was a blend of a spicy citrus and musk. An unlikely combination that was sensual and provocative. The fragrance was Martin Cole.

"Dr. Lopez had a report of your disability delivered to your employer this morning, and if you want I'll have someone go to your apartment to pick up something for you to wear. Unless you don't mind modeling my T-shirts."

Glancing up at him over her shoulder, Parris frowned, shaking her head. "I thought not," he said, laughing.

What he did not tell her was that he had hired a private investigator to uncover her connection with Owen Lawson. That would remain his secret.

He rubbed several strands of her hair between his thumb and forefinger, examining the blunt-cut ends. Her hair was in good condition. He had noted her manicured hands and her coiffed hair Saturday night. He had also taken in the tasteful design of her dress and recognized her designer handbag and shoes. Parris Simmons was a woman who pampered herself and her vanity was manifested when she saw herself as ugly because her face was bruised and swollen.

He hadn't lied to her. She was the most beautiful woman he had ever met and the two things that had attracted him to her in the first place were temporarily flawed—her face and her voice.

"Have you made plans for dinner, Parris?"

A hint of a smile crinkled her eyes. She was tempted to nod yes. The expectant look in his eyes stopped her. She shook her head.

Lowering his head and his lids, he stared down at her. His penetrating gaze was as dark and powerful as he was. "Will you share dinner with me, Parris?" She nodded the affirmative and he pulled her back to rest against his body.

Martin held her, not wanting to move or to let her go. He dared not forget she was with him because she was an invalid. But she wouldn't remain an invalid for very long. Luis explained that she was young and in excellent health, and that meant she would heal quickly.

How long could he hope to keep her—two weeks? Maybe three at the most.

He studied her delicate bruised face. "Are you familiar with computers?" he questioned. She nodded. "Good," he continued, "because I brought a laptop home for you. Using the laptop should be easier and faster than your pen and pad method."

Closing his eyes, Martin tried to shake off the feeling that once Parris left he would never see her again.

He didn't know why, but as soon as the thought entered his head he recalled the quote from his college newspaper. *'I'm going to have a piece of everything I want. Some of it may not work out, but I'm still going to have a piece of it anyway.'*

Right now his everything was Parris Simmons.

Chapter 4

Parris did not remember the day the swelling in her face went away or when the bruises faded. She had lived with Martin for two weeks and in that time she looked forward to sharing breakfast with him before he left for his office. He usually left the house at seven so that meant she had to wake up early, shower and get dressed by six.

Her breakfast was pureed fruits with wheat germ and a multivitamin while Martin filled his plate with any fresh fruit that was in season, a bowl of Grape Nuts and a cup coffee. On the weekend his menu varied to eggs, with a choice of bacon, ham or sausage or whole wheat or buttermilk pancakes.

Dinners were very different, and what she didn't know was that Martin left the office before five to be with her.

No one at ColeDiz said anything, at least not to his face, but rumors were circulating about who was she that had him rushing through the front doors before quitting time. His unusual behavior even had Joan Shaw wondering if the rumors were right this time. Wagers were taken that Martin would announce his engagement before Christmas.

Parris heard the sound of Martin's car and opened the front door at the same time the automatic garage door slid up.

She had never been outside of the West Palm Beach self-contained community of two and three-bedroom town house condominiums but knew everyone entering or leaving the development had to pass through a security checkpoint.

The beautifully landscaped community had its own swimming pools—two for children and two for adults, tennis courts and health club. A recreation hall was available for anyone who wanted to use the facility for any event larger than an intimate dinner party or for family or holiday celebrations.

Martin's two-bedroom unit contained an expansive living-dining room, a large modern kitchen with a pantry, two full bathrooms, one half-bath, a laundry room, a family room and a patio spanning the length of the rear of the house. Sliding glass and screened doors from each bedroom led out onto a second-story balcony.

Martin explained that he had moved in in March, but hadn't had time to decorate his home because of the time he spent traveling.

She made suggestions, communicating with him by using the laptop computer he had brought home from his office. They'd sit together "talking" for what seemed like hours until her fingers tired from punching keys on the small power notebook.

Ruby Johnson no longer slept over, but came every day before Martin left in the morning and stayed until he returned in the evening. He still had not felt comfortable leaving her home alone until she could talk.

Dr. Lopez made house calls every other day and examined Parris's face. His gentle hands moved lightly over the delicate bones along her jaw, pleased that she was healing quickly. His prognosis cheered and saddened her at the same time. She wanted to be able to talk normally and eat solid foods, but she also didn't want to leave Martin.

She was astonished at the sense of fulfillment he offered her. He had saved her life, protected her and had asked for nothing in return.

Martin saw Parris in the doorway. It was the first time she had ever waited for him to come home, and the sight should've pleased him yet it didn't. The typed report the private investigator gave him during lunch lessened his enthusiasm. There were questions he had to ask Parris and he wanted answers to those questions.

The garage door closed quietly behind him as he turned and walked toward Parris. He halted, staring down at her upturned face, taking in the pinpoints of green in her clear brown eyes. It was the first time he noticed the green lights in her eyes since he was introduced to her.

His gaze swept quickly over her face, her shampooed hair and her slender body under one of his T-shirts she had paired with her own well-worn faded jeans. Even though he had gone to her apartment and picked up clothes and any other personal item he thought she needed, she continued to favor his oversized T-shirts. Again, he'd decided against having someone associated with ColeDiz run his personal errands.

Parris wiggled her fingers at him. It was her way of greeting him. "Hello back to you too," he said, curving an arm around her tiny waist. Without warning, he pulled her to his chest and touched her mouth with his. The kiss was only a brushing of the lips but both of them were shocked by the static caused by the casual touch.

Martin wanted to deepen the kiss. He wanted to devour her mouth and…

Shocked at his thoughts, he pulled back. Parris's eyes were wide, staring at him in disbelief. He opened his mouth to apologize but closed it as quickly. Why the hell should he apologize for something he wanted to do ever since he met her, and at that moment he realized he'd lied to Brittany when he said he didn't want to sleep with Parris Simmons.

Maybe he hadn't wanted to sleep with her two weeks ago. However if Brittany asked him now—today he would say yes.

He wanted to do more than sleep with Parris. He wanted to see her—every day *and* every night. He wanted to see her when he woke up in the morning and he wanted her waiting for him when he came home at night, and he wanted her to live with him.

He wouldn't ask that she give up anything for him except not leave him.

Forcing a smile, he hugged her. "What do you want for dinner?" Parris shrugged her shoulders. "How does fettuccine with a garlic sauce sound?"

She pinched her nose with a thumb and forefinger, then waved her hand in front of her mouth.

Martin laughed easily at her pantomime. It was his first real laugh since he read the P.I.'s report. "Don't worry about having bad breath. We'll use a mouthwash."

Parris stood beside Martin at the cooking island in the kitchen, stirring a pot of creamy garlic sauce while he dropped freshly made fettuccine into a large pot of boiling water.

He handed her a long-handled fork. "Please stir the pasta while I get some bacon." Registering her glare, he said, "Don't worry, Parris. I won't ask you to stir anything else." She curtsied, smiling at him.

Her gaze lingered on his back as he reached into the refrigerator. She had never met anyone like Martin. He appeared so sure of himself and his rightful place in the world. When, she thought, had he acquired his self-confidence? Or had he been born with it? Did he consider it his god-given privilege because he was who he was?

Straightening, he turned and caught her staring. "Are you stirring, my dear?"

Nodding her head slowly, Parris forced her attention back to the cooking island and stirred the sauce and the pasta.

He placed three strips of bacon on the stove's grilling surface and within minutes the kitchen was filled with the fragrant aroma of bacon and the savory garlic sauce.

Martin tested the pasta, finding it *al dente*. He removed a portion for himself, but cooked the remaining fettuccine until it was soft and mushy.

"You can stop stirring the sauce, Parris." She put down the spoon and retrieved the laptop from the countertop. Her fingers moved quickly over the keys. She positioned the screen for Martin to read what she had typed.

He read her request quickly. "No, Parris. It has to be pureed."

Her fingers went to the keys. *I'm sick and tired of sipping everything through a straw!*

He noted the frown marring her smooth forehead, wanting to lean over and kiss it away. "If I don't put your food in the blender, how are you going to chew the bacon?"

I won't eat the bacon.

Staring down into her clear brown eyes, Martin noted the glassy sheen of unshed tears and something tightened in his chest. He could feel her frustration, her impatience.

Once more he experienced an overwhelming need to take care of her, and he wondered who was she, this woman, who pulled so achingly at his heart?

"Okay. I won't puree it," he conceded.

Parris surprised him and herself as she pressed her body to his. His arms went around her waist and he held her close as she buried her face against his throat.

The slim arms around his neck, the fragrant smell of her skin and the soft crush of her firm breasts sent a warming shiver through his body.

Suddenly he was conscious of where his warm flesh touched hers and the differences in their bodies. He was aware that Parris Simmons was a woman, but it was only today that he saw her as wholly female.

Physically she was his counterpart.

Parris registered the subtle changes in Martin's body—the tightening of his fingers along her rib cage, the quickening of his pulse, the growing hardness against her middle and her own body tingling from the intimate contact.

Her arms slipped from his neck and she pulled out of his embrace, head lowered.

Cradling her chin in his hand, Martin raised her face. His warm breath feathered over her lips. Leaning over, he placed a kiss on either side of her mouth. "Let's eat," he whispered.

* * *

Parris left more pasta and sauce on her plate than she swallowed. The creamy noodles slid down the back of her throat without her tasting the fragrant garlic and herbs.

Placing her spoon on the table, she stared over Martin's head at the towering palms trees in the distance. She enjoyed dining outdoors on the patio.

"Is that all you're going to eat?" he asked.

She nodded, folding her arms over her chest.

Frowning, Martin put down his fork. He registered an expression of tired sadness pass over her features.

Damn, he thought. He shouldn't have listened to her. He should have pureed her food. She hadn't eaten more than four spoonsful of pasta

He knew she had lost weight. Her cheeks were gaunt and the bones of her collarbone were more sharply pronounced.

"Are you ready for dessert?"

Leaning against the back of her chair, Parris shook her head.

"You have to eat something," Martin insisted.

She shook her head harder, staring intently at him. Reaching for the laptop, she typed, *I don't want anything else to eat. Thank you for dinner.*

He read her reply. "I don't need your thanks, Parris. You didn't eat."

I did eat, she typed.

Suddenly his expression was grim. "You didn't!" he shouted.

Parris was stunned by his outburst. She recovered quickly. Her fingers raced over the keyboard. *Don't you dare yell at me unless I'm able to yell back! Do you understand me clearly, Mr. Cole?*

Martin's black eyes impaled her after he read the acerbic reprimand. She stiffened as the air between them vibrated with static electricity.

"I understand you quite clearly, Miss Simmons," he responded after a lengthy silence.

Averting his head, he hid the smile crinkling his eyes. Fragile and mute, she still challenged him, and when he turned back to her there was a gleam of admiration in his gaze.

Rising to his feet, he moved over and pulled back her chair. "You must be stuffed," he crooned near her ear. "What do you say we go for a walk to burn off a few calories."

Her head came up quickly and she stared up at his wide grin. She couldn't laugh aloud, but her shoulders shook uncontrollably as she laughed until tears streaked her cheeks.

Dusk had fallen by the time they began their stroll around the track surrounding the health center. There were a half-dozen couples also circling the track, some casually and a few jogging at a moderate pace.

Martin held Parris's hand, pulling her close to his side. He tightened his grip on her slender fingers and she glanced up at him. They shared a secret smile. A smile lovers usually reserved for each other.

They logged a half mile around the track, then walked along the wide avenue back to the house.

He knew he couldn't put it off any longer. He had to talk to Parris about Owen Lawson.

Parris was surprised when Martin knocked on her bedroom door and walked in, carrying the laptop. The slight arching of his sweeping eyebrows should have warned her that what he wanted to "talk" to her about was serious. She had learned to gauge his facial expressions and body language to monitor his moods.

"I'd like to talk to you about something," he began, sitting on the chair beside her bed.

Parris nodded, smoothing the sheet out over her knees. Since living in Martin's house, she had taken to wearing a nightshirt to bed. Normally she slept in the nude. She took the laptop from him, switching it on.

She felt him studying her profile as she stared at the small screen. Tilting her chin, she glanced up at him from under her lashes.

"I want to know why your ex-husband tried to kill you."

Her eyes widened until he could see fear in their depths. Her lips formed a silent "no."

Moving quickly, he sat down on the bed, pulling her to his chest. "You have to tell me, Parris. How else can I protect you from him."

Parris stared out across the bedroom. She catalogued each item in the room as if she had never seen them before.

The furnishings in the bedroom were an eclectic mix of Scandinavian and French provincial. She lay on a queen size sleigh bed in a gleaming mahogany. A double dresser and chest-on-chest were constructed with straight lines reminiscent of the popular Scandinavian styles.

"Parris."

Martin calling her name pulled her from her reverie.

You don't have to protect me.

"Yes I do," he argued.

No you don't because you don't have to get involved.

"It's too late for that, Parris. I became involved the moment I hit Owen Lawson to keep him from drowning you. I became involved the second I carried you over the threshold of my home. I am involved because I asked a doctor to compromise his professional ethics and risk losing his license when he put your face back together on a countertop in my kitchen instead of on an operating table at a hospital."

I am involved because I want you in my life, he said to himself. He was involved because he thought perhaps he was falling in love with her.

He was angry with me, she typed, countering his tirade.

"Why?"

Because I left him.

"Why?"

I can't tell you that.

Martin's jaw hardened. He took a deep breath. "How long were you married?"

Parris felt a surge of anger and resentment. He was interrogating her as if she had committed a crime. It was Owen who tried to kill her not the reverse.

Not long.

"How long is not long?"

We lived together for a month.

"Did he ever hit you while you lived together?"

Parris shook her head. *We argued a lot, but he never attempted to hit me.*

Martin wanted to hold her close, reassure her that her ex-husband would not hurt her again but he curbed the urge to comfort her. She had to learn to trust him; trust him enough to know that he would use everything at his disposal to protect her.

"When were you divorced?" he asked, knowing the answer to the question before asking it.

The marriage was annulled last December, she typed.

"How old were you when you married him?" Another question he knew the answer to.

Twenty.

"You married him while you were still in college?"

She shook her head. *I had graduated,* she typed. *I was in an accelerated program in high school so I entered college at sixteen.*

"What about your parents? Did they approve of you marrying him?"

My mother said he was too old for me, but I reminded her that my father was fifteen years older than she was when they married. It didn't matter whether she approved or not because I married Owen three weeks after she died in a traffic accident.

"What about your father, Parris?"

I don't remember my father. He died when I was three.

Martin stared at the words crowding the small screen, focusing on the blinking cursor. He wondered if Parris had married because she felt the need to rebel against her mother's authority or if she had married Owen because of grief and she didn't want to be alone or...

He couldn't form the words. He wanted to know if she had ever loved Owen, and if she had could she learn to love again. He had thought about her hostility at the table in the restaurant. Had she seen him as her husband? Had she built a wall around her to keep all men at arm's length?

Martin felt vulnerable for the first time. He had to ask one more question. "Do you love him, Parris?" She shook her head. "Did you ever love him?"

Her eyes filled with tears, but she blinked them back. She would not shed a single tear for Owen. He wasn't worth it. He had stopped being the man she loved the moment she discovered he was a substance abuser who refused to go into a treatment program. She had only uncovered his clandestine activities after she saw him inhaling a white substance in their bathroom when he thought she was asleep. That single act ended their marriage and changed her forever.

The amber words filled the screen. *I loved him at one time.*

He took the laptop from her lap, shutting it off and placing it on a bedside table. Then he pulled her into his embrace, pressing a kiss to her forehead.

"You'll never have to worry about him hurting you again, baby." She trembled and he tightened his hold on her body.

"Nothing matters now," he crooned.

He wanted to say that what did matter was that Owen Lawson was a highly decorated police officer with the West Palm Beach police department. It mattered that the man had just been promoted to the rank of lieutenant. And it mattered that he had tried to kill his ex-wife and would probably try again if given the opportunity.

What did matter was that Lawson had the protection of a police department and that of a federal judge. He was the son of Lowell Lawson, Florida's first black federal judge who was rumored to have his sights set on a Supreme Court appointment.

"I'll take care of you," Martin promised. He whispered his promise over and over to himself, for if he said it enough he would believe it. And at that moment he did.

Chapter 5

A week later Parris waited for Martin to come home. She found it difficult to contain her excitement. She could talk. Not clearly, but enough to make herself understood.

She was tired of "talking" to Martin on the laptop. It seemed as if her thoughts always raced faster than her fingers. The front door opened and she rose from the black and white striped sofa, smiling.

Martin placed his leather case and suit jacket on a table near the door, his gaze fixed on Parris's smiling face. She was waiting for him as she had been doing for a week. And it had been a week since they discussed her ex-husband, the highly decorated police officer who now was on a medical leave.

He walked over to her and she did not disappoint him when she put her arms around his neck and pressed her lips to his cheek.

Closing his eyes, Martin held her close, inhaling the distinctive Chanel No. 5 clinging to her skin. At first he thought she was too young for the sophisticated fragrance but the scent was her. At twenty-two Parris Simmons claimed a sensuality many women twice her age had not acquired, and coupled with the sensuality was an innocence he couldn't see but he could feel.

There were times when he felt the seven-year difference in their ages was twice that amount. But he had to remind himself that she had been married; married to a man who could be her father. Parris was twenty-two while Owen Lawson was thirty-nine.

Pulling back, Martin stared down at her upturned face. He didn't think he would ever get used to her natural beauty. Her satiny golden-brown skin, her luminous eyes and her lush passionate mouth. A mouth he yearned to devour.

"How are you?"

Martin's soft voice sent chills racing up and down Parris's spine. The green lights in her eyes darkened as her hands moved to cradle his smooth lean cheeks, her thumbs tracing the curve of his high cheekbones.

"I'm fine, thank you." The four words were low, coming haltingly from her unused vocal chords.

He blinked at her in disbelief. It had been so long—too long since he had heard her low breathless voice that he thought he was imagining it.

"Does it…does it hurt when you move your jaw?" His fingers traced the outline of her cheek.

"It's a little stiff," she admitted. "And I feel a little tingling behind my ear. But at least I can talk."

Lowering his head, Martin pressed his mouth to her earlobe, his lips feathering over her neck and jaw. He was too caught up in the silky feel of her skin and the haunting fragrance of her body to note her trembling.

Parris felt a rush of heat singe her body followed by a vibrating liquid between her legs. Emotions she had only glimpsed in the past were back. Stronger than ever.

Abandoning herself to the whirl of sensations, she moaned as Martin's mouth covered hers. The kiss was soft, gentle, as if he feared hurting her. She felt the tightening muscles in his upper arms under the crisp fabric of his laundered shirt, heard the rush of breath from his delicate nostrils and she registered his maleness hardening and throbbing against her thighs.

It ended as quickly as it had begun and Parris felt weak, lightheaded. She clung to the front of his shirt, breathing heavily.

Holding her tightly, Martin buried his face in her hair. He had been ready to swing her up in his arms and take her to his bed. He wanted her with a hunger that had exceeded any he had ever experienced.

She's mine, he claimed silently and possessively. No one would ever take her from him.

"I think this calls for a very special celebration," he whispered in her ear. She nodded, her nose pressed against his chest. "Do you want to go out for dinner?"

Her body went rigid. In the three weeks she had lived with Martin she hadn't thought about the world outside of the private community. It was as if she was resigned to live behind the walls where she felt safe and totally protected for the first time since she left Owen.

"Not yet," she rasped breathlessly.

Pulling back slightly, Martin stared down at her face, seeing fear and uncertainty in her eyes. "Everything will be all right. You'll be safe with me."

I hope you're right, Martin, she mused. Swallowing back her fear, she said, "Where are we going?" She prayed it wasn't to a place that she had frequented with Owen and his friends.

"A seafood place in Lauderdale. Have you ever been to Boston?" She nodded. "Have you eaten New England clam chowder?"

"Yes."

"Then you're in for a treat. The chef can out-chowder the best New England chowder ever created."

Parris gave him a skeptical look. "I don't believe you."

"Believe me, baby," he said, pressing his lips to her forehead. "Believe me."

What Parris couldn't believe was how happy she felt sitting next to Martin as he drove southward to Fort Lauderdale. She lost count of the number of pleasure crafts she saw bobbing on the water along Florida's gold coast.

The calendar said Fall, but the weather still said summer. The warm tropical air filtering through the Jaguar's open windows caressed her face and ruffled her hair before it settled back to the lines of the professional cut.

She wiggled her bare toes in a pair of neutral-colored espadrille sandals with fabric ties circling her ankles. The footwear was appropriate for the sleeveless cotton dress in a black, orange and tan jungle print with two wide straps crisscrossing her bare back to the waist.

Martin maneuvered into one of the last spaces at a restaurant whose backyard was a pier where diners moored their boats while they ate.

He held Parris's hand possessively as he helped her from the car and led her to the restaurant's entrance. Shielding her body from the crush of patrons crowding the waiting area, he smiled at the hostess. Two minutes later the owner gestured to him.

She couldn't ignore the hostile glares from the other people who were resigned to wait up to half an hour before they were seated while Martin tightened his hold on her waist as he smiled and nodded like a politician as the crowd parted for him. They were seated in a booth in a corner which afforded them maximum privacy, and given menus.

She scanned the menu quickly. "Do they serve baby food?"

The small candle on the middle of the table highlighted the gold undertones in Martin's brown skin as he smiled at her, and once again Parris found it hard to believe his masculine beauty.

His black hair was pulled off his high intelligent forehead and secured at the nape of his neck. He had exchanged his business attire for a collarless linen shirt in a small-checkered tan and white print and tobacco-brown linen slacks and brown loafers. She hadn't decided whether she liked him better in a business suit or in his casual attire.

Reaching across the table, he held her hands firmly. "Don't worry, Parris. I'll make certain you won't have to chew anything."

Parris spent the next two hours thoroughly enjoying Martin's charming company and the most delicious New England clam chowder she had ever tasted, mashed potatoes with just a hint of grated romano cheese and a creamy lemon sorbet that was so tart it tingled her palate with each spoonful. Martin had given the waitress explicit instructions that everything they prepared for her would have to be strained and pureed until it was smooth and free of lumps.

He enjoyed his own lobster bisque, grilled salmon and sweet cole slaw while watching Parris as she tentatively spooned small amounts of food into her mouth.

Seeing her under the glow of the candlelight he noted things about her face he had missed before. Her hair wasn't black, but a dark brown with reddish highlights, the corners of her eyes tilted slightly upward and her earrings were tiny balls of gold in her pierced lobes. So fragile, so beautiful and so sensual, he mused, leaning back on his seat.

His dark eyes widened in astonishment as she reached for his wineglass, took a, sip, then handed it back to him with a smile.

"Would you like a glass?"

"Yes, please."

She didn't know what made her agree to share a glass of wine with him. She hadn't lied when she told Martin that she didn't drink very much. She had seen too many of her friends in college drink until they passed out. Their hangovers were always worse. The nauseating smell of undigested food and souring alcohol in the dormitory bathrooms turned her off alcohol where she could count the occasions when she would accept a drink.

She drank the single glass of white wine and felt its effects immediately. Her body was loose and relaxed, reminiscent of what she had felt earlier when Martin kissed her. She wanted him to kiss her now; she wanted him to do more than kiss her.

She wanted him to make love to her!

Closing her eyes, she pressed back against the leather seat. She wanted the man who had given her back her life. The man who had permitted her a second chance to live out her life the way it had been deemed from a higher power.

She wanted the man who made her feel safe and protected.

She wanted the man sitting across from her, and she wanted

the man she knew she had come to love in the three weeks she had lived in his house.

She wanted Martin Diaz Cole.

Martin watched Parris's lids lower until her lashes swept the curve of her cheekbones. It was apparent she wasn't much of a drinker. He signaled for the check and left a generous tip for the waitress and guided Parris out of the restaurant to the parking lot.

"I don't drink much," Parris slurred as he settled her onto her seat and adjusted the seat belt over her chest.

"I know, darling." He pressed a kiss to her temple.

He was smiling as he took his own seat and started up the car. Her confession that she didn't drink revealed a lot about Parris Simmons. She was a talented interior decorator who travelled all over the country. Business was usually discussed over dinner yet she probably did not drink during these business meetings. She was an enigma. A mysterious woman who had come out of the night and into his life.

Parris woke the next morning on her bed and fully clothed except for her shoes. Peering down at her dress, she remembered what had happened. She had fallen asleep during the ride back from Fort Lauderdale.

Turning her head, she stared at the clock on the bedside table. It was eight-thirty. She had missed Martin!

Her movements were slow as she pushed her body off the bed and headed for the bathroom, deciding to take a bath instead of her usual shower.

An hour later, dressed in a pair of shorts and one of Martin's T-shirts, she walked down the staircase to the living room. Glancing around the large space, she looked for Ruby Johnson. She usually found her in the living room watching the early morning talk shows.

Her bare feet were silent as she made her way across large blocks of white glazed tiles. Martin had confessed that he hadn't decided how he wanted his house decorated so the living and dining area only contained a black and white cotton striped sofa and matching love seat, an entertainment grouping with a television, VCR and stereo electronic components and a formal dining-room table with seating for eight, a glass-front china cabinet and a buffet server.

She always felt a little tingle of excitement whenever she thought about decorating the spaces. She hadn't offered her services to Martin, thinking perhaps he wanted to use his own decorator. But she had begun making notations on a pad, hoping he would ask her. She would design an incredible showplace for the man who had saved her life.

Walking into the kitchen, Parris stopped short. Martin stood at the cooking island humming along with a song coming from speakers hidden within the walls. He wore a pair of shorts and a tank top, and like her his feet were bare.

It was the first time she had seen so much of his flesh exposed that her mouth went dry as she noted the thick black hair on his strong legs. Her gaze moved up and he turned to face her.

"Good morning, sleepyhead."

She missed his dimpled smile as she stared at the thick mat of hair on his chest. She found herself mute again.

"What…what are you doing here?" Her normally low voice had dropped half an octave.

"I live here."

Her face heated up. "I didn't mean that."

He registered her embarrassment. "I took a much-needed day off."

"Where's Mrs. Johnson?"

Martin turned back to beating an egg mixture with a wire whisk. "Mrs. Johnson won't be coming back anymore. You're able to talk now and Luis says you should be completely healed in another couple of weeks."

"I don't need you to look after me," she said, thinking perhaps he thought she needed help because she possibly had a hangover.

His hair shielded his face with black damp curls as he concentrated on preparing breakfast. "I don't intend to look after you, Parris. What I *am* going to do is enjoy my home for the first time. I'm going to try to get in a game of tennis, do a few laps in the pool and lift some weights at the health club before I sit out on the patio and watch the sun set." He stared at her. "Does that meet with your approval, Miss Simmons?"

Embarrassment turned to humiliation. "Yes, *sir.*"

Martin laughed loudly, compounding her uneasiness. He laughed harder as she turned and walked across the kitchen and out to the patio.

She sat on the patio enjoying the feel of the warm sun on her face until Martin appeared and served breakfast.

Parris finished reading a paperback book Martin had brought from her studio apartment when he had gone there to retrieve her clothes. The novel was one she had picked up at the West Palm Beach airport the day she had flown to San Francisco.

Laying aside the book, she thought about her position with the architectural and design firm. She had been away three weeks and she wondered who had covered for her. Would she lose her coveted position with the West Palm Beach branch or would she be forced to move to another city wherever there was an opening. West Palm Beach was her home and she wasn't ready to leave it—not yet.

West Palm Beach was where Martin was and she didn't to leave him—not yet.

Martin watched Parris close her eyes, preferring to stare at her instead of the setting sun. He'd spent the day swimming and playing a strenuous game of racquetball instead of tennis. The tennis courts were crowded with women who were more interested in flirting than hitting the ball over the net. The vigorous exercise on the racquetball court substituted for the workout in the weight room.

The exercise had been fun for him. It had relieved him of the tension he felt whenever he was near Parris. He recognized the tension for what it was—sexual.

He wanted her the way he never wanted any other woman. Not only did he want to make love to her, but he wanted to keep her in his life forever.

He thought of the role he was to play in less than a week. He would be best man to a friend who would pledge his love and life to a woman when they married.

Marriage!

The word caused a shudder to shake him from head to toe. For twenty-nine years he never thought of marrying a woman, and now the pull was so strong it unnerved him.

Could he marry Parris?

Did he love her?

Did he want to spend the rest of his life with her?

He held his breath, then let it out slowly. The answer shook him to the core. Yes!

Chapter 6

Martin noted that Parris was unusually quiet during dinner. She appeared distracted and anxious.

"Is something wrong, Parris?"

Her head came up quickly, and she shook her head. "No. I guess I'm not very hungry."

He pushed his own plate away, rising to his feet. "Do you want to go for a drive?"

"No." Her voice was low, expressionless.

Circling the table, he reached out to touch her but she shrank from him. "What's the matter?"

She stood up and folded her arms around her body. "I want to go home."

The thing he had been dreading had manifested itself. She wanted to leave. "But you're not well enough…"

"Stop it, Martin. I can be alone and you know it. I stay here alone—all day."

"It's different here."

Her gaze searched his face, missing the pain in his jet-black eyes. "Why is it so different?"

"You're safe here."

Her chest rose and fell heavily as she bit down on her lower lip. "I can't spend the rest of my life hiding behind a walled community. Don't forget I have a job that I'll be returning to in another two weeks, and there are no walls to protect me when I travel, Martin."

Martin pulled her to his chest, his arms tightening around her body as she struggled to free herself. "Listen to me, Parris." She stopped struggling. "I don't want you to leave. I want you to live with me."

Closing her eyes, Parris buried her face against his hard shoulder. She had to leave—now. She had to leave before she couldn't.

It had taken nearly four weeks, but she knew she had fallen in love with Martin.

He had saved her life, protected her, taken care of her every need and in return she had secretly given him her heart.

She looked forward to seeing him each morning, and she couldn't wait for his return each evening.

She yearned for his touch and his kiss.

She wanted Martin with an intensity she never felt with the man she had married. There were times when she even forgot that Owen had ever been a part of her life. Yet she could not forget his assault; however, if Owen ever came near her again she would follow through on the threat she'd made if he'd refused her demand that they annul their marriage. She'd threatened to disclose his substance abuse problem to his superior officers at the West Palm Beach Police Department.

"Parris?"

"I can't." Her reply was weak and trembling.

"Why not?" His lips grazed an ear. "Do you despise me that much? Have I been unkind to you? What is it you want me to do for you?"

Her eyes filled with tears. "It's not you, Martin" she replied, her voice breaking.

Closing his eyes, Martin felt the breath rush from his lungs, leaving him breathless. He prayed silently that it wasn't Owen Lawson.

"Who is it?" he gasped.

A hot tear rolled down her cheek, wetting his T-shirt. She had spent the day fighting the realization that it was her driving need for Martin that made her want to run as fast and as far away from him as she could.

"It's me," she cried, giving way to a rush of heartbreaking sobs.

Martin cradled her face between his hands and stared down at her. Something clicked in his mind. He couldn't bear the thought that she feared him.

"Are you afraid of men, Parris?" She shook her head vigorously. "Do you hate me?"

She sniffled loudly, once again pressing her nose to his chest. "No-o-o."

His heart started up a double-time rhythm. "Do you at least like me?"

Her sobbing subsided and there was complete silence except for their labored breathing. Parris felt as if she had run a race. She was exhausted from her emotional ordeal.

"Yes."

Martin wanted to shout, cry. He needed to do something to relieve the band of tension tightening his chest. Dropping a light kiss on her forehead, nose and finally her mouth, he whispered, "Now, was that so hard to admit?"

Parris smiled through her tears. "No."

He returned her smile, flashing deep dimples. "You can always talk to me, darling. You must always let me know what you like, don't like, want and don't want."

What she wanted to say was that she needed him. She needed Martin to make her feel like a woman.

He brushed away her tears with his fingers, kissing each inch of her face his hands caressed. "I don't ever want to see your beautiful eyes fill up with tears again unless they are tears of joy," he crooned, holding her close to his heart.

Passion pounded through his chest and body, and it was herculean control that prevented Martin from blurting out his true feelings for the woman he held to his heart.

* * *

The next time Parris shed tears, they were tears of joy. She dabbed her eyes carefully with a tissue as Brittany and Jon exchanged vows in the tiny white church whose walls and towering steeple were covered with climbing ivy and fragrant white roses.

She stared at Martin's profile before he turned to follow the smiling bride and groom down the red-carpeted aisle to the doors of the church. He caught her stare and flashed her his sensuous smile. Lowering her spiky wet lashes, she returned the smile.

She hadn't agreed to live with Martin yet she hadn't returned to live at her studio apartment, and each day she stayed she found it more and more difficult to leave.

Their relationship was easy and unencumbered. Martin hadn't asked anything from her except that she not leave him, and she hadn't—not yet. Not leaving him was a small price to pay when she compared it with his saving her life or perhaps a more serious injury than a broken jaw.

Filing out of the church with the other guests, Parris made her way down a flight of stairs to a room set up with small round tables decorated with deep rose pink and white tablecloths.

"Hello, Parris."

She turned and smiled at the man who had sat on her right at the restaurant the night of the engagement party.

"Hello, Bill."

Bill Dobbs, a used car salesman, had grown up with Jon Grant. His booming voice, florid face and easy laugh enhanced his image as a natural-born salesperson.

He extended his arm. "May I have the pleasure of your lovely company once again?"

Parris took the proffered arm, smiling. She had come with Martin but he would sit at the bridal table with the bride, groom and the matron of honor.

Two other couples joined her and Bill at the table, everyone extolling the beauty of the ethereal ceremony and Brittany's exquisite dress.

Her gown was a sheath of ivory organza and Alençon lace, and she had decided to forego the traditional veil, dressing her pale hair with a spray of miniature white roses and baby's breath.

As the wedding party gathered on the church lawn for photographs, a quartet played familiar tunes while waiters served trays of hot and cold canapes.

Martin's smile did not falter as Barbara Alexander pressed her firm breast against his arm. He couldn't wait for the photo session to end where he could disengage himself from Brittany's sister without causing a scene.

Barbara and Brittany shared the same ash-blond hair and cool-gray eyes, but that's where the resemblance ended. Whereas Brittany was delicate and demure, her older sister was lush and provocative.

Barbara had flirted with him during the rehearsal and at the dinner which was given afterwards at the home of the Alexanders' but he'd ignored her. What Barbara didn't know was that her fair coloring, pale hair and gray eyes were "too cool" for his tastes. He preferred women of color with dark hair and skintones in varying shades of brown, ranging from cappuccino cream to a rich mahogany.

"That just about does it," the photographer announced.

Martin was certain Barbara could hear his sigh of relief as he took her elbow, escorting her back to the church's social hall.

His gaze swept around the room and he saw Parris sitting with Bill Dobbs. The man was more annoying than fly paper. He had latched on to Parris again. The only thing which prevented him from warning Bill that Parris was "off limits" was that she would go home with him.

Martin seated Barbara next to Jon, then took his own seat beside Brittany. He couldn't pull his gaze away from Parris as she smiled at something Bill said. He found her more beautiful than the first time he met her.

A long sleeve silk jersey sheath in a warm orange flattered her body and her coloring. She had blown out her hair and pinned it up in a sophisticated French twist, leaving a few errant curls to grace her forehead and ears.

He had driven to her apartment to pick up the dress and a pair of shoes, and as he gathered other items she requested he'd tried to get a glimpse of who Parris was when he surveyed her apartment.

He had found it neat yet impersonal. Her bed was a convertible sofa and the small kitchen contained a bistro table and two chairs. There were no photographs or diplomas on the walls. A steamer trunk with a woven Navaho rug doubled as a coffee table and tablecloth. It was on the trunk that he found a stack of mail the landlady had left in the apartment whenever it wasn't picked up for more than two days.

He'd checked her answering machine; no one had called or if they had they didn't leave a message. If it hadn't been for the business suits, blouses and dresses hanging neatly in a small closet off the entrance and a toothbrush in the bathroom, Parris Simmons would not exist.

Martin placed a hand over Brittany's, squeezing her fingers gently. Turning, she smiled at him. Happiness shone from her gray eyes and he was pleased that she had married his friend. She was good for Jon, who claimed she mellowed him to where he'd given up his dream of racing cars to join his father's lucrative law practice.

"How did Parris meet Owen Lawson?" he asked her without preamble.

The blood drained from her face before she recovered. "I warned you to leave her alone." Her tone was sharp and waspish.

Martin's darker hand tightened on her fingers. "I can't leave her alone. She's going to be my wife."

Brittany's eyes widened until they resembled large silver dollars. "No," she whispered. She attempted to rise to her feet but he stopped her.

"Sit down." The two words were spoken quietly but said with such authority that Brittany obeyed him immediately.

"I am going to marry her," he repeated with emphasis. "But I need to know what happened between her and Owen Lawson."

"There's not much to tell," she whispered. "Parris met him when she was eighteen. Her car blew a tire one night and he came along and helped her fix it. He was off-duty so she didn't know he was a police officer. He took down her plate number and got her address through DMV. As a cop he had his ways of securing her unlisted telephone number and he called the next day. They dated a few times that summer and I thought it was over when we went back to Savannah for the fall semester.

"But whenever he had time off he drove up to see her. He was a lot older than she was and even I had to admit that he was very, very charming. He asked her to marry him and a few months after she graduated they were married. I felt she should've waited to marry him because she still was very broken up over losing her mother in a horrible car crash. But Owen didn't want to wait so they married and a month later it was over. She had to grieve twice, Martin. The breakup of her marriage and her mother's death."

"You don't have to worry about her anymore, Brittany. I'll take care of her and make her very, very happy."

She stared at him as if he'd grown two heads. "Those were the exact words Owen said the day he married her."

Martin's jaw hardened. Taking care of someone was not the same as trying to kill them, he thought.

He released Brittany's hand and smiled over her head at Jon. Jon's dark blue eyes were sparkling with excitement and his face was flushed from several glasses of champagne.

Raising his own glass of champagne, Martin saluted Jon before he drained the glass. He couldn't wait for the wedding reception to end so he could take Parris home.

Chapter 7

Parris danced through the front door, curtsying deeply to Martin. "You owe me a dance, Mr. Cole."

Martin closed the door, took her in his arms and waltzed her over the living room floor, humming.

"You hum nicely, but how about putting on some music?" she suggested, staring at the waning sunlight coming through the windows.

He noted the dreamy expression on her face. "What's your pleasure?" Martin spun her around and around until she begged him to stop. Grasping her hand firmly, he led her over to the shelves of compact discs and cassettes. "Something slow, fast or a little salsa?"

"Salsa."

He retrieved a cassette and inserted it in a tape deck, then removed the jacket to his tuxedo before he pushed the play button. Tossing the jacket across the room, he swung Parris against his body, molding her breasts to his chest.

"You've chosen the dance of passion and fire," he whispered, lowering his head until his warm breath swept over her mouth. "Are you familiar with passion, Parris?"

Staring up at him, she nodded mutely. She had glimpsed passion the few times he'd kissed her.

"How about the fire?"

"No. Not the fire," she admitted breathlessly.

The slow rhythmic pounding of conga drums filled the living room and Martin moved fluidly to the beat as she followed his expert lead.

She felt the muscles in his thighs flexing and unflexing with each step. Closing her eyes, she floated with him as their bodies were joined, chest to knees, swaying and calling to each other.

The two glasses of champagne simmered in her blood and she felt the rising inferno coming from Martin and spreading to her until she wilted in the heat.

Her slender arms moved from his shoulders to his strong neck and she held onto him like a straw tossed on an ocean wave.

Registering her feminine heat and the rising scent of her body, Martin pulled her closer, trying to absorb her into himself. He was certain she could hear his increased respiration and feel the hardness he was helpless to control. His fire and passion were raging and spreading—out of control, and he did to her what he didn't do the first time he tasted her lips. He devoured her mouth.

One hand held her chin gently as the other searched for the zipper at the back of her dress. Forcing himself to go slowly, he lowered the zipper to her waist, exposing her bare back. Martin didn't want to hurt Parris nor did he want to frighten her.

Both hands feathered over her naked skin until his hands grazed the cotton panty of her pantyhose. She moaned once against his invading tongue as one hand gathered the hem of her dress to her waist.

Parris was lightheaded with her rising desire and her hands were as busy as Martin's when she untied the deep rose pink length of satin from around his neck. The bow tie floated to the floor.

A low tortured groan was swallowed up by the drums the moment Martin's hand slipped under the waistband to her panty-hose and he found her hot, wet and pulsing.

"That's the fire, baby," he crooned against her moist lips. "You are the fire."

His hand claimed her womanhood, one finger searching

between the succulent folds and finding her ready. Her pulsing flesh closed on his finger and he swept her up in his arms, taking the stairs two at a time.

Placing her on the center of his bed, Martin didn't take his gaze off her face. He recognized the flood of desire flushing her features. Her dress, bunched up above her waist and down around her shoulders was a twisted ribbon of orange. Silken nylons shimmered on her long legs and the variegated colors of orange, purple, pink and red on the snakeskin high heels on her narrow feet contrasted sharply against the white bed sheet.

Undressing quickly, his trousers, cummerbund, socks and shoes were pooled on the carpeted floor. Seconds later his briefs joined the pile, and he stood above her, naked, proud and magnificent in all of his throbbing male splendor.

Parris wanted to look away but couldn't. She could not believe the perfection of the body poised above her. Martin Cole was larger, much larger than she thought he could possibly be. His broad chest was covered with thick black curling hair which tapered to a thin line before disappearing into an inverted triangle of even coarser hair, from which throbbed a long, thick length of hard dark-brown flesh nestled between strong muscled thighs.

She closed her eyes, registering the overwhelming heat from his body as he sank down to the bed. She curled her fingers into tight fists as he removed her dress, shoes and then her pantyhose, opening them only when she heard Martin's breath explode from between his compressed lips.

Every muscle in his body screamed and vibrated. The smell of her perfume on her skin and hair rose sharply in his nostrils, making his blood rush hot and uncontrollably in his veins.

Martin laid his right hand, fingers outstretched over her flat belly. She inhaled deeply and her firm golden breasts with their dark nipples trembled noticeably above her narrow rib cage. He lay down beside Parris, pulling her to his side. He had to force himself to go slow; slow enough so he wouldn't spill out his passions before he claimed her body.

"I am going to love you, Parris. Love you until you forget any other man ever existed. Love you until you want me as much as I want you." Moving over her, he supported his weight on his elbows and lowered his body.

Her arms curved under his arms and grasped his thick shoulders. "I want you, Martin. I want you so very, very much," she confessed.

He kissed her forehead, her nose, her mouth, then moved lower to her neck, his tongue tasting and savoring her flesh. "Oh, baby," he moaned before his mouth closed over a breast. He devoured the breast, his teeth tightening on the nipple, then moved over to give the other one equal attention.

Parris swallowed back the sobs threatening to spill from her throat. She ran her hands up and down his damp back, feeling the muscles contracting under her fingers. She did gasp when his tongue traced a path downward between her breasts to her ribs and further down to her stomach.

His hot breath scorched the furred triangle between her thighs and she arched instinctively. Her body squirmed beneath him once his finger found her again, her hips moving erotically on the sheet.

The temperature of her body alternated between hot and cold. The pleasure Martin wrung from her was pure and unrestrained.

The dormant sexuality of her body had been awakened and she craved his possession, her desire rising quickly. She groaned in frustration when he left her, but she smiled when she saw him reach into the drawer of the bedside table and withdraw a small packet.

Breathing heavily, she waited until he withdrew the latex covering and rolled it down the length of his rigid flesh.

Her breasts tingled against his hair-roughened chest as he moved over her again and positioned his length between her thighs.

Martin found her opening and pushed gently. He increased the pressure until a small cry from Parris halted him. She was wet enough but he hadn't thought she would be so tight.

"Relax, baby," he crooned. He kissed her mouth, renewing her desire. Her fingers fastened in his long hair, pulling the heavy curls from the confines of its elastic fastening.

Moving down her body, he kissed her belly, leaving heat as his hot mouth seared her naked flesh. Settling himself at the foot of the king-size bed, he tasted the honey flowing from between her legs.

Parris gasped in sweet agony, unable to believe the pleasure whirling and spiraling, screaming for release.

She couldn't disguise her body's reaction as his tongue searched where his finger had been and she surrendered to the ecstasy shaking her uncontrollably.

She was so caught up in the wonder of fulfillment that she barely registered the sharp invasion of her body. Arching, she cried out as Martin again sought entry into her tight flesh.

Martin went still. She couldn't be, he thought. She just couldn't be!

He withdrew and removed the latex condom. A spurt of desire made him harder, and he wanted her even more.

His own need for fulfillment matched Parris's as he pulled back and drove his starving flesh into hers. He felt the resistance give way and seconds later he was lost in the fiery force of vibrating liquid fire, pulling him in where he was helpless to resist the ecstasy hurtling him to another dimension.

Parris felt the rigid fullness taking up every inch of her body and she responded to the rocking motion of her womb. The involuntary tremors began, taking her higher and higher until she thought she would surely die.

Her fingernails bit into the firm muscles in his buttocks and she buried her face against his shoulder. Her teeth claimed the flesh below his throat and she cried out shamelessly as she abandoned herself to the sweet burning joy of completion.

Martin was aware of the moment her body flowered and closed around his sex and he was lost. He exploded, filling her womb with his love and his passion.

Parris felt his weight, registered his heat and felt the soreness between her thighs, savoring the feeling of satisfaction that left her unable to move. Closing her eyes, she succumbed to the sleep of a sated lover.

Martin loathe to withdraw from her body. He wanted to lie between her thighs—forever.

But he did withdraw, his brow furrowed in confusion. Reaching over, he turned on the lamp on the table and stared down at the dark red stains on the sheet and between Parris's thighs.

Sitting back on his heels, he shook his head. How could she be? How could Parris be a virgin when she had been married?

Even though she had lived with Owen Lawson for a month—surely that should have been time for her to share her body with her husband.

He picked up the unused condom and tossed it on the floor. Sinking down the bed beside her, he exhaled and closed his eyes. He didn't know what to think, and again he wanted answers from the woman asleep under his roof.

The answers would have to wait; wait until she woke up.

Parris woke, not knowing the time or the day. The vertical blinds were drawn and the bedroom was bathed in a soft pink light. Turning over, she realized she was not in her bedroom.

She sat up and Martin moved from where he sat in the shadows to stand beside the bed. "What time is it?"

"Nine-thirty."

She saw the direction of his gaze and she pulled the sheet up over her naked breasts. "How long have I been asleep?"

He took in her heavy lids and the huskier than usual sound of her voice. She was even sexy after making love. "A little bit more than three hours." Reaching out, he pulled the sheet from her loose grip. "I ran some water for your bath."

Parris was forced to let go of the sheet and hold onto his neck as he scooped her from the bed. Burying her face against his strong neck, she kissed him behind the ear.

Martin stumbled slightly and tightened his grip under her knees. "Don't do that." He tried to sound angry, but chuckled when she ran the tip of her tongue around the outline of his ear.

"You have sexy ears, Martin." She fastened his curling hair behind his ears. "Why do you wear your hair so long?"

Studying her face thoughtfully for a moment, he said, "It's my way of rebelling."

"Against who?"

"Against those who think they know who I am," Martin answered truthfully. "When it comes to business and finance I can walk the walk and talk the talk with the best of them. But that's where the similarity ends. When I work a deal everyone at the table knows which is mine because I've given it my signature. In other words it is the same but it looks different."

A slight frown of confusion appeared between her eyes. "I don't understand."

He walked into the bathroom and settled her into a sunken tub of swirling warm water from pulsating jets. Stripping off his jeans, he joined her in the black marble Jacuzzi.

"You're a designer. What's makes your work different from someone else's?"

She luxuriated in the healing water, sinking down to a depression along the side of the tub. Moisture beaded quickly on her face and curled her hair.

"My preference for certain color combinations and fabrics. I'm known for working with light walls, natural woods and mirrors."

"These features are your signature, Parris. One of these days I'll have you read a proposal, then ask you to identify my signature."

She watched Martin run a wet hand through his hair, pushing the heavy curls off his forehead. "How will I know which is or isn't yours?"

"You've lived with me for a month. You should've learned something about me in that time."

Her expression still registered confusion. *Don't you know that I'm in love with you, Parris?* Martin screamed silently to her. *Don't you know that I want to marry you?*

He waded over to her, pulling her against his chest. The warm water heightened the color in her face. Lowering his head, he kissed her tenderly.

Her legs floated between his and Parris didn't have to look down to see his rising desire. She felt it against her bare thighs.

"Put your legs around my waist," he ordered quietly.

She complied as he lifted her easily and entered her newly

opened flesh. The water warm helped ease the sore muscles she never had to use before.

Holding onto his neck, she leaned back in Martin's strong embrace and once again experienced a shimmering moment of uncontrolled passion. Her eager response to his raw sensuousness shocked the both of them as she collapsed against his chest, her breath coming in long, surrendering moans.

Deep shuddering groans escaped Martin's parted lips before they faded away when he repeated her name over and over like a litany.

He recovered enough to retrieve a thick terry wash cloth and a bar of scented soap and lathered her body, taking special care with the area between her legs.

Parris returned the favor as she lathered his large body, her teasing fingers lingering between his thighs.

He scooped a handful of water over her hair; she sputtered, then splashed his face. It ended with a passionate kiss that left the both of them breathless.

Martin stepped out of the tub, extending his hand and pulling her up in one strong motion. He wrapped her in a large thick bath sheet, rubbing her body until her skin glowed and tingled.

"Remind me not to share a bath with you again," she murmured. Her hair was soaked and limp strands had escaped the pins she used for her French twist.

"I thought you enjoyed it."

"I enjoyed everything except the dunking."

He towel-dried his hair, grinning at her. "Then we'll repeat everything except the dunking."

Martin dropped his towel to the floor and reached for her. Tilting her chin, he made passionate love to her with his eyes. "Parris, why didn't you tell me you were a virgin?"

Her eyes widened and her breathing halted, then started up again. Her gaze was directed to the base of Martin's throat where her teeth had left a dark red bruise.

"You didn't ask me," she replied.

"I assumed you wouldn't be one because you'd been married."

"You assumed wrong."

Martin noted the hostility in her voice. "What the hell did Lawson do to you?"

Parris pulled away from him, taking a backward step. How could she tell Martin that Owen hadn't been able to make love to her because his addiction made him impotent? She couldn't tell Martin about Owen's impotency without breaking her promise to Owen that she would never tell anyone about his addiction if he gave her her freedom.

"You said that I should let you know what I don't want and don't like. I don't want or like to discuss Owen Lawson."

He stiffened as though she had struck him. She had given him back his own words. Nodding slowly, he said, "I'll respect your request."

She gave him a smile, moving closer and curving her arms around his neck. Martin felt the soft crush of her breasts, but they failed to arouse him. He would never mention her ex-husband's name to her again, but some unspoken voice whispered that the man would turn up again to threaten Parris and drive a wedge between them.

Chapter 8

Martin had successfully concealed his anger. He had been in San José for a week, having completed his negotiations with Raul Cordero-Vega, but not without a few concessions. ColeDiz International Ltd. had pledged a million dollars to support the preservation of Costa Rica's rain forest.

Interior Minister Raul Cordero-Vega was relentless in his demands. It was as if the retired colonel had taken perverse pleasure in making the heir apparent to ColeDiz International Ltd. wait two days before granting him an audience; then he would not concede to lowering the tariff for exports until Martin threatened to shut down production and withdraw all ColeDiz business dealings from the Central American nation.

Martin's call to Samuel Cole elicited a string of colorful expletives from the elder Cole who promised he would make Cordero-Vega pay for his dictatorial demands.

"A million dollars is nothing compared to what ColeDiz will lose if we halt production before we're able to set up in Belize," Martin countered.

"You're right, Martin," Samuel agreed, "but I hate to have Cordero-Vega think he can hold ColeDiz hostage while he exploits us for what we both know is his personal illegal scam. The man's probably amassing a fortune to raise a private army to overthrow the Costa Rican democratic government."

"Whatever his plan for the future let's hope we're operating in Belize if he decides to replay this scenario."

"Why don't you see if you can set up an appointment with the Belize officials before you return home."

"I've confirmed a meeting with their interior department for the end of the month."

There was a pause before Samuel Cole replied. "Why wait three weeks, Martin? You're right there."

Martin ran a hand over his face in a gesture which indicated weariness. "I'll meet with them after I get back. Raul took more than a year to set us up for this ploy and I don't think he'll squeeze us again for a while."

"I don't want to wait for him to set us up again," Samuel argued.

"I said I'll finalize everything when I get back," Martin insisted.

"Get back from where?"

"I'm taking a week off."

"Where the hell are you going?"

Martin's jaw tightened as he closed his eyes. Fatigue, frustration and annoyance swept over him in a rush. Cordero-Vega had manipulated him, his father was pressuring him and he had been away from Parris for more than a week. All he wanted was out of San José and in Parris's arms on a beach far enough away from Florida and anything which vaguely resembled ColeDiz International Ltd.

"I'm going on vacation, Father. I'll have a report of this trip on your desk before I come back." He depressed a button not permitting Samuel a chance to interrogate him further or offer an apology.

Punching in several numbers, he dialed the exchange to his home. He counted the four rings before the answering machine was activated. A slight frown creased his forehead. Parris hadn't answered the call.

Checking his watch, his frown deepened. It was nearly ten o'clock in Florida and he wondered if perhaps she was asleep or in the bathroom. No, he thought. Even if she had been in the bathroom she would've heard the telephone. He had installed telephones in every room in the house.

Martin lay down on the bed and folded his arms under his head. He wasn't scheduled to leave San José until early the following morning and he needed to hear Parris's voice.

He had convinced her to stay at his house until he returned. She had agreed and he looked forward to his nightly telephone calls with her. Hearing her velvety voice coming through the wire each night dissolved his tension and made him look forward to concluding his business negotiations and returning to her as quickly as possible.

Half an hour later he rang his house again. This time Parris picked up the receiver. "Hello."

Martin's entire body warmed to the sultry greeting. "Hello back to you too," he replied. "How are you?"

"Good. How's everything going?"

"Everything's concluded. I'm coming home in the morning."

There was silence. "I'm glad to hear that Martin," Parris admitted. "I've been a little lonely around here by myself."

Martin managed an easy smile for the first time in a week. "Are you saying that you miss me?"

"I miss you a lot," she confessed.

He chuckled. "How would you like a vacation?"

"I've been vacationing for five weeks, Martin."

"A real vacation."

"Where?"

"Jamaica."

"Remember, Martin, I have to go back to work in another week."

"I'll have you back in time for you to return to work. I'll make the flight arrangements as soon as I hang up."

"When do you intend to leave for Jamaica?"

"Tomorrow. I'll call you in the morning to let you know the time of our flight."

"I have to get my passport and pick up some clothes…"

"We'll just have time to pick up your passport, Parris," he interrupted. "I'll buy you what you need to wear once we get to Jamaica."

"Martin…"

"I'm sorry to end this call," he said, cutting her off again, "but

I have to make reservations for our flight. Good night, darling. I'll see you tomorrow."

What he didn't say was that not only did he miss her but that he loved her. That was something he would tell her when he saw her again. A week away from her had intensified his feelings to where he knew he wanted to spend the rest of his life with Parris Simmons.

The weather on Jamaica was warm, soothing and healing, and Martin experienced a feeling of well-being as he sat beside Parris in a well-preserved Land Rover as the hired driver sped across the island.

Pulling Parris to his side, he pressed a kiss to her temple. "I don't think you'll get to wear half of what you bought," he whispered against her ear.

She had spent more than two hours browsing in trendy shops in Kingston. Many of the business owners in the Jamaican capital recognized his face and name and Parris was afforded the courteous attention reserved for the wealthy privileged residents of the Caribbean island.

"Why not, Martin?" Turning her head slightly, she stared up at him.

"Because we're going to spend half of our time on the beach and the other half in bed." He laughed aloud as she lowered her gaze.

"I don't intend to spend my vacation in bed," she countered quietly, staring at the back of the driver's head.

"We'll see about that," he teased.

"Do you think we can squeeze in a night of dancing in between the bed and the beach?"

Lowering his head to her shoulder, Martin held her close. "So you want a little reggae to go along with the salsa? I'll be more than willing to accommodate you, darling."

Parris leaned into his strength, one hand searching and undoing the buttons on his shirt. Her fingers grazed the muscled hardness of his furred chest, eliciting a slight gasp from him.

"I wasn't talking about that kind of dancing, *darling,*" she crooned.

His fingers caught her wrist, pulling her hand away from his fevered flesh. They hadn't made love before leaving Florida. There was only enough time after his connecting flight from Miami landed in West Palm Beach to pick up Parris, then drive to her apartment where she picked up her passport before they returned to the airport for their flight to Miami and a connecting one to Kingston.

His body was on fire, his flesh throbbing. He wanted her with a passion which bordered on hysteria. He wanted to bury himself in her hot, tight body, becoming one with her. He wanted Parris Simmons as his wife and as the mother of his children.

"Where are we going?" Parris asked after a long comfortable silence.

"Ocho Rios."

"Do you have vacation properties there?"

"No. We're going to stay at a friend's place."

"Will this friend be in attendance?"

Martin chuckled, ruffling her hair. "You're full of questions, aren't you?"

"I just want to know what to expect."

"This friend will not be in attendance. He's in Germany."

Tilting her chin, Parris smiled up at him. "So it's just going to be the two of us."

He lowered his head and kissed her awaiting lips. "You, me, the ocean and the sand and all of the tropical fruit we can pick," he murmured against her moist mouth.

Nodding, she settled against his chest and closed her eyes, not opening them again until the driver parked the Land Rover in front of a house in Ocho Rios.

Martin's friend's home was a two-storied white stucco structure that was wholly West Indian in character: red Spanish tiled roof, white tiled floors surrounding the house and Creole jalousie shutters. Exotic flowers and trees added to the lushness of the property.

She walked around to the rear of the house while the driver unloaded Martin's luggage and her purchases from the roof of the rugged vehicle.

The fruit trees were pregnant with ripened fruit, bananas, mangoes, oranges and lemons swaying gently from an ocean breeze.

Turning around and shielding her eyes from the brilliance of the setting sun with a pair of sunglasses, Parris noted that there wasn't another structure in sight as a stretch of white sand and the blue-green ribbon of the Caribbean in the distance served as the backdrop for the exotic setting.

She heard footsteps and turned. Martin moved toward her, a smile deepening the dimples in his cheeks.

"How do you like it?" he asked, his gaze sweeping over her face and body in a single glance. The sea breeze lifted her hair while molding a pale yellow silk blouse to her breasts.

Winding an arm through his, she returned his smile. "It's beautiful."

"You're beautiful, Parris." His compliment seemed to shock her as her jaw dropped slightly. He felt her fingers tighten on his arm. Reaching up, he removed her sunglasses and stared down into her clear brown eyes. There was enough daylight left to see the mysterious, hypnotic green lights in their depths.

"Don't," he urged as she attempted to turn away from him. "Look at me, Parris. That's it," Martin crooned when she tilted her chin to stare up at him. "I will never lie to you. Never."

Parris inhaled, her chest rising and falling with a delicate shudder. "You think I'm beautiful, Martin." Her voice held a hint of disbelief.

He nodded slowly. "Quite beautiful."

Her full lips softened with a smile. "Then that makes two of us because I find you to be quite beautiful."

Martin laughed, shaking his head. "Men aren't beautiful."

"You are."

"I am not beautiful."

"If you're not beautiful, then what are you?"

"I'm average-looking," he replied, shrugging broad shoulders. "Let's go for a walk. We'll unpack later."

Parris fell in step beside him, her arm going around his waist. "Did I embarrass you?"

"What about?"

"Your looks."

"No," he replied quickly.

She glanced up at his distinctive profile. She could tell by the throbbing muscle in his jaw that he was uncomfortable and that she had embarrassed him.

"I never thought you would be so modest," she continued, unable to resist teasing him.

Martin increased the pressure of his arm around her narrow waist. "I've been called a lot of things, but never modest."

"What have you been called?"

"Names which I won't repeat."

Parris thought of the names Owen had called her that she could never repeat. It was as if he had blamed her for his substance abuse problem. He blamed the differences in their ages, saying he felt more like her father than her fiancé. He claimed he felt like a pedophile each time he kissed her or attempted to touch her body, the groping encounters ending with her trembling in sexual frustration and Owen stalking out enraged because he was unable to make love to her.

Pushing memories of Owen to the deep recesses of her mind, Parris followed Martin as they headed in the direction of the beach.

Martin sat down on the sand, pulling her down with him. He slipped out of his loafers, unbuttoned his shirt and shrugged out of it, then pushed off his slacks.

Parris stared at him. "What are you doing?"

"I'm going swimming."

"Aren't you going to put on bathing trunks?" He'd removed his briefs.

"No. This is a private beach. No one will see us."

Rising to his feet, Martin stood before her dark and powerful as an African fertility totem. He held out his hand and she shook her head.

"I can't."

Martin stared at her as she sat on back on folded knees, head lowered and both hands clasped tightly together on her lap. Suddenly it hit him. How quickly he had forgotten. It wasn't modesty that made her unwilling to shed her clothing and swim naked with him, but her near-drowning at the hands of her ex-husband. It was still too soon and too real for her to forget the attempt on her life.

Hunkering down to the sand beside her, he pulled her to his chest. He felt her trembling.

"It's going to be all right, Parris. You're safe with me. I won't let anyone or anything hurt you."

Parris inhaled the cologne on his chest. She knew she was safe. As long as she was with Martin she would always feel safe.

"I…I'm sorry, Martin," she stammered. "It's just that all of it came back…and…and I could…" She couldn't continue.

"If you don't want to go swimming it's fine with me."

"It's not you," she insisted. "It's me. When you held your hand out to me I saw it as Owen's. I'd put my hand in his, trusting him when all he wanted was to kill me."

"How could I be like him, Parris? I saved your life."

"I know," she said, sighing heavily. "And I'll never be able to thank you enough for that."

You will thank me, Martin thought. You'll become my wife. Releasing her, he reached for his slacks, but he was momentarily surprised when Parris's hand stopped him. He tried seeing her expression in the waning light.

"I've got to stop reliving that night, Martin. I have to go forward and forget what Owen did to me. I'll go swimming with you."

Cradling her face between his palms, he brushed a light kiss over her lips. "You don't have to if…"

"I *have* to," she interrupted.

Her hands were shaking as she attempted to unbutton her blouse and Martin pushed them gently aside and helped her undress. Her blouse, matching skirt and underwear lay on the sand beside his clothes. He kissed her deeply then swung her up his arms and walked across the pristine white sand and into the warm water. They rode the waves and splashed like little children as the sun dropped below the horizon and stars lit up the tropical sky like diamond dust.

Parris floated over to Martin and held onto his neck. "I'm turning into a raisin," she laughed, breathing heavily.

He nibbled at her neck. "I love raisins."

She giggled like a little girl, but all of the teasing stopped when his mouth covered a breast. She gasped and buried her face against his shoulder.

"I think we'd better go back," he mumbled against the soft mound of flesh.

"Please," Parris pleaded, succumbing to the sensual spell Martin had spun.

Chapter 9

Martin waited until their third night in Ocho Rios to reveal the depth of his feelings for Parris. He hadn't made love to her because he knew she was never responsive after their having made love.

He sat up in bed, his back pressed against the elaborately carved headboard, holding her as she lay on his chest between his outstretched legs, his large hands caressing the silken skin over her flat belly.

"Are you enjoying your vacation?" he asked softly.

"It's been perfect," Parris replied, not opening her eyes.

"Open your eyes." Martin held Parris's gaze. "I want you to be my wife."

His voice, warm, soft and silky, chilled her to the bone. Her delicate jaw dropped slightly. "You're not asking me to marry you?"

"I am." He cradled her face between his palms. "I'm going to ask a lot of things of you. I want you to live with me, marry me, decorate our home and have my children. These are things I've never asked of another woman, Parris."

Parris's eyes widened in surprise before she closed them tightly. "No," she replied, trying to shake her head.

Martin tightened his hold on her head. "I love you."

"Don't!"

"Don't tell me how to feel, Parris." Anger was evident in his voice. "Look at me," he ordered. Her lids fluttered up. "I can't help the way I feel about you." His voice was quieter, softer. "I didn't plan to fall in love with you, but I did. This is all so very new to me, darling. All I know is that I want you and I want to spend the rest of my life with you."

Parris masked inner turmoil with deceptive calmness. "I can't give you what you want, Martin." There was no way she could marry him. She did not want a repeat of her short-lived marriage to Owen.

She had fallen in love with Owen and agreed to marry him, and despite Owen's claim that he wanted to wait to marry her before he made love to her she loved him blindly. Everything was so perfect until their wedding night.

Martin Diaz Cole was everything Owen Lawson wasn't. He was secure and virile. Yet there was an unknown component in Martin's personality that frightened her. An unspoken peculiar characteristic which said that if she married him her life would be inexorably changed forever.

"What can you give me?" he questioned, successfully concealing his disappointment.

"I will live with you and decorate your home."

Dammit, he raged inwardly. He could get any woman to live with him and contract with any design firm to decorate his home. But what he wanted most from Parris she withheld.

He had to accept what she was willing to give him—for now.

His gaze dropped from her eyes to her shoulders and finally to her full breasts pressed to his chest. He was certain she could feel the runaway beating of his heart.

"Do you love me, Parris?"

Martin's voice was so soft that Parris barely heard his query. She studied his lean dark-skinned face, her answer radiating from her gaze before she spoke.

"Yes, Martin, I love you."

Anchoring his hands under her arms, he pulled her up higher

and fastened his mouth to her breasts, his teeth and tongue wringing spasms of desire from her wet, throbbing core.

Reversing their positions, he moved over her, his hair swinging forward and brushing her face. She inhaled his cologne and the subtle male scent that was Martin's and Martin's alone. She would be able find him in a darkened room filled with a hundred men.

His hands slipped under her hips, cupping her buttocks as she guided his rigid sex into her hot, inviting body.

Parris was unmindful that Martin hadn't stop to reach for the small packets he kept on the bedside table as she gave into the fiery sensations of his thrusting hips. Each thrust was harder and deeper than the one before it and she tried thinking of everything but the rising desire threatening to stop her breath where she would die in Martin's arms.

Martin was lost in his own world of sexual hysteria. Each time he made love to Parris he was rewarded with an unselfish offering where she held nothing back.

She never faked her responses and her slender body demanded wordlessly from him what he had never given another woman— all of himself.

He moved his mouth over hers, caressing her lips before they parted to his searching tongue. His tongue matched the rhythmic cadence of his pounding hips, both moving with a frenzied thrusting motion that left Parris moaning and gasping for air. She whispered his name, the sound of her husky voice penetrating the fog burning his brain.

"Take all of me," he pleaded over and over, as her body stretched to accommodate his prodigious size. "Take it. That's it, baby. "That's it," he repeated.

She took him—every inch of length and width of his blood-engorged sex until she felt him touch her womb.

She screamed his name, the sound of it floating to the ceiling and it was swallowed up by the whirring sound of the blades from a ceiling fan.

Martin felt the room spin, the light from the lamp dim and the strong milking suction of Parris's body as she pulled him in until they ceased to exist as separate entities.

He loved her and she loved him. That was all that mattered as he exploded, leaving his seed buried deep within her body.

Chapter 10

Martin and Parris returned to the States at the end of a week tanned and relaxed. They strolled through the West Palm Beach airport, hand-in-hand, following a red cap pushing a cart filled with their luggage out of the terminal to an awaiting taxi.

"Martin!"

He turned in the direction of a feminine voice and was temporarily blinded by the flash of a bulb. He blinked several times to clear his vision, then noted the surprised expression on Parris's face.

"Thanks, darling," crooned the petite woman with the camera.

Parris stared at the woman's retreating back, her pulses racing. "Who was that?"

"She's a photographer with the *West Palm Beach Post.*"

"Why did she take your picture?"

Martin's arm circled her waist, pulling her closer to his side. "She took *our* picture. Natalie's been trying to get some "dirt" on me for a long time. And if I know Natalie she'll probably make up something lewd for Renata Baldwin's gossip column."

"I hope not," Parris replied. She didn't want her association with Martin Cole advertised in the local morning newspaper.

His dark eyes registered her distressed look. "Does it bother you to be seen with me?"

Tilting her chin, she stared up at him. The hot Jamaican sun had burned his skin to a rich mahogany brown, accentuating the inky blackness of his hair and eyebrows.

"No," she said. What bothered her was that there was no valid reason to advertise their liaison to all of the citizens of West Palm Beach. Those interested in Martin Cole would discover soon enough that she was living with him even though she was less concerned with propriety than she was about having lies printed about her.

A taxi pulled up to the curb and the red cap opened the rear door. Martin settled her on the seat, then waited until their luggage was loaded in the trunk of the car before giving the driver his destination.

He pressed a bill into the red cap's hand. "Thank you, Mr. Bennett."

"Thank you, Mr. Cole. And you have a good evening," the elderly red cap said with a smile.

Martin returned his smile. "You do the same, Mr. Bennett."

"Who don't you know, Martin?" Parris asked when he was seated beside her.

"You. I don't know you, Parris Simmons."

"You know all you need to know about me. Where are we going?" Parris asked as the cab left the airport in the opposite direction from Martin's housing development.

"I have to pick up a car for you," Martin explained. "If you're going to live with me you're going to need a car to get to work."

Parris glanced down at her watch. "It's Saturday night, and it's seven o'clock. Where are you going to buy a car at this hour?"

"I didn't say I was going to buy a car, Parris. I said I was going to pick up a car."

"Where?"

"At my parents' house."

"Martin!"

He could hear the panic in her voice. "You look wonderful."

"I'm not concerned about how I look. I'm just not prepared to meet your parents. What are you going to tell them about me?"

"I'll tell them the truth. That we've been living together for over a month and that we're in love with each other."

A flicker of uneasiness coursed through her. "You can't come out and say that."

"Why not? It's the truth."

Why not? she said over and over to herself as the taxi pulled into a circular drive leading to a large house designed in Spanish and Italian revival styles with barrel-tiled red roofs, a stucco facade and balconies shrouded in lush bougainvillea and sweeping French doors that opened onto broad expanses of terraces with spectacular panoramic water views. The magnificent structure was surrounded by tropical foliage, exotic gardens and the reflection of light off sparkling lake waters.

Martin directed the driver to leave their luggage by the front door as he pushed it open and let Parris proceed him into an entrance with an African slate floor. Her professional gaze catalogued the Dutch ebony and gilt table dating to the eighteenth century cradling a Baccarat vase with a profusion of snow-white roses.

She registered the sound of footsteps and turned to find a tall slender woman dressed in pink silk with short graying black hair staring at her. There was no mistaking who the woman was. She and Martin shared the same delicate features.

The older woman's surprise was short-lived when she smiled at her son. Her dimpled smile was Martin's.

"Darling," she crooned, her voice soft and caressing. "It's nice that you decided to share dinner with us. But you should've let us know that you were bringing company."

Martin gathered his mother to his chest and kissed her cheek. "We didn't come for dinner. I came to pick up a car."

Marguerite Josefina Diaz Cole registered the "we" and arched her sweeping black eyebrows. Pulling away from Martin, she gave him a questioning look. "Can't you stay for a few minutes? I was just telling Sammy that I haven't seen you in weeks."

Martin grasped Parris's hand and squeezed her fingers. "Mother, I'd like you to meet Parris Simmons. Parris, my mother, Marguerite Cole."

Parris managed a smile for the tall elegant woman. "My pleasure, Mrs. Cole." Even though she and Martin's mother were of equal height, Marguerite seemed to stare down her thin delicate nose at her.

"Please call me M.J." She turned her attention back to Martin before Parris could acknowledge her as M.J. "You don't have to eat, Martin. Just stay a while and have some coffee. You know that Saturday nights are always informal."

Martin glanced down at Parris and she nodded. "Okay. We'll have coffee."

He released her fingers and curved an arm around her waist. "Come, I'll show where you can freshen up."

Martin led Parris up a flight of twin staircases and down a hall. She barely had time to note the furnishings which were predominately French. She saw a pair of Louis XVI wing chairs upholstered with Scalamandré silk and a bench of the same period covered in Bergamo silk in a sitting room off a second floor bedroom.

"Even though I don't live here any longer I haven't removed everything from my apartment. This house has twenty-four rooms and four apartment suites," Martin explained. "I think my parents planned on having six children, but stopped at four. I'm the oldest. I have two sisters and one brother."

"Do they live here?"

"Only David. Nancy and Juliana are married and live in Palm Beach."

She followed Martin into a bedroom suite that was a startling departure from the other rooms in the house. Martin's apartment was dramatically contemporary from the furnishings to the stark blacks, whites and grays of sofas, chairs and rugs. The suite contained a sitting/dressing room, a bedroom and an adjoining full bathroom.

She had her answer in what period to decorate his home—a blending of contemporary with a few Art Deco and antique pieces.

Parris examined her face over the lighted sink in the bathroom. Her cheeks were beginning to fill out again and the dark shadows under her eyes had disappeared. The week in Jamaica had darkened her golden-brown skin where it shimmered with a glow of good health. She unpinned her hair and brushed it then repinned it in a twist with a feathering of bangs across her forehead. Searching the depths of her handbag, she found a tube of burnt-orange lipstick and applied a coat of color to her lips.

After washing and drying her hands she turned to leave the bathroom but ran into Martin. His hands went out as he steadied her.

"Careful, darling." He stared down at her face, his eyes moving slowly over her mouth. "You look beautiful," he whispered reverently.

She had barely caught her breath when he took it again as his mouth covered hers, his tongue pushing gently against her lips. Her lips parted and his tongue worked it magic as it searched, caressed and communicated delicious sensations of what she could expect when they returned home.

Parris pressed her breasts to his hard chest, her arms going around his neck. "Home." It was strange that she could think of Martin's house as her home; she realized home wasn't a structure of wood, slate or stucco but Martin. He was home. Being with him afforded her shelter, protection and security.

Her arms came down and she pushed against his broad chest with both hands. "Martin," she gasped. "Your mother is waiting for us."

Curbing the urge to kiss her again, he said, "You've met beauty and now it's time you meet the beast. The beast is my father."

Parris didn't know what to expect from Samuel Cole, but it wasn't the tall, muscled man with a head of shocking white hair and a booming voice.

Her smaller hand was lost in the huge one Samuel extended to her. "Welcome, welcome." He pumped her hand vigorously. "It's been a while since Martin has brought a girl home to meet us, but if you're the reason for this auspicious occasion then you're welcome here anytime."

"Thank you, Mr. Cole." Parris felt the heat in her face when Samuel Cole stared openly at her.

"Call me Sammy. I've made it a rule not to stand on ceremony in my home."

Parris smiled up at the man with the rich sienna-brown coloring.

Looping her hand over his arm, Sammy led her out of the living room to a loggia. Martin followed, escorting M.J.

The loggia opened out to a courtyard and beyond the court-yard gardens. Lighted overhead Spanish lanterns spilled golden light onto a table of twisted rattan set with dining for six.

Martin seated his mother. "Who else are you expecting?"

"David said he might come back in time to eat with us." M.J. offered Sammy her attractive smile. "We're ready, dear."

Martin moved to stand behind Parris's chair after his father had seated her. The fingers of his right hand trailed lightly over her bare arm. The gesture was barely perceptible but neither of the older Coles missed its possessive significance.

The two men retreated inside the house, leaving Parris with M.J.

Sammy reached for a large wooden bowl filled with salad greens. "How serious is this, Martin?"

He stared at his father, his gaze never wavering. "It's very serious. We've been living together. And if she'd have me I'd marry her tomorrow."

Sammy crossed thick arms over his chest. "That's serious," he replied in awe.

Sammy removed a large glass bowl of seafood salad from the refrigerator and several bottles filled with salad dressings. The two men were silent as they returned to the loggia.

Martin was relieved to find Parris chatting amicably with his mother. He had found on occasion that M.J. tended to intimidate people with her formal presence. She had grown up as a member of pre-revolutionary Cuban aristocracy, and even after more than thirty years the breeding and privileges afforded her class had not faltered or vanished.

"Parris tells me that she is a decorator," M.J. said to her husband.

"Who do you work for?" Sammy asked after he was seated.

"Chadwick, Ferguson and Solis."

Sammy stared, his hand halting as he poured wine into crystal glasses. "They're the most prestigious architectural and design firm in the country. You must be very talented to have secured a position with them."

Martin watched Parris as she filled her plate with a small serving of salad greens and another plate with a seafood salad of shrimp, lobster and crab. Both of them had eaten on the plane. He also noted that the glass of white wine at her place setting went untouched.

"Are you originally from West Palm?" M.J. asked.

"Yes."

Sammy reached over and covered M.J.'s hand with his. "Martin and Parris are living together."

Parris thought M.J. was going to faint as color drained from her face, leaving it a sickly sallow shade under her naturally burnished-gold complexion. Reaching for her wineglass, M.J. took a sip of the chilled liquid. Her hand shook when she put down the glass. "You're too young to start living with *men.* I'm certain your mother…"

"My mother's dead," Parris interrupted. "And I'm not too young to live with a man. I lived with a man when I was married."

Martin shifted his eyebrows as his parents turned their startled gazes on him. They wanted answers and apparently they were not prepared for the truth.

"Why live together?" M.J. continued. "Why not marry?"

"We'll marry when it's time to marry," Martin replied, staring at Parris's profile.

"I agree with Martin," Parris stated, smiling at him. "We'll both know when the time is right."

Sammy and M.J. exchanged a subtle look of amusement when they realized their son had fallen in love, but what had surprised them was that Parris Simmons wasn't the type of woman they had expected him to marry.

Chapter 11

"*W*hen is she going out of town again?"

"I don't know."

"I pay you good money to know."

"She's been reassigned."

"What's that suppose to mean?"

"She won't be travelling. It looks as if she's going to work out of the West Palm Beach home office."

"Get her out of town. I don't care how you do it, but I want her whacked."

"But, sir, what if I can't…"

"I don't pay for can'ts and won'ts. Get her the hell out of Florida and away from Martin Cole."

The connection ended abruptly, and the man with the throbbing vein in his forehead swore savagely under his breath. He needed the money he was being offered to kill Parris Simmons, but getting her out of the state was more difficult than he first thought. If it was up to him he would follow her, then pop her when she was getting into or out of her car. One clean shot to the head with a hollowed-out bullet. Quick, clean and simple. He had to get her, and soon, because his gambling debts were adding up. Parris Simmons would be his ticket to freedom,

*because if he didn't come up with enough money to cover his
bets both of them would be found floating along the Intra-
coastal Waterway.*

Parris woke up disoriented. She glanced at the clock on the
bedside table. The red numbers read twelve-thirty. She had been
asleep for more than six hours.

A deep-seated hunger gripped her stomach, reminding her
that she had skipped lunch. Turning to her right, she shook
Martin.

"Wake up!" she whispered.

He sat up, reaching for the lamp. "What's wrong?"

Parris laid a hand over her flat middle. "I'm starving."

He pushed his hair off his forehead. "You should be. You
slept through dinner." Reaching out, he pulled her across his lap.
"What do you want to eat?"

She ran her fingertips through the hair on his chest. "Lobster."

"What!" The word exploded from his mouth.

"I have a craving for lobster."

Hooking a finger under her chin, Martin raised her face. His
sweeping eyebrows lifted. "Are you certain you aren't pregnant?"

She laughed at his bemused expression. "Of course not. I just
want lobster."

Martin released her and picked up the telephone. He dialed a
number, then waited. "Frank, Martin. How late are you going to
stay open? Yes, tonight. Good. I'll be there within the hour." He
smiled at the expectant expression on Parris's face. "Lobster.
Thanks." He hung up, saying, "Put some clothes on, darling.
We're on our way to Fort Lauderdale."

It was another two weeks before Parris thought about what
Martin had asked her the night they drove to Fort Lauderdale for
lobster. She had missed her period.

Her forehead was furrowed in concentration as she sat at her
desk staring at a calendar showing the past three months.

She hadn't had a menstrual flow since the beginning of October. But nothing in November. It was now the second week in December and she was very late.

Her fingers beat a rapid staccato tapping on the desk. When? When could it have happened? Martin had always protected her except for the first time, and that was the end of September.

How? When?

The question screamed inside of her head until she was mindless with confusion. Ocho Rios!

A gasp escaped her constricted lips as the realization washed over her like an icy shower. The night Martin had asked her to marry him; the night they had confessed their love for each other; the night their unbridled passions began a new life inside her body.

Burying her face in her hands, Parris blinked back tears. She wasn't ready to be a mother; she wasn't ready to bear Martin's child; she had too many other things to do with her life.

Maybe she wasn't pregnant. Maybe something else was wrong with her. Opening her appointment book, she looked up the number to her gynecologist. She was in luck. The receptionist reported that someone had cancelled and if she could be at the office at five-thirty the doctor would see her.

Parris was numbed when she stumbled blindly out of the doctor's office to her car. The doctor had confirmed her worst fear: she was pregnant. He had tactfully told her about the alternatives, but if she decided to see the pregnancy to term her baby was due the middle of July.

She sat in the car, staring at the pamphlets the nurse had given her. Books explaining how her body would change and what to expect during each trimester.

She laughed and the sound was strange even to her own ears. Laughing seemed to relieve some of the tightness in her chest. Martin had won it all. He had gotten her to live with him and decorate his house. Now he would also get a wife and child.

Parris hadn't decided how she would tell Martin about the baby. No matter how she would rehearse it she knew it would never come out right.

I'll give him a gift, she thought. Suddenly she couldn't wait to see his face when he opened the tiny box with a pair of newborn booties.

Twenty minutes later, Parris maneuvered into an empty parking space in a large mall. The parking lot was crowded with cars. The Christmas shopping season was in full gear.

She opened the door to get out, but something held it shut. It wasn't until she saw the outline of a man's body and the barrel of a gun pointed at her that she began to shake.

She couldn't see the man's face clearly, but she understood his raspy order when he told her not to move.

Parris was frozen in place as the man opened the door and pushed her over on the seat, letting out a cry of pain when the gear shift on the console stabbed her hip.

"Crawl over me and drive," he ordered. "I'll tell you where to go. And if you make any stupid moves I'll blow your brains out where you sit. I've been paid to kill you, but I won't because I have a soft touch for kids, even those who aren't born yet. Yeah, I know you're carrying Martin Cole's kid. So if you don't want him lying in a lake without a face you'll do what I tell you to do. Do you understand me?"

Parris nodded. How was she to drive when her hands were wringing wet. How did he know about Martin? How did he know about her baby?

"Drive."

"Where?" Her voice was barely a whisper.

"To the airport. You're going to take a little trip."

"I…I can't. Martin's expecting me home by…"

"Shut up! Now drive!"

She didn't know how she managed to drive without causing an accident. Several times she swerved too close to other cars, but the pressure of the gun barrel against her ribs shocked her into awareness.

"Who's paying you?"

"Shut up!"

The one time she tried turning her head to see her kidnapper's face he pushed the gun savagely into her side. "Don't. I told you before I have a soft spot for babies."

She kept her eyes straight ahead. "This is some kind of joke, isn't it?"

"No way, lady. This is for real. I was paid to get you out of Florida and I'm doing it. I'm also suppose to kill you once we cross the state line. But just between you and me I'm not going to do that. Because of your baby. I don't murder no babies. And that means once you leave you can't ever come back. Because if I hear that you're back or you've contacted your boyfriend I'll make you sorry you were ever born. And if you ever tell Martin Cole about our little meeting and chat, I'll cut him up until there's nothing left of him."

The rest became a blur. Parris remembered driving into the airport and being told to stop in the section of the airport where private planes were parked. She was blindfolded and helped into a small aircraft, then lost track of time the moment the craft was airborne.

Martin paced the floor like a caged rat. Parris had been missing for more than forty-eight hours and the police had no clue to her whereabouts. They told him what he already knew: she had left her office at five and her locked car was found at the airport parking lot.

He tried over and over rethinking the last time they'd been together. Had he said something to anger her? Was she upset about something he had done or said?

Everything had been wonderful. They talked about Christmas and going away together for a long weekend. She hadn't sounded as if she was unhappy. Or was she?

He began to think that maybe he had pressured her into living with him. Had he in some way made her feel guilty that he had saved her life?

The had he, maybes and whys attacked him day and night. They attacked him at Christmas and even harder in the new year. Emotionally he was drained and the second week in January he walked into his father's office and told him he was taking a month's leave of absence.

A month became three months and when Martin Diaz Cole walked back into the offices of ColeDiz International Ltd. he was a different man. The shorter hair and moustache was not as startling as the change in the man.

He moved his office to the wing with the other corporate officers, and his closed door was a constant reminder that he was no longer available or approachable.

PART TWO

Chapter 12

Joshua Kirkland's expression hadn't changed as he listened to Martin talk about Parris Simmons. "What are you going to do, Martin?"

Martin glanced down at the black and white photographs, his jaw hardening. "I'm going to New York."

Joshua nodded. "Do you need me for anything else?"

"No. And thanks, Josh." He watched Joshua rise to his feet and walk out of his office, closing the door quietly.

Leaning back on the chair, Martin closed his eyes and let feelings he hadn't felt in years sweep over him. He sat for half an hour before he pushed the button on the intercom.

"Joan. Call the airport and have the jet fueled and ready for a flight to New York. I'd like to leave early tomorrow morning."

He barely heard Joan's acknowledgment as he sat at the desk until the sun set and the office was shadowed in darkness.

Mentally and emotionally he was ready for Parris Simmons.

"Mommy, it's snowing!" Regina came to a quick stop in the middle of the narrow utility kitchen. "Do you think they're going to close the school?"

Parris secured the top to a thermos, giving her daughter a wary glance. "I know I'm not hearing Regina Simmons talk about playing hooky from school, am I? I would think after the grade you managed to *earn* on your last math test you'd want to go to school on Saturdays and Sundays."

Regina pushed out her lower lip. "Aw, Mommy, it wasn't so bad."

Parris's eyebrows shot up. "Forty-two?"

"Tanya Davis is the smartest girl in the class and she got twenty-seven," Regina mumbled.

"Regina Simmons happens to be my daughter, not Tanya Davis, young lady. We'll let Mrs. Davis worry about Tanya's twenty-seven, thank you."

Regina shuffled over to the butcher block table in the dining area. She frowned at a bowl of steaming cereal. "I hate math and I hate oatmeal."

"And I'd hate for you to repeat the fourth grade, Miss Simmons."

Regina flopped down on her chair and groped for the spoon beside the bowl, not bothering to raise her gaze. The *Miss Simmons* said it all. Her mother was angry.

"I'm sorry, Mommy. I promise to study real hard. Every day," she added. Closing her eyes, she grimaced and swallowed a spoonful of oatmeal.

Parris turned her attention back to preparing Regina's lunch, while glancing over at the expanse of glass in the dining area. The first snowfall of the winter had hit the northeast, and there was still another three weeks before Christmas.

Her clear brown eyes saddened with the thought of Christmas. It had been exactly ten years ago that she had been forced to leave Florida and Martin Cole. She had spent that Christmas alone, alone and weeping unconsolably in a strange furnished room in New York City.

However, many things had changed in ten years. She was a mother of a beautiful child, she had purchased her own condominium apartment and she had secured a position as a freelance decorator for a consortium of local antique dealers. Freelancing allowed her the flexibility to schedule projects around Regina's school vacations and class trips.

"I'm finished, Mommy. Breakfast was very good. Thank you."

Parris hid a smug grin. The applesauce concealed at the bottom of the bowl had been a bonus. "You're welcome." Regina had eaten her cereal and toast and drank her juice in record time this morning. Usually the child lingered over her food each morning, testing the limits of Parris's patience.

"Don't forget to brush your teeth, then get the comb and brush and I'll do your hair, angel. How would you like it this morning?"

Regina's large dark eyes sparkled with laughter. "Two French braids."

She took the bowl from her daughter and dropped it into the sink filled with soapy water. Leaning over, she kissed the end of Regina's nose. "Two French braids coming up."

Staring at Regina's skipping figure until she disappeared from view, Parris's eyes narrowed in concentration. Every time she saw the child's dimpled smile she was reminded of Martin Cole. Regina had inherited Martin's hair, eyes, quick smile, dimpled cheeks and his loose-limb grace. As long as she lived Parris would never completely be exorcised of her child's father. He lived in a smaller, feminine image that was Regina Simmons.

She walked into the living room and sat down on the sofa to wait for Regina. Her decorating trademarks were everywhere. Each room had been created to evoke a different atmosphere, and each one possessing its own personality.

Nineteenth-century English gas lamps punctuated the sophisticated living room setting. The texture of woven fabric in sand beige covered the walls and the upholstered furniture set on an antique French parquet flooring. A patterned area rug in shades of sand beige, terra-cotta red and chocolate brown complemented the neutral furniture. Recessed ceiling lights cast a warm glow throughout the apartment despite the gray, bitterly cold stormy weather outdoors. Massive potted plants filled both the living and dining rooms, making the space an oasis of verdant lushness.

The doorbell chimed. "Parris, are you sending Regina to school?" came a cheery voice, followed by three rapid knocks on the door.

Parris crossed the room and opened the door. Stephanie Edwards smiled at her neighbor clutching a mug of hot cocoa in one hand. A young boy clothed in a ski hat, suit and boots stood beside Stephanie.

Stephanie's dark-brown rounded face, framed by a profusion of shoulder-length braids, was blooming with her impending motherhood.

"My daughter happens to need every minute of schooling she can get," Parris informed a smiling Stephanie.

Scott waddled into the Simmons's apartment, holding both arms outstretched. A backpack containing textbooks bumped against his back. Stephanie pulled the apple-green colored knitted cap from his head.

"If I fall down I won't be able to get up," he whined. "You put too much clothes on me, Mom."

"Too many, not too much. And stop complaining, Scotty," Stephanie scolded in a soft voice. She followed her son into the living room.

Scott tugged at the zipper under his neck. "But I'm hot, Mom."

"I need to have my head examined," Stephanie groaned. She sat down heavily on a love seat. "What do I need with another baby when this one refuses to grow up?"

Parris glanced down at her neighbor and best friend's belly. "Under another set of circumstance, I'd gladly change places with you." What she wanted to say was that if she had married Martin Cole, she was certain they would have had more than one child.

"That's highly unlikely. Especially since you're practicing celibacy," Stephanie said, smiling broadly.

"What's cellackbessie?" Scott asked, waddling around the living room like a duck.

"Never you mind," warned his mother.

"How's a kid to learn something?" he mumbled.

Stephanie stared at her son, biting down on her lower lip. "Celibacy is when a man or a woman…when a man and a woman…" Her gaze shifted to Parris.

Parris returned her stare, unable to believe what she had just heard. Scott was nearly ten and Stephanie was to give birth to her second child within a month yet she was too embarrassed to broach the subject of human sexuality with her prepubescent son.

"Celibacy is when a man or woman do not engage in sexual relations of any kind," Parris said, completing the explanation.

"Oh." Scott pulled down the zipper of his ski suit, his curiosity waning quickly once he was given an answer. "I know about sex," he volunteered, "but not about cellackbessie."

Regina walked into the living room, carrying a jacket with a pair of matching ski pants. "Hi, Scotty. Do you want to make a snow castle in the playground behind our building after we come home from school?"

Scott's eyes widened. "Girls can't make a good snow castle. The one you made last year melted before you put the tower on it."

"You're mad because my castle was better than yours," Regina retorted with a blaze of temper.

"It was not!"

"Enough, kids," Parris interrupted, ending the debate. She motioned to Regina. "Let's go, snow bunny. I need to comb your hair before the bus arrives."

Regina stuck out her tongue at Scott when he thumbed his nose at her, and both mothers rolled their eyes upward.

Ten minutes later, Regina, bundled in a bright red jacket and matching pants with her two French braids tucked under her red knitted cap, and Scott trudged out to wait in front of the modern apartment complex for their school bus. Both of them stomped through the falling snow, laughing when they left footprints on the untouched cover of whiteness.

"I think your daughter intimidates my son." Stephanie followed Parris into the kitchen.

"Only because he can't resist teasing her." She plugged in the coffee maker while easing her tall, slender frame down onto a high stool. "Blessed peace."

Stephanie rubbed her lower back. "Amen to that." She duck-walked over to the dining area, easing her body down onto an armless chair.

"What are you going to do with four weeks vacation time on your hands?"

Parris, crossing her arms under her breasts, smiled a full-mouth, relaxed smile. "Four weeks sounds like a lot of time but a month will go by before I know it. I decided to save my vacation time because I'm thinking of taking Regina away for Christmas."

"But you always go away for Christmas."

Parris nodded. What she didn't tell Stephanie was that this Christmas was a special one. It marked the tenth anniversary of her flight from Florida. Ten years was a long time to be away from her home and the man she loved.

"I have an open ticket to fly anywhere in the continental forty-eight States, but I haven't decided where I want to go."

"Regina's been talking about Disney World."

"Disney World will probably be too crowded. I was thinking of the new family attraction in Vegas," she answered instead of telling Stephanie that she could never go back to Florida.

"When we get back I suppose I'll be ready to babysit Scott when you go into the hospital for your new arrival."

"Forget it," Stephanie protested, shaking her neatly braided hair. "You work yourself into the ground all year and when you get a chance to have a month to yourself, I'm not going to ask you to care for another child. Calvin's mother has already bought her ticket to come up for a few days before Christmas. And I certainly don't want to cheat her out of the extraordinary opportunity to look after her most delightful grandson, whose name I will not mention at this time."

Parris ran the palms of her hands down the denim fabric covering her thighs. "Scott will change once the baby comes."

"The kid's obnoxious, Parris."

"He's normal, Stephie. He's just a little boy."

"I've waited too long between pregnancies."

"Stop complaining and enjoy your family," Paris suggested.

Stephanie did not miss the fleeting look of sadness sweep over Parris's face. She did not know all there was to know about Parris Simmons, but knew Parris had no one else besides Regina.

When Parris moved into the neighboring apartment three years earlier she told her she was divorced and both her parents had died before Regina's birth. Parris had never once spoken to her about Regina's father, and respecting her neighbor's right to privacy, Stephanie hadn't asked any questions.

Stephanie rose slowly to her feet. "I'd better get ready for my doctor's appointment. Somehow it takes me forever to get myself together."

Parris saw Stephanie massage an area in her lower back. She didn't think her friend was going to make it through December. "Do you want me to drive you?"

"No, thanks. I'll see you later."

Stephanie made her way slowly across the living room, Parris following. She opened and closed the door behind Stephanie, mentally assessing what she had to do on her first day of her four-week vacation.

Her thoughts were interrupted when there came three rapid knocks on the door for the second time that morning. The three knocks were Stephanie's signal.

Don't tell me Stephanie's baby is coming earlier than pre-dicted, she thought, opening the door quickly.

Parris couldn't believe her eyes. She became rigid, unable to move. Her breath came in short pants as she leaned against the door frame, her body sagging weakly.

"No," she moaned, pressing a fist to her mouth. She was dreaming; that's it, she was dreaming and when she awoke everything would be as it was. He wasn't in New York—he just couldn't be. She'd eluded him for ten years, even though a part of her wanted him to find her; not for herself but for Regina.

She shifted as he pushed the door. Parris had not thought of trying to close it or lock it. It would've been useless to lock a door against Martin Cole. She knew he simply would've kicked it open. The cold, hard look in his eyes said it all.

She jumped slightly when he stepped into her living room, dropping two soft leather carry-on bags to the floor.

"Martin," she whispered, not knowing where she garnered the strength as she made her way over to the sofa that faced a matching love seat.

Closing her eyes, Parris rested her head on a plump cushion, willing her mind blank.

Chapter 13

Martin Cole had called himself every kind of fool only moments before he knocked on the door to Parris's apartment. He had run from trouble all of his life, not sought it out. He knew going after Parris Simmons again was more than trouble; it was certain disaster.

He had stood out in front of the building complex waiting and watching the school bus pick up the children gathered on the corner. He had recognized his daughter immediately, even though her hair was covered by a red knit cap. It was one thing to see her face in a photograph and another to see the image in the flesh.

Raising his hands, he laced his fingers over the thick black hair curling on the nape of his neck. His hair was still damp from the falling snow. His right hand moved down his face and a long, tapered forefinger grazed the neatly barbered moustache concealing his upper lip. If Parris had opened her eyes she would have recognized the gesture. The gesture was familiar to all who knew Martin Cole well. Whenever he was deep in thought the right forefinger toyed with his upper lip; and the black moustache covered a sensual mouth many had not seen in nearly ten years. He had grown the moustache just after Parris disappeared from his life, and its presence had become a constant reminder of how much she had altered his life. What he was unaware of was that the moustache enhanced his Afro-Cuban heritage.

Martin Diaz Cole, the eldest of four offspring of Samuel and Marguerite Cole, had inherited the superior genes of both his parents: Samuel's impressive height and rich sienna-brown coloring; and Marguerite's delicately sensual features and curling black hair. Some men claimed Martin's looks were too refined, while most women adamantly disagreed with them. Whatever their opinion of him, both sexes were drawn to and captivated by his looks and commanding manner.

Martin had registered Parris's breathless whisper when she called out his name. He'd always loved the timbre of her voice. She had the lowest, huskiest, sexiest feminine voice of any woman he had ever met. He found it cloaking, velvety, and soothing.

But Parris's voice wasn't the only thing that had captivated him. It was also the woman herself. And as in the past, he suspected Parris was completely unaware of the spell and power she wielded over him.

Parris opened her eyes, staring at Martin as if she had never seen him before. Although Parris hadn't changed much over the past ten years, Martin had changed drastically. His inky-black hair no longer flowed to his shoulders but was short, close to his scalp, while a sprinkling of gray sparkled throughout the ebony strands, reminding her of his rapid approach to forty. The black well-defined eyebrows above his expressive dark eyes were the same, as well as the tiny lines around those deep, penetrating eyes; however, slashes on his lean cheeks, around his nose, and the thick growth of a moustache were new.

Instinctively, Parris knew these new changes were not only due to maturity, but to a hardness and determination she recognized immediately in the man who had once captured her heart.

Martin shrugged out of his coat, dropping it on the opposite end of the sofa. Rather than sit beside Parris, he decided to sit on the love seat. His gaze moved leisurely over her straightened hair which was pulled off her face and secured in an elastic band. Unsecured, her hair was long enough to sweep over her shoulders.

He had never forgotten her soft almond-brown coloring, her large clear brown eyes with the dark green centers, her pert nose and her lush full mouth. Parris looked no differently than she had years before, except for her eyes. They were older, wiser, haunted and guarded.

"You know why I'm here," he said without hesitation.

Parris couldn't help smiling. "You always were direct, weren't you, Martin?"

"That's the only way I know how to be," he replied, unsmiling. "I want you and I want *my* daughter."

She successfully concealed a shudder. "Why now and not ten years ago? What took you so long to come after me?"

Martin rose to his feet and walked over to the expansive window that covered an entire wall from the living room to dining area.

A pair of gray wool slacks, a matching gray cashmere V-neck sweater over a pale blue silk shirt emphasized a muscular, proportioned six-foot three-inch frame, and testified that his clothes had not come off a department store rack. Martin Cole was a man who would only grow more attractive with age.

Parris, having recovered from the shock of seeing Martin again, replied, "I want you to leave."

Turning around, he glared at her. "I'm not leaving until I get some answers."

"Answer my question first. What took so long to come after me? Don't tell me that you woke up this morning and decided to look up Parris Simmons because she just happened to cross your mind."

Martin let out a deep sigh. He returned to the love seat and sat down. A hardness touched his jaw as he said, "I hated you for running away from me, Parris. It took me a long time to get over your deceit. But with time the memories faded and so did the hurt. It was only a few weeks ago that I paid someone to find you."

"Why?" She was surprised at her own outward display of calmness although her stomach muscles churned and knotted in apprehension.

"I want a wife," he admitted, deciding on honesty. He'd never lied to her and he didn't want to begin now.

Parris ran a hand over her hair. "You wanted a wife ten years ago."

"Wrong." He frowned. "I needed a wife ten years ago. I needed you."

"You needed me for all the wrong reasons, Martin," she managed to state in an even tone.

His face flushed under the deep rich color of his tan. "Why do you think I wanted to marry you? I just wanted to give you what your husband did not give you. I wanted to show you that being married to me would not have been the same as being married to Lawson. Things haven't changed that much in ten years because I still want to marry you."

"You always said you got whatever you wanted. You weren't content to just sleep with me. You had to have it all."

Martin covered his face with his hands. "Damn you!" he whispered savagely. "Nothing has changed, has it?" His hands came down and his eyes danced wildly. "You've had ten years to think of something new, Parris." His chest was now rising and falling heavily. "What excuses have you given my daughter?"

Parris schooled her features not to reveal the panic spinning out of control within her. "Her name is Regina. I've created no excuses. Your family despised me and made no attempt to conceal it. And as for Regina, I told her that you lived in Florida; and although I had no intention of ever returning, I would make certain she would meet you one day."

He moved from the love seat, his right hand lashing out to grip her left wrist. "When? How many more years would she be forced to wait?"

Martin relinquished his hold when he saw her impassive expression. He couldn't believe this was the Parris Simmons who had haunted him for years. Her indifference and ability to hide her emotions frightened him. *When had she changed? Was she a cold, unemotional mother? Had a part of her died, leaving no room for love?*

He released her wrist and Parris stopped herself from massaging the area where his fingers had burned her flesh. Her sculpted eyebrow lifted slightly. "I don't know," she replied.

Martin moved back to his original position on the love seat.

"That doesn't matter anymore. I'm not leaving New York without my daughter. Or without you."

Parris was grateful to be sitting, because she knew if she had been standing she would've fainted. His promise was not a promise but a threat. A threat she knew Martin intended to carry out.

Rising to her feet, she walked into the kitchen. She had to get away from him, even if it was only a few feet.

She took down two coffee mugs and poured freshly brewed coffee into them. She was back in control by the time she returned to the living room and handed Martin a cup.

He murmured a low thanks and stared down into the black depths of the strong brew, looking for answers to questions he found difficult to ask.

"Why did you leave me, Parris?" he asked softly.

She cupped her hands around her coffee mug, feeling its warmth seeping into her icy-cold fingers. Ten years and twelve hundred miles and countless sleepless nights when she prayed she would be able to forget him. It still had not been enough. There were times when she was successful, but many more when she wasn't. Sometimes she reached for the telephone to dial Martin's number, but became physically ill whenever she remembered the threat against her life.

"Would you believe me if I said I was afraid to remain in Florida?"

"I don't know what to believe, Parris. All I know is that your ex-husband tried to kill you."

"I couldn't stay." What she couldn't say was that her life, their lives, had been threatened.

Martin's expression changed, becoming one she recognized immediately. His anger was apparent.

"Did Lawson have anything to do with your leaving me?"

He was asking questions she was unable to answer. "If he did, what would you do, Martin? Would you go look for him and kill him this time? What do I tell Regina? Do I tell her that her father is a murderer?"

Martin's mouth twisted under the moustache as he glared at

Parris. It was apparent she was upset as well. There was just a hint of green in her clear brown eyes.

"I've never murdered anyone, Parris. So don't think of me as a killer."

She refused to back down. "Of course you wouldn't kill anyone. You'd pay someone to kill him the same way you paid someone to find me." She registered his quick intake of breath.

Martin refused to rise to her baiting. "You're spoiling for a fight, aren't you?" He gave her a crooked smile.

She ran her tongue over her lower lip. "No. I don't want to fight with you."

He placed his cup on an end table and moved over to sit beside her. The knuckles of his right hand grazed the silken flesh of her cheek. His obsidian gaze caressed the delicate bones of her jaw. The same jaw that had been shattered and healed, leaving no trace of a scar.

His gaze lingered on the length of her lashes and the curve of her high cheekbones. His fingers spread out and wound through the hair which fell from the elastic band to grace her long neck. He leaned closer until his face was only inches from hers.

"Do you still love me?" Her breath quickened against his throat.

"No," she whispered. The heat of his body flowed into hers and she shivered noticeably. "No, Martin," she repeated, shaking her head and praying he believed her.

His fingers feathered over her neck and she stiffened, pulling away from him. Feelings she had repressed sprang to life.

"Don't, Martin. Please don't touch me."

He released her, staring at her pained expression. Hunching over, he rested his elbows on his thighs. He knew Parris was lying to him, but why? Who was she trying to protect?

He wanted to tell her that he hadn't begun searching for her two weeks ago, but ten years ago. After the police closed their investigation on her disappearance he hired private investigators to look for her. The result was the same: Parris Simmons had vanished without a trace.

He suspected Owen Lawson had something to do with her disappearance and paid someone to follow him. But that also proved fruitless. The investigator's report read that there was no reason to suspect that the recently promoted Captain Owen Lawson of the West Palm Beach Police Department had anything to do with the disappearance of his ex-wife. The last sentence in the report proved more intriguing than the conclusion of the investigation. Owen Lawson had remarried and his wife had given birth to a baby boy.

"Please call a cab for me, Parris. I need to check into a hotel."

She jumped up, too relieved to hear the resignation in his voice. Martin had walked back into her life like a tornado, without warning or a respite.

She made the call, asking which hotel he was checking into, and replaced the receiver.

"The taxi will be here in ten minutes."

Martin stood up and retrieved his overcoat, slipping his arms into the sleeves of the cashmere garment. His gaze was fixed on her face. "When can I get to meet Regina?"

"You make it sound so simple, Martin. You just can't walk in here and disrupt her life. She'll have to be prepared to meet you. I'll talk to her and when she's ready I'll call you."

"How long will that take?"

Parris struggled to control her temper. "I don't know."

He gave her a withering glare before he picked up his bags. She opened the door and without a word he walked out.

She closed the door, and only when she turned the lock did she find her way back to the sofa on trembling legs and collapse for the second time that morning.

The dread and danger she now felt would not permit her to experience the joy she felt of seeing and touching Martin once again. She loved him the way she could never love another man. He'd given her all she needed to exist as a woman; but all of that vanished ten years ago.

The stranger, a slightly-built pale man with a raspy voice, had changed her life forever. He had blindfolded her before he put her on a plane to New York City. She was blindfolded again when the small private jet landed, and she was driven to midtown

Manhattan. Before she was put out of the car, she was given a coat and an envelope; and it wasn't until she had checked into a hotel did she realize her ex-husband may have been involved in her kidnapping.

She believed he had employed his own method of revenge. The envelope contained an amount equal to what she had received as a divorce settlement from Owen Lawson.

Chapter 14

Closing her eyes, Parris let her mind wander. Although she had been six weeks pregnant when she left Florida, she refused to accept her condition until she was unable to fit into her clothes. She had been well into her fourth month before she sought out a New York doctor.

Her physical state fared a lot better than her emotional state. Even though the envelope she had been given contained enough money for her to exist comfortably for a year, she rented a small furnished apartment and refused to venture out of her sanctuary until it was time for her to shop for food or to keep an appointment with her doctor.

The first time Parris felt the new life move within her, she broke down, crying until her eyes were no more than slits and sleeping in the same clothes for three days.

She cried for her father, Charles Simmons, who had died of a stroke before she had a chance to know him, and she cried for her mother whose delicate beauty faded quickly with the long, hard hours Ada Simmons worked to support herself and her only child; however, she had her mother for twenty years until an automobile accident claimed Ada's life after she fell asleep at the wheel due to exhaustion from working a double shift at the county hospital where she was a staff nurse.

The pain of losing her mother had not faded when her abductor threatened to kill Martin. Fleeing Florida had not only saved her life, but Martin's and Regina's.

Opening her eyes, she stared out through the window as her delicate jaw settled into a stubborn line. If she hadn't accepted her blackmailer's challenge ten years ago she was certain not to tempt fate now that she was responsible not only for her own life but Regina's.

Rising to her feet, she suddenly felt tired. Emotionally she was drained. How was she to tell her daughter that her father wanted to meet her? How would Regina react? How would Martin react?

She made her way across the living room and down a hall to her bedroom. Standing in the doorway, she examined the furnishings that were the trademark of her profession. As the decorator she had selected pieces from her favorite period—Victorian Revival.

Decorating her home offered a sense of fulfillment she never was able to achieve when she designed spaces for clients. Each piece of furniture in her home had been selected with meticulous care to satisfy her moods: from the large bed with a massive mahogany headboard and side chairs covered with an intricately designed tapestry pattern, to the round antique table, desk, and chair. The mood was regal with patterns of pink and beige intricate paisleys and florals. Lacy panels, which once covered long tables hung at the windows while the table skirt matched the pattern of the bed sheets and pillow coverings, and a carpeting of creamy ivory repeated the color of the wall covering.

The sparse Christmas cards on the desk served to remind her of how solitary her life had become. Aside from the Edwards and the antique dealers she contracted with she had no family or close friends in New York.

But Regina did have a family: paternal grandparents, two aunts, an uncle and at least a half-dozen cousins.

She wondered how much longer she could keep Regina away from them once they were made aware of the child's existence. But more importantly, she wondered if Regina would resent her for keeping her from the only family she had.

* * *

Martin lay on the hotel bed, staring up at the ceiling. Joshua had done what he had asked him to do: he found Parris Simmons. But in finding her, he had opened a wound, forcing him to feel the ache, causing his heart to bleed.

He wondered if the separation had been as painful for her as it had been for him. *No,* came a nagging little voice somewhere in his head. She left him.

Martin Diaz Cole offered Parris Simmons what he'd never offered any other woman—his name.

She didn't want his name. She only agreed to live with him and decorate his house, refusing to become his wife or the mother of his children. It was after this that he cursed Owen Lawson.

He'd tried to forget Parris—with other women, alcohol, and parties that went on for days. Afterwards, he would wake up in a drunken daze, feeling worse than before he began poisoning his body with mind-distorting alcohol.

He spent thousands on investigators to look for her, lost weight, couldn't sleep and spent weeks at a time drifting along the Atlantic in a rented sloop. It took a year for him to finally convince himself that Parris wasn't coming back.

A satisfied smile lifted the corners of his mouth and deepened the creases in his cheeks. She was back because he had found her; and she was the mother of his child.

Folding his arms under his head, he closed his eyes. Whatever reason Parris had for running away was no longer important to him. He had found her, and she would never hide from him again.

Parris heard Regina's distinctive laugh through the door before the child rang the doorbell, and wondered if the child would continue to laugh after she told her about her father.

She had spent all morning trying to form the words she would use to tell her daughter that the man she had loved and continued to love had come to find them.

Opening the front door, Parris smiled down at Regina as she stood with Scott, both children holding snowballs.

Regina held a piece of paper in one gloved hand. "There's no school tomorrow, Mommy."

"Lucky you," Parris said, pulling the knitted cap from her daughter's head.

"Mommy, can I spend the afternoon at Scotty's house?"

"Yeah," Scott agreed. "We can look at videos until the night."

"I'll see," Parris replied, not committing herself.

The door to the neighboring apartment opened and Stephanie looked out. "There's no school tomorrow, Mom! There's snow in the school yard up to the sky," Scott said excitedly.

"How wonderful," Stephanie replied, winking at Parris.

"I'll see you later, Scott," Regina promised as she made her way into her own apartment.

Parris waved to Stephanie and closed the door. "Put that snowball in the sink, Regina. I don't want water tracked over the floors."

"Can I put it in the freezer, Mommy?"

She stared down at the expectant look on her child's face, amazed at how much Regina resembled her father. Seeing him again had verified the startling similarity of their features. It was as if she had nothing to do with the creation of this child except carry her to term.

"Yes, you may."

Regina dropped her backpack and raced to the kitchen. "How long do you think it'll stay a snowball?" she asked after placing it in the frost-free freezer.

"I don't know, angel."

"All winter?"

"Perhaps." Parris's voice was soft, her manner distracted.

"Can we make cookies, Mommy?"

Whenever Parris took time off from work she and Regina had made it a habit to bake cookies. Baking cookies and visiting museums together was their way of bonding.

As a working mother Parris had to make many of the sacrifices that other mothers made, but she tried to make the precious time she and Regina spent together quality time.

"What kind of cookies this time?"

"Double chocolate chip raisin oatmeal," Regina replied.

Parris pulled at a fat silky braid hanging over the red ski jacket. "Now that sounds like a monster cookie. Change your clothes and wash your hands and I'll get all of the ingredients together."

Forty-five minutes later, Parris watched Regina as she carefully removed several large cookies from a cookie sheet and placed them on a rack. Her mouth was compressed tightly in concentration and Parris was shocked when she saw the expression. Everything that was Martin Cole swept over her at that moment. Like Martin, Regina loved to cook. He was most comfortable in the board room and in the kitchen.

"I think that just about does it, Mommy." Regina stepped back and surveyed her handiwork. Large cookies, at least six inches in diameter, were stacked up like saucers in a cookie jar.

"I believe you're right." She smiled, knowing she couldn't avoid the inevitable. She had to tell Regina about her father.

"Do you think one cookie and some milk will spoil my appetite for dinner, Mommy?"

Parris glanced at the clock on the oven. "Not if we eat a late dinner."

"I'll fix the table," Regina volunteered.

Waiting until after Regina set the table, Parris poured two glasses of milk and placed two cookies on a large plate. She sat down at the table and held the child's hand.

"Regina, I have something very important to tell you."

"What, Mommy?" She took a bite of a moist cookie, then raised the glass of milk to her mouth, taking a swallow of the cold liquid.

"It's about your father."

Regina's eyes widened as she slowly replaced the glass on the table. "What about him?"

Parris was certain Regina could hear her heart pounding outside of her body. "He's come for you. He's here in New York."

"Why, Mommy?" Her lower lip trembled while her eyes filled with tears. "Is he coming to take me away from you?"

She didn't know what to expect, but it had not been fear. Why would Regina fear a man she had never met?

Pulling the child from her chair, she cradled her on her lap, holding her close. "No, angel. He's not here to take you from me. Why does that bother you?"

Burying her face against her mother's breasts, Regina sniffed back tears. "I don't want my face on a milk carton, Mommy."

Suddenly it all came together. Regina didn't want to become a child who had been abducted by an angry, resentful parent.

She kissed her hair. "Your father would never take you from me, Regina. You're my child."

"But…but he's my daddy."

How was she to explain that Martin was her father biologically and not legally. She had not listed Martin Cole as Regina's father on her birth records.

"You don't have to meet him if you don't want to. But if you feel you want to talk about him at another time we can. Okay, baby?"

Regina nodded, her arms tightening around her mother's neck.

Parris held her until she was calm. Somehow she had thought Regina would be pleased to meet her father. She had no way of knowing that the child harbored fears of being abducted by the other parent.

Both of us have our fears, Parris mused. When would it ever end?

Parris had just turned out the lamp in her bedroom when the telephone rang. She answered it before the second ring.

"Hello."

"Did you tell her?"

Her pulse raced quickly at the sound of the familiar quiet Southern voice. "I said I'd call you when she's ready to meet you."

"Did you tell her?" Martin repeated.

"Yes, I told her."

"And?"

"She doesn't want to see you."

"Why the hell not?"

"Because she's afraid of you!" Parris didn't realize she was shouting.

Martin's labored breathing came through the telephone line.

"Why should she be afraid of me, Parris? What have you told her about me?"

"I haven't told her anything except that you're here in New York and that you want to meet with her. She's harboring some kind of fear that you'll snatch her from me and that her face will appear on a milk carton as a missing child."

"That's preposterous!"

"Tell that to a nine-year-old who's told constantly that she shouldn't talk to strangers…"

"I'm not a stranger, Parris. I'm her father."

"You're still a stranger, Martin. She doesn't know you."

"And who's fault is that?"

"If you start with the accusations I'll hang up on you," she threatened.

There was a profound silence before Martin spoke again. "Talk to her, Parris. Convince her that I won't take her away from you. All I want to do is see her. I won't even touch her if she doesn't want me to."

Registering Martin's plea, Parris found difficulty in swallowing. "Give her time, Martin."

"How much time?"

"As much as she needs. I'm going to take her away for Christmas, and maybe that will give us the time we need to build the trust she'll need to confront you."

"Where would you be going?"

"To Las Vegas."

Again there was silence from Martin. "I'll wait for your call."

"Why don't you go back to Florida," Parris suggested. "I'll contact you there if she changes her mind."

"I'm not leaving New York until I meet my daughter."

Parris listened to the break in the connection as Martin hung up abruptly. There was no mistaking his intent, and something told her that Martin Cole would spent the next ten years in New York if he had to, waiting for Regina to come to him.

He was used to waiting. He had already lost ten years waiting for her to become his wife.

Chapter 15

Regina crawled into bed with Parris, waking her up. She opened her eyes and peered over at the bedside clock. It was only five-thirty.

"What are you doing awake so early, Regina? You don't have to go to school today." Her voice was husky with sleep.

"I was dreaming too much," Regina replied, snuggling closer to her mother.

"What were you dreaming about?"

"The man who said he was my father."

Suddenly she was alert. "What did you dream about him?"

"He was calling me, and he couldn't find me because I was hiding from him."

You weren't hiding from him, Regina, Parris thought. *I was.*

"What did you do?"

"I let him find me."

"What happened after that?"

"We were laughing. You, me and my father. All of us were laughing."

Reaching over, Parris pulled Regina's head to her shoulder. "Is that what you want, angel? Do you want to laugh with your father?"

Regina bit down on her lower lip. "I do, but...but then I'm afraid."

"There's no need for you to be afraid of your father, sweetheart. He's wonderful."

"If he's so wonderful why isn't he with us?"

"Something happened a long time ago before you were born and I couldn't stay with your father. When I left him I didn't let him know you were growing inside of my body."

"Why not?"

"I didn't have the time. Something important happened and I had to leave Florida right away."

Regina stared up at her mother's face. "You're not going back to Florida, are you?"

Parris met her gaze. "No."

"Does that mean my father is going to live in New York?"

"I don't know," Parris answered honestly. "He says that he's going to stay in New York until he sees you."

Regina picked at the lacy eyelet trim on the comforter, her sweeping eyebrows furrowed in a frown. She compressed her lips and twin dimples dotted her cheeks.

"I'll let you know when he can see me."

Parris nodded, holding her daughter close to her heart. Martin would have to wait until the child was ready, hoping it would come soon. She wanted it over so that she could get on with her life.

It was another three days of waiting before Martin picked up the telephone and heard Parris's voice. Regina wanted to meet him.

He panicked! He raced out of the hotel and drove his rental car to the nearest mall and bought the largest stuffed bear they had available, but once he returned to his hotel room he had second thoughts.

He couldn't buy the child's affections. All he had to present was himself and either she accepted him or she rejected him.

He vacillated about bringing the bear, but in the end left it in the car once he parked in the visitors parking section at Parris's housing complex.

The bite of the cold December wind chilled him through layers of wool and cashmere. His blood was too thin to withstand the harsh, bitterly cold northeast winter.

He rang the bell to Parris's apartment, then pushed his gloved hands into the large pockets of his overcoat. The door swung open and he was momentarily stunned by the woman standing before him.

Her hair was curled and caught up in a ponytail that trailed over her shoulder like a dark ribbon. The familiar fragrance of Chanel No. 5 wafted from her body as she moved aside to let him enter. It had taken ten years for her to grow into the sophisticated scent.

"Come in."

Her velvet voice beckoned him like a specter in a dream. He moved past her and walked into the living room, the heat from a crackling fire behind a decorative screen thawing his chilled body. It was the first time he noticed the room contained a fireplace.

Parris extended her hand. "I'll take your coat."

Removing his gloves, he slipped out of his coat and handed it to her. He examined her slender figure as she hung the coat up in a closet.

She wore what he had considered her favorite attire: bare feet and a pair of well-worn jeans with a white long sleeve T-shirt. Her body was still slim, still perfect.

Parris took her time hanging up Martin's coat, trying to catch her breath. He was as dramatic as the first time she met him. Again he was dressed all in black: a wool turtleneck, slacks and shoes, and she concluded his short graying hair and moustache complemented his handsome face.

His footsteps were muffled in the deep pile of the cream carpeting as he walked over to the fireplace and extended his hands toward the heat.

A slight smile softened her mouth. "How are you surviving the cold weather?"

He turned and smiled at her. "Just barely. How long did it take you to get used to these temperatures?"

She was slightly taken aback by his sensual smile when the attractive lines fanned out around his large dark eyes. He still had the power to make her insides go soft and mushy.

"Just one winter. But if you make it through February you can consider yourself a veteran."

"I don't plan to be here in February," Martin remarked confidently.

That remark reminded Parris why Martin Cole was standing in her living room. "I'll go and get Regina for you."

She turn to leave but Martin moved quickly, capturing her arm. "Parris." Tilting her chin, she stared up at him. Touching her, inhaling her fragrance conjured up memories of their passionate lovemaking; a lovemaking that transcended the limits of sanity. A coming together he had never experienced before her or since she'd left him.

"I don't want you to leave us alone. I think Regina would feel a lot more secure if she saw us together."

Parris felt a warm glow flow through her. Martin had unselfishly considered Regina's feelings even before meeting her. He didn't want his daughter to fear him; he wanted the child to feel safe. The same way he once made her feel safe.

"Thank you, Martin."

He released her arm and she made her way to Regina's bedroom, recalling the time Martin had saved her life, cared for her while she convalesced from her ex-husband's attempt on her life and protected her until she was forced to leave Florida. If he had known someone had been stalking her she knew he would have taken measures to keep her safe.

Regina sat on a rocking chair, her legs crossed in a yoga position, reading.

"He's here, Regina."

She glanced up from the book and laid it aside. She looked younger than nine with her hair plaited in two thick braids falling over her flat narrow chest. She was tall, even though her young body had not begun to show any indication of the onset of puberty.

Parris held out her hand and Regina rose to take it. Hand-in-hand they walked into the living room where Martin stood with his back to the fireplace.

Parris released Regina's hand, staring mutely at the drama

unfolding before her eyes. She could hear the sound of her daughter's and her former lover's breathing as they stared at each other.

Martin's gaze widened. Nothing he had ever experienced could have prepared him for the young child. Her hair was almost a blue-black, and curling around her face where it hadn't been secured in the thick braids falling over her narrow shoulders. She had inherited his eyes, the curve of his eyebrows and his nose. Even the mouth was his. She bit down on her lower lip and her dimples were displayed.

Martin felt his pulses racing. His daughter was a feminine version of himself! She's beautiful, he thought. It never mattered whether his thoughts were compromised by vanity, but she was truly magnificent.

Clasping his hands behind his back, he smiled at her. "Hello, Regina."

"Hello." Regina's voice was low and soft.

Martin's startled gaze shifted to Parris. The child had her mother's voice.

"How are you?" Regina questioned, still not moving.

Martin could hardly contain himself. "Cold." He couldn't think of anything else to say. "I'm not used to cold weather," he explained.

"Don't you have winter in Florida?"

He smiled again. "We have winter but it's not like your winters. The temperature rarely goes below freezing, and when it does it doesn't stay there for a long time."

"Don't you have snow?"

"Hardly ever. Florida is known as the "Sunshine State" because the sun shines most of the time. But in the summer it gets very, very hot. That's when everyone goes swimming two and sometimes three times a day."

"I don't know how to swim yet," Regina admitted.

Martin walked over to the love seat and sat down, not taking his gaze off his daughter. "Maybe one of these days I'll teach you how to swim."

Regina, seemingly drawn to the tall man who was her father,

moved over to the love seat and sat down at the opposite end from Martin. Parris took a seat on the sofa.

"Will you teach me in Florida?" Regina continued.

Martin draped one trousered knee over the other, the gesture almost too elegant for a man of his size. He shook his head. "You don't have to go to Florida to learn how to swim. You can learn anywhere."

Regina nodded, staring at her folded hands on her lap; she had run out of questions.

Martin glanced at Parris, giving her a smile and nod of approval. She had done a wonderful job with the child. She was an excellent mother.

"What is it you like doing best, Regina?"

Regina's face brightened with animation. "I like to cook. Mommy and I made monster cookies the other day."

Lowering his leg, Martin leaned forward. "I also like to cook. I used to cook for your mother."

"Do you want to taste Mommy's and my monster cookies?"

Martin affected a frown. "These cookies won't turn me into a monster, will they?"

Regina placed her hand over her mouth and giggled like a normal nine-year-old. "No. They're just so big that we call them monsters."

"If that's the case I'd love to taste your monster cookies."

Parris rose quickly to her feet. "I'll get the cookies and make some hot chocolate." Regina and Martin seemed comfortable enough with each other for her to leave them alone together.

She made her way to the narrow kitchen and opened the refrigerator to take out a carton of milk. The faces of two missing children stared back at her, and she thought of Regina's fear that Martin would spirit her away from her mother.

Parris hadn't known Martin very well yet instinctively she knew he would never try to take Regina away from her. He didn't want the child without her mother.

She heated the milk carefully, then poured it into three mugs filled with powdered cocoa. The mugs were topped off with a froth of whipped cream and placed on the dining area table with a plate of monster cookies.

"Everything's ready," she called out to Martin and Regina.

Regina escorted Martin to the table, holding his hand tightly. "See, monster cookies."

"Good gravy!" he gasped, feigning astonishment. "You expect me to eat all of that?"

"That's not too big, Daddy. I can finish one by myself."

Martin and Parris registered the *Daddy* at the same time and were stunned at how easily it came from Regina. The title had acknowledged that she thought of him as her father.

They sipped the rich delicious hot chocolate and ate cookies while the sky darkened and Parris turned on an overhead chandelier in the dining area. The soft light highlighted the abundance of gray in Martin's short hair and the rich dark color of his face.

He truly is beautiful, she mused. She remembered she had called him beautiful once and embarrassed him.

Martin couldn't take his gaze off his daughter and he wondered if it was possible to love someone on sight. She was beautiful, charming, engaging and bright, and he felt a tugging of love from within his body that made it difficult to control his feelings.

He and Parris had created a perfect child.

He drank his chocolate and ate his monster cookie, declaring both delicious. Glancing at his watch, he rose to his feet. He had stayed for nearly an hour.

"I have to go," he announced. It was only a half-truth. He wanted to stay forever, but he had to place an international telephone call.

Regina stared up at him. "When are you coming back, Daddy?"

He winked at her. "I'll call you tomorrow and we'll make a date."

"I'm too young to date," Regina squealed.

"You're never too young to date your father."

Parris stood up and tugged at one of Regina's braids. The initial meeting had gone well.

"I'll get your coat," she said to Martin.

The three of them of stood at the door staring at one another.

Hunkering down, Martin pressed a kiss to Regina's cheek. "I'll call you tomorrow." He straightened and leaned down and repeated the action with Parris. "Thank you," he whispered near her ear.

He opened the door and then he was gone.

Regina wrapped her arms around her mother's waist, smiling. "He's nice, Mommy."

Parris dropped a kiss on the top her head. "That he is, angel."

What she didn't say was that she still was in love with Martin. She'd never stopped loving him.

Chapter 16

Regina woke up the following morning, complaining of a headache yet insisted on going to school because she was scheduled to present her project on invertebrates in her science class. Science and English were her favorite subjects.

Parris tied a scarf around her daughter's neck, pressing her lips to Regina's forehead. "You feel a little warm. I want to take your temperature."

"I'm going to be late for the bus, Mommy," Regina whined.

"Okay, sweetheart. But if your headache doesn't go away have the nurse call me and I'll come and pick you up."

"See you later, Mommy." She raced out of the apartment to wait for her school bus.

Parris spent the morning changing bed linen and putting up several loads of wash. She had just completed vacuuming all of the rugs when the telephone rang.

"Parris," came a familiar male voice.

"Martin." She couldn't help the breathless quality in her voice.

"I'd like to thank you."

Her brow furrowed. "For what?"

"For the child. She's delightful."

Her frown vanished. "She's quite a joy." There came a beeping sound, indicating an incoming call. "Hold on, Martin. I have another call." She depressed the hook and picked up the call. It ended quickly and she depressed the hook again. "Martin, the school nurse just called. Regina has a fever and I have to pick her up from school."

"Wait for me, Parris!" he shouted.

"I can't, Martin."

"Wait for me!" he insisted, then hung up.

Parris didn't know how Martin got to her house within the time it took her to change her clothes and run a comb through her hair, and as she stepped out of the apartment he was already striding up the path to her building.

He took her arm and guided her to his car. He practically shoved her into the car and slammed the door. He slipped behind the wheel and shifted savagely into gear.

"How do I get there?"

Parris gave him the directions and he exceeded all of the speed limits, coming to a screeching halt in front of Regina's school.

He followed Parris into the school, pacing the floor as they waited for the nurse to bring Regina to the front office.

Regina emerged, walking slowly, her face flushed. "My head still hurts, Mommy."

Parris gathered her to her chest. "It's all right, baby."

Martin went to his knees and pulled Regina from Parris. He picked her up, his dark gaze searching the tiny face so much like his own. "We're taking you home, cupcake."

Regina dropped her head to his shoulder. "I don't feel well, Daddy."

Parris signed the release form, then followed Martin and Regina out of the school building. She sat in the back of the rented car, holding Regina as he retraced the route back to her apartment.

Parris put Regina to bed, then called the pediatrician. She listened intently to his instructions. She returned to Regina's room and saw that Martin had pulled the rocking chair next to the bed. He cradled one of her hands in his. The scene was reminiscent of the time he had sat by her bed when her jaw was shattered.

She gestured to Martin and he rose to his feet and followed her out of the bedroom. "The doctor says she probably picked up a virus. He says to give her plenty of fluids and take her temperature every four to six hours. He says she's going to feel pretty weak until her fever breaks."

"Has he recommended any medication?"

"I have an aspirin-free medication he wants me to give her every four hours."

His black eyes, filled with concern, impaled her. "Are you sure she's going to be all right?"

"She's been sick before, Martin. She'll recover."

He ran a hand over his hair, closing his eyes briefly. "This is all so new for me. I suppose being a father is going to take some getting used to."

Parris patted his muscular shoulder. "You'll make it."

He tried smiling but it looked more like a grimace. "Do you mind if I come back to see her in the morning?"

"She'll probably be out of it for few days. I'll call you when she's feeling better."

"I still want to come."

"Martin…"

"Don't Martin me, Parris. She's my child and I want to see her."

Parris felt her temper rise quickly. "This is not about what you want, Martin. It's about what's right. You walk in here and declare that you want me for your wife while you expect me to fall in your arms and give you my consent; and now you demand to see a sick child who needs as much rest as she can get without you distracting or upsetting her."

Martin grasped Parris's arm, guiding her into the living room. He sat down on the sofa, pulling her down beside him. He held her hand, not permitting her to escape him.

"I wanted to marry you ten years ago, Parris, and I haven't changed my mind. Do you want to know why?" He didn't wait for her response. "Materialistically I have it all: money, fancy cars, custom-tailored clothes, a recognizable face, and a family name with enough clout to frighten those who displease me.

But none of it means spit because I don't have what really matters to me.

"I never knew what it meant to give of myself until you came into my life. Suddenly I wasn't the only person in my universe because I had someone else to share it with. You were that someone else, Parris."

Parris shook her head, trying not to hear what he was saying. There was no room her life for Martin. She had changed; she was a different person.

"We can't pick up the pieces, Martin. What we had is over. I've changed and you've changed."

"The only thing that's changed is ten years and Regina. We now share a child."

"Wrong!" She inhaled deeply. "Why don't you want to face reality? I don't love you," she lied, feeling a lump rise in her throat as soon as the words were said.

Martin leaned closer, his gaze unwavering. "How can you love Regina without loving me?"

"I can love you without being in love with you," she argued.

His classically handsome features froze moments before his mouth curved into a smile. "Oh, please. Spare me the psychoanalytic prattle. I think you've been watching too many T.V. chat shows."

A shadow of rage crossed her face and Martin recognized it immediately. He released her hand, rising to his feet. Gathering the coat he had tossed on the love seat, he slipped his arms into it.

"I'll call you," was all he said before he opened the door and walked out of her apartment.

Parris sat where she was, replaying Martin's confession. If her feelings for him hadn't changed in ten years there was no reason why his should've changed.

She had been only twenty-two when she fell in love with Martin, and she had been mature enough to know what they'd shared was a love that had been so strong and profound that it was destined to last a lifetime.

She had tried dating a couple of years ago, but each encounter ended with her date promising to call her again. They never did. No man wanted to see a woman who wouldn't let them touch or kiss her.

The doorbell chimed, followed by three rapid knocks. "Parris. It's me." Parris opened the door for Stephanie.

A slight frown marred Stephanie's normally smiling face. "Is Regina all right? Scotty said she didn't come home on the bus?"

"I picked her up early," Parris explained. "The doctor says she probably has a virus. I'm going to keep her home for the rest of the week."

Stephanie took a backwards step. "I'm not going to come in. The last thing I need is not feeling well on top of being humongous. A sick fat pregnant woman is not the nicest person to be around."

"Just hope Scott doesn't get it."

"The only thing Scotty ever gets is a stomachache when he overeats. I don't know whether to say anything," Stephanie continued, lowering her voice, "but I saw a tall man coming out of your apartment yesterday and…"

"The man you saw is Regina's father."

Stephanie tried to look embarrassed as she glanced away. Her braided hair was swept up in a ponytail, making her look a lot younger than thirty.

"I kind of knew that," she admitted. "Regina looks just like him. And I hope you don't mind my saying it, but he's hot, Parris."

Parris recalled Stephanie's assessment of Martin as she lay in bed, her mind blocking out the sound of the newscaster's voice on the all-news radio station.

She smiled. Martin was hot. And it was not only his looks.

Martin had the power to make her want him every day and at any time. She never seemed to tire of him.

He never made love to her and she never made love to him—they always made love to each other. From the first time they shared a bed they shared whatever they had to give the other. There was no pretense, no guile.

She had given him her innocent body and he treasured the gift, reciprocating with his offer of marriage.

She had turned down his marriage proposal, but what Martin didn't know was if she hadn't been forced to leave Florida she would've married him after she discovered herself pregnant. She had grown up not remembering her father. She didn't want the same for her unborn child.

However, that decision had been taken out of her hands the very night her pregnancy was confirmed, and Regina had lived the first nine years of her life not knowing who her father was.

Parris turned off the radio and snuggled under her blanket. She fell asleep immediately, and just as quickly the dreams began. She dreamt of Owen Lawson shouting obscenities. Owen dragging her into the ocean. Owen hitting her and the excruciating pain in her face. She dreamt of Martin holding her, kissing her. She dreamt of floating and responding to the fire of Martin's powerful lovemaking. The nightmare ended with the raspy voice of the man who threatened to put a bullet in her head, killing her and the child in her womb. She remembered his promise to cut Martin into little pieces before he threw what was left of his body into a lake filled with alligators.

She woke up, her body drenched with moisture and her mouth screaming a silent scream. Then she cried. It had been ten years since she cried, and when the tears no longer flowed she lay on the wet pillow and fell into a deep dreamless sleep.

Parris heard the ringing of the telephone through a thick fog. She picked up the receiver, swallowing to relieve the dryness in her throat.

"Hel-lo."

"Parris. Are you all right?"

Falling back to the pillow, she closed her eyes. "What time is it, Martin?"

"It's eight o'clock. How's Regina?"

The cloudiness in her brain cleared instantly. Regina! She replaced the telephone receiver and jumped from the bed.

Her heart was pumping uncontrollably as she raced into Regina's bedroom. Holding a hand to her chest, she walked over to the four-poster bed and stared down at the sleeping child.

She pressed a hand to Regina's forehead. Thankfully it was cooler than the night before. She would let her sleep.

It was only after she'd returned to her bedroom that Parris remembered she had hung up on Martin. She dialed the number to his hotel room, listening as the phone rang and rang. Shrugging her shoulders, she hung up and made her way to her bathroom to shower.

Parris covered her feet with a thick pair of cotton socks before she slipped into a pair of laundered jeans. The jeans had been washed so many times that they were now a pale blue shade. She pulled on a light gray sweatshirt, then brushed her hair, securing it in an elastic band.

She checked on Regina again and found her awake. "How are you feeling this morning?"

"My head still hurts a little bit." Her voice came out in a croaking sound.

Parris removed a thermometer from its case and inserted it under the child's tongue. She sat down on the side of the bed. "I'm going to see if you still have a fever, then I'll run some water for you to take a bath and change your bed. You're going to have to drink a lot of juice and water." She watched Regina wrinkle her nose when she mentioned water. The child did not like to drink water.

She removed the thermometer. One hundred point two. It was down from the previous one hundred and two, but Regina still had a fever.

Parris and Regina were startled by the ringing of the doorbell and the pounding on the front door.

"Stephanie," they said in unison.

Parris raced to the front door, but before she could open it she heard his voice calling her.

She flung the door open, shouting at the same time. "Are you mad?"

A coatless Martin pushed past her. "Where is she?"

She stared at Martin glaring down at her. "What are you talking about?"

"Is Regina all right?"

"Of course she's…"

"Why did you hang up on me?" Martin asked, cutting her off.

Heat suffused her face in embarrassment. "I'm sorry. Your call woke me up and when you mentioned Regina I remembered she was sick and I guess I kind of hung up on you."

Martin ran a hand over his hair. "You kind of hung up? When you slammed the phone down in my ear I thought something had happened to her."

"I tried calling you back," Parris countered.

"I probably was on my way over here."

"And without your coat."

Martin stared down at his running shoes, jeans and sweater as if he'd never seen them before. "I suppose I panicked." His head came up slowly and he smiled, the dimples in his cheeks deepening as Parris returned his smile.

"Can I see her?" he asked shyly.

"Wait until I give her a bath and change her bed. Then you spend as much time with her as you want."

Martin spent the entire day with Regina, sitting on the rocker and reading to her as she dozed on her bed. He gave her her medication, coaxed her into drinking water and shared the lunch Parris had prepared for the both of them.

Parris spent most of her time in her bedroom, sitting at her desk and going over a stack of photographs she had taken of the furnishings of an estate she'd catalogued for a client. The large Dutch manor house overlooking the Hudson River had yielded priceless treasures dating back to the early seventeenth-century. Most pieces of furniture had found their way to the New World via the Dutch West India Company.

Her gaze narrowed as she stared down at the photographs of several pairs of silver candlesticks. She considered candlesticks to be one of the most essential pieces of silver to own; the Dutch patron who commissioned to have the manor house built had a passion for them which had been handed down through subsequent generations.

Parris had catalogued a pair of five-shell-base circa 1760 Georgian candlesticks; circa 1880 Baltimore repoussé candlesticks from Samuel Kirk. The extreme rococo curves of a pair of circa 1885 French first standard candelabra by Armand Gross were only matched in bravado by a pair of 1825 Warwick vase wine coolers. An exquisite 1860 sterling bowl with matching serving pieces crafted by silversmith John Wendt rounded out the exquisite collection.

What puzzled her was that the five-shell-base Georgian candlesticks were quintessentially Southern. What was a New York Hudson River Valley family doing with pieces of silver that were usually seen only on a formal Southern table? She was taught that Southerners have very different tastes in silver from Easterners. Southerners liked silver that reflected very understated, conservative tastes, and collected for style, not for name.

Parris felt the pull of his energy and presence before looking up. She didn't know how long he'd been standing in the doorway to her bedroom, waiting and watching, but something impalpable raced through her. Glancing up, she met his dark eyes.

She wanted to run away, hide, but his emotions kept pulling her back; back to where she was unable to resist him, and back to love him. Martin was a thief: he'd stolen her love and her heart.

Their gazes held, and a whispered silence was broken even though no words were spoken.

She remembered every inch of his large body as if it had been only the night before. Her hands and mouth had explored his flesh, drawing moans of pure unbridled pleasure from him whenever she led him to heights of spiraling fulfillment. Martin had been an excellent teacher, and she an apt student.

She tried ignoring the once-familiar throbbing in the lower part of her body. It had occurred so quickly she wasn't able to hide the shattering reaction from him. Her lips parted and she closed her eyes while sighing audibly.

Martin's heart pumped painfully in his chest as he watched the color rise under Parris's golden-brown skin. His hands tightened into fists as another part of his body tightened and pulsed with desire.

He'd lied to himself; he'd told himself that he could be rational. He could see her and remain in control. He was wrong. He wanted her; he wanted to sleep with her.

"I'm leaving now," he said quietly. "I'll call you tomorrow."

Parris nodded, not moving or saying anything. For if she would have spoken she would have asked him to stay—to spend the night.

She opened her eyes and stared at the spot where he had stood seconds before.

"He knew," she whispered to the empty space. He knew she wanted him. Martin was right. Nothing had changed. Everything had remained the same, except for Regina.

Chapter 17

Regina's fever broke after forty-eight hours, leaving her with a cough that wracked her thin body every time she took a deep breath.

The cough bothered Parris more than the fever because it was debilitating. The doctor had prescribed a cough elixir which suppressed the cough while leaving her drowsy and sleeping most of the time, and instead of her missing three days of school it had become seven days.

Parris had held off confirming her reservations to go to the MGM Grand extravaganza in Las Vegas because she didn't know whether Regina would be up to the exhausting activities associated with a family vacation resort.

Martin waited until Regina had gone to bed when he asked the question that had been nagging at Parris for days.

"Are you still going away for Christmas?"

She stood at the wide window in the living room, staring out at the lighted Christmas tree in the center of the courtyard of the housing development.

"I don't know," she answered honestly. He crossed the room and stood behind her. She could feel the heat of his body and the whisper of his breath on the back of her neck.

"I want you and Regina to come to Jamaica with me."

She spun around, her eyes wide with surprise. Didn't he know he had gotten her pregnant in Jamaica?

"No."

"Why not?"

"It just wouldn't work, Martin."

He frowned. "What are you talking about?"

"Us, Martin. We can't relive what once was."

The forefinger of his right hand swept over his black moustache as he smiled. "That week will never be repeated, Parris. I'm enough of a realist to accept that.

"You'd planned to take a vacation anyway and Regina needs a warm climate so she can get rid of her nagging cough," he continued, watching her face as she registered his carefully chosen words.

"And you're tired of the cold weather, aren't you?" she asked perceptively. His expression was boyish when he bobbed his head up and down.

"I'm always freezing," he admitted.

Unconsciously, her brow furrowed. He wasn't thinking of a romantic liaison. He only wanted a family vacation.

"Let me think about it."

His luminous eyes widened in surprise. "Don't take too long because I have to make arrangements for the flight."

Sure you do, Parris thought. If she had given him an affirmative Martin would have her racing to the airport within the hour. She remembered when she only had time to pick up her passport before they rushed to the airport for their flight. He hadn't even allowed her time to pack her clothes.

Passport! She gasped audibly. "I don't have a passport for Regina."

"That's not a problem. I'll get her through customs," Martin replied.

"But what if you can't?"

"Then we'll go to Puerto Rico." Leaning over, he kissed her cheek. "You worry too much. Good night."

Her fingers grazed her face where his warm mouth had touched. It was only the second time in two weeks that he showed any affection, and both times it was the feathery pressure of his mouth on her cheek.

"Good night," she said softly, watching him leave.

* * *

Parris felt the warmth of the Caribbean sun caress her face through the window of the small private jet. She glanced over to her left when the strength of a large hand enveloped hers.

"How are you?"

She managed a warm smile for Martin. "Good."

The pilot's voice penetrated the incessant roar of the aircraft's engine. "We're approaching the Kingston airport. Please prepare for the descent and landing."

Martin squeezed her fingers briefly, then moved across the aisle to wake Regina while Parris turned to gaze down at the rapidly approaching patch of verdant lushness surrounded by the bright green waters of the Caribbean.

She was transfixed by the stretch of beaches covered by pristine white sand and the tall palm trees. A feeling of quiet solitude swept over her. The sight of the palm trees evoked poignant memories of Florida.

The jet landed smoothly on a private strip of runway, and within minutes the baggage was unloaded. They found themselves whisked through customs and spared the customary search reserved for all arrivals on the island.

Martin exchanged words with a slight, dark-skinned Jamaican. The man's casual white shirt and trousers were a startling contrast against his rich, dark complexion. It was apparent he had been waiting for Martin as he directed them out of the noisy airport crowded with tourists arriving for the start of the peak season.

The sights, smells and the sounds of Jamaica paled when they were led to the black sedan Martin had used when he first brought her to the island. Standing beside the sedan was a tall, slender man.

At first glance, there was something about the man that reminded Parris of Martin. But as she neared him she realized the only characteristic they shared was equal height. Whereas Martin was dark, this man was fairer under his extraordinary tan. His close-cut hair was so blond it appeared platinum. His eyes were a strange shade of pale green, which at first appeared nearly transparent.

It was difficult to determine his age, yet he possessed an ominous quality she had never encountered in anyone she had ever met; not even in her abductor. If she thought of Martin as dark and dangerous, this man was lean and lethal.

Martin and the man embraced warmly. Martin turned, smiling. "Joshua, this is Parris Simmons and her daughter, Regina. Parris, Joshua Kirkland."

Parris found her hand enveloped in a firm grip as she mumbled a greeting. Joshua smiled, if a parting of his lips could be called a smile, Parris thought.

"Welcome to Jamaica, Parris." His voice soft and controlled and his pale eyes never left her face. "I find Jamaica to be the most sensuous, enticing island in the Caribbean, and I hope you'll enjoy your stay. I extend to you the enchanting hospitality the island is known for."

Martin pulled Regina from Parris. Joshua hunkered down to Regina's level and extended his hand. The child gave the hand a long quizzical look before she took it.

Joshua's gaze softened as he examined the young girl who looked so much like her father. "Nice to you meet you, Regina. How would you like to get out of those heavy pants and into a swimsuit to splash in the ocean," he suggested.

Regina's wariness vanished quickly. "Can I really swim in the ocean?"

Joshua straightened and led her to the vintage Mercedes Benz. "The ocean is only several hundred feet from the house where you'll be staying. Let's see how fast I can drive to get you there." Regina scrambled willingly into the seat beside Joshua.

"I'm ready, Mr. Kirkland."

Parris and Martin smiled as they too settled back in the spacious interior of the old car. Martin reached out and held her hand. He relaxed when she didn't pull her hand away. They were silent throughout the trip which took them west through the historic community of Spanish Town, each lost in past memories of their trip ten years ago.

Parris found Joshua less forbidding, and then charming, as he related stories about the history of the island to Regina. He would insert a bit of mythical folklore, when appropriate, keeping her and Regina deeply engrossed in his strangely-accented phrases. Parris finally concluded his speech was truly accent-free, but it was his inflection which gave rise to the foreign-sounding intonations.

Martin was snoring lightly as they neared Ocho Rios, and Joshua explained to Regina that the word was not Spanish for *"eight rivers,"* but a bungling of *"chorreras,"* a word meaning spout or waterfall which applied to an entire coastline where a series of rivers or waterfalls flowed from the mountains onto limestone rocks to form spectacular cascades. He assured Regina that her father would take her around the island to show her the more beautiful and famous haunts of the many of the past and present celebrities who had made Jamaica their home.

Joshua stopped in front of his house and Regina stared out of the window in awe. Her mouth formed a perfect O. Joshua helped her out of the car while Parris shook Martin gently to wake him.

His eyes opened slowly, and for a few seconds he stared at her from under half-lowered lids. His gaze said everything and she registered his private message before glancing away. The realization struck her with the force of the rushing waters of the waterfalls they had passed on the northward journey. Martin was special. He had been from the first time she saw him, and she found herself a prisoner to the memories and of her own emotions. She wanted and needed Martin the way a woman needed and wanted a man.

Martin helped Parris from the car, his arm circling her waist and pulling her to his body. She swayed slightly and he steadied her. He lowered his head to kiss her, then he pulled back. The impulse to kiss her had been so strong it left him shaking. Dropping his arm, he turned away.

Parris stared at Martin, unaware that Joshua was staring at her. His pale eyes lingered briefly on her face before they caught fire when an utterly beautiful young woman came out of the house.

The slender woman was of medium height with large dark slanting eyes set in a flawless tawny-brown face. Black shiny curls framed her face, flowing to her shoulders. Her full mouth and high cheekbones only enhanced her delicate, exotic beauty. A simple white cotton dress with a full skirt made her look delicate and innocent.

The woman spied Martin and smiled. She closed the distance between them and threw her arms around his neck. Martin picked her up, kissing her cheek.

"Sable, you get more beautiful every time I see you. If Joshua and I weren't so close I'd attempt to steal you from him," he teased.

Sable clucked her tongue and kissed Martin soundly on the mouth. "I would never leave my Joshua. Not for all the money in the world, Martin." Her lilting accent made his name sound like Mar-tine.

Joshua stared over Sable's head at Martin. "Would you be willing to give up Parris for Sable, my friend?"

Martin's dark eyes blazed into Joshua's challenging gaze. He released Sable, pushing her gently toward Joshua. *"Never, my friend."*

There was a moment of strained silence before Regina tugged impatiently at Joshua's arm to get his attention. "Mr. Kirkland, can I go swimming now?"

Joshua gave her a warm look. "You can if you stop calling me Mister Kirkland and call me Uncle Josh."

Regina looked at her mother for approval while Parris glanced over at a frowning Martin. He nodded and Joshua led Regina toward the house.

Parris turned to Sable, extending her hand. "Men sometimes forget their manners. I'm Parris Simmons."

Sable gave the taller woman a dazzling smile. She shook the proffered hand. "I'm Sable St. Clair. Welcome to Jamaica. Come into the house out of the heat. I'll show you which room you'll have during your stay."

Parris followed Sable into the house, leaving Martin to unload the luggage from the car. The room chosen for her was the same one she had occupied with Martin during their first trip to the island.

Sable busied herself closing shutters to block out the heat from the sun when Martin entered, carrying several bags under his arms. She fluttered around the room like a delicate moth and within seconds she was gone, the door closing behind her.

Perspiration plastered Martin's shirt to his chest and back and Parris felt her mouth go dry as he unbuttoned it. It seemed like minutes even though it had only been several seconds by the time he shrugged out of his shirt and dropped it to the floor. She stared mutely at the thick mat of black curling hair on his chest.

"Which side of the bed do you want?" he asked smoothly.

Chapter 18

"**Y**ou're kidding, aren't you?" Disbelief was apparent in the tone of her voice.

Martin sat down on a rocker and unlaced his running shoes, the muscles in his back rippling sensuously under his brown skin as he bent over. He removed the shoes and slouched down in the rocker, stretching out his long legs and crossing his bare feet at the ankles. From where he sat his face was hidden in the shadows.

"Will it make you uncomfortable to sleep with me again?" he asked, completely ignoring her query.

"Yes," she spat out.

He shrugged his bare shoulders. "What do you want me to do?"

"Move into another bedroom."

"Regina's in the other bedroom."

"Then she'll move in here and you can take her bedroom."

Martin sat up straight. "Is that what you want, Parris?"

"Yes."

Martin rose from the chair, gathering his shirt and shoes. He picked up his bags and quietly walked out of the bedroom, leaving her luggage behind.

It really wasn't what she wanted, but it was the way it had to be. She couldn't fall back into Martin's arms and his bed and pretend nothing had happened in the ten years they were apart.

She took the rocker he had vacated, burying her face in her hands. They would spend the week in Ocho Rios, relaxing, then they'd leave to go their separate ways and pick up the pieces of their lives. She would return to New York and Martin would go back to Florida.

She wouldn't keep him from seeing Regina, and if they wanted to take a family vacation again it could be in Jamaica, Puerto Rico or any place in the world except Florida.

Her hands came down the moment she heard Regina's voice. "Daddy said I have to sleep with you."

She smiled at her daughter. "Daddy's right. You and I are going to have a slumber party every night."

"I need my bathing suit. I'm going swimming with Uncle Josh." Regina was more interested in swimming than her parents' sleeping arrangements.

She unpacked, finding Regina's suit, then put away all of their clothes in the large armoire. Regina raced out of the house, dressed for swimming, and Parris decided she needed to change out of her own jeans and blouse and into something cooler.

She walked into the adjoining bath, remembering the room's delightful charm with a large claw-foot blue-veined marble bathtub hidden behind an Oriental ornamental screen. An oval basin sat on a decorative pedestal. White wicker pieces, covered with cushions in aquamarine green added a tropical accent to the space. Hidden away in a far corner was a shower stall.

Parris turned on the tub's faucet, letting the water run clear, then added pale green crystals from a large glass jar on a shelf near the basin. The cloying fragrance of lilies filled the room, and she quickly stripped off her clothes and stepped into the tepid water and rising bubbles.

A quarter of an hour later, she emerged from the bathroom, her hair twisted in a knot on the top of her head. Dressing quickly, she pulled on a pair of lace underpants under a swingy cotton dress. The loose-fitting garment bared her shoulders and narrow straps crisscrossed her back to the waist.

She left the bedroom through a door which led out to the gallery. Stepping out into the sultry tropical air she was met by the thick scent of wild orchids and magnolias.

Closing her eyes, Parris moved into the strong sunlight, turning her face up to the healing rays. The heat penetrating her body was a soothing balm and she smiled at the calming languid feeling entering her limbs.

"Too much sun too quickly can be dangerous."

Parris opened her eyes to find Joshua Kirkland leaning against a wrought iron railing about ten feet away from her. She smiled at him. Surprisingly, his skin was deeply tanned. *He should take his own advice,* she thought.

"I'll be careful," she remarked.

Joshua moved closer, crossing his arms over his chest. A short sleeve white cotton shirt and shorts highlighted his tropical tan and sharp features, making Parris aware that her host was a very attractive man. His face was unlined, and she guessed he was somewhere between thirty-five and forty. His hair was thick, coarse, and worn close to his scalp. She thought his hair was closer to silver rather than gold.

She shifted uncomfortably as he continued to stare at her with a pair of deep-set ice-green eyes, shivering in spite of the torrid heat. His gaze was mesmerizing and she struggled to free herself from its spell.

"Where's Martin?" she breathed out in a throaty whisper.

"You're a beautiful woman, Parris," Joshua stated quietly, not answering her query. "I can't decide which I like more—your eyes or your voice."

Two pairs of eyes—one light and one dark held. Joshua moved closer, his compelling eyes riveting her to the spot. She felt the movement of his breathing and her heart hammered wildly in her ears.

He's like Martin, she thought. Joshua had the same appeal as Martin where the very air around her seemed electrified until she had trouble drawing a normal breath.

She wanted to run, but couldn't. Their gazes were locked as

their chests rose and fell in unison. There was something about the man that frightened yet fascinated her.

Let me go, she implored him silently.

"Aren't you going swimming with us, Mommy?" Regina's voice shattered the stillness of the afternoon.

Joshua lowered his gaze and Parris was mercifully freed from his hypnotic spell as she sagged weakly against the railing.

She managed a smile for her daughter. Regina's hair hung like a thick rope down her back. "Not right now, angel. I'll go later this afternoon."

Regina laughed and shook her wet hair. The braid snapped like a wet tail. She giggled when both her mother and Joshua stepped out of the path of spraying moisture.

"Well, Daddy wanted me to tell you that it's time to eat."

Joshua reached over, grasping Regina's braid and wringing out the excess water. "Let's say you and I swim again after we eat and relax."

"I say yes," Regina agreed.

Parris followed Joshua and Regina to the back of the house where Sable had set up a large table. Martin was helping Sable bring out dishes filled with chilled fresh melon, large boiled shrimp, a piquant sauce for dipping, an array of fresh lettuce leaves, boiled eggs and creme caramel puddings served with blackberries in a cognac and vodka liqueured sauce.

"You can sit here, darling," Martin said to Parris. He pulled out a chair for her.

She gave him a tender smile and sat down.

The five dined alfresco under the sweeping branches of an ancient banana tree. Brightly colored birds chatted and squalled, hopping nimbly from branch to branch.

Regina was given a coconut shell filled with tropical fruit juices while the four adults sampled a chilled potent concoction of tropical juices liberally laced with one hundred proof Jamaican rum. Parris tasted her sparingly. She had never acquired a fondness for alcoholic beverages.

The heat, food and an ounce of the drink lulled her into a state

An Important Message from the Publisher

Dear Reader,

Because you've chosen to read one of our fine novels, I'd like to say "thank you"! And, as a special way to say thank you, I'm offering to send you two more Kimani™ Romance novels and two surprise gifts – absolutely FREE! These books will keep it real with true-to-life African American characters that turn up the heat and sizzle with passion.

Please enjoy the free books and gifts with our compliments...

Glenda Howard

For Kimani Press

Peel off Seal and Place Inside...

FREE GIFTS
EDITOR'S SEAL
THANK YOU

We'd like to send you two free books to introduce you to Kimani™ Romance books. These novels feature strong, sexy women, and African-American heroes that are charming, loving and true. Our authors fill each page with exceptional dialogue, exciting plot twists, and enough sizzling romance to keep you riveted until the very end!

KIMANI ROMANCE ... LOVE'S ULTIMATE DESTINATION

Your two books have a combined cover price of $11.98, but are yours **FREE!** We'll even send you two wonderful surprise gifts. You can't lose!

2 Free Bonus Gifts!

Two Kimani™ Romance Novels
Two exciting surprise gifts

YES!

I have placed my Editor's "thank you" Free Gifts seal in the space provided at right. Please send me 2 FREE books, and my 2 FREE Mystery Gifts. I understand that I am under no obligation to purchase anything further, as explained on the back of this card.

PLACE
FREE GIFTS
SEAL
HERE

168 XDL EZRP   **368 XDL EZSP**

FIRST NAME	LAST NAME

ADDRESS

APT.#	CITY

STATE/PROV.	ZIP/POSTAL CODE

FOR SHIPPING CONFIRMATION

EMAIL

Thank You!

Offer limited to one per household and not valid to current subscribers of Kimani™ Romance books. **Your Privacy**—Kimani Press is committed to protecting your privacy. Our Privacy Policy is available online at www.KimaniPress.com or upon request from the Reader Service. From time to time we make our lists of customers available to reputable third parties who may have a product or service of interest to you. If you would prefer for us not to share your name and address, please check here ☐. **Help us get it right**—We strive for accurate, respectful and relevant communications. To clarify or modify your communication preferences, visit us at www.ReaderService.com/consumerschoice.

BUSINESS REPLY MAIL

FIRST-CLASS MAIL   PERMIT NO. 717   BUFFALO, NY

POSTAGE WILL BE PAID BY ADDRESSEE

THE READER SERVICE
PO BOX 1867
BUFFALO NY 14240-9952

NO POSTAGE
NECESSARY
IF MAILED
IN THE
UNITED STATES

of total relaxation, and Martin had to repeat his statement before she was able to respond. Nodding in agreement, she stood up.

"A nap sounds like a good idea," she replied. Her words slurred together in a singsong fashion.

Martin smiled and Joshua studied his long delicate fingers before both of them rose to acknowledge her departure as she led a protesting Regina to their bedroom. Sable also retreated to the house while the two men sat at the table sipping the rum-laced drink.

Martin glanced over at Joshua from under half-lowered lids. "What do you think of her, Josh?"

Joshua's expression displayed none of what he was feeling as he stared across his property, watching the gentle lapping of waves against the beach. "She's perfect. Almost too perfect," he confessed. "Have you told her?"

Martin shook his, head, a frown creasing his forehead. "Not yet."

"Why?" The single word sounded like a shot.

Martin stirred his drink with a straw. "I don't know," he said slowly. "I know I can't wait too much longer," he admitted, trying to shake off a feeling of uneasiness.

Martin had planned to seduce Parris, but soon came to realize that she wasn't the same woman he knew ten years ago. She was no longer a girl in a woman's body but a full-fledged woman who was in complete control of her life.

"Somehow I have to convince her that I want to marry her because I still love her. Getting her to marry me will probably be less of a hurtle than convincing her to return to Florida with me. And there's no way I can predict how she'll react when I tell her that she may be the next first lady of the state of Florida."

"You managed to get her to come to Jamaica with you, why not Florida?" Joshua questioned.

Martin assumed the familiar gesture of steepling his fingers and bringing his right forefinger to his mouth, but his relaxed stance did not fool Joshua. Martin was not as confident as he appeared.

"She didn't have much of a choice," he confessed. "It was because of Regina." He quickly related how Regina had come down with a virus and hadn't recovered as quickly as the doctor originally predicted.

"You're using the child," Joshua accused him harshly. He thought of a time in his own life when he'd become a pawn between his parents.

Martin caught Joshua's meaning immediately and failed to check his quick temper. "Wrong! Don't forget that I love Parris and that I acknowledge Regina as my child."

He tossed his cloth napkin on the table and stood up. He stared down at the pale hair and the bold profile, registering pain in Joshua Kirkland for the first time.

"I'm sorry, Josh."

Joshua sat motionless, only the prominent veins in his slender hands revealing his tension.

Sable came out of the house. She knew all was not right the moment she saw Joshua's face. He seemed to be carved out of marble.

Martin touched her shoulder and whispered, "I said something I shouldn't have said. Try to get him to forgive me."

Sable nodded and smiled. "Don't worry, Martin. I'll take care of everything."

Martin walked along the beach, staring out at the sea. He wanted to go to Parris and tell her of his plans, but couldn't. Insecurities wouldn't permit him to tell her of the campaign which he hoped would put him in the Governor's Mansion in Tallahassee.

The men who had approached him six months ago had presented him with their recommendations: they wanted Martin Diaz Cole to oppose the incumbent governor. Of the nine men, six had voiced reservations as to his marital status. They delicately suggested he would be a better candidate if he had a wife.

He had laughed and told them to forget it. He had no intention of ever marrying. That decision had been taken out of his hands when Parris Simmons left him.

However, the notion of marrying continued to haunt him whenever his thoughts strayed to Parris. At twenty-two, she had been able to weave her spell over him the way a woman twice her age had been unable to do.

After the meeting with the political strategists, he found his thoughts filled with memories of Parris's voice and her smile. At business meetings he began seeing images of her flushed face after they had made love and the awe of fulfillment darken her eyes whenever he confessed his love for her. And he also remembered the flashes of fear stealing across her features whenever he mentioned marriage.

She had never disclosed why she had ended her brief marriage to Owen Lawson or why she had come to Martin a virgin. The life she had shared with her ex-husband had remained a closely-guarded secret.

The images of her grew stronger, and his patience shorter until he contacted Joshua Kirkland; the one man whose counterintelligence training made him one of the best in the world had used his own methods to find Parris Simmons for him.

Martin once stood on a beach watching Parris as her ex-husband attempted to drown her. Now he stood on another beach, his heart pounding relentlessly. He was going to marry Parris and he was to become a candidate for governor of Florida.

An undefined emotion swept through his body, and he shuddered violently. He would have both! He refused to think of one without the other.

Chapter 19

Parris lay down beside a sleeping Regina, closed her eyes and fell into her own deep slumber. Within minutes the dream flashed vividly in her mind, the frightening sequences emerging like so many flickering frames on a roll of film: Owen, the black angry waves, Martin making love to her until her mind floated beyond her body, the raspy-voiced abductor, and the unmistakable pressure of the gun barrel biting into her ribs.

She sat up, covering her mouth, whimpering.

It was the second one within two weeks. The nightmare had returned more real than in the past.

Pushing aside the mosquito netting draping the bed, Parris stumbled across the room and opened the door leading out to the gallery.

Sinking down to the white tiles surrounding the house, she pressed her back to the wrought iron railing and closed her eyes, trying to slow down the runaway beating of her heart. She was in the same spot when Martin returned from his walk along the beach.

Martin knew something was wrong the moment he saw her strained profile. Quickening his step, he went to his knees and pulled her limp body to his, cradling her face against his shoulder.

"What's wrong, Parris?" His hot breath seared her ear.

"Nothing, Martin." Her voice was low, her tone flat and expressionless.

"Are you sure?" Martin asked, not believing her.

"Yes." There was nothing wrong *now.* She was awake and the nightmare was gone.

"If nothing's wrong, then what are you doing sitting out here in the sun?" The thumb of his right hand swept over her cheekbones, feeling the build-up of heat in her face.

"I just couldn't sleep," Parris admitted. Why, she thought, why had the nightmares come back? She hadn't had one in ten years, but now that Martin had walked back into her life they also were back. Were the dreams a foreboding? Did Martin's presence foreshadow a danger to her and Regina? Or to all three of them?

Martin rose to his feet, pulling her up with him. "Why don't you come swimming with me?"

Her head came up quickly and she stared at him, remembering the first time they had come to Ocho Rios ten years before and swam nude. They had spent a week at the house and never used their bathing suits.

Martin smiled sensuously, also remembering their early morning and late night playful encounters in the water.

"I'd rather not, Martin." She did not want a repeat of anything which brought back memories of her life with Martin before she was forced to leave him.

Martin hid his disappointment well. "How about going for a walk?"

Parris shook her head. "Regina's still asleep."

"I'll ask Joshua and Sable to look out for her."

"They're not her baby-sitters," she argued softly.

His fingers tightened around her bare upper arms. "I don't think either of them will mind looking after her for what—an hour or less. Go get your shoes and I'll tell Joshua we're going for a walk," he suggested when he noted her indecision.

He released her, letting out his breath slowly as she turned and retreated into the house. He knew he couldn't intimidate Parris. He had never been able to do that. But he had been able to seduce her; now even seduction was a part of their pasts.

He still wanted her; wanted her with a burning which wouldn't permit him to sleep; a burning which made him feel edgy and ill-tempered; tense and off-balanced.

He had suggested the trip to Jamaica as much for himself as for Regina, thinking that if he returned to the place where he had confessed and poured out his love for Parris it would right all of the wrongs of the past ten years.

It was almost like returning to the scene of a traumatic incident wherein one would be forced to come to grips with what had happened. On the other hand their first trip to Ocho Rios had been anything but traumatic. Ocho Rios was where he had gotten Parris pregnant.

After Joshua revealed Parris had had a child—his child, he sat at his desk, trying to remember when it had happened, when had he gotten her pregnant.

Replaying every day, each time they had made love he finally recalled the night he had asked Parris to marry him. She had turned down his proposal, enraging him. The slender thread between rage and passion merged and he took her quickly, without protecting her, and buried his flesh so deeply in her wet, hot, tight body that he thought he was going to faint.

His heated blood scalded his skin as it raced in his veins like molten lava while his heart nearly exploded when he exploded in her body, his release stronger and longer than any he had ever experienced in his life. He hadn't wanted to admit it but he knew the moment a new life had begun in her body.

Pushing his hands into the large pockets of a pair of white cotton loose-fitting pants with a drawstring waist, Martin refused to think beyond the moment. He had less than six weeks to announce his candidacy. The day would coincide with his fortieth birthday; and when he made the announcement he wanted Parris standing by his side as his wife.

* * *

Parris sat beside Martin, their backs supported by the sturdy trunk of a palm tree. A cooling breeze ruffled the massive fronds bowing gracefully above their heads. She stared at the broken pieces of a coconut, feeling Martin's fiery black gaze on her face.

"How long have you known Joshua?"

Her question seemed to startle Martin, and he shifted his eyebrows. "Almost eighteen years."

"How old is he?"

"Thirty-four. Why?"

Turning her head slowly, she stared back at Martin. "He looks young, but there's something about him which says he's so much older. Are you close friends?"

"Very close," Martin replied softly.

"Is he always so serious?" she continued with her questioning, remembering Joshua's expressionless face.

"Yes." Martin crossed his arms over his broad chest and closed his eyes.

There was only the sound of the rolling waves and an occasional gull screeching wildly as it competed with another gull for a morsel of sea life left on the beach.

Parris, placing a hand on Martin's shoulder, shook him gently. "Why are you so mysterious about Joshua?" she asked as he opened his eyes.

Martin unfolded his arms and reached out, pulling her over to sit between his outstretched legs. He tightened his grip under her breasts as she attempted to break his loose hold on her slender body.

"Joshua is a very private person, Parris. And that means he'll only reveal what he wants someone to know about him. I respect his right for privacy, and because I do we've remained close friends. Relax, Parris, I'm not going to attack you."

"I know you would never attack me," she countered confidently. "You're not Owen." The moment she mentioned her ex-husband's name she knew she had made a faux pas.

This time his arm did tighten, halting her breathing momentarily before it relaxed. "I wasn't talking about that kind of *attack*. Is that why you left me? Did Lawson come after you again?" he asked savagely.

"Don't ask me about Owen."

"Did he?"

"I said don't ask me anything about Owen Lawson," she warned between clenched teeth.

They sat, Martin holding her until her body relaxed and she pressed her back to his chest. He registered the slight rising and falling of her breasts on his arm and he successfully controlled his rising desire for her.

He delighted in her closeness, her slight weight and the familiar curves of her slender body. Pressing his lips to her hair, one hand was busy searching the dark brown strands, removing the pins securing it at the top of her head.

"Martin…"

"Shush, baby. I just want to see you with your hair down." He removed the last pin and combed his fingers through the wealth of sweet-smelling strands falling around her shoulders. "I like you with longer hair."

Parris stopped his hand. "It's too long. I should've cut it months ago."

"Don't. Please. Let it grow," he urged softly.

Turning in his embrace, she stared up at the smoldering fire in his coal-black eyes. "Long hair is for little girls." Her voice was a seductive whisper.

Martin's reply was to lower his head until his mouth hovered above hers. He inhaled her moist breath seconds before he captured it as his lips moved sensuously over hers.

The feel of the thick silky hair on his upper lip shocked Parris into an awareness of his blatant masculinity. The delicious touch of his lips moved down the slender column of her throat before returning to reclaim her mouth.

His hands spanned her waist, lifting her effortlessly until she straddled his thighs. His desire rose quickly and there was no way he could control the hardness pressing up against her hips through the thin cotton fabric of her dress.

Parris melted against his body and her world was filled with Martin Cole. She groaned once as his hands cupped her breasts through her dress, his thumbs sweeping back and forth over her distended nipples.

Pushing gently, his tongue parted her lips. She felt the aching between her thighs, clenching and unclenching them when the familiar throbbing grew stronger and hotter.

Martin knew exactly when they were going over the edge and he pulled back and buried his face in her unbound hair.

A smile curved his mouth, his hands moving up and down on her bared back in a comforting motion. "I'm sorry, baby. I shouldn't have done that," he apologized.

What he had wanted to do was take her where they lay, on the sand and in full view of the heavens and the ocean. He wanted Parris more than at any time in his life. He wanted and needed her.

But he had time. Plenty of time to show her that he still loved her. They had a week.

Pulling back, he cradled her face between his palms, examining the features which assailed his passions, illusions and fantasies. Parris Simmons had haunted his dreams for ten years.

He noted the gold undertones in her smooth skin that appeared velvet and poreless.

His thumbs traced the fragile curve of high cheekbones which afforded her an exotic appearance along with the upward slant of her luminous eyes.

The short nose which he found alluring whenever he recalled the number of times he placed a kiss on its rounded tip. And her mouth, full, lush, soft, hot and giving, was swollen and pouty from his passionate kiss.

His gaze moved slowly over her features, never wavering. Her beautiful delicate face, stripped bare of makeup, was exquisite.

Joshua had confirmed what he'd known the moment he saw Parris walk into the private room at the West Palm Beach restaurant what now seemed so long ago—she was perfect. If possible—too perfect.

"Martin."

He registered the breathless sound of his name, and their gazes caught and held in a pregnant silence before she spoke again.

"I'm going back to the house. I want to be there when Regina wakes up."

Martin nodded and helped her to her feet. He held her hand protectively as they retraced their steps back to the house.

Parris hoped Martin didn't feel the slight tremors still coursing throughout her body. She hadn't expected him to kiss her and she hadn't resisted him either because it had been a long time, too long, since she'd felt any hint of real passion; and it was only now that she had begun to recognize her own needs; however, it was her own need for Martin that shocked her.

A smile softened her mouth and she shrugged a shoulder. What did she have to lose? She would enjoy his kisses, and after a week she would return to New York, her apartment and her profession.

Chapter 20

The weather decided not to cooperate. It rained steadily every day, letting up and finally stopping a day before Martin, Parris and Regina were to return to the States.

Their plan to take an excursion around the island on Sable's brother's charter boat was cancelled. Martin's plan to take Parris and Regina to Dunn's River Falls was also cancelled, and Martin's promise to teach Regina to swim was put off until the rains stopped.

Regina complained that she was bored. She wanted to swim; she wanted to sail on a boat; and she wanted to leave the house and go out—anywhere.

Parris spent her time reading and watching countless American reruns and British sitcoms on one of the few channels broadcasting on the island while Martin spent hours bending over his power notebook typing a report of his last business trip and a draft of a proposal for a resort development in Belize. It had taken ten years for ColeDiz International Ltd.'s Belize investment to equal their Costa Rican counterpart, which was undergoing a process of downsizing.

Parris brushed Regina's hair and braided it in a single plait. She wound an elastic band around the curling end. "You're all finished. Now we're ready to go."

Regina turned, staring up at her mother. "Mommy, would you be mad if I didn't go shopping with you and Sable?"

Cradling Regina's chin in her hand, Parris lowered her head and brushed her nose against her daughter's. "What do you want to do?" she asked slowly.

Regina smiled. "I want to go swimming."

Parris let go of her chin. "You'd rather swim than go shopping?"

"I have to learn how to swim. When I go back to school I'm going to tell everyone in my class that I went to Jamaica on vacation, and that I learned to swim in the ocean."

Parris returned her smile. "But what if you don't learn to swim in one day. Remember, we're going back home tomorrow."

Regina tilted her chin and stared down her thin delicate nose, nodding slowly. "I will learn to swim in one day," she stated confidently, arching her eyebrows.

The gesture and her confidence was so much like Martin's that Parris smiled. "No, I won't get mad if you don't go shopping with me. But when I get back I want you to show me how well you can swim."

Regina curved her arms around her mother's neck and kissed her cheek. "Thanks, Mommy."

Sable settled herself behind the wheel of Joshua's Mercedes and she and Parris waved goodbye to Martin, Joshua and Regina, then set out for their drive to Montego Bay where they strolled about the restored Georgian structures on Church street and the public market on Fustic. The market was alive with a carnival-like atmosphere, and Parris felt herself caught up in the festive spirit.

She was shown breadfruit, ackee and callaloo. She sampled a spicy hot meat pattie and curried goat. Sable quickly recommended soursop, a delicious drink much like a milkshake to cool her overstimulated taste buds.

The two women smiled shyly after two young men offered to take them sightseeing. "Never you mind the honey words, Tomas," Sable scolded mildly at the taller of the two. "I've heard about your tours, man. You take the ladies for a tour of your bedroom where all she sees is the cracks in the ceiling and your hairy chest."

Tomas and his friend retreated quickly, hoping no one overheard Sable's damning statement. Both of them earned a profitable living *giving tours* to wealthy women vacationing in Jamaica.

Parris laughed as the gigolos raced out of the plaza. She glanced at her watch. They had spent more than five hours shopping and sightseeing.

She smiled across the table at Sable. "I want to thank you for everything you've done for us this past week."

Sable waved a hand. "It was nothing. Joshua and I rarely have guests so it was good to have some female company. Since I left my job as a secretary for a Kingston export company and moved in with Joshua I find that I miss the noise and the crowds of the big city."

"How long have you lived in Ocho Rios?"

"A month," Sable replied, blushing attractively. "Even though Joshua and I aren't married I feel like a newlywed," she admitted.

Parris thought of the months she had lived with Martin and the memories elicited a smile. "I wish you and Joshua happiness and a lifetime of love."

Lowering her head, Sable murmured thanks. "Is there anything else you want to see?"

Parris patted her straw bag filled with gifts for Martin, Regina, her New York neighbors Stephanie, Scott and Calvin Edwards and her Jamaica hosts.

"No, I'm ready to go back now."

It was Christmas Eve and Parris felt an exhilaration and a sadness as it came time to say good-bye to Joshua and Sable.

She hugged Sable, then kissed her cheek. "Merry Christmas. I left a little something for you with Joshua," she whispered in her ear. She had bought a gold bangle bracelet for Sable after she saw the longing look in her eye after she'd tried it on in a little jewelry shop in Montego Bay. She knew the semi-precious stones circling the bracelet would be spectacular against Sable's tawny-brown skin.

Sable blinked back tears. "Thank you. Be happy with Martin."

"Thank you." She gave her another hug, then turned to Joshua, extending her hand. "Thank you again for your hospitality. It's been a wonderful week."

He took her hand, squeezing her fingers gently. "You're always welcome to come back with Regina. You don't have to wait for Martin to bring you." It was his way of saying that he was aware that she and Martin had not shared a bedroom during their stay.

Parris registered his open invitation, nodding.

Martin kissed Sable and embraced Joshua. "Thanks, buddy."

Joshua bent down to pick up Regina. Her black hair was a striking contrast to his shimmering silver. She wound her arms around his neck. "What am I going to do now that my best girl is leaving?"

Regina rubbed her nose against his smooth cheek. "You still have Sable, Uncle Josh. She'll take good care of you."

Joshua stared at Sable, his pale gaze registering her smiling face. "You're right about that, Regina."

"We're cleared for takeoff," Martin informed them the moment he registered the pilot's signal from the private jet.

There came a chorus of good-byes before Martin, Parris and Regina entered the aircraft.

Parris seated Regina and secured her seat belt before taking her own seat. From where she sat she could see Joshua and Sable standing arm-in-arm, watching the aircraft taxiing for takeoff. She waved through the small window and they returned her wave.

A smile lifted the corner of her mouth when Joshua's arm circled Sable's shoulders, bringing her cheek to his chest. And in the moment before the plane picked up speed, Parris saw Joshua lower his head and kiss Sable's awaiting lips.

"What are you smiling about?"

Parris glanced across the aisle at Martin. "Joshua and Sable. I was just wondering that if they ever marry whether they would elect to live in the house in Ocho Rios or live somewhere else."

"Don't tell me you still believe that superstition about the house being cursed?"

"I really don't believe it."

"Either you do or you don't, Parris."

"I don't."

"Good." Martin pushed a button on his seat, lowering it to a reclining position once they were airborne. He crossed his arms over his chest and closed his eyes.

Some time later Parris did the same.

"Wake up! Parris, wake up!"

She came awake immediately, blinking in the darkness of the cabin. "What is it?"

"We…"

Whatever Martin was going to say was cut off as the jet dropped several hundred feet.

"We can't fly into New York," Martin managed to say before the aircraft dipped and rolled again. "There's a winter storm sweeping the coast from Georgia to Maine."

Parris looked around for Regina. The child was still asleep, oblivious to what was going on around her.

"Where are we? Do we have to turn back?" The questions tumbled from her lips.

Martin made his way across the aisle, his hand going to the ceiling of the plane to steady himself before he sat down next to Parris and secured his seat belt. His eyes appeared abnormally large and bright in the muted light coming in through the windows. He held both of her hands in one of his, not permitting her to pull away.

"We're going to put down in Florida."

"No!"

Martin registered Parris's scream of fear. He felt her shaking and tightened his hold on her hands.

"Don't fall apart on me, Parris."

Tears flowed unchecked from under her tightened eyelids. "Don't, Martin. Please."

"We have to, Parris." His voice was very gentle, almost coaxing. "It's going to be all right, baby. Everything's going to be all right. I'll protect you from Owen Lawson," he promised. "He'll never hurt you again."

Martin held Parris while she cried silently, and he never thought it was possible but he felt her pain. Her pain and her fear. He had promised to protect her; and he would even if it meant giving up his own life; he loved her just that much.

He had paid Joshua to find her, and now he would pay Joshua to protect her. Parris was never to know that she would have an invisible bodyguard.

There was no rain in Florida as the pilot prepared to land at the West Palm Beach airport but high winds made the landing rough and bumpy.

Regina, having slept through the turbulence, woke up and looked out of the window. "Where are we, Mommy?"

Parris, eyes closed and jaw clenched tightly, could not answer.

Martin moved over to his daughter, staring down at her questioning gaze. "We're in Florida."

Her smile was dazzling. "Are we going to Disney World?"

Martin laughed, releasing some of his own tension. "No, cupcake. We're going to visit my family."

Her forehead furrowed. "Who in your family?"

"My mother and father. Your grandparents. You'll also meet my two sisters, my brother and my sisters' children. My sisters are your aunts and my brother is your uncle."

"Like Uncle Josh?"

Martin stared at the expectant expression on his daughter's face. Tenderness softened his gaze. "Yes," he replied slowly. "He's like Uncle Josh. And you'll also get to meet your cousins. Some are near your age but most of them are older than you."

"How old?"

"Twelve and thirteen."

"How long are we staying in Florida, Daddy?"

Martin stared at Parris. Even though the aircraft had landed she still was seated, belt secured and her eyes closed. He had promised her that he would protect her but he knew she didn't believe him.

"I don't know, Regina.

"We can't stay too long," Regina stated. "I have to go back to New York and tell Scotty and my class that I learned to swim in the ocean."

Martin sat, staring at his parents, frowning. His fingers tightened on the arms of the delicate chair, his grip threatening to snap the fragile gilded wood.

"I thought we could discuss this like three somewhat intelligent adults, but apparently I was mistaken. I intend to marry Parris, and it will not matter whether you approve or not."

"How the hell do you expect me to react, Martin…"

"Sammy, please," Marguerite Josephine Diaz Cole interrupted softly.

Samuel Cole paced the floor of his sitting room, his eyes wide with anger. "Not this time, M.J. Don't expect me to act like a puffed up snob when he comes in here with that kind of news."

M.J. rose gracefully from the matching chair that Martin occupied. Within seconds she composed her aristocratic features. "Don't leave, Martin," she pleaded softly as he stood up. A slight smile touched her mouth when he stayed his departure. "Your father and I are not opposed to your marriage," she stated quietly. M.J. glanced over at her scowling husband. "It's just that we're somewhat surprised by your impulsiveness."

Martin couldn't help smiling as he turned to face his mother. "Ten years is hardly what I would call impulsive, Mother."

"Why can't you wait, Martin?" M.J. continued. "I can't believe Parris won't wait…"

"Don't start in on Parris, Mother," Martin said, cutting her off in an acid tone.

Samuel Cole glared down at his eldest son. Thick white eyebrows met in a frown. "Why do you want her after what happened, son? There are at least twenty other women I could think of who would make a better wife for you."

Martin inhaled sharply, reminding himself that these two people were his parents. They'd been responsible for him when he was a child. Now he was a man. Only he was responsible for running his own life.

"I suggest we drop this subject—right now," he warned. "And if she'll have me, I'm going to marry Parris and you *will* respect her as my wife whether you like her or not."

Rising to his feet, he turned on his heel and walked out of his parents' sitting room.

Parris stood in the middle of Martin's bedroom. She had to pinch herself to believe all that had happened since the jet touched down on a runway at the West Palm Beach airport under gale wind conditions.

Martin had not taken her and Regina to the house they had shared ten years before, but to his family's home. He'd calmly informed her that he'd sold the town house condominium after she left him.

The Cole family home was as beautifully decorated as it had been ten years ago. M.J. had selected each furnishing with the precision of a professional decorator. Silk wall coverings, Aubusson rugs and a plethora of French antique pieces filled the twenty-four room mansion.

She remembered the first time she had come to the Cole estate, surprising Samuel and Marguerite Cole when Martin revealed he and Parris had been living together. The elder Coles exchanged knowing glances, realizing she had enamored their oldest son the way no other woman had done before.

Regina let out a soft sigh on the large bed, and fell into a deep sleep.

"You're back."

Parris recognized the voice immediately. Turning, she saw Marguerite Cole who was as strikingly beautiful at sixty-one as she had been at twenty when she married Samuel Claridge Cole. The once raven hair was now silver and stylishly cut, complementing a smooth, unlined tanned face.

As the daughter of a wealthy cigar manufacturer, M.J.'s classical features and dimpled smile was renown during pre-revolutionary Cuban society.

"Yes, I'm back, M.J." Parris confirmed, smiling confidently.

M.J. arched a curving eyebrow, stepping into the bedroom. "For how long, Parris? Have you come back to make my son's life a living hell again before you disappear for another ten years? I heard about how you married that wonderful police officer but left him after a month. Then you latched on to my son and left him. What kind of a woman are you anyway?"

Parris felt M.J.'s equal for the first time. "I'm a woman who happens to love Martin," she confessed to M.J.

"Mom—my."

M.J.'s gaze went to the bed for the first time and she recoiled as if she'd been slapped as Regina sat up, rubbing her eyes. Parris almost felt sorry for the woman.

Parris sat on the bed, pulling Regina to her side. "I suppose it's as good a time as any for you to meet your granddaughter. This is Regina." She had no way of knowing that Martin had not told his parents about Regina. The natural color drained from M.J.'s face as she moved slowly toward the bed, staring mutely.

"Madre de Dios," M.J. whispered, reverting to her native tongue. She placed a trembling hand over her mouth. "I didn't know. I didn't know," she mumbled over and over, staring at the child who had gone back to sleep.

Parris left the bed, moving quickly and holding the older woman as M.J. groped for a nearby chair. "M.J., are you all right?"

M.J. nodded, tears streaking her face. "Yes-s."

She stepped back when M.J. blotted her cheeks with a delicate linen handkerchief. Her display of concern was the closest Parris had ever come to sharing any emotion with Martin's mother.

"I'm sorry I fell apart." A squaring of the shoulders indicated M.J. was back in control. She stole a quick glance at Regina. "Seeing the child came as somewhat of a shock. She's so much like Martin."

"That she is, Mother." Martin walked into the bedroom, flashing a dimpled smile. His right arm curved around Parris's waist.

M.J. raised her chin. "Why didn't you tell us about the child?"

Martin released Parris. His gaze met hers as she gave him a questioning look. "You and Dad were too busy badmouthing Parris, and telling me why I shouldn't marry her." M.J. flushed and stared down at the toe of her expensive shoe before she rose to her feet.

She walked toward Martin who took her arm gently. They stepped outside of the bedroom. "I'm going to say this only once, Mother," he began softly. "Parris is to be treated with respect for as long as she resides under this roof. I will not tolerate anything less from you or from the people you employ. Do I have your word on this?"

M.J. looked every inch a queen as she responded, "You have my word." Smoothing down the slim black silk dress over her flat middle, she arched a curving eyebrow. "Dinner will be served promptly at eight."

Parris waited until Martin returned to the bedroom, saying, "You can't intimidate her into respecting me." She had over-heard their conversation.

"I'm not asking her to love you or even to like you, Parris," he countered, his voice laced with annoyance. "I simply will not tolerate the hostility I know she's capable of exhibiting toward you. And she has to get used to you because you and Regina are a part of my life, and I don't want to let either of you go."

She turned her back, her gaze fixed on Regina. The child was curled in a fetal position, snoring lightly. Could she take the chance? Could she trust Martin? Trust him enough to protect her from Owen?

"If I come back to you, Martin, would you be able to protect me from whatever is out there that frightens me? Do you possess the power to make me feel safe?"

Martin moved behind her, his arms going around her waist and holding her protectively. "I would give up my life for you," he whispered fervently in her ear.

And I've given up ten years of my life for you, Parris told herself.

She loved Martin but she couldn't tell him she loved him. Not yet.

Chapter 21

Divine intervention had forced her back to Florida. The winter storm sweeping the Atlantic coastline pushed winds to hurricane proportions and all airports from Georgia and northward to Maine were closed because of highs winds or snow drifts.

She hadn't had time to ponder her fate once the small jet touched down at the West Palm Beach airport. A driver waited for their arrival and within half an hour they arrived at the Cole residence.

She had swallowed back her fear because of Regina. Parris knew she could not project her fear on to the child. When, she thought, would she ever stop being the sacrificial lamb for those she loved?

Martin held Parris, his arms offering protection and comfort. It had happened so easily. She had come to him without his coaxing or seduction. A power beyond his control, beyond the control of any mortal—the weather—had forced Parris back to Florida and back into his life.

"You're going to have to wake Regina up within the hour to get her ready for dinner," he informed Parris. "Christmas Eve dinner is usually a festive affair when everyone comes together to eat and exchange gifts."

Closing her eyes, Parris nodded. "We'll be ready," she replied, shivering slightly as Martin pressed his lips to the back of her neck.

"I'll have someone unpack for you and iron whatever it is you want to wear for dinner."

"Thank you, Martin." Her voice was low, her tone resigned. It was as if her destiny had been determined for her. She was back in Florida and a part of Martin's life whether she wanted it or not. She was scheduled to share her first Christmas Eve dinner with the Coles while introducing her daughter to the family Regina never knew she had.

She had extracted Martin's promise of protection, and a sense of strength came to her as her fear lessened. She loved, Martin and had always trusted him, hoping that would be enough, enough to allay her fears so that she could remain in Florida.

Parris stepped into the drawing room on Martin's arm, her gaze sweeping around the lavish space filled with a pair of exquisite Louis XV fauteuil chairs, upholstered with a pale blue, cream and peach tapestry. The chairs framed an eighteenth-century French bouillotte table. The tapestry pattern was repeated on a luxurious sofa and love seat filled with dark-haired Coles whose ages ranged from toddlers to middle-age adults. The bouillotte table cradled several family photographs in leaded crystal frames and a priceless collection of Russian icons.

The soft murmur of voices stopped the moment gazes were directed at Parris. The tight smile on her lips relaxed when David Cole, Martin's younger brother, crossed the room, arms outstretched. She offered her cheek for a kiss as he gathered her tightly to his chest.

"Welcome back, Parris."

She smiled up into a pair of jet-black eyes in the devilishly handsome face of David Cole. "Thank you, David."

David released her, reaching for Regina. "Is this the beautiful princess my brother has been bragging about?" He ignored Regina's frown, picking her up. His lopsided dimpled grin revealed large white teeth as he pulled at the profusion of a long curling ponytail flowing from a dark green satin ribbon. "In ten years you're going to be a real heartbreaker, Regina."

Regina held herself stiffly in her uncle's embrace, her dark eyes examining his long waving hair secured with an elastic band at the nape of his neck and the twinkling diamond stud in his left earlobe.

Of all the Coles, David had been the only one to befriend Parris. At seventeen he had been too enamored with the opposite sex to view her as an enemy. Parris noticed that the ten years had added fifteen pounds to his lanky frame. David Cole had become a devastatingly attractive man.

"Which one of these dark-haired beauties belong to you?" she asked David.

David shook his head, his black eyes sweeping over his many nieces and nephews. "Not a one. I'm not married, and I have no desire to get married and have children at this time in my life."

"Uncle David, you didn't tell me whether you'll be my show and tell when I go back to school," whined a young girl with a distressed expression marring her lovely face. She stood at his side, glaring up at Regina. David lowered Regina to the floor and the two girls stared at each other.

"I can't be your show and tell, Evelyn, because I'm not a rock star," he said gently. "There's a big difference between being a rocker and a jazz musician."

"But you play music, Uncle David," the girl insisted.

David hunkered down to her level and held her hand. "I play jazz, honey, not grunge or anything that resembles the heavy, driving guitar-playing rhythms you're talking about."

"Can you play that?" Evelyn questioned.

"I suppose I could if had the music."

"Then you can be my show and tell," Evelyn stated smugly, kissing her uncle's cheek.

David groaned under his breath, rising to his feet. "I've been had," he murmured softly to Parris. She smiled at him and he returned her smile.

Her smile faded as she stared at Martin's two sisters, Juliana and Nancy, making no attempt to approach them. The two women had always been fiercely protective of Martin, expressing openly that they had never met a woman whom they felt was worthy of their brother.

"Hello, Parris," Juliana forced a smile, her facial expression and body language an exact replica of M.J.'s.

"Juliana," Parris returned, with a slight nod of her head.

Nancy held back, staring coldly at Parris and Regina.

"Let Regina meet her cousins, David," Juliana urged. She held her arms out to Regina and she went into her aunt's embrace. Soon Regina was surrounded by her aunts and her many cousins.

Parris hung back as Martin urged her forward. They had not accepted her, and would never accept her. Regina was a Cole because she was Martin's child, and with the Coles blood ties were viewed almost fanatically.

She noted the children who had been preschoolers were now young teens, and were quick to chastise younger siblings and cousins. Juliana and Nancy had given their parents nine grandchildren between them. Regina had become the tenth grandchild.

Martin and Parris approached Samuel and M.J. at the same time a uniformed household employee walked into the room and nodded to M.J.

"Dinner is ready," M.J. announced softly. Samuel put down his drink, taking his wife's arm. He escorted her to the dining room, everyone following their lead.

"Loosen up, love," Martin whispered over Parris's head, seating her.

Her eyes flashed him a look which he interpreted immediately. *Not until I'm out of this house.*

"What the hell do you think you're doing, David?" Samuel bellowed across the room.

"Sammy, please," M.J. admonished. "Not only do your children swear like riffraff, but the grandchildren are beginning to use your foul language."

Samuel Cole refused to let his wife's admonition ruin his enthusiasm. "Not another word, M.J., or I'll really let loose." He motioned to Regina. "You sit here." He patted an empty chair to his left where he sat at the head of the table. "Next to your grandfather."

Regina looked at David who winked and nodded his approval. She gave him a smile and circled the long table to sit beside her grandfather.

Samuel's booming voice matched his large body. Even his approach to life was pompous. If Samuel Cole couldn't do it big he didn't attempt it; his showy style had turned the money his father gave him into a figure many hundred times that amount; and the wealth M.J. brought to her marriage ballooned his worth to enormous proportions.

Martin had inherited his father's expertise for making money, but by more unobtrusive means. Whereas Samuel Cole had been the plodding elephant Martin was the sleek, cunning panther. Business rivals became unsuspecting prey until Martin dealt the last card.

Parris glanced down the table at David. His long hair and pierced ear solidified his image as a popular jazz musician. His obsession with music had earned him a degree in music instead of the business and finance his father had insisted upon. As the youngest of the Coles, David had always been fiercely independent and followed the beat of a different drummer.

She remembered Martin encouraging his younger brother to control his own destiny and would occasionally fill in for a missing member of his brother's fledgling group whenever they needed a keyboard player. Samuel would explode with a stream of colorful expletives when he reminded M.J. of her insistence to expose her children to music. Neither had expected the works of Mozart or Brahms to lead to all-night jazz sessions.

Parris silently admired the formal dining room as she barely tasted the fragrant white wine in a fragile glass. Twenty Regency-style chairs, upholstered in silk, surrounded a Louis XV Bodart pearwood dining table set with what she recognized as Bloor Period, Royal Crown Derby plates and doré candlesticks festooned with red tapers.

The aroma of fresh pine cones and tree boughs on a side table wafted above a roast turkey stuffed with cornbread dressing, candied sweet potatoes, a glazed Smithfield ham, mixed greens, okra succotash, sweet pickles and fluffy parkerhouse rolls. Pecan pies, spiced peaches in brandy and praline awaited those who saved room for dessert.

Everyone was casually dressed, the men foregoing jackets and ties and the women choosing tailored blouses with their slacks or skirts. Parris wore a white silk blouse with a pair of gabardine slacks in a rich burgundy red with a pair of matching burgundy patent leather low-heel shoes. She had washed, blown-out her hair and pinned it into an elaborate chignon on the nape of her neck.

She listened to the sounds of the soft drawling Southern speech patterns as she filled her plate with turkey, okra succo-tash and candied sweet potatoes. She had missed so much: the tradition of eating fried fish and grits on Sunday morning, the few friends she had made, her position with Chadwick, Ferguson and Solis, and the mild winters and sultry summers. She had missed her home.

Smiling at Martin when he covered her hand with his, Parris willed her mind to relax, admiring Sammy's and M.J.'s tolerance of the younger children spilling gravies and sauces on the heirloom lace tablecloth while waving forkfuls of food in the air. Regina, caught up in the festive atmosphere joined her cousins in their childish antics, exhibiting the outgoing charm Parris observed in Martin.

She felt a measure of pride as she witnessed her daughter's interaction with the Coles, laughing and talking easily. No, Parris thought. I cannot take her away from this. She may have been Regina's mother but the Coles were her family.

It was after midnight by the time the entire household settled down to sleep, and Parris was exhausted by all that had happened that day.

She sat in the middle of the king-size bed in Martin's bedroom, staring down at his Christmas gift to her. A small white velvet box contained a pair of earrings with round emeralds sur-rounded by three rows of brilliant diamonds.

"They're beautiful, Martin."

Her low breathless voice swept over Martin and he smiled. "I've been waiting a long time to give you those," he admitted.

Her head came up and her gaze met his. "What are you talking about?"

"I bought those earrings ten years ago, Parris. They were to be your gift for our first Christmas together. I sold or gave away everything I owned after you left me except for the earrings, the tapestry we bought at that auction, the Saarinen table you selected and the Steinway."

She was unable to respond. Martin had hung onto her. Even though she had disappeared without a trace, he continued to hang on to her memory.

"And I'd like to thank you for your gift, Parris. It's the most appropriate gift I've ever received."

She smiled at him. "You're welcome." She had purchased an elegant black Montblanc Meisterstuck fountain pen and inkwell at a boutique in Montego Bay. She had had both the pen and inkwell engraved with Martin's full name. The accompanying gift card read, 'For Your *Signature.*'

Martin knew the *signature* to be his influence on any business transaction, not his handwriting.

He rose from a plush pale gray chair and walked over to the bed. Staring down at Parris, he said, "We're going to have to sleep together tonight." Her head snapped up. "Every room and every bed has someone in it," he explained. "I'll be back in half an hour." Turning on his heel, he walked out of the bedroom, closing the door.

Three minutes later, Parris still saw his collarless white silk shirt and black slacks when she finally propelled her body off the bed. The day had begun with her preparing to leave Jamaica to return to New York, and would end with her back in Florida, at the Cole residence, in Martin's bedroom and in Martin's bed.

She brushed her teeth, showered and covered her body with the most modest nightgown she could find. It was sleeveless, reaching her ankles, the bodice made entirely of lace and embroidered with tiny pink French knots. Staring at her reflection in the mirrored wall in the bedroom's adjoining bath, she concluded the white cotton garment was not conducive to seduction. Unpinning her hair and braiding it in a single braid, she returned to the bedroom and slipped under the crisp sheet. Minutes later, she fell asleep.

Martin returned to his bedroom and saw the outline of Parris's body on the bed in the soft glow of a table lamp. His attempt to share a bed with her on Jamaica had been thwarted. Having her that close and not being able to touch her had been torture. He had kissed her once, the first day on the beach, and any opportunity he may have had after that vanished when they were forced to remain in the house because of the torrential rains sweeping the island.

Let everything unfold naturally, a little voice taunted him. All he had to be was patient. He headed to the bathroom and prepared to go to bed.

Chapter 22

Parris moved toward the source of heat and fell into a deeper sleep. There were no dreams of gaping mouths cursing her or the pressure of cold steel against her body. She felt the comforting embrace of strong arms around her and a soft sigh escaped her parted lips. Something feathered across her nose and lips but she did not wake up.

When she did wake up she found herself sprawled over Martin's chest, one leg cradled intimately between his. Her head came up slowly and she realized what had been tickling her nose. Her face had been pressed to the solid surface of Martin's hairy chest.

His large eyes were open, staring down at her. "Merry Christmas."

"Merry Christmas back to you," she mumbled, as heat burned her face. She tried easing off his body. He tightened his hold. "Let me go, Martin," she pleaded softly.

"Why should I, Parris? You crawled on me last night, and I managed to get exactly two minutes of sound sleep. Now that you're rested you want to leave? I'll let you go when I feel like letting you go," he taunted.

She stared up at him. The dark smudges under his eyes verified his admission that he hadn't slept. The shadows under his dramatic dark eyes and the faint shadowing of a beard on his unshaven cheeks made her breath catch in her throat.

This dark naked man whom she was sharing a bed with still had the power to touch her the way no other man had been able to do. A look, and only a look, was enough to make her tremble with desire.

He shifted slightly until she lay by his side. Both of them exhaled audibly. Martin grasped her hand, threading his fingers through hers. The gesture was a familiar one. Years before they'd laid in bed, fingers joined, talking.

"If I stay with you, Martin," Parris began quietly, "I'm going to lose everything I've worked for over the past ten years."

"What will you lose?" he asked, hoping he didn't sound selfish.

"My home, my job."

"You can always buy another home and secure another position with any design firm you want. You're an expert in your field, Parris. If you wanted to you could go into business for yourself."

"What about Regina? She'll be uprooted from everything that has been familiar to her."

"She'll be leaving *friends,* Parris. You cannot measure her loss of friends to her finding her family." He lowered his head and kissed her hair. "I'll buy you a house, darling," he crooned. "Anywhere you want. You can pick it out and decorate every inch of it. If you want to work I'll hire you to work for ColeDiz. You can decorate the villas and bungalows we plan to build in Belize. Regina could attend the same school as her cousins so she won't feel so alienated when she changes schools."

Martin had all of the answers. He had planned his statement the same way he prepared for a business meeting.

"I don't know, Martin. I've spent ten years building a life that is exactly the way I want it."

"I, Parris. You speak of I but what about Regina? Isn't she entitled to have her father in her life? You grew up without your father because he couldn't be there for you. You don't even remember him. Do you want the same for our child?"

Closing her eyes, Parris turned toward Martin and pressed her face to his muscled shoulder. "You know I don't."

Releasing her fingers, he cradled her to his chest, inhaling the perfume on her warm flesh. "I'll take care of everything, darling. The sale of your home and car. I'll arrange for storage of anything you want to keep. I'll…"

Parris placed her fingertips over his mouth. "You have it all planned out, don't you?

"Because I'm methodical and practical, Parris. I have to think of Regina's future. Every child a Cole brings forth into this world is provided for, and a plan is put into place for them the moment the infant draws their first breath. It's always been and always will be that way."

Parris lay motionless, reflecting that if she married Martin it would make her a Cole and afford her all of the privileges which would give her the protection she needed for herself and Regina.

"Okay," she whispered. "I'll stay with you."

Martin felt lightheaded with relief. "Does that mean you will marry me?" he asked slowly.

She nodded, biting down on her lower lip. There was a moment of strained silence before she said, "Yes."

Martin moved over her body, supporting his weight on his elbows as he cradled her face between his hands. His gaze made a slow journey over every inch of her face.

"When?" he asked.

Parris stared back at him, registering the leashed tension in his body and the apprehension in his gaze. "Soon."

He flashed his dimpled smile as tiny lines fanned out around his eyes. "How about New Year's Eve?"

She shrugged a delicate shoulder. "It sounds good to me."

She savored the pressure of Martin's body as he pressed her down to the mattress, his mouth busily exploring her neck and shoulders.

"Everything will be different this time," he murmured.

"I don't want it to be different, Martin," Parris gasped as the heat from his mouth seared her breast. "I want it to be better than before."

He heard the sound before she did and he sprang from her body, sliding down on his pillow and pulling the sheet up over his chest. Regina stood in the doorway, staring at her parents.

"I knocked," Regina said quickly, staring at the two pairs of eyes watching her.

Parris recovered quickly, gesturing. "Come here, angel." She patted the space between her and Martin.

Regina raced across the bedroom and crawled onto the bed. She lay atop the sheet between her parents.

Martin pulled her unbound ponytail and kissed her forehead. "Merry Christmas, cupcake."

Regina kissed his stubbled cheek. "Merry Christmas, Daddy." Turning to Parris, she kissed her cheek. "Merry Christmas, Mommy." She held up her left arm and peered at the watch on her wrist.

"Daddy, did you know that as of today December twenty-fifth that Mars is in conjunction with the sun, over 225 million miles away from the earth?"

Martin shifted his sweeping eyebrows. "Does your watch tell you that?"

Regina compressed her lips in a gesture of annoyance. "Don't be silly, Daddy. The watch can't tell me that. I just know that," she said smugly.

Martin looked embarrassed. "What does the watch tell you?"

Regina stared at her mother's Christmas gift to her. "It can tell you all of the phases of the moon at any time of the month. It can also tell you what time it is in any part of the world at any time. My watch tells me the day, date and of course the time."

He was impressed. "Tell me more about the planets."

"Mercury will begin the new year at the edge of the morning twilight, and dives deeper toward the sun as the month passes. Near the end of January it will be an evening star. Venus starts the new year as a brilliant evening star."

Martin stared at his daughter, his mouth gaping slightly. "Good gravy, where did you learn all of this stuff about the stars and planets?"

"Mommy took me to the planetarium in New York City. She bought me some books and I did a lot of reading."

"You like astronomy?"

Regina rested her head on his pillow. "I like science. I'm not sure what I want to be when I grow up."

"You can be whatever you want to be," Martin reassured her.

"It's been a good Christmas," Regina said, smiling.

"It's going to be a better new year because we're all going to be together," Martin stated, smiling at his daughter.

"Really?"

Parris pressed her head to Regina's and told her that she and Martin were getting married. Regina didn't seem as excited about her parents' upcoming nuptials as she was about living in Florida. It had taken less than twenty-four hours for her forget about returning to New York to inform her classmates that she had learned to swim in the ocean while vacationing in Jamaica.

"Who do you think you are coming here?"

"*I am* whomever the hell you want me to be, *old man.*"

Samuel felt an uncontrollable rage he could never explain whenever he encountered Joshua Kirkland. There was something about the younger man that reminded him too much of himself when he was Joshua's age. They were both so much alike it was frightening. However, it still could not explain his hatred for the arrogant human being who dared to defy him again and again.

The blood rushed to Samuel's face, as a tic tortured his left eye. He could barely tolerate Joshua's presence, but M.J. could not. Why of all days did he have to show up?

"You picked a bad time to come visiting. We're having a private family gathering, and you're not welcome."

Joshua's feral grin should've been a warning as his left hand moved with startling speed, applying deadly pressure to Samuel Cole's exposed throat, thumb and forefinger tightening against the vital area. He achieved his desired reaction as the large man slumped weakly against his body in pain.

"I've been invited to a wedding, Sammy," Joshua whispered savagely. He supported the older man's massive bulk. "Not you or anyone else will keep me from attending." He released Samuel's throat. "Stay the hell away from me or so help me I'll make M.J. a widow."

Samuel, gasping, tried filling his lungs with much needed oxygen while Joshua brushed past him to take the staircase leading to Martin's apartment. The maid who had answered the door stood watching in horror. When she had opened the door she silently admired the tall, slender, well-dressed man, never thinking he would try to murder her employer.

"What the hell are you looking at?" Samuel shouted at the startled woman. "Get out of here!"

M.J. walked into the entry just in time to hear her husband shouting. "What's going on, Sammy?"

Samuel shot his wife an angry glare. "Martin invited him."

"You're not making sense, Sammy."

M.J.'s soft voice grated on Samuel's taut nerve endings. "That Kirkland bastard."

Her thin nostrils flared in rage. "How could he, Sammy? It's not enough that Martin's marrying *that* woman, but he also has to have that…that…" M.J. was unable to come up with an appropriate description. Her slender manicured hands curled into fists, her dark eyes narrowing. "The sooner this is over, the better."

Her heels mirrored her anger as they clattered noisily on the marble flooring as she stalked away from her frowning husband.

The sun shone brightly for Martin and Parris's wedding, yet for Samuel and Marguerite Cole the day had become as gloomy as a dark, storm-swept sky.

It was her wedding day and Parris hadn't begun to change out of her jeans and blouse and into her dress. She heard footsteps and turned to find a pair of pale green eyes watching her. She took in the suntanned face, bleached hair and the lithe body in an expertly tailored dark suit.

"Hello, Joshua." She was surprised at her calm greeting when her heart was racing erratically. A week's absence had made him more attractive, and disturbing, than she'd remembered.

He inclined his blond head. "Parris."

She gestured to him. "Come in. Please sit down."

Joshua folded his lean body down onto a plush armchair, crossing one leg over the other. "How do you feel?"

Parris moved over and sat down on a matching chair. "Great." Her brown eyes sparkled. "Do you think I'll make a presentable bride?"

Joshua nodded. "Your tan looks terrific," he remarked. "How's Regina?"

Parris stared at the denim fabric covering her knees. "She's like Martin. Everyone loves her." Her head came up and she met Joshua's gaze. "I hardly get a chance to be with my own daughter. If she's not visiting with an aunt or uncle, it's her grandparents and cousins."

Joshua reached over, holding her hands gently within his. "Don't worry too much. Having a family is still new to her. You'll never lose her."

"Let's hope you're right." She smiled when his lips parted in a warm smile for the first time.

"I know I'm right." Leaning over, he kissed her cheek. "I'll let you get dressed for your big day."

Parris was shocked by his show of affection. He didn't appear as frightening as he had before.

"Martin's in the library," she called out when Joshua stood up to leave.

She left the chair and moved over to the bed, staring at her reflection in the mirrored doors of the wall-to-wall, floor-to-ceiling closets. Her hair and face had been done earlier that morning when M.J. offered the services of her personal stylist. She was going to refuse then thought better of it because her soon-to-be mother-in-law had been overly polite and respectful whenever they encountered each other over the past week. A frenzy of activities had kept the two women apart from each other except at times whenever they shared an occasional evening meal.

Regina had been equally entertained, spending several days at Juliana's and Nancy's homes. She attended a recording session with David at a Miami studio, bubbling effusively when Regina realized her uncle was a popular musician.

She and Martin had discussed Regina's education, deciding to enroll her in a private school in West Palm Beach until they moved to their permanent residence.

Parris favored Fort Lauderdale and Martin barely acknowledged her recommendation with a shrug of his broad shoulders. This attitude was evident whenever she asked for his opinion, and she stopped asking.

It was as if they'd reversed roles. Now he was the private person. She saw what she didn't see three weeks ago. The ten-year separation had changed Martin when she found herself waiting for bits and pieces of information to filter down to reveal his plan for their future. The open, spontaneous man was now cautious, even secretive.

She had agreed to leave New York, her home, her job and all that had been familiar for the past ten years for her daughter's emotional well-being. She had become the martyr while Martin had become a stranger.

Martin had become the nervous bridegroom while she'd managed to forestall the attack of jitters she experienced twelve years ago. She couldn't help but parallel this wedding day to the one when she married Owen. His moods had vacillated from depression to euphoria and she blamed it on nerves, for the both of them.

Tears filled her eyes, and she blinked them back before they stained her carefully made-up face. What no one knew was that her honeymoon never began because Owen had been unable to consummate his marriage. He tried day after day, then gave up all pretense, falling asleep beside her tense body.

She had accidentally stumbled upon the reason for Owen's impotency when she awakened late one night and saw him in the bathroom, bent over her dressing table, inhaling several lines of white powder on the formica top. Suddenly everything was clear to her. Her husband was addicted to cocaine. She now knew the cause of his mood swings, his lack of appetite and his impotency.

She confronted him and he stared at her with a silly smile on his face. He lied, saying it was his first time trying it and she wanted to scream at him for thinking she was that naive. She issued an ultimatum: go into treatment. She gave him exactly thirty days to sign himself into a drug abuse program or she was going to annul their marriage.

The lies and the excuses continued until she began packing. Then she issued her last ultimatum: give her a divorce or she was going to his superiors at the West Palm Beach Police Department. Her freedom for her silence. Owen finally agreed, her lips sealed with his secret.

But this day was different. She was marrying a man she loved. Joshua would be their witness and Regina her bridesmaid. Other than Brittany and Jon Grant, who'd relocated to the west coast, she had no other close friends or family members to invite.

Martin walked into the bedroom and Parris turned, smiling at him. "Tradition says it's bad luck to see the bride before the ceremony," she teased.

"Since when have we ever been traditional, darling? We've lived together, have a nine-year-old child and reside together under my parent's roof without the benefit of marriage. All that in the face of tradition." Extending his hand, he pulled her from the bed. He kissed the end of her nose. "If you ever get traditional on me, I'd go crazy with boredom."

Parris pressed closer to his chest, wrapping her arms around his waist. The smell of soap and after-shave clung to his smooth cheek. "I won't change on you, Martin."

Martin pulled back. He stared down into the clear brown eyes with just a hint of green in their depths. She wore his Christmas gift in her pierced ears. No jewel or amount of money could come close to the love he felt for her. His black eyes touched her glossy dark hair, curled, pinned up and festooned with delicate baby's breath. His heated gaze added color to the soft plum blush on her high cheekbones.

"I love you, Parris. I love you more than life itself," he admitted passionately. "Parris…" He hesitated. He couldn't begin their life together knowing he owed it to her to reveal his political aspirations. "I've got to talk to you," he continued.

She reached up, straightening the navy and silver striped tie under the collar of his stark-white shirt. "I have to get dressed. Everyone's waiting for us."

"They can't have a wedding without the bride and groom, can they?" he questioned.

Parris registered the sharp retort. Suddenly she felt his tension. "What is it, Martin?"

He pulled her down to the bed beside him, holding her hands tightly. "I'm leaving the family business."

Her eyes widened at this disclosure. "Why? Who's going to succeed you?"

This time Martin did not hesitate. "I've been grooming David to take over…"

"But he's a musician," Parris interrupted.

"He's a Cole, Parris. He's inherited Sammy's instinct for business whether he wants to admit it or exploit it. He's learned more in three months than I ever did in five years of college." There was a lethal calmness in the obsidian eyes. "I'm going into politics," he declared.

"Politics?" An icy chill shook Parris, and she wanted to wrap her arms around her body. "Is that what you meant when you said you needed a wife?"

"No, Parris," he started. "You don't understand."

"I don't understand, Martin." Her voice was low, filled with anger. "You don't really love me. All those years…"

Martin released her, rising to his feet and towering over her bowed head. "What I feel now was what I felt ten years ago. I *want* you because I love you. And my wanting or needing you has nothing to do with Regina or politics."

Parris stood up. "Well, Mr. Politician, it looks as if you've managed your first fait accompli. I don't like being treated as if my feelings or opinions don't matter. You completed this deal without letting your opponent know the terms that were to be negotiated."

"You're not my opponent, Parris."

"Of course not, Martin," she drawled. "I'm only the woman you *need* to marry. And because you need a wife, you're going to get one. Let's go and get his farce over with."

The moustache hid Martin's intense upper lip as it tightened. He didn't know what to expect, but it certainly hadn't been Parris's apathetic attitude to becoming his wife.

"You don't like it, so why the hell are you marrying me, Parris?"

"Because of Regina," she said coldly. "And because I'm a fool for loving you, Martin Cole."

She had declared her love for him but instinct told Martin that, just like Owen Lawson, his entrée into politics would serve as a wedge to keep them apart. He would have Parris the wife and not Parris the woman.

Chapter 23

Parris stood beside Martin, repeating her vows as the judge performed the private civil ceremony in the cooler, shaded magnificence of the loggia.

The setting was ethereal. Large baskets of white flowers in every variety crowded the travertine flooring and the bright orange rays of the setting sun reflecting off the lake threw a strange fiery glow on coral columns and exposed beams and any light-colored surface.

A dress of white organdy, with a large scalloped collar, exposed the smooth length of Parris's long neck, meeting at a deep V at the hollow of her breasts, flamed like gold. Full sleeves with three inch cuffs, a two-tiered scalloped full skirt and a wide white sash emphasized the narrowness of her waist and created an aura of innocence and unabashed sensual femininity.

The taste of brandy on Martin's lips was heady and pleasant when he gathered her to his chest, sealing their troth. Handing her bouquet of white roses and lilies to Regina, Parris leaned down to kiss her.

Regina stared up at her mother. "You look pretty, Mommy."

Regina's black hair was a curling mass falling down her back to her waist. Miniature white carnations on mother-of-pearl combs held the curls off her face.

Parris smiled. "Thank you. You look very beautiful too, angel."

"I'll see you later, Mommy." Regina's attention was diverted as she waved to a cousin who had called out to her. "Bye, Daddy."

Samuel touched Parris's arm. "Welcome to the family." He pulled her into an embrace, kissing her cheek. His body was still hard, solid for a man who had recently celebrated his sixty-fifth birthday.

"Thank you, Sammy."

Samuel's gaze swept quickly over her face. "My son has exceptional taste in women."

Parris's smile was soft and inviting. "Like father, like son?"

"No lie," Samuel gushed loudly.

M.J., stunning in a dress of black and gold silk, smiled. "Well, it looks as if I got the third daughter I always wanted."

Parris returned her smile, offering her cheek for M.J.'s kiss. "Thank you."

M.J. signaled the hired caterers, and the silent, efficient waiters began setting the twisted white rattan tables with food. Patterned coral and white cushions on the many chairs and love seats were quickly filled with Coles and close friends of the family.

Parris smiled graciously, accepting handshakes, kisses and the good wishes from the assembled. After a while she felt as if her face was going to crack from the continuous effort. She lost count of the names of well-wishers and felt strangely relieved when she, having lost Martin in the throng, found herself face-to-face with Joshua. She permitted him to lead her to a deserted area of the loggia. A large potted palm concealed them from the view of the noisy crowd.

She smiled up at him. "I feel like a wooden puppet with a hideous grin painted on my face."

Joshua nodded, his expression unreadable. His light green eyes caressed her face briefly before his lids shuttered them from her gaze. "Get used to it, Parris. As Martin's wife you'll smile when you least want to."

Martin's disclosure that he was going to enter the political arena chilled her with Joshua's statement. "Let's hope you're wrong," she whispered.

Joshua held her left hand, examining the circle of graduated marquise-shaped diamonds in a gold setting on her delicate finger. His left hand moved to her chin, raising her face to his. "You're a Cole now, Parris." His voice was soft, almost coaxing. "Surely you're aware of what's expected of you. You have it all: beauty, charm, money. Those are the prerequisites, and you've succeeded with Martin where so many other women have failed." He released her hand, but not her chin. "Martin's taste in jewelry is almost as exquisite as his choice of a wife." Leaning over, he kissed her cheek. Joshua released her and walked away.

Parris leaned against a column of coral marble staring at the space where Joshua had been. He had disappeared like an apparition. His words tumbled over themselves in her head. `Surely you're aware of what's expected of you.'

A tremor coursed through her body and she turned, meeting the dark accusing stare of her mother-in-law. Glancing away, Parris searched for Martin, finding his broad shoulders under the jacket of his gray suit as he stood with the judge and his father, talking.

She accepted a glass of champagne from a passing waiter and gulped it down. She returned the empty glass to the tray, reaching for another. The cool sparkling liquid numbed her quivering nerves. Looking around at all of the smiling, talking people she felt alone. Aside from Regina, Martin and Joshua, these people were strangers to her. She recognized names and faces, but she actually did not know them. All of them were Martin's family and friends and she felt like an outsider. Regina was a Cole by birthright, and she had become one only through her marriage. She wondered if she would ever feel close to this large, peculiar clan.

The celebrating continued, everyone eating, drinking, dancing and talking incessantly. Some of the younger children were escorted protestingly to bed, Regina among them, while the adults became more animated with the approach of the new year.

Parris felt light and carefree after her second glass of champagne. The oysters she had eaten did little to counterbalance the alcohol in her blood. She swayed to the beat of a popular love song. The hired band had a repertoire ranging from Big Band tunes to the latest club favorites.

Her body stiffened. She detected the familiar fragrance of a specially blended masculine cologne and the warmth of the large body pressing against her back. Fatigue and the champagne had lowered her resistance to where she couldn't move to escape him. Common sense dictated she not forgive him for his deceit, but all traces of prudent and sound judgment had vanished when she agreed to stay in Florida and marry Martin.

She'd blamed it on Regina, knowing the child wasn't solely the reason. Martin's memory had been strong enough for Parris to keep men at a distance, and his love for her strong enough to repress the fear of the blackmailer's threat until he mentioned politics. Campaigning would not permit her to maintain her privacy or an attempt to achieve a measure of anonymity.

"Promise me you'll protect me," she pleaded. The words slipped from her tongue against her will.

Martin's fingers tightened around her upper arms. "I told you I would, Parris."

She turned, staring up at his frowning expression. Her fingernails bit into the tender flesh on his wrists. "Promise me!"

Martin felt the fine hairs rise on the back of his neck. He hadn't noticed any hostility between her and his parents, and could only think of one person who could generate that much panic in her voice. Owen Lawson.

His hands went to her shoulders. "It's Lawson, isn't it?" His eyes flashed danger like a cornered animal. "You've seen him. He's bothering you."

Parris's hands slipped down to his chest and she tried leaning against Martin, but he held her fast. He was asking her questions she couldn't answer. Who was it? Owen? Her abductor? Her blackmailer?

"It's not Owen."

"Then, who is it?" He shook her gently.

Her fingers curled into tight fists. She was not successful in concealing their trembling when Martin saw them shake. "I don't know who it is. Promise me, Martin," she insisted. "Just promise me."

"Damn it, Parris!"

"Say it!"

"I promise," he said, his voice thick and unsteady with tension. He released her and Parris rose on tiptoe, capturing his mouth and seeking and drawing what she needed from him. His gasp of surprise was momentary as he crushed her body to his, desire straining to break loose at any second. She was controlling him and he didn't care. As long as she loved him he would attempt to walk on water for her. He could not deny Parris anything.

His mouth devoured her luscious full lips, and like a starving man he wanted more; he wanted all of her. "Let's get out of here," he panted as he pulled his mouth away from hers.

"We haven't cut the cake," Parris sighed, her body throbbing with passion.

Martin ran a forefinger over her swollen lips. "You're being traditional, darling."

The corners of her mouth curved in a seductive smile. "You're right." She was still smiling as she followed him through the garden to the garage where he had parked his car.

Parris felt like a virginal bride as she reentered the bedroom. Martin stood with his back to the sliding glass doors, waiting for her. He'd surprised her when he drove down the coast to the little beach front cottage where they would spend their honeymoon. They had not talked about a honeymoon, and she simply had put the idea out of her head. The one-bedroom guest house had been stocked with food, and somehow Martin had gotten her dress size and purchased an elaborate trousseau without her knowledge.

He drew one hand out of the pocket of his robe. "Come here." His soft command sent tremors along her spine. She walked toward him, trancelike. Black eyes, like polished jet, noted everything: her damp hair curling around her neck, the untanned swell of golden-brown breasts rising above the lace of the satin floor-length nightgown, and the undisguised look of love in her eyes.

The soft chiming of a clock on the bedside table penetrated the thick layer of desire gripping Martin. He continued to stare at the woman he had married, listening for the final chime signaling the beginning of a new year.

It was the beginning of many things: being a father; a husband; severing his professional association with his family's business enterprises, and challenging an incumbent who held the political reins of the state tightly within his grasp.

Martin smiled. He would succeed; only because of the woman standing inches from him.

He watched the play of emotions cross her lovely face. This woman, above all women, made him aware of himself as a man as no one ever had before or since. It was as if Parris had the power to make him physically cognizant of his compelling need to surrender all he had to her.

She, alone, possessed the key to unlock his heart, baring his soul until all of him lay open, raw and penetrable. He was powerless to resist her, and he had not stopped to ponder whether it was physical. If it was it would not have mattered.

The tension in the room was hot and volatile. Their unspoken passions increased and shimmered like waves of heat. Parris ached for Martin: his nearness, his protection, his possession and his love. With Martin she was never rational. Her reaction to his lovemaking from the very first time had always been strong and uncontrollable.

Reaching out, her fingers slipped to the opening in his robe, untying the belt at his waist. The white silk robe parted silently, and her hand moved over his flat belly with agonizing slowness, her fingers brushing over the tight thatch of black hair to encircle the rigid tumescence jutting majestically from between his muscled thighs. Martin was ready for her; he was fully aroused.

She continued caressing the thick velvet softness, smiling as it jerked and pulsed strongly against her palm. Martin closed his eyes, gritting his teeth against the exquisite torture.

His hands moved up to her shoulders, increasing the pressure on her delicate bones as his chest rose and fell in shuddering gasps.

She changed the rhythm and his grip on her shoulders lessened as his fingers swept down to remove the thin straps holding up her gown. One delicate strap ripped when her hand inched lower, fondling and cradling the taut sac filled with his seed.

Parris stared up at the blatant carnality gripping his handsome features. She never knew when the fabric sheathing her body floated to the floor in a whispering shimmering shower of creamy satin.

His fingers began their own exploration as they grazed her breasts, thumb and forefinger tightening on her full, bursting nipples.

"Love me, Martin. Love me the way I love to be loved." Her litany filled the room.

They had shared a bed Christmas Eve but not since then. He had waited ten years for her. He would wait a little longer.

"No, Parris. Not yet." His ragged breathing indicated Martin's control was slipping away as quickly as hers.

Picking her up in one smooth motion, he placed her on the middle of the bed. His body followed quickly, his mouth fixed on hers, demanding and savoring all she had to give him. His fingers slid down her belly and thighs, parting the moist folds concealing her womanhood.

Parris moaned aloud. Shivers of pure pleasure shook her entire body as his fingers plunged deeper.

"Tell me what you want, baby." Her eyes opened, the tear-filled, green-flecked brown orbs, imploring him to take her. "Tell me what you want," he crooned near her ear.

"No…no," Parris cried out when he removed his finger. He smiled. He had no intention of stopping. His finger found her again and again, and her body arched again and again against his hand and questing fingers. The waves of desire crashed down, drowning her with their rushing, heated force.

Martin waited for Parris, cradling her to his chest. She felt the strong pounding of his heart under her breasts as her tongue tasted the salty wetness of his throat, then explored his body as it made circular motions over his hair-matted chest and flat belly.

Every muscle in his body tensed and screamed when her

mouth closed on him with a claim that made Martin faint in burning surrender. He smothered a savage growl, throwing his forearm over his face. She was driving him crazy. Her mouth sent violent jolts through his system, and he sat up suddenly.

"Don't! Not yet! Please!"

Parris glanced up at Martin, recognizing the desperation in his command and the naked fear of loss of control. She slid up the length of his damp body, rubbing her breasts against his, while kissing him fully on the mouth. His hands traced the length of her spine, and he shifted until she straddled him. He cupped her buttocks whenever he rose to meet her, establishing a fierce driving rhythm.

"Yes, Martin. Oh yes. Yes-s-s." The sound of her husky approval gripped him and his ardor spiraled out of control.

His world tilted, careened, and he gave into the hot tides of love and passion sweeping him out to a sea of bright lights and weightlessness. He was afraid to open his eyes to look up at Parris; stunned by the raw sensuousness she had offered him and afraid of the power she wielded and what she would do if she ever realized it. He never thought he would fear a woman—especially if that woman was his wife.

Chapter 24

Parris had been married a month when she sat at her husband's desk in the offices of ColeDiz signing a stack of papers.

Signing the documents signaled a change. It was the last day in the first month of the new year; it was Martin's fortieth birthday; warm winter temperatures had vanished, leaving the early mornings and late nights cool and crisp, and all traces of the Christmas holidays had vanished, the decorations and the parties.

Her neat signature and the date glided across the last document: Parris S. Cole, January thirty-first. "That should do it."

The pale, wiry attorney pushed the documents into a leather portfolio. "Thank you, Mrs. Cole. I believe everything's in order. I'll file the necessary papers to change your daughter's name in the morning, and I'll call the real estate agent in New York for a date to finalize the sale of your property."

Martin fingered a sterling silver letter opener. "Thanks, Phil." He smiled at the man who headed the corporate legal department. Normally one of the associate attorneys would have done the legwork, but this was too personal to entrust to someone other than Philip Trent. "After you return from New York, why don't you take a few weeks off. I heard you had a good time in Costa Rica."

Philip Trent blushed, then blanched. He ran a hand over his neatly brushed light brown hair. He offered Martin a weak smile.

"No thanks, Martin. It was too hot…" He glanced over at Parris, unable to complete his statement.

Martin steepled his fingers to his mouth, hiding a grin. "Was it the heat or the women, Phil?" The middle-aged bachelor's golden-brown eyes were downcast as he rushed out of the office, Martin's laughter following his stiff back.

"Martin!" Parris couldn't believe his teasing the obviously embarrassed attorney.

Martin stood up. "Let's go, honey. I don't want to be late for my birthday celebration."

"Do I have time to change?" she asked, watching him slip on his suit jacket.

Martin examined the lightweight navy blue wool suit she had paired with a gold silk blouse. "You look beautiful," he murmured, his arms curving around her waist.

"If I wore nothing you'd say the same thing."

"Wrong, Mrs. Cole. I wouldn't say anything, but I sure would *do* something."

Picking up her handbag, Parris walked out of Martin's office, smiling at his secretary. Joan Shaw returned her smile.

Things were progressing quickly. Regina's name would be changed from Simmons to Cole, her apartment had a buyer and Martin was to officially announce his candidacy for the gubernatorial race that evening. All that remained was finding a house she wanted to live in. She'd refused to think as far as the next January when they could possibly live in Tallahassee instead of Fort Lauderdale.

The number of cars crowding the garages and driveway indicated many of the guests had already arrived at the Cole residence by the time Parris and Martin returned to the house. Aside from family members, selected members of the press had been invited.

"Give me fifteen minutes, and I'll be down," Parris flung over her shoulder at Martin as she raced up the stairs to their suite.

It took only ten minutes for her to apply a fresh coat of lipstick, buff the shine off her nose and change into a pale peach wool sheath with a squared neckline. She hadn't bothered to change the navy blue lizard pumps.

Reporters and photographers mingled with family members as they huddled together in small groups, talking quietly. The light of twin chandeliers in the large living room gleamed like jewels as serving carts were rolled in, filled with crudités and beverages.

Martin's candidacy had been a well-kept secret. Only a few were privy to his plans, and Parris suspected the press was in for quite a shock.

Martin had joined his father's company at twenty-five, taken over as president at thirty, and now at forty was ready to enter politics. What would he, she thought, want at fifty? Sixty? When was too much ambition dangerous?

"He's going to be a tough act to follow," David remarked near Parris's ear. He leaned over, kissing her cheek.

"Don't try to be Martin," she suggested. "Just be David Cole."

"A major in music and a minor in business doesn't quite prepare me to assume control of ColeDiz International," he admitted, smiling his lopsided grin.

Parris stared at David's wavy hair laying heavily on his wide shoulders covered in black silk. The long hair and black attire would soon become a part of his past when Martin officially resigned. Being lead singer and drummer for Night Mood would soon become a sparkling memory for David. Memories he would one day relate to his children.

David ran his fingers through his hair, pushing it back off his forehead. "Dad doesn't like this, but there's little he could do once Martin decided to go ahead with his plan. He hates politicians. He says he doesn't trust them."

"He'll change his mind once Martin's elected."

"Let's hope you're right…" David broke off as he caught the eye of an attractive photographer who stared openly at him from across the room. "Excuse me, Parris. I think I see someone I know."

All conversation ceased, and Parris turned to find Joshua Kirkland leaning against the arched entrance. A myriad of expressions crossed the faces of the Coles.

Parris was stunned by their reaction. Why were they treating Martin's friend like a leper? She broke the spell, walking across the room and holding out her hands to him. The uncomfortable silence ended once the low babble of voices started up again.

"Hello again, Joshua."

He took her hands. His smile was cold, not reaching his eyes. "Nice to see you, too, Parris."

Martin came over to join them. He grasped Joshua's hand firmly. "Now that you're here, we can begin."

Samuel Cole waited until there was complete silence. His snow-white hair and eyebrows were an attractive contrast to his rich sienna-brown coloring. Brilliant dark eyes flashed like burning coals in his lean, sculpted face. "I'd like to offer a toast to my son." He extended a glass filled with an amber-colored liquid. "May the next forty years bring you everything you could ever wish for in your life on this earth. It is not often a man can achieve perfection in his lifetime." Pride flowed from the dark eyes under thick bushy white eyebrows. "I'm proud to say that I've come close to it. You, Martin, have helped me to gain that measure of perfection."

Martin acknowledged his father's praise with a nod. His right arm curved around Parris's waist and she could feel his excitement. He nodded at his mother, giving her a warm smile.

M.J. returned a matching dimpled smile. It was her turn to speak. Her voice was soft and very controlled. There was just a hint of a lingering accent. "Martin is very special to me. Not only because he is my first born, but because he taught me how special motherhood can be. So special I repeated it another three times," she added, a touch of color staining her cheeks.

Parris laughed with the others present. Juliana and Nancy offered their toasts to their older brother, unable to conceal their love and admiration.

Appearing before an audience was nothing new for David, and he waited until he felt the pull of everyone's attention. "To my older and slightly used brother. Now that you're no longer available for the single women, may I please have your black book?"

All laughed at his sorrowful expression and plea. David Cole had amassed groupies everywhere he traveled.

Martin winked at David. "Sorry to disappoint you, kid. I never had a black book. If she was worth seeing again I always memorized her number."

Then Parris felt the attention directed at her. She knew it was time for her to offer a toast to her husband. Her gaze was fixed on his face, mentally telegraphing her deep feelings. His midnight eyes seemed to draw her into him, and she felt as if he'd devoured her soul. Hypnotically, he seemed to trap her within his mind, and the words fell unbidden from her lips.

"To Martin—my husband. The man who has given me the freedom to be myself and the freedom to love freely. I'm willing to share my life, my dreams and your destiny with you. Happy birthday, darling." His face swam before her eyes, then his mouth covered hers in a quick, demanding kiss.

Joshua, who had not attended a Cole birthday celebration in the past, raised his glass to deliver his toast. A light gray jacket hung elegantly from his shoulders, tapering at his narrow waist. He gave each person a penetrating stare, then spoke.

"To Martin, the man to whom I entrust my life." He paused briefly, staring at Martin. "I'd like to put Governor Eliot Howard and his corrupt administration on notice. Start looking for a new place to live next January. Ladies and gentlemen—Martin Diaz Cole, the next governor of Florida."

Parris lost track of the number of times she heard Governor Eliot Howard's name mentioned once Martin had announced his candidacy. The activities of his corrupt administration had become the topic of all dinner table conversation. The list of allegations against the incumbent governor were endless: bribery, kickbacks, theft of services, patronage jobs and blackmail.

Parris had come to hate her role as candidate's wife and the race itself. She had come to loathe both when she noted Martin was coming home later and later each night. This night was no different as she lay in bed, waiting for him.

She had dozed off but came awake the moment he slipped into bed beside her. Her body stiffened as he curved an arm over her waist. Glancing at the clock on the beside table, her jaw tightened. It was three-ten.

"Why did you bother to come home?" Her voice was low and vibrating with repressed rage.

"Parris…"

"Don't!" she said, cutting him off. "Don't give me excuses, Martin. And dammit, don't mention Eliot Howard's name."

"Parris," he began again, "I'm sorry."

Sitting up, she turned on a lamp. "You're not sorry, Martin."

He sat up, the sheet falling down around his waist, appearing larger and darker in the muted light. He ran a large hand over his face. "What do you want me to say? What do you want me to do?"

Pulling her knees to her chest, Parris rested her forehead on her folded arms. "I want a husband, Martin. And I want a father for Regina. She sees you less than I do. When she gets up and leaves for school you're gone, and when she goes to bed at night you're still gone.

"I want out of this house," she continued. Raising her head, she glared at him. "I want my own home. You promised that I could buy a house—anywhere. We've been married for more than two months and I'm still living under your parents' roof."

Reaching out, he pulled her forcibly to his side, burying his face against her breasts. The stubble of whiskers on his chin scraped her tender flesh. "I'll cancel a meeting I have tonight and the three of us will go out for dinner. And as soon as I can clear my calendar I'll take a few days off and we'll go house hunting."

"Don't make promises you can't keep, Martin," she warned.

"I promise," he groaned, increasing his grip on her body.

Parris lay in his arms, her gaze on the ceiling. She didn't believe him. "Go to sleep, Martin."

Martin registered the coldness in her voice. He released her and settled back to his pillow. She reached over and turned off the lamp.

Both lay, their backs to each other, motionless. It was the third time that week since they had ever shared a bed that they slept without touching.

Martin read the written notice on his desk at his campaign office: *Tonight's meeting cannot be rescheduled.* He cursed violently under his breath. He wouldn't be able to have dinner with Parris and Regina.

Picking up the telephone, he called Parris. Other than her greeting when she picked up the receiver there was silence from her. He told her he couldn't cancel his meeting and she hung up. He listened to the droning dial tone until an ear-piercing sound came through the instrument forcing him to hang up.

"You tell me if it's worth it, Josh?"

Joshua continued his perusal of the typed data on the desk, checking off a listing of contributors. "Is what worth it?" He answered Martin's question with one of his own.

"Losing Parris."

Joshua's head came up quickly with the mention of her name. What he had suspected was finally confirmed. Martin's lackadaisical approach to the campaign was beginning to worry him. He had neglected to comment about it because he knew intuitively Martin would confide in him.

"Has she threatened to leave you," he questioned in his direct manner.

Martin covered his face with his hands, then ran a hand over his gray-streaked hair. "No, she hasn't," he confessed. The words slipped out slowly. "She doesn't have to leave me to shut me out of her life. This past week has been a living hell for me, Joshua."

He closed his eyes, seemingly trying to erase the image of Parris's closed expression whenever he slipped into bed with her only hours before dawn. "We're two strangers who happen to share a bed. She calls me a stranger, and she's right. There's no argument I can invent to make it any different."

Joshua had pledged his support to Martin, and all Martin knew was winning. Neither of them knew how to lose.

Chapter 25

Owen Lawson. It was late March when Parris saw him. He was impeccably attired and wearing his usual dark glasses to shade his eyes from the sun and the world.

"Go, Mommy!" Regina urged. "Everyone's honking at you."

He hadn't seen her as he crossed the street and entered a building, but it still did not matter as his name and face followed Parris on her trip from West Palm Beach to Fort Lauderdale to look at a house.

Her gaze followed the road; seeing and not seeing.

Since her return to Florida, Parris discovered Owen had retired from the police force, remarried and was the father of two young boys; sons who could have been theirs if they had stayed together.

"I'm hungry, Mommy," Regina whined.

"We'll eat later," she mumbled. She couldn't look at the child sitting next to her.

Regina fidgeted with her seat belt. "I'm thirsty, too."

"Please, Regina." She couldn't argue. Perspiration had soaked her blouse and cotton pullover. Parris alternated wiping her wet palms on her jeans whenever her fingers slipped from the steering wheel. The fear was like a cobra, coiled, poised and ready to strike.

"After we see the house, we'll get something to eat," she stated, hoping Regina didn't register the quivering in her voice.

"I want a steak."

Parris took her eyes off the road, glancing quickly at her daughter's animated features. "I thought you and your father decided it was going to be pizza." Neither of them were dressed for a fancy restaurant.

Regina clapped a hand over her mouth. "Oops. I forgot." She picked up the book on her lap and began reading. Knowing they were going out for pizza temporarily assuaged her thirst and hunger.

The structure was an architect's masterpiece.

"Is this where we're going to live, Mommy?"

Parris held Regina's hand, leading her up the flagstone path to the opened front door. "Yes," she replied confidently. She loved the house even without seeing the interior. The smooth lines and free and easy spaces of the beach front house went beyond her imagination.

"Martin?" Her voice carried and echoed in the entryway.

"I'm in the back," came his reply.

Regina ran through the living room. "Where are you, Daddy?"

Parris moved slowly as she stared up at the high-ceiling entry and more than fifty square feet of livingroom space. She wandered through a full-size ultra modern kitchen and several bedrooms with adjoining baths. Glass walls along the rear of the house afforded an idyllic view of the Atlantic Ocean.

"How do you like it?" Martin asked when she found him in the master bedroom.

"I love it." Her smile mirrored her approval. "How did you ever find it?"

"A guy at the campaign office told me about it."

Parris wound an arm through his. Her tongue flicked over his moustache. "Thank him for me," she crooned.

Martin frowned. He pulled her to his chest. "Not like that I hope."

"Where's my room, Daddy?"

Martin peered over Parris's head, smiling at Regina. "Which one do you want?"

"One where I can see the water."

"Take the one next to this one. After you see everything, then we'll go out and have that pizza you wanted."

Regina wrinkled her nose. "What's all that stuff?"

Martin used a plastic fork, pointing out the toppings on the pie. "Mushroom, green pepper, onion, sausage, black olive, pepperoni, anchovy and garlic."

"Ughh-h garlic!"

"Before you turn up your nose, young lady, why don't you taste it," he suggested to Regina.

Regina shook her head. "It looks yucky."

Martin reached over, taking her slice. "I guess there will be more for me."

"Daddy!"

Martin gave Regina a long look. His stomach made a flip-flop motion when he noted the tears in her eyes. She was so delicate, vulnerable, and he found, like her mother, he couldn't deny her anything. Without realizing it, he had spoiled her.

"What if I order a slice with only cheese?"

Regina's smile was radiant. "Thanks, Daddy."

Martin motioned to the waitress and ordered two slices with extra cheese. He glanced down at his daughter as she inched closer to him, her cheek resting against his arm. He pulled her onto his lap, cradling her head to his chest. He had to hold her close because within two months he was scheduled to begin his campaign tour and she would be left behind.

Since he had announced his candidacy, the pace had accelerated to where he was spending as much time with his political strategists as he did in his office at ColeDiz. David had cancelled his personal appearances with Night Mood to study policy and procedures for the holding companies yet Martin hadn't felt confident enough to let go of the reins of ColeDiz and transfer complete responsibility to David.

Parris kissing him that afternoon was the first display of affection she had shown him in weeks although they continued to share a bed; they existed like married strangers.

She had accused him of becoming a stranger and that she didn't know him anymore, and he knew she was right. Taking two days off to look for houses did not remedy his frequent absences, but he had to make the attempt. He would do anything to recapture the love and warmth missing in his marriage.

"Not only is she back, but she has a child. You told me she was dead."

"I didn't tell you she was dead. I told you she was gone."

"I pay you to do exactly what I tell you to do. Now I want her dead!"

"What about the kid?"

"Forget about the kid. Just take care of the mother."

"Do you want her taken care of out of the state?"

"I want her dead. I don't care if you kill her in front of thousands in Disney World! I want her d-e-a-d."

"Killing her this time should be a lot easier, sir."

"That's what you told me the last time."

"This time I won't miss," the man with the prominent vein in his forehead promised.

He hung up and cursed, violent, savage expletives. That little frog-voiced weasel told him Parris Simmons was never coming back to Florida. Well, she was back and with her kid! Damn! He couldn't get the weasel to try again because she might recognize his face. He had to plan everything very carefully. It was only a matter of time before Martin Cole would find himself a widower.

Parris dug her bare feet into the plush softness of the creamy short shag carpeting. With the installation of the carpets, another phase of her decorating project had been completed. The walls were done two days before, and with the window dressing and the delivery of furniture she would finalize her decorating the immense and exceptionally beautiful place she was to call home.

It had been too many years since she created spaces for her personal lifestyle, and she had forgotten the flutter of excitement when she surveyed the harmonizing of colors and textures. Soft shades of sand beige with a touch of mauve on the walls created a cool effect in the living and dining areas. High, wood-beamed ceilings would allow for hot air to rise high above the carpeted floors and light from a clerestory window illuminated the open expanse of the dining room.

She had elected to decorate the rooms in neutral colors to produce an appearance of coolness of the interiors during the long hot summer season.

Her regular trips to the house after Regina left for school gave her a temporary respite from her silent war with Martin.

She sank down to the carpeted floor and bit down on her lower lip. Just when she thought her life had formed some semblance of order it was going to be torn asunder with their being catapulted into the media's spotlight with Martin's upcoming public appearances.

The sound of a car's engine brought her to her feet. She was surprised to see Joshua striding up the path. She hadn't seen him since the night when he'd made his announcement of her husband's candidacy.

His cold gaze swept over her bare feet, faded jeans and oversized khaki shirt. "I want to talk to you."

His command slapped at her, and she bristled. "Did Martin send you?"

He leaned against the door, arms folded over his chest. "This visit is my idea."

"Then why don't you wait for an invitation."

"Don't play cat and mouse games with me, *Mrs. Cole.* I want to know why you're behaving like a spoiled child instead of the woman you're supposed to be?"

Parris's temper flared and she turned her back. "Get out!"

Joshua closed the distance, capturing her arm and spinning her around. His eyes were devoid of color and Parris couldn't control her fear. Joshua Kirkland had shown her what few saw—rage.

"Don't you know what you're doing to your husband? Are you bent on destroying the man—piece by piece, day by day? When November arrives there'll be nothing left for Governor Howard to defeat. Does it give you a sick thrill to know that you can ruin

Martin only because you don't agree with him? Don't you know that you have more power over Martin than the highest elected official in the state. You outrank the governor, Parris!"

Her jaw jerked spasmodically before she was able to get the words out, her rage matching his. "Don't you dare speak to me of something you know nothing about. If I choose not to go along with everyone's scheme to make Martin the dragon-slayer when he defeats the most corrupt governor this state has ever elected, that's *my* business. And I won't allow you or anyone else to question my motives."

"He needs your support, Parris!" Joshua ranted, his face becoming a mask of fury.

Parris tried escaping his punishing hold on her arm. "Take your hand off me." He released her. "He doesn't need my support when everyone in his family and *you* are helping him."

Joshua took a deep breath. "You're the only one who matters, Parris. Don't you know by now how Martin feels about you?" he asked in a softer tone.

"You're wrong, Joshua. Martin may love me, but he needs me more. I know he needs to dispel his playboy image with a wife and child."

"That's where you're wrong. Martin's image is not an issue. He hasn't even begun to tour the state and already he's ready to quit. Quit because of you." He registered the quickening of the pulse in her throat. "Since we've issued the press release, money and verbal support have been pouring in from all over Florida. Bumper stickers, campaign buttons and posters have been printed and distributed, while campaign headquarters are being mobilized in every county from Dade to Escambia. For the first time in Florida's history an Independent Party candidate has a chance of winning the gubernatorial. Meanwhile Martin is talking about dropping out."

She shook her head. "No."

"Why no?"

Closing her eyes, Parris chewed her lower lip. "Martin doesn't give up that easily," she whispered.

A knowing smile softened Joshua's features. "Now, we're back to square one, Parris. You hold the key. When are you going to tell Martin you're ready to help him? And that you're willing to make the personal appearance that's required of a candidate's wife?"

"I'm scared to death," she confessed as Joshua reached out, pulling her to his chest. "When I think of the crowds and the reporters, all I envision is running away and hiding."

In a nightmare she saw the face of her abductor in a crowd, leering and waiting. "For Martin this is easy." She blinked back the tears forming behind her eyelids. "I need my privacy, Joshua. Martin's isn't offering me a choice when he expects me to follow him all over the state smiling and speaking when I least want to. It's unfair."

Joshua's fingers caressed her back in a comforting gesture. "There's no shame in admitting you're afraid," he replied softly.

Raising her tear-filled eyes, Parris stared up at him. There was something about this man that said he feared nothing or no one. "I can't believe you'd ever be afraid of anything," she said, smiling.

His eyes glowed with a strange fire. "There are some things that frighten me, but I try to conquer the fear and not have it conquer me."

She wanted to believe him. She'd been trying for years to conquer her fear. "Will you help me?" she asked timidly.

"That's why I'm here, Parris. I'm here to help you and Martin." What he didn't say was that he was there to protect her.

Cupping her face in his palms, he kissed her forehead. "I'll make certain you'll come through this with passing grades. In the end, we'll all be winners."

"I don't want to be in any stupid play," Regina stated, pouting.

"But, Mrs. Adams is counting on you, Regina," Parris coaxed. "The spring play is a very important event at the school."

Regina pushed out her lower lip. "I don't want to be the old queen. I want to be Alice."

Parris picked up one of her daughter's braids and wound it around her finger. The curling ends spread out like black velvet.

"Regina," she began patiently. "We've gone over this before. Beth is going to be Alice…"

"Only because she has blond hair," Regina countered. "I have to be the queen because I have black hair."

"That's not the reason, angel. Mrs. Adams selected you to be queen because you were the best when you said 'off with her head.' You were very dramatic."

Regina's eyes brightened with pride. "Did Mrs. Adams say that?"

"That's what she told me," Parris confirmed, breathing somewhat easier now that Regina warmed to the idea of playing the queen in *Alice in Wonderland.* "She said you're a very talented little actress."

Regina clapped her hands. "Maybe I'll be an actress."

Parris laughed, pulling her close and kissing her cheek. "What happened to becoming a scientist?"

Regina reached up, piling her braids atop her head like a crown. "I'd rather play a queen and give orders to chop off heads," she drawled in an authoritative tone.

She had been appropriately named Regina: the queen. "Well, Your Highness, off to bed with you."

"Good night, Mommy." Regina squeezed her mother's neck, leaving a moist kiss on her cheek. She settled down to the pillow, cradling her arms over her head. A slight smile touched her lips. Within minutes, she was asleep.

Parris turned off the lamp and slipped quietly out of the room. She stifled a cry of surprise when she bumped into Martin. She hadn't expected to find him lurking outside of Regina's bedroom. He placed a large hand over her mouth.

"Hi," she said after he'd removed his hand. Her voice was breathless with surprise.

"Hi back to you." Martin smiled down at her. "You handled that quite nicely." He led her down the hall to their bedroom.

"Thank you. What are you doing home so early?"

He closed the door to the bedroom. His fingers circled her upper arms, pulling her to his chest. "Is there some law which states I can't come home early to my wife and daughter?"

Parris peered up at him through her lashes. "No."

Martin lowered his head, his warm breath brushing her lips. "Are you glad to see me?"

"Yes," she whispered. "Very." Her arms went to his neck, bringing his head down. He tasted her mouth, then with a burning that promised to consume them both, gathered her tightly, recapturing the fire eluding them for months.

Minutes later, their clothes lay in a pile on the floor as they lay on the bed in a tangle of limbs. All talk and thoughts of the campaign and election faded as Martin parted her thighs with his knee to tell her wordlessly and leisurely that he loved her in a way he was never able to verbalize.

Parris slept; however, sleep was not as kind to Martin. His head was still reeling from their lovemaking. How could he have neglected her? But he knew the answer to his question even before his mind formed it.

Ambition.

A driving ambition which would continue to haunt him until he assuaged it with victory—or defeat.

He had never been one to turn down a challenge. It had been one of the reasons why he had followed Parris the night he met her. She had turned down his invitation for a date, and his wounded pride would not accept rejection. From the moment he saw her he had to have her.

He had her, then lost her. And if he wasn't careful he would lose her again.

Priorities. His campaign manager had pointed that out to him. Who or what was more important?

He owed it to the secret circle of powerful men who backed him to fulfill his promise to challenge and defeat Eliot Howard; but he also owed it to Parris to be a husband, and to Regina a father.

He had made a choice. He was going to take a week off to be a husband and a father. He would take the time and he would defeat Eliot Howard. He would succeed only because he had never failed nor had he ever been defeated.

Chapter 26

Parris slipped quietly from bed the next morning and made her way into the bathroom. It felt strange to find Martin beside her when she woke up. He had come home early the night before, they had made love for the first time in more than a month and she felt as if she had won a small victory. She had gotten her husband back. Even that was temporary because she knew she would have to share him with the people of Florida when he began to tour the state.

She showered, dressed, then saw to getting Regina ready for school.

An hour later she returned to the bedroom. Martin was still asleep, his face pressed to the pillow. He was exhausted. Even without his saying he was tired, all of the visible signs were apparent: he had lost weight and his eyes were shadowed and deeper.

Returning to an alcove in the large bedroom she and Martin used as their sitting area, she gathered her handbag and the leather case containing fabric samples for the dining room chairs she wanted to purchase.

"Going somewhere?"

She looked up and saw Martin. Both of his hands were hidden in the pockets of a wine-colored paisley-print robe.

Parris smiled. "Shopping."

"Anywhere in particular?"

"I'm going to order the fabric to cover the dining room chairs, and then visit a few shops on Worth Avenue in Palm Beach."

"Do you mind company?"

She opened her mouth to ask whether he was going into his office then changed her mind. "Not at all."

Shifting an eyebrow, he gave her a sensual smile. "Good. Give me half an hour and we'll be on our way."

She sank down to one of the chairs after he'd walked into the bathroom, smiling. The last time she had Martin all to herself was on their honeymoon.

The three days they'd spent at the beach front cottage was a repeat of their first trip to Ocho Rios. They spent half their time on the beach and the other half in the bed. Martin concocted monstrous breakfasts and exotic dinners, which they shared over candlelight.

Martin had begun to teach her to speak Spanish, and he spent at least an hour a day conversing in Spanish, gesturing or pointing to whatever object she didn't understand. The lessons had continued each night when they retired for bed until he announced his candidacy.

"Ready, Parris?" He'd readied himself in twenty minutes.

Martin had shaved, showered and was dressed in a pair of khakis with a dark green short-sleeve Lacoste polo shirt and a celery green V-neck Lacoste cardigan. He wore his favored Gucci loafers in a dark brown. He looked nothing like the president of a corporation or a candidate for an elected office.

"My car or yours?" she asked as they made their way down the staircase and through a corridor leading to the garages.

He took her case and handbag. "Mine."

"I'd like to be back in time for Regina when she gets in from school," she reminded Martin after he'd pulled out of the driveway.

Martin patted her knee. "I'm not going to abduct you, darling. We're just going to spend a few hours together."

Her eyes widened and the breath caught in her throat the moment the word was out of his mouth.

Abduct. It had been a while since she had relived the nightmare. Even after seeing Owen she expected the dream to return but it hadn't. She knew she wouldn't feel completely safe until she moved to Fort Lauderdale.

Exhaling softly, she pressed her back to the leather seat in Martin's late model Jaguar. Closing her eyes, she said, *"¿Qué hora es,* Martin?"

He glanced at the clock on the dashboard. "It's ten…"

"¡En español, Martin!" she teased.

He rattled off the time in Spanish, grinning. It had been a long time, too long, since he had practiced speaking Spanish with her.

Glancing over at her delicate profile, he launched into a monologue, the words spilling fluidly from his tongue. Out of the corner of his eye, he saw Parris staring at him.

"I don't think I understood more than five words," she admitted. "What did you say?"

"I apologized for neglecting you, Parris. I've missed your voice, your face and your body. I've missed lying in bed with you, holding your hand and teaching you Spanish. I miss seeing you smile and I miss hearing you laugh. I've missed loving and tasting you."

His voice lowered. "When we made love last night it was like I'd been dying of thirst and you were an oasis. I need you, Parris. Not just your body, but all of you. Without you I'm only half of what I should be."

Her cheeks were burning from his passionate confession. "Martin…"

"I adore you, baby." The fingers of his right hand curved possessively over her thigh. "I'll try to make it up to you. Just remind me when I get too demanding."

Parris covered his hand with hers and they exchanged a tender smile.

They arrived in Palm Beach and Parris and Martin split up after agreeing to meet back at the car within the hour.

Parris couldn't remember when she had spent a more pleasant day. She ordered her chairs for the dining room, shared lunch with Martin, then browsed through several stucco fronted shops on Worth Avenue. She showed a particular interest in an antique shop located off Worth Avenue but declined to buy anything.

"You showed a lot of interest in those silver candlesticks," Martin said once they were seated in his car.

"Seeing the candlesticks reminded me of the last project I worked on before I left New York. I catalogued a collection of candlesticks from a Hudson River Valley estate that was extraordinary."

"Do you miss New York?"

"I miss my neighbor and her family. I manage to call her several times a month." She paused. "She had a baby girl. It was born on New Year's day."

"Do you want another child, Parris?" He didn't know why he'd asked because whenever they made love neither of them used any contraception.

Their gazes met and Parris managed a wry smile. "I don't know," she answered truthfully. "I want a baby, but not now. Our lives are too unsettled. We're still living with your parents, you're running for a political office which if you win will mandate that we move across the state and live there for at least four years…"

"You're right," Martin said, cutting her off. He was forty and he was getting older, not younger. He wanted another child before he turned forty-five. "Speaking of moving, Jon and Brittany are moving back to Florida. Both of them have had enough of Los Angeles. I think the last earthquake helped them make up their minds."

"It'll be good to see my old roommate again." When she had asked about her friend, Martin told her that the Grants had moved to Los Angeles after Brittany was offered the position of assistant curator with a museum featuring Pre-Columbian art. Jon left his father's law practice and followed his wife, securing a teaching position at a local community college.

"We'll probably be in our new house by the time they return. It will give us an excuse to throw a party," Martin said with a wide grin.

"You'll have to wait until I finish decorating it."

"If you're not finished we can throw something outdoors. A pool party should be fun."

"I will not have people in my house when it's half-done."

They argued good-naturedly on the return trip, exiting the car arm-in-arm. Martin thanked Parris for her company and she graciously accepted his thanks by pressing her mouth to his in a chaste kiss.

"We'll continue this later," he promised.

"I can't wait," she said saucily, proceeding him into the house.

Parris lay in bed, reading. She was waiting for Martin to come home. It had been six weeks since they had shared a glorious week together before he returned to his campaign activities. He was scheduled to begin touring the state the first week in May. That was only a week away.

She looked up as he walked into the bedroom. "Hi." She curbed the impulse to spring from the bed and cradle him to her breasts. He was past being fatigued.

"Hi back to you." He gave her a tired smile.

Lifting the sheet, Parris patted his side of the bed. "Come to bed before you fall on your face."

She watched as he undressed, leaving his suit on the floor, and staggered toward the bed.

"Where are you going?" she questioned as he turned back to his clothes.

"I want to you give you something." Reaching into the inner pocket of his jacket, he withdrew a flat box wrapped in gold foil paper. He handed her the box. "Happy birthday, darling."

Her eyes widened in surprise. She thought he had forgotten her birthday. "Thank you."

He groaned aloud as he lowered his body to the bed. "Tomorrow you'll begin a makeover session where you'll be fitted for a new wardrobe for our personal appearances." He peered up at her. "Yes, Parris, you'll have to dress up. No more jeans and jogging shoes. I'll make all the arrangements with Mr. Ray."

Those were his last words as he closed his eyes and turned his face into his pillow.

She removed the paper from the box and opened a black velvet case. The light from the bedside lamp caught the fiery light of a necklace set with emeralds encircled with brilliant blue-white diamonds. The necklace was the match to the earrings he had given her for Christmas.

"Martin," she whispered. His answer came in a soft snore. She closed the box and put it on the table, wondering if he had also bought the necklace ten years ago.

Martin gave her everything but what she wanted most. She wanted him and only him while he wanted her and the state of Florida.

Mr. Ray, as he was referred to by his staff, met Parris personally. His smoldering dark gray eyes looked her over quickly, professionally, assessing what needed to be altered. He smiled a quick, nervous smile. "Come right this way, Mrs. Cole."

"Please call me Parris.

Parris followed the slender man who had become the most sought-after stylist along Florida's east coast. He wasn't much taller than she was, but rumors of Ray and his numerous affairs with his clients were rampant in the gossip columns, and she wondered whether it was his artistic expertise they sought or his philandering.

Ray led her into a large room with mirrored walls. Turning, he buttoned several buttons on his body-fitting white shirt. Parris stared at his profile. He wasn't good-looking. There were too many sharp angles in his face yet there was something about the man that drew women to him.

He displayed another nervous smile. "Mrs. Cole…Parris. You've probably heard stories about me—nasty little stories." He smoothed back a thick lock of honey-blond hair. "Don't believe them," he added quickly. "Your husband is a wealthy man, and a very powerful one."

Parris stared at him. What was he talking about? He hadn't

made a pass at her so she didn't know why he was attempting to apologize. "What is it?"

"A friend of your husband's came here yesterday." He buttoned another button. "Well, in not too many words he *warned* me not to get *familiar* with you. Not that I would," he protested.

She was more confused than before. "Who?"

"He didn't leave his name."

"What did he look like?"

"Tall, over six feet with blond hair."

"Joshua," Parris whispered. Had Martin sent Joshua to threaten the stylist? She managed a smile although she did not feel like smiling. Martin would hear from her.

"I don't think we will have a problem, Mr. Ray. I'm here because my husband feels I should change my image. You're the professional, so I'll go along with whatever you suggest."

Ray took her hand, bowing over it and kissing her knuckles. "Thank you for your confidence." He released her hand. "We'll start you out with a sauna and massage."

Ray slipped out of the dressing room, smiling at a masseuse. He had lied. He did have affairs with the wives of the wealthy men who paid for their excesses, but Martin Cole's wife wasn't worth the risk.

He discovered she was an attractive woman who could be beautiful after he changed her hair style and taught her how to apply makeup to emphasize her eyes and mouth. She would be a head-turner just by stepping into a room; however the image of Parris Cole's protector was still too vivid for him to maintain the confidence and charm he had spent half of his life cultivating. He was only thirty-eight, and he looked forward to enjoying his glittering jaded lifestyle. Parris Cole was safe with Ray Lewis.

Chapter 27

Parris was so relaxed the masseuse had to shake her several times to make certain she was still awake. "Mrs. Cole, it's time for a snack."

"I'm not hungry," Parris mumbled, not moving.

"You must have something, Mrs. Cole. You'll be here another three to four hours and you'll need some nourishment."

Parris raised her head from her folded arms. "What else has to be done?"

The masseuse helped her into a fluffy white terry robe. "You'll get a facial, manicure, pedicure and your hair and face done."

She was escorted into another room where a half dozen women sat eating and chatting with one another. One went on excitedly about the highway sniper who used passing cars for target practice and had successfully evaded the police. Another woman topped the story by saying her sister's car was hit by a bullet just two days before.

The bored idle rich. Parris nibbled on pieces of low-fat, low-sodium cheese and fresh fruit slices, wondering how often they came to have their bodies and faces pampered.

A slight frown furrowed her forehead. After decorating her own home what else would she have to do? Even if Martin won the election she knew she had to see about her own career. There was no way she wanted to end up like these women.

Ray's gaze met Parris's in the reflection of the mirror. His fingers tested the strands of her shoulder-length dark brown hair. "Your husband's campaign colors are red, white and blue, and your wardrobe will be coordinated as such."

"I hardly ever wear red," Parris protested.

Ray rested both hands on her shoulders. "You should. You have a clear complexion with rich yellow undertones. Warm colors in the red range: soft russets, terra-cotta, clear reds or peach are perfect for daytime. Cool colors—roses and pinks are great for the evening."

"What are you going to do with my hair?"

"I'm going to soften the color, then cut it into a style that will be easy to manage whether you decide to curl it or blow it straight."

Parris thumbed a magazine, counted the number of bulbs in the track lights and admired the black and white furnishings in the popular salon as Ray worked on her hair.

Four months before she had been Parris Simmons, mother, single parent and interior decorator. Now she wasn't sure of who she was or what she would become.

Two hours later she couldn't believe the transformation. Her hair had been cut to chin-length and curled softly around her face. The highlighted strands accented the gold undertones in her complexion. She turned her head and the curls bounced with the slight motion.

"It looks good with or without makeup, don't you think?" Ray questioned with pride.

Parris nodded, still shocked. Even without makeup she looked feminine, but sophisticated and worldly.

"Let's see to your makeup and that will complete our session."

Esther, a tiny bird-like woman stopped Parris as she gathered her handbag to leave. Her small dark eyes darted quickly over her body. "Mrs. Cole. You must try on your clothes."

Parris stared at the woman with the small pointed face and thinning hair pulled back in a bun as if she had spoken in a foreign tongue. She glanced at her watch. It was after five. She'd spent the day in the salon. "What clothes?"

"Right this way. Your husband already paid for them. I need your measurements, then I'll have everything delivered to your home."

The boutique adjoining the salon was filled with designer originals and copies. Parris suffered through trying on blouses, dresses, gowns and undergarments.

"Mrs. Cole, you should wear that dress home."

Parris looked down at the printed red and white silk crêpe de chine pleated dress. The drop yoke styling emphasized the slimness of her body. She nodded, too exhausted to change into the dress she had put on that morning.

"Is there anything else?" she asked, afraid that there were more surprises in store for her.

"Shoes."

For shoes she could sit. Parris lost count of the number of shoes she tried on. She was grateful for the snack she'd eaten earlier because now her stomach was beginning to grumble loudly.

"Thank you," she mumbled to the woman whose name she'd failed to catch when she introduced herself, gathering the bag containing her dress. She all but ran out of the boutique before someone else stopped her.

The parking lot was still crowded with cars as Parris walked over to her Accura. She sat behind the wheel, staring through the windshield into the darkness. What she'd thought would take only a few hours had turned into a six hour ordeal.

Turning on the ignition, she flicked on the headlights and maneuvered out of the parking lot, skirting Mercedes Benzes, Porsches, Jaguars and Lexuses. The warmer weather was returning, but she decided against turning on the air conditioning.

Parris made good time returning to West Palm Beach as she avoided the heavily-traveled highway. She glanced up in her mirror as the bright lights of a car behind her obscured her vision. The driver had his high beams on.

Lowering her chin, she tried avoiding the blinding glare. Slowing and moving over to the right lane, she waited for the car to pass her. The driver also moved to the right lane and continued to follow her.

"Idiot!" The word mirrored her mood. She was tired and in no way did she want to play highway tag. She increased her speed and the car following her kept pace.

A shiver of fear snaked up her spine. The local road was dark, with light vehicular traffic and she doubted whether she could find a police cruiser on this stretch of road. Most of them were probably looking for the highway sniper.

Sniper! The single word slapped at her. What if the driver in the car behind her was the sniper?

The question had barely formed in her mind when the back of her car was rammed and she lurched forward. Her foot instinctively floored the accelerator.

"No!" she screamed as the back of her car was rammed again. Shifting from the gas pedal to the brake, she jerked the wheel of her car to the right, the heel of her left hand fastened to the horn. Seconds later, she skidded off the road and stopped when her car crashed into a wooded area abutting the roadway.

She had unclasped her seat belt and scrambled across the gear shift when the crack of a bullet shattered the glass on the driver's side. Pressing her cheek to the seat, Parris eased her body down into the small space between the front passenger seat and glove compartment. She covered her head with her arms and prayed.

She waited for a second shot, but it never came.

She was still cowering on the floor when the car door swung open.

"Parris, are you all right?"

Never had she been so relieved to hear that deep, powerful voice. Trembling, she crawled up to the seat, hands and legs shaking uncontrollably.

"No!" she screamed when she saw the black, deadly handgun pointed at her.

"It's all right, Parris."

Eyes wide with fright, Parris stared at the gun in Joshua's hand. Tears filled her eyes and stained her face. "Why?" she asked weakly. "Why, Joshua?"

Joshua replaced the nine millimeter automatic handgun in a shoulder holster concealed under his jacket, then reached for Parris. "He's gone," he said quietly. "He can't hurt you now."

Parris didn't remember Joshua leading her to his car, or his placing a call to the police on his cellular phone. She lost track of time of the trip as he drove her home. She smiled numbly at M.J. when the older woman met her as she climbed the staircase to her bedroom, saying she had a headache and she was going to bed.

However, it was when she sat on a chair in the bedroom that the frightening scene replayed in her mind. Placing a hand over her mouth, she cried silently until she was drained.

Martin shook hands with the men who were responsible for his Jacksonville campaign office.

"Pardon me, Mr. Cole. There's an important call for you. The caller is a Mr. Kirkland. Shall I put it through here, or would you prefer to take it in the office?"

"I'll take it in the office," Martin informed the maître d'. "Excuse me, gentlemen." He followed the maître d' through the dimly-lit restaurant.

"Through that door, sir."

Martin pushed the door open and walked into a room filled with Italian provincial furnishings. Wrinkling his nose at the ornate display, he picked up the telephone receiver that lay on a table.

"What's up, Josh?"

"Someone tried to kill your wife."

"What the hell are you talking about?" His fingers tightened on the receiver.

He listened as Joshua related how someone forced Parris off the road, then fired a shot at her.

He tried easing the tightness in his chest as a wave of moisture washed over his body. "Where is she?" he asked, closing his eyes.

"She's at the house."

"I'll be back within the hour."

"She's safe, Martin."

"Either pick me up or have a driver waiting for me," he ordered. Martin slammed down the receiver, retraced his steps, a grim expression signaling his dinner meeting was over before it began. "I'm sorry, gentlemen. I have a family emergency," he explained quickly. "I must return home."

"When will we meet with you again?" asked the group's spokesman.

"One day next week," Martin flung over his shoulder as he raced out of the restaurant.

The four men seated at the table stared at Martin Cole's broad-shouldered back. They had waited weeks to meet with their candidate, and his return to West Palm Beach was interpreted as a snub. They stared at one another, and a silent communication was registered. Martin Cole would eat humble pie before they scheduled a meeting with him again.

Martin took the stairs two at a time. He hadn't been able to rid his mind of the stranglehold of fear since Joshua's telephone call.

He missed seeing Regina in her bed when he raced past her bedroom to enter his own. He sagged against the door in relief. She *was* there; she *was* safe.

Martin couldn't bring himself to believe Joshua until he could see Parris with his own eyes. She was asleep on a chair, her feet drawn up under her body.

He smiled as his gaze lingered on her hair. She was lovely. No, beautiful. The soft curls fell over her forehead and grazed her silken golden-brown cheek. There was no girl left in her. This Parris was all woman; sensual and alluring.

She came awake as if sensing his presence. Her eyes widened, unable to believe he was smiling down at her.

"What are you doing here? I thought you were staying over in Jacksonville."

Reaching down, Martin gathered her in his arms. He kissed her nose as she stifled a yawn. "I missed you too much to stay away," he lied smoothly. He held her tightly, feeling her warmth and inhaling her familiar fragrance.

Parris tightened her hold on his neck. Never had she needed Martin as she did now. He didn't know how close he had come to losing her. "Hold me," she pleaded, her velvet voice breaking with emotion.

The tension lining Martin's mouth and forehead eased, and he was able to draw a normal breath for the first time in an hour.

He laid Parris on the bed, sinking down beside her. "Go back to sleep, darling. I'll be here all night."

Chapter 28

"Can't you do anything right? You had her where you wanted her and you still couldn't kill her. I'm beginning to believe either you're incompetent as well as stupid or she has nine lives. Now which one is it?"

"I had her but some guy came along and pulled a gun on me and I had to get out of there before I could finish her."

"Did he see you or get your plate number?"

"There was no way he could see me. It was too dark. And as for the license plate—I stole it off a pickup truck."

"At least you did something right."

"You think this is easy? She's not a hooker whose job it is to walk the street where she's a sitting duck."

"You're paid well to follow orders, not ask questions. The next time I talk to you I want to hear some good news for a change."

"The good news is that the police arrested someone as the sniper. I guess the copycat wannabe got his five minutes of fame when the newspapers did a story on him."

"The only thing I want to read is Parris Cole's obituary."

"I'll get her."

"My boss is getting tired of your promises and excuses."

"`Why does he want her dead?"

"I'll forget you asked me that question. Just do the job!"

* * *

Martin tightened his grip on Parris's waist, leading her through the lobby of the hotel. "Ready, honey?"

Parris nodded. She would never be ready for the reporters and the photographers. She had been saved from their questions and microphones when she and Martin stepped off the plane at the Orlando airport.

Martin fielded their barking questions, saying he would give a news conference prior to a fund-raising dinner later that evening, although most of them seemed more intrigued by Mrs. Cole's close brush with death at the hands of the 'Palm Beach Sniper.' Flashbulbs distorted her vision long after she was seated in the spacious limousine that took them from the airport to the hotel.

One member of their security team preceded them through the lobby, while two others lagged behind as Martin and Parris walked the carpeted floor to the elevators.

She and Martin were scheduled to stay in Orlando for two days before moving on to Altamonte Springs.

The elevator ascended quickly to the eighth floor and within minutes they stepped into a suite of rooms filled with all of the amenities one could find at home.

"Very nice. Quite nice indeed," Martin remarked, looking around the suite.

"We'll be across the hall if you need anything," one of the men offered.

Martin waited until the door closed behind them, locking it and placing the key on a table. He slipped out of the jacket to his dark blue suit. "Why don't you try to get some sleep before Olga Ramirez arrives to brief you about the issues."

Parris wasn't going to argue with him. She had been up before dawn, unable to sleep when she thought about leaving Regina. Martin made certain their departure was smooth and unemotional. They shared breakfast, reassuring Regina they would return in a week. The child smiled when Martin told her they were going to Orlando. She made them promise to bring her souvenirs from Disney World and Universal Studios. So much for their daughter grieving for her parents.

Parris walked into the bedroom and closed the drapes, shutting out the bright May sunlight. Their clothes had arrived earlier that morning, and a nightgown lay across the large bed. She would take the time given her before she spoke with the woman who had been assigned as her press secretary.

It took only minutes to cleanse the makeup from her face and slip into the gown. She lay on the bed, recalling the television newscast about the man who had been arrested as the 'Palm Beach Sniper.' The police had reported that the man had chosen his targets randomly—lone women in cars.

Parris and the entire populous of Palm and West Palm Beach did not relax completely until the arrest had been made. It had taken Parris a little longer to relax because she still wasn't able to let go of all of her fears.

Closing her eyes, she drifted off to sleep.

Parris emerged from the bedroom dressed in a navy blue linen gabardine coat dress with a contrasting white collar and lapels and navy blue and white spectator heels, mentally prepared for her briefing with Olga Ramirez.

Martin sat on a sofa with the slender woman with dark curling hair and intelligent dark eyes. He rose to his feet as Parris gave him a smile. His shirt was unbuttoned at the throat and the stubble of a beard shadowed his lean cheeks.

"Parris, I'd like you to meet Olga Ramirez. Olga, my wife, Parris."

Olga stood up and shook Parris's hand. "Hello."

"It's nice meeting you, Olga."

Wonderful voice, Olga thought, quickly assessing the woman whom she was to work closely with for the next six months. Parris Cole was the youngest and most attractive woman she'd been assigned to work with in the twelve years she had been a political consultant and analyst. It usually made her job easier when a political couple visually complemented each other because she always preferred to sell the "package" rather than each person on their own merits. Now if Parris Cole was as intelligent as she was physically attractive, then her assignment would be an easy and rewarding experience.

There was something about the woman Parris liked immediately. They were about the same age, however Olga's firm handshake, unmade-up face and her severe business suit could not disguise the warmth in her friendly smile.

Martin squeezed Parris's shoulder possessively, smiling. "I'll see you later. It's been nice talking with you, Olga."

"Same here, Martin," Olga replied.

Both women sat down at a small round cherry wood table covered with a vase of fresh flowers, a carafe of coffee and several cups and saucers as Martin disappeared into the bedroom.

Olga withdrew a stack of papers from a folder on one of the chairs. "How much interest do you have in politics?" she asked Parris.

Parris studied Olga's short curling hair, her smooth olive-colored skin and her even features. Her face was plain except for her eyes. They were large, dark and alert. They missed nothing.

"Aside from voting, absolutely nothing."

Olga smiled. "Good."

"Good?"

"It's always better for me when I don't have to deprogram a person. In other words you won't come to me with preconceived prejudices. Our only problem will be is making certain you'll be knowledgeable enough about the issues. Both the Democrat and Republican candidates' wives are political campaign veterans. Russell Baker and Eliot Howard share more than forty-two years of political experience between them, and their wives have been with them since the beginning of their political careers. Martin is new at this and so are you."

"Should that make a big difference?" Parris questioned.

Olga shook her head. "Not in the least. In fact, you can use your political inexperience as a platform to create a new trend in a tired old arena. Politics is a lot like movie-making. It's all hype and marketing. In other words, it's whoever has the most beautiful face, sexiest smile and the most drama and glamour in their lives.

"You and Martin look like the perfect couple. You're young, tall, thin—and you know how Americans are obsessed with being thin—and you're gorgeous. Even your profession as an interior decorator reflects beauty. The people of Florida will watch you very closely. They'll want to know what you're wearing and what your house looks like. They're going to want to know why Martin married you and not some other woman. They are going to want to know *everything* about Parris Cole."

"And they'll probably want to know why I waited ten years to marry Martin even though I'd had his child."

Olga stared intently at her, then said, "That was going to be my first question to you."

Parris had rethought the question many times and had formulated a response she could repeat in her sleep. "Martin and I had a difference of opinion, and I left Florida."

Olga asked other questions about her family and past.

Parris spent an hour with Olga, listening and asking questions. The first of many briefing sessions ended when Martin returned to the sitting room, shaved and impeccably groomed in a tailored navy blue suit with a faint pinstripe.

At exactly six fifty-five the campaign security personnel rapped on the door and escorted Parris, Martin and Olga to the hotel's grand ballroom for the fund-raising dinner.

The soft whisper of breathing and the crisp rattling of the early morning edition of the newspaper was the only audible sound in the room. Everyone watched Vince Daniels as his eyes raced over the outspread newspaper.

Miraculously, the campaign committee kept up with the hectic schedule: six cities within eight days. They had covered Orlando, De Land, Altamonte Springs, Sanford, Deltona and Daytona Beach.

The committee, consisting of speech writers, photographers, publicists and security personnel gathered for early morning breakfast, late morning brunch, midday lunch and late night dinner. All were kept busy attending mall openings, fund-raising dinners and high school and college forums.

During the sweep of these cities Parris saw another side of Martin she had never encountered. Rumors of his compelling persuasive manner in the corporate board room became apparent as he wooed the undecided and uncommitted voter with his scathing criticism of the suggestion of corruption that had followed Eliot Howard from every hamlet in the state since his entrée into the political arena nearly thirty-five years before. Martin became an actor in a role, giving his best performance to a captive audience.

Martin's press secretary cleared his throat, flashing his candidate a smile. "It's not page one, but then five isn't too shabby either." He examined the article quickly, a broad grin softening his round face.

" 'A storm has blown across Central Florida, and what is so strange is that it's not the season for tropical storms. Martin Diaz Cole, of West Palm Beach, who formally declared his candidacy for governor four months ago, has all of the qualifications to be a most formidable opponent for the incumbent governor Eliot Howard.

" 'Forty-year-old Cole has the striking good looks of a soap opera idol, a smile reminiscent of Billy Dee Williams and the charisma of the late President John F. Kennedy. The dynamic West Palm Beacher uses the stage much like a dancer, utilizing every inch of it while his mellifluent voice sways the reluctant supporter to his camp of ever-increasing loyal followers.

" 'His verbal assault on Howard and his constituents was delivered with the force of a blitzkrieg, labeling the governor as Typhoid Mary in that he's responsible for the spread of corruption throughout the state while not coming down with any of its ill effects himself. Incredibly, Cole enumerated the extensive list of individuals and agencies, indicted or investigated, who have been politically linked to the incumbent over the years the controversial boss has been leader of his party. Cole then listed the items of his platform, policies that the capacity-filled convention center agreed would be good for Florida. Cole reminded the crowd of Howard's claim that he's never taken a dishonest dollar in his life, countering that Howard is incapable of distinguishing honest from dishonest.

" 'The thunder of applause and stomping feet reverberated throughout the convention center like cannon fire. Many had come to observe Martin Diaz Cole out of curiosity, and left transfixed by the magical spell woven by a man who dared to challenge the political juggernaut of a veteran politician rumored to possess power equal only to the President of the United States.

" 'Floridians cannot ignore this new force in Florida's political arena, and neither will gubernatorial hopeful Russell Baker and Governor Eliot Howard.' "

Martin laughed, slapping his press secretary on the back. "Are you certain you didn't write that piece, Vince? It sounds too much like you not to have your by-line."

"He probably paid his friend to write it," Olga teased.

Vince flushed to the roots of his orange hair. Since Olga joined the committee as Parris's press secretary, he and Olga had become embroiled in a constant battle of wills.

"It's still better than plagiarizing someone else's work." Vince's retort was lost on Olga with the level of noise in the hotel room.

"People, people." Olga tapped the handle of a teaspoon against her coffee cup. "Good folks, before we celebrate prematurely about our esteemed candidate, allow me to inform you that Martin isn't the only Cole to receive press coverage."

She shot a smug grin at her obviously embarrassed counterpart, snapping open her edition of the paper with an exaggerated flip of the wrist. " 'Parris Cole addressed a luncheon of the Ladies Auxiliary of the Daytona Beach Beautification Committee and quickly dispelled the image of being a hothouse flower who was totally incongruent to her dynamic wealthy husband.' "

Parris raised her eyebrows and met Martin's obsidian stare. They had become strangers once again. Traveling together and sharing the same bed. The warmth and intimacy in their marriage had decreased as the pace of campaigning increased. They were cool to each other and overly polite, but presented themselves as the perfect couple to the residents of the state of Florida.

" 'Mrs. Cole demonstrated a command of all topics when she conducted a question and answer session following the luncheon, delighting the attendees when she lingered beyond her allotted scheduled appearance. Committee members concluded it was an enthusiastic afternoon, filled with the delightful presence of an intelligent and radiant woman.' "

Chapter 29

Martin watched the shadowy figure of his wife as she leaned against the wall separating their terrace from the adjoining hotel suite. He knew she would be up waiting for him. Over the past two weeks she had been unable to sleep unless he took her to bed and held her until exhaustion claimed her tense body.

Lately, everything had begun to annoy her: the heat, crowds, personal appearances and the accelerated pace of covering as many as ten cities within a week.

Insomnia wracked Parris until she appeared gaunt and fragile. Photographs captured the haunted look in her large eyes, giving her the appearance of a runway model with the graceful hollow of cheeks under delicate, high cheekbones.

The hectic pace was taking its toll on everyone involved with the campaign. Olga Ramirez, one security person and two speech writers had all succumbed to exhaustion. And as much as he tried, Martin found it virtually impossible to retire for bed before midnight.

Eliot Howard had begun his counterattack and he was compelled to spend more time trying to convince the voters that his political inexperience was not a major issue.

Glancing at his watch, Martin winced as he mentally predicted Joshua's reply when he woke him out of his much needed sleep at one in the morning. He didn't hesitate as he picked up the telephone and dialed the number. It took less than sixty seconds to relay his instructions.

Sliding back the screened door, Martin stepped out into the humid blackness. His hands circled Parris's tiny waist. She was thinner than she was when he met her ten years before.

"Parris, you've got to try to get some sleep."

"I can't sleep," she mumbled weakly, floating against his stronger body.

He picked her up, shocked by her weight loss. He placed her on the bed, lying beside her and drawing her into his body's warmth. Burying his face in her freshly shampooed hair, Martin kissed her neck. "Do you want me to get a doctor to prescribe some pills to help you sleep?"

"I don't need sleeping pills, Martin. I need a husband, not a man I have to share with millions of other people. I feel betrayed. I thought I married you, not the state of Florida."

"You have me, baby. You have all of me."

"I only have a little piece of you, Martin. The little piece that's left over after you've given everyone else the charm, wit and your grand plan for overhauling the state's political machine." Pulling out of his embrace, she glanced up to find him staring at her. "I'm tired, Martin. I'm tired of microphones being shoved in my face and flashbulbs distorting my vision.

"I'm sick and tired of smiling and trying to be gracious to people who make snide remarks about you breaking up my marriage to Owen. I need a break from this circus." She massaged her eyes with her fingertips. "If I don't get away from the madness for a few days, I'm afraid I'm going to go crazy."

His lids came down swiftly, masking his disappointment. Didn't she know that it was her presence that gave him the motivation to keep the pace he'd set to attain his goal? It was her he came back to to renew himself for the next battle. His need to defeat Howard and Russell had become a burning obsession, raging out of control. It had come down to a personal war instead of a battle of political ideology.

"I'll have Joshua take you home tomorrow." His voice lacked emotion. "He's to stay at the house until I come back on Saturday." Martin ignored her soft sigh of relief. "You're to remain in Fort Lauderdale until Regina is out of school. She only has three weeks before the terms ends so it'll have to be your decision whether you want to remain at my parents' house during the weekdays with Regina or permit her to stay with Mother, Nancy or Juliana until the end of the school year. The next three weeks should give you enough time to recuperate, finish decorating the house and anything else you feel you want to do.

"After that, you'll be expected to hold up your end of this cause, Parris. It will only become more fierce and ugly the closer the day of reckoning approaches." The burning light in his midnight eyes belied his flat tone. "I hope this meets with your approval, Mrs. Cole?"

She dropped her gaze, staring at his bare chest. "Yes, it does, Martin. Thank you," she whispered.

Martin gathered her close, feeling alone and empty even before her departure. Their marriage had become one of convenience and betrayal. She was right. He had betrayed her. He needed her; he needed her so much; but more than that he loved her. He held her until her breathing deepened and she fell asleep.

You've used her. The three words attacked him relentlessly until he clenched his teeth to stop his denial from spewing out. The three words continued to haunt while he slept and taunted him the following morning long after Parris had returned to Fort Lauderdale.

Parris watched the fast moving cumulus clouds race across the bright blue sky as a strong breeze from the ocean cooled her moist skin. After two days of rain the sky brightened with sunshine and warmth. She dangled her bare feet in the warm pool water, leaning back on her hands and enjoying the cooling air. The stiff fronds of the overhead palm trees caught the wind and bowed majestically from their towering height.

"We're finished, ma'am."

Parris was reluctant to look at the man who supervised the landscaping crew. A large prominent vein throbbed visibly under the pale flesh stretched across his forehead. She finally stared at him until he looked away, seemingly embarrassed by her obvious repulsion.

Joshua watched Parris watching the man. "Send the bill to Martin Cole," he said.

"Will do, sir." The landscaper nodded at Joshua and walked back to his truck and crew.

Joshua sat down beside Parris, examining her intently. "Is something wrong?"

"That man," she said quietly.

"What about him?"

She shivered despite the heat. "He was staring at me." A shiver of panic swept through her as fearful images of her abduction came back to haunt her. "Every time I came out of the house I found him standing there, not doing anything. I tried to ignore him but he kept watching me."

"Have you ever seen him before?"

She shook her head slowly. He couldn't be the man who had accosted her in the mall parking lot. He was too tall. The man who had stalked her was slightly-built and was close to her own height.

"No," she finally admitted.

"It's been rough on you, hasn't it?"

"What has?" She pretended ignorance.

He leaned closer as the wind ruffled his now longer silver-blond hair. "Don't pretend with me, Parris. I know you crave your privacy and wish for some kind of normalcy in your marriage. You want to be able to breakfast every morning with your husband before seeing him off to work. And after Regina leaves for school, you'd love to go to an elegant little shop that has been set up for your decorating business.

"You want to come home after work, see Martin and Regina and share what's left of the day with them. You probably want another child and I can safely guess that you detest this nasty game of politics Martin has become involved in."

Parris stared at his grim expression, feeling her own temper rise. "With a friend like you Martin doesn't need any enemies, does he?" she asked bitterly.

Joshua raised his eyebrows. "You doubt my loyalty to your husband?" His pale eyes burned into her. Placing a long elegant hand on her shoulder, his fingers tightened. "You'll desert him before I will," he predicted.

She jerked out of his grasp. "If you're such a loyal friend, why are you saying these vicious things about Martin?"

"I just want you to be aware of your position, Parris." He shifted, staring out into the ocean, his gaze following a flock of circling gulls. "Martin loves you and I know you love him. But sometimes love can obscure reality. Before you agree to go any further with this campaign think about the consequences. Make certain all of the successes will be worth what you'll have to sacrifice to achieve it."

Parris sat, trailing her feet in the pool long after Joshua returned to the centrally air-cooled interior of the house. She was aware of his anger because he had been forced to baby-sit her until Martin returned; and it had not made her feel any better to have him constantly watching over her.

Wherein Joshua was restless and bored since they had returned to Fort Lauderdale, she hadn't been. She spent a day shopping for food to stock her pantry, and for linens for the bedrooms.

Decorating the bedrooms allowed her a taste of reality and stability. In keeping with the tropical locale, she'd decorated the spaces in light, airy romantic colors.

The bedroom she would share with Martin contained a graceful white brass and iron king-size bed with a white embroidered comforter and sheets of eyelet and lace. She wondered about Martin's reaction to sleeping in the frilly, feminine bedroom, but dismissed it as soon as the thought entered her head. He probably wouldn't notice; defeating Eliot Howard and Russell Baker were his only priorities.

She hadn't been able to resist the graceful dips and curves of the head and footboards when she saw them in the manufacturer's warehouse. Glass and wrought iron tables, live potted plants and palms and a pale green rug completed the furnishings. An adjoining dressing room held two massive oak armoires and dressers.

Regina's room was filled with wicker furniture, handwrapped over welded iron tubing frames in a delicate light green. The double bed with a wicker headboard, matching aquamarine, apricot and cream bed dressing enchanted the child when she first saw it, but failed to sustain her interest as she complained she had "nothing to do by herself."

Regina had been ambivalent about coming down to Fort Lauderdale. She whined that she missed her cousins and grandparents, and Parris retraced the fifty miles to take her back to M.J. Regina would remain in West Palm Beach during the week and return to Fort Lauderdale on weekends.

Parris couldn't relax enough to remain in West Palm Beach; the thought of running into Owen had become a constant threat she couldn't ignore.

She refused to permit Regina's wish to stay in West Palm Beach to dampen her relief of being away from the frantic pace of campaigning. She was able to sleep soundly and the shadows under her eyes disappeared quickly.

She no longer had to concern herself with what to wear, makeup or jewelry. In Fort Lauderdale, with Joshua beside her, she strolled the streets in complete anonymity, comfortably dressed in her worn jeans, oversized T-shirts, frayed sandals or jogging shoes and sunglasses.

Joshua walked into the kitchen, surprising Parris when he smiled at her. "You're not cooking tonight. We're going out, and it'll be my treat."

She returned his smile. Apparently their earlier confrontation was forgotten. If he was offering her an olive branch she would accept it. "Only if I can wear what I have on."

Joshua glanced at her slim white cotton skirt, red T-shirt and white espadrilles. "You don't have to change."

He drove to a popular downtown restaurant with a patio bar, waterfall and an abundance of tropical foliage. The fragrance of grilling steaks on an open hearth filled the air with a mouth-watering aroma.

"What would you like to drink?" Joshua asked her after they seated themselves.

"Something cold with a mixture of tropical juices."

"You don't trust me enough to order something alcoholic?"

She stared at him. "Whether I trust you or not is inconsequential. Martin trusts you."

Joshua smiled again, and he looked like a different person. She had been wrong when she thought him cold and unfeeling. Joshua Kirkland was as human as she was, only he was an expert when it came to hiding behind a wall; a wall he let few penetrate.

"That's because Martin is special to me, Parris. Very special." He walked away to order their drinks.

Resting her chin on the heel of her hand, Parris smiled as Joshua was waylaid by two attractive young women as he made his way back from the bar with their drinks. They sandwiched him in a corner, each hanging onto an arm. Joshua gave them a solemn expression, motioning with his head in her direction.

Parris puckered her lips, blowing him a kiss. The women turned and glanced in her direction. She raised her left hand and wiggled her ring finger, and Joshua was allowed to escape.

He sat down opposite her, letting out his breath. "Thanks."

Leaning forward, she said softly, "What did you tell them?"

He managed a sheepish grin. "I told them I was married and had six kids at home."

Parris speared a cherry tomato from one of the two bowls of salad a waitress had left on the table, giving him a skeptical look. "Six kids?"

He frowned. "Three sets of twins."

She laughed aloud, and to her surprise so did he.

"How's the drink?" he questioned.

"Perfect." She glanced around the crowded restaurant. "This place is charming, yet relaxed. Thank you for inviting me."

"My pleasure, Mrs. Cole."

A slight frown creased Parris's smooth forehead as she put down her drink. "Why do you insist on calling me that?"

"Aren't you Mrs. Cole, Mrs. Cole?"

"Yes, I am," she replied. She glanced away, feeling somewhat uncomfortable. "But Mrs. Cole makes me sound prim and staid."

"You're a challenge, Parris. That's why Martin was attracted to you."

First she was shocked, then wary. How did Joshua know so much about her? About her and Martin? Had Martin told him about their relationship?

A waiter approached the table to take their order, interrupting their conversation.

Parris sipped her drink and ate half of her salad in silence. She declined Joshua's offer of another drink, and waited for him to reorder his before gathering enough nerve to ask him the questions which had plagued her since she was introduced to him.

"How long have you known Martin?"

"Seventeen years," came his direct reply.

"Did the two of you go to school together?"

Joshua leaned back in his chair, staring at her, his gaze now cold and forbidding. "No. Martin grew up with a silver spoon in his mouth while I grew up in what is known as Little Havana."

"Do you speak Spanish, too?"

He nodded. "Spanish, Italian, French, German, Russian…"

"What's left?" she interrupted, laughing.

"I haven't mastered Japanese or any of the Chinese dialects."

"Where did you learn all of these languages?"

"I learned Spanish at home from my mother. The others I learned while traveling."

Parris shifted delicate arching brows. "Your mother is Cuban?"

He nodded again. "My mother was Cuban, and my father's African-American."

"Was?"

"She died last year."

Parris thought of how much she missed her own mother. "I'm sorry, Joshua."

His jaw tightened as he lowered his head and stared at the salad in front of him. There were many more questions she wanted to ask, but didn't when he deliberately put up a wall to shut her out.

Parris unlocked the door and turned off the sophisticated electronic security system. Joshua preceded her into the entry and dimmed the lights after she reactivated the system.

She stared up at his shadowed features. "Martin will be home tomorrow. Will you stay over this weekend?"

He took her elbow and led her into the living room. "No. I'm scheduled to fly down to Jamaica. Sable hasn't been feeling well and I think I'd better look in on her."

She had almost forgotten Joshua was involved with Sable. "Give her my love and best wishes."

Joshua smiled down at her. "I will. Good night, Parris." He turned and walked in the direction of his bedroom in the guest wing.

Parris made it to her own bedroom, humming to herself as she slipped out of her skirt and shoes. A smile curved her mouth when she thought about Martin coming home. He would pick up Regina and the three of them would be together as a family in their new home, and for the first time since returning to Florida she would feel like a wife and mother.

Chapter 30

Pulling her T-shirt over her head and slipping out of her underwear, Parris walked into the adjoining room and turned on the water in the shower stall in the raspberry and powder blue bathroom. She rinsed her hair and body, then adjusted the water temperature and let lukewarm water sluice down her body as she closed her eyes in total relaxation.

Why couldn't Martin understand that Parris wanted simplicity. She didn't need fancy cars, expensive jewelry, a mansion behind high gates or outrageously priced clothes.

Stepping out of the shower stall, she patted her hair and skin lightly with a towel and reached for a robe from a brass hook on the wall. As she belted the satiny midnight blue garment, she saw something move.

Watching the shadow near a potted palm near the door, Parris moved closer, hoping to see what was causing the rustling noise at the base of the large straw planter. It became a game of hide and seek as she crept silently toward the plant, hoping not to disturb what was seeking refuge there. She thought of the possibilities: lizard, frog, cricket or maybe even a field mouse. Whatever it was, she thought, she would allow it to escape unharmed.

Parris gasped loudly, unable to control the rush of fright paralyzing her body. The flickering tongue emerged, followed by the spade-shaped head. The diamond markings in black, brown and white clearly distinguished the *thing* as a rattlesnake.

Her mind froze as well as her body when the angry sound of the reptile's rattle signalled its means of escape was threatened.

Moisture soaked her body, and Parris could smell the raw, acrid scent of fear rising from her pores. Although she saw only the head of the snake above the planter, she could visualize its thick coiled body with the upright tail writhing with its length of vibrating rattles.

It became a matter of who could move faster—she or the snake. The rattler was positioned between her and the door. If she called out for Joshua, would he be able to hear her at the other end of the house? If the snake bit her, would she die instantly or would it be a slow painful death? Would she ever see Regina or Martin again?

Closing her eyes, Parris prayed silently. She was helpless. Her voice was frozen in her throat and she couldn't move. The muscles in her legs were beginning to cramp and twitch from her rigid position. Fear compounded fear, and she began to hum to herself. She hummed the tune over and over, not recognizing it as a lullaby she used to sing to Regina when she was a baby. She had no recollection of how long she repeated the verse. Each time she started over she realized she was still alive. The humming stopped and her eyes flew open as she registered the heat of a body.

"Don't move, baby. No matter what I do—don't move," came a soft warning.

Parris wanted to turn around to see Martin; to make certain it was him and not her imagination. She managed to quell her curiosity and obeyed his softly spoken command.

She saw the shadow of another body on her right. She stared straight ahead, her gaze widening when the snake uncoiled itself, slithering along the base of the wall.

An explosion erupted in her head. There was another explosion before she disobeyed Martin and sank against his body.

Martin caught Parris before she slid to the floor, carrying her limp body out of the bathroom and into their bedroom. He laid her gently on the bed, watching the fluttering pulse in her throat.

Her breathing was shallow although her face was flush with unnaturally high color.

He gathered her to his chest, rocking her back and forth. He decided to return home a day early, surprising Parris, but after entering the bedroom he heard Parris humming and the the angry, disturbed rattle of the snake coming from the bathroom.

He'd raced to the other end of the house to get Joshua. He shocked Joshua when he told him that there was a rattlesnake in the house. Joshua was two steps behind him as he quickly retrieved a handgun. It had taken less than sixty seconds for Martin to return to Parris before the reptile was sighted and killed.

Joshua emerged from the bathroom, an automatic cradled in his left hand. His expression was that of horror and disbelief.

"How is she?"

Martin pressed his lips to Parris's forehead and closed his eyes. "She'll be all right. I'm going to stay with her for a while." Joshua nodded and walked out of the bedroom.

"Martin?" Her voice was low and weak.

"It's all right baby. It's gone."

Parris struggled to sit up. "Where is it?"

"It's dead."

Her heart slowed to a normal rate and her head fell limply to the pillows cradling her back. "How did it get into the house?"

"It must have wandered in. You rest here while Joshua and I get rid of it."

Parris closed her eyes, smiling. "Martin?"

His gaze swept over her delicate face, then down to the silky robe covering her slender body. "Yes."

"I love you."

"I love you, too," he confessed, his voice thick and unsteady. He did not want to think of what would've happened if he hadn't come home when he did. He didn't know what he would do if he ever lost Parris.

Martin rested his elbows on his knees, shaking his head. He and Joshua had disposed of the venomous reptile. "I keep telling myself that it wandered into the house, but a nagging voice in the back of my head says differently."

A frown furrowed Joshua's forehead. "I don't believe it wandered in either. I think it was deliberately dumped here."

"What do you think?" Martin questioned.

The light from a lamp slanted over Joshua's near-white hair, creating harsh shadows on the planes of his lean face. "I think someone wants your wife out of the way."

Martin straightened, his eyes boring into Joshua's. "Why?" The single word sounded like the crack of a rifle.

"I don't know why. But things are just not adding up. The police claim they arrested the Palm Beach Sniper."

"They did," Martin argued.

"They arrested someone who used a different weapon than the one who shot at Parris. The man the police charged as the sniper was picked up with a rifle that was loaded with thirty-threes. The round I picked up off the floor of Parris's car was from a forty-four."

"There's been no more sniping since that guy was arrested," Martin countered, not wanting to believe that someone wanted to kill Parris.

Suddenly he felt tired, old. The pressure of the last month had taken its toll—on his mind and his body. And he wasn't ready to face the possible danger lurking in the shadows.

"Parris asked me to protect her the day we were married. The only person I could think of who she'd want me to protect her from is Owen Lawson."

"Her ex-husband."

Martin nodded. "He'd tried to kill her."

"Tell me about it," Joshua ordered. He sounded like an interrogator. Martin did, leaving nothing out. He digested this new information, his face a mask of stone. "I want you to stay away from Lawson," he warned Martin. "If he's behind this, I don't want you involved."

"The son of a bitch is trying to kill my wife, and you don't want *me* involved." Martin sprang to his feet. "Forget it!"

"You don't know for certain if he's trying to kill her now. And don't you forget you want to be governor. Murderers usually don't run for public office," Joshua reminded him. "You've been lucky, Martin. Howard hasn't begun to attack you personally. There's only been the rumors that you were seeing Parris while she was still married to Lawson. Both you and Parris will have to develop thick hides when Regina's illegitimacy becomes front page news."

"That's common knowledge. I haven't tried to hide the fact that Regina was born out of wedlock."

"You can't hide it. And Howard knows that. He's just waiting for an opening where everyone in the state will also know it. But nowadays it's accepted a lot more readily than it was years ago."

"It can't hurt me," Martin replied. His voice was filled with confidence.

"But becoming embroiled in a confrontation with your wife's ex-husband can. No one, not even Lawson, suspects you were responsible for attacking him, and that's how it will remain. You've asked me to protect Parris and I will."

Martin slipped his hands into the pockets of his slacks. Parris's words came rushing back. *Would you believe me if I said I was afraid to remain in Florida. Promise me you'll protect me.* She was crying out to him and he'd ignored her plea.

Joshua stood up. "I'll stay with Parris until you pick up Regina tomorrow. Good night, Martin." He walked out of the room, leaving Martin staring at the chair he had vacated.

Martin clenched and unclenched his teeth, his jaw throbbing, while he paced the floor. Never had he felt so helpless. He didn't want to believe that Parris was in any danger. Ten years and nothing had changed. When would it ever end?

Parris dropped a light kiss on Joshua's smooth cheek after giving Martin a lingering kiss on his smiling mouth. She took the chair facing the glass wall where she viewed the pool, deck, beach and the ocean. The rising sun did not brighten the sun porch until mid-day, making for the perfect spot to greet the morning.

"Good morning, Mommy." Regina skipped into the room,

already dressed for swimming. Parris held out her arms, and Regina climbed onto her lap. "Will you go swimming with me?"

Parris smoothed back raven-black hair from Regina's cheek. Closing her eyes, she pressed a kiss to her daughter's forehead. "Sure, angel." Regina did not know how close she had come to losing her mother. Opening her eyes, she smiled at Martin. Silently, she thanked him. He nodded, acknowledging her unspoken gratitude.

Joshua placed his napkin on the table. "I'd better be on my way if I'm going to make my flight."

"When are you coming back, Uncle Josh?"

Joshua rose to his feet, smiling down at Regina's upturned face. "For you, Monday."

Regina scrambled from her mother's lap. "I'll walk you to your car, Uncle Josh."

Parris waited for Joshua to leave, then directed all of her attention to Martin. He'd lost weight yet he had become more attractive than she had ever known him to be. His gray-streaked black hair was longer, brushing his shirt collar and his moustache was fuller, obscuring his upper lip. The band of paleness on his left wrist where he usually wore his watch, intensified the richness of his dark skin. He exuded an aura of power and sexual masculinity that made her unable to control her heart, mind or body. His physical presence was overwhelming.

"I noticed the schedule you put up on the board in the kitchen, Martin." She glanced away from his smiling face, watching a gull glide with the wind currents before swooping down to skim the water in search of food. "Why have you changed your itinerary?"

"If you think I'm going to leave you for three weeks you're insane, darling. There'll be enough activity between Fort Lauderdale and Miami to keep the momentum going until you're ready to rejoin the campaign."

Parris shrieked in delight, rushing from her chair and throwing her arms around his neck. He pulled her down to his lap. "Thank you, Martin." She kissed him soundly on the mouth.

His hand curved around the back of her head. Slowly, deliberately, he tasted her mouth. "You're welcome."

Parris inhaled the cologne on his smooth cheek. "I thought I'd lost you. When I saw that snake all I thought about…"

"Don't," Martin whispered, interrupting her. "It's gone."

Pulling back, Parris stared at the new lines around his eyes. Campaigning was taking its toll. There was no trace of boyishness left in Martin Diaz Cole; hardness, determination and something else she couldn't identify was evident by the steely look in his eyes. Her finger traced the curve of an eyebrow, the length of his nose and his lower lip.

His arms tightened on her body, and they held each other until Regina returned, breaking the spell where they had offered the healing they both sought.

Parris lay on a lounge chair, in the shade of several palm trees, watching Martin as he pretended to race Regina across the pool. Regina swam half the length of the pool before tiring. She squealed as he filled his mouth with water and sprayed her face.

They had spent the day swimming, picking up shells and finding a sand dollar along the beach. Martin barbecued franks, hamburgers and spareribs after they decided to picnic outdoors.

"No more, Daddy," Regina screamed. "Mommy, make him stop!"

"Stop, Martin." Parris was too full and too relaxed to sound effective.

Martin settled Regina on his shoulders and waded across the width of the pool. "Stop, Martin," he mimicked, hoisting Regina out of the pool. "Everyone out of the water, cupcake, or you're going to turn into a raisin."

Regina climbed out of the pool, racing toward the house, Martin staring at her tall thin body.

He made his way over to Parris, sitting down on a matching chair. "She's growing up so quickly it's frightening. Every time I see her she's changed."

Parris shifted, noting Martin's tortured expression. "Children don't wait, Martin. We can't tell them to put their lives on hold while we make our plans. They go on with growing up, and when we turn around they're gone."

He lay down, peering through the fronds of the overhead trees. "I'll have her for such a short time. In eight years she'll be eighteen, and by then I won't the only man in her life. Then it'll be a boyfriend, fiancé, college or whatever else a young woman is usually involved with. The years I've missed I'll never be able to recapture."

"You can't recapture the past," Parris countered.

He sat up, staring at her. "Who do I blame? Myself?"

Parris shook her head. "I accept the blame. All of it. I left you, not the other way around."

"Why?"

She swallowed painfully. She had to choose her words carefully. Sitting up, Parris swung her legs over the chair. "I was a coward," she admitted. "I wasn't brave or mature enough to stay and fight for you. It should not have mattered that your family didn't approve of me or that I wasn't married to you when I discovered myself pregnant. And because I was a coward, I ran and hid. I'd be hiding now if you hadn't come for me."

Martin stood up, pulling her up with him. He cradled her face between his hands. "Are you still hiding, Parris? Are you still afraid?"

"No," she confessed truthfully. "As long as I'm with you I'm not afraid."

Chapter 31

Martin walked into the bedroom and stopped short. Parris stood beside the bed, wearing only a pair of black lace bikini underpants. His body reacted violently.

She had carried and delivered a baby yet her belly was still flat and her hips firm. Only her breasts had changed; they were fuller, the areola darker and larger. She folded her hands on her hips, pulling back her shoulders and her breasts jutted out, heavy and lush as ripened fruit.

"I like the red," he said in a strangled voice, surprising her as she spun around.

She smiled at him. "There's not much to it."

He returned her smile. "That's why I like it."

She picked up a red silk strapless dress with a flaring skirt, holding it up in front of her. "It's rather risqué, don't you think?"

"You're risqué, Parris Cole," he teased. His eyes glittered when he remembered their rapacious lovemaking earlier that morning.

He continued to watch her as she stepped into the dress. Her long legs seemed to go on forever in the narrow red satin heels that added an additional three inches to her five-foot-eight-inch height.

"Hook me up please."

Martin moved closer to Parris, inhaling the cloying perfume on her glistening satiny brown skin. And for the first time since he'd begun campaigning he wanted out. It had taken only two days for him to settle into his new home and experience what it meant to be a husband and father—and he loved it.

Lowering his head, his lips feathered across the width of her scented bare shoulders. "You only have ten minutes to fix your face and hair before we leave."

Turning, Parris smiled up at him through her lashes. "I'll be ready." She kissed his cheek and pushed him gently. "Go, please."

Martin watched the swell of breasts rising and falling above the revealing décolleté of red silk. She's perfect, he mused. A perfect wife and a perfect mother.

"Martin!" Parris pleaded. His eyes revealed his hunger for her. If he didn't leave their bedroom neither one of them would attend the scheduled fund-raising event at a Fort Lauderdale sports complex.

She let out her breath as he turned on his heel and walked out of the bedroom. The phone rang and she picked it up after the first ring.

"Hello." There was only the sound of breathing. "Hello," she repeated another two times before she hung up. She wished she had a whistle to blow into the receiver. It would serve the pervert just right if she blew out his eardrum.

Parris sat down at her dressing table, quickly and expertly making up her face and styling her hair. She was ready when Martin returned to the bedroom.

Parris rose to her feet with the sixty thousand other spectators in the sports complex, cheering the musicians who gathered for the fund-raising event. As many as ten groups, Night Mood included, had combined their musical talents to host the Musicians for Cole extravaganza. She squeezed Regina's hand gently, smiling when noting the awe-struck expression on the child's face.

Regina cupped her hands to her mother's ear. "When is Uncle David coming on?" she shouted.

"He's up next."

A roar went up from the crowd from the upper deck of the

stadium and Parris glanced over her left shoulder. Several rows behind her, her gaze met those of the man with the large vein in his forehead. He smiled at her, nodded, then turned his attention back to the stage as shafts of light highlighted the members of Night Mood.

Parris turned her attention back to the stage, breathing heavily. What was he doing there? Had he followed her?

Don't lose it, Parris, she told herself. She couldn't start screaming in front of sixty thousand people that a man was stalking her because he wanted her dead. She didn't know him other than that he worked for a landscaping company she had contracted to put in her lawn and flower garden. She could not allow her fear to replace common sense. The man had every right to be where he was. He had paid his money to attend a fund-raising event.

The flashing lights ringed David Cole's raven hair in an aureole of gold. He held up his arms for silence. "Is everyone having a good time?" David crooned into a microphone. A deafening roar ensued.

I was, Parris thought, *having a good time until I saw the landscaper smiling at me.*

"Well, we aren't finished yet," David continued. "We have a very special guest here with us tonight." There was an eerie silence in the open-air stadium as the spectators waited in the humid air blowing off the Atlantic.

"I know that most of you have heard this man speak, but I wonder how many of you have heard him play. Perhaps if he decides to give up politics he could always play backup keyboards for our band."

David strutted across the stage like a peacock in a black tank top, black jeans and a pair of low-heeled ostrich-skin boots. He ran a hand through his hair and the light glinted off the gold hoop in his left ear. A woman screamed out his name. David paused, smiling. "Why, bless you." The stadium erupted in laughter. "I'm somewhat biased when it comes to our special guest because he happens to be my brother. Ladies and gentlemen, Martin Diaz Cole!"

Parris forgot about the man as her heart pounded relentlessly in her ears when she watched Martin make his way across the stage. The blazing spotlight followed his progress, illuminating his longer dark hair, midnight blue silk jacket, collarless shirt and linen slacks. He smiled at David, extending both arms above his head and giving him a high-five handshake.

The two brothers, tall, lean and muscled electrified the audience as screams shattered the night.

"Speech! Speech!" The word was chanted in the sultry air.

David shook his head, raising the microphone to his mouth. "No speeches tonight. Just music and your vote in November." He moved closer to the edge of the stage and blew a kiss to Parris and Regina who were seated only five rows from the stage area.

"Tonight Night Mood is going to give you a taste of soul and salsa." He placed the microphone on its stand and took his position behind a set of congas. His fingers moved like softly falling rain as they caressed the stretched surface of the drums and the rhythmical sounds of Africa and the Caribbean filled the stadium.

Parris watched, transfixed as the rhythm of the drums throbbed passionately, reaching inside of her and sweeping away her tension and fear where she was transported back to the land of her ancestors. The beat was fluid, restrained and sensual.

She recalled the time she had heard the musical composition and she closed her eyes, reliving the first time she'd danced with Martin. He had asked her if she was familiar with *the fire.* She'd admitted she hadn't been but he soon changed that. She felt the fire and her world shook.

Martin was the consummate lover, always making certain she was fulfilled before taking his own satisfaction. He was selfless in bed.

She couldn't take her eyes off him as his fingers rippled across the double keyboard like flowing water. The music pulsed from the powerful sound system, lights flashing wildly in various colors. Every seat in the stadium was empty as the crowd swayed and gyrated in the aisles.

The sounds of the jungle were hypnotic, spellbinding. The

force of the music had everyone stomping, clapping and dancing in a powerful grip beyond their control.

Parris wasn't certain when it all ended because she found herself screaming as much as the others. Only Joshua's hand on her shoulder broke the spell.

Suddenly she wondered if anyone had observed her reacting like a star-struck adolescent. Clutching Regina's hand, she followed the stadium security personnel to the stage. The flared red silk dress swirled around her long legs and a chorus of whistles followed her progress across the stage. Her knees were weak and her hand shook as she extended it to Martin.

He pressed her to his chest, his heart pounding like jungle drums. She stared up at his face and recognized the wild glazed look in his eyes. It was as if he had been injected with a powerful stimulant. Martin Diaz Cole was high. High on power!

Regina stood between her parents, trying to hide from the thousands of people staring at her from out of the darkness of the warm spring night. Martin leaned over and picked her up, raising her arm to wave at the people who had come to enjoy a night filled with music, and to catch a glimpse of a candidate they could relate to.

Without warning, hundreds of red, white and blue balloons were released from an overhead net and they floated out over the stadium. The crowd, momentarily distracted, did not see Martin, Parris and Regina when they were escorted backstage.

Stepping over cables and skirting lights, they left the stadium and walked to where Joshua waited by a car. He helped Regina and Parris into the automobile.

Martin shook his head in amazement, grinning. Joshua, feeling his excitement, gave him a quick rough embrace.

"How did it feel, buddy?"

Martin laid his hand on Joshua's shoulder. "Good, Josh. Damn good!"

"I've got her set up."

"That's what you told me the last time."

"I have a schedule of all of their public appearances."

> "Which means what?"
> "Everything can be planned in advance."
> "It sounds good. Do it soon."
> "I plan to."

Parris thoroughly enjoyed the three week respite she had been given from campaigning with Martin. He had changed his schedule where he made public appearances in many of the major cities along the east coast but returned home each night.

His campaign manager, while agreeing to the arrangement, had become uncomfortable with his candidate's unavailability. He wanted an at-home taped interview with Martin, his wife and daughter, but Parris quickly disagreed. She would not allow television cameras or personnel into her home. However, she agreed to accompany Martin when he resumed his fast-paced stops across the state June first.

She dressed with special care for a West Palm Beach fund-raising dinner. It would the last time she and Martin would appear publicly in their former hometown until the election.

"I must admit that you look lovely, Parris."

Parris smiled at her mother-in-law's reflection in the mirror. "Thank you, M.J." She studied her own reflection, adjusting the heavy beaded necklace of lapis lazuli with a center of pear-shaped lapis lazuli, mobé pearls and diamonds. Elegant mobé pearl drop earrings, suspended from diamonds, hung from her lobes. Her strapless dress in organdy with a beaded pearl-seeded bodice and two tiers of ruffles banded in cobalt blue satin flowed into yards of pristine white, ending several inches above the floor in the same blue satin that covered the top of the bodice, belt and ruffles.

M.J. pursed her crimson mouth, while lightly powdering her nose. "It's about time Martin decided to do something in his hometown. Too many people were saying that he acts more like a musician than a politician."

Parris shot a baleful glance at the woman exquisitely gowned in white crêpe with shimmering triangle insets of bugle beads along the shoulders and at her neckline.

"The Gold Coast is not the state of Florida. All of the money in Palm Beach won't get Martin elected if registered voters don't go to the polls and vote for him."

"I'm afraid you misunderstand me, Parris," M.J. said quickly. Her face was flushed with embarrassment. "I merely meant that Martin must be highly visible if he's to win."

Parris picked up her sequin evening purse. She and M.J. had managed to be civil to each other since she had moved to Fort Lauderdale and, wanting to please Martin, Parris was more than happy to have it remain that way.

M.J. sighed in relief, smiling her attractive dimpled smile. "We'd better get back to the ballroom before Sammy and Martin send out a search party for us."

Both women left the powder room at the West Palm Beach Polo Club, rejoining the invited guests at the elegant fund-raising gala event. Speeches and dinner behind them, the large crowd danced, or stood around in small groups talking and drinking. When the affair had been advertised, the thousand dollar-a-plate dinner was sold out within days. West Palm Beach did not hesitate to rally behind its native son.

Parris smiled and nodded as she made her way across the ballroom. Smiling had become as natural to her as breathing.

"Do you think you could save a dance for an old man?"

Parris focused her bright smile on Samuel Cole and linked her bare arm through the muscular forearm covered by the black fabric of his tuxedo. From the heightened color in his red-brown face, she suspected he had exceeded his quota of his favored scotch and soda.

"Fishing for a compliment, Sammy? I'd put my money on you any day than on a man twenty years younger."

Samuel gathered her in a firm embrace. "Tell that to my wife," he whispered against her cheek. He led Parris into the quick smooth steps of a foxtrot. In spite of his large bulk he was light on his feet and as graceful as a professional dancer. "My son has everything he could ever want."

Parris pulled back slightly, staring up at her father-in-law.

"Why would you say that?" She registered the faraway expression in his dark eyes.

"He has the woman he always wanted for his wife and a beautiful child he can claim as his own."

"I don't think you've done too badly, Sammy."

He blinked several times, then gave her a sad smile. "You're right, Parris." She thanked him effusively when the dance number ended and followed his lead to the bar.

"A little champagne, Parris?"

She nodded, and he asked the bartender for her champagne and a scotch and soda. She sipped the dry bubbly wine while Samuel downed his drink. Over the rim of her glass she spied Joshua and smiled. He acknowledged her greeting with a slight nod of his head. He also was dressed in formal attire and appeared to be as comfortable in it as he was in his casual clothing. She beckoned for him and Samuel frowned when he noted her gesture.

"I must get back to M.J.," he explained, walking away from Parris.

She couldn't understand Samuel's need to get away from Joshua, and she still couldn't understand the Coles' disdain of Martin's friend. Nancy and Juliana ignored Joshua completely while David tolerated his presence. Samuel and M.J. were openly hostile, seemingly unable to remain in the same room with him.

Joshua's right arm curved around Parris's waist. "You are exquisite, Parris." His pale green gaze swept over the crowded room. "It's better than we could have ever expected. Everything seems to be falling into place with nothing short of perfection. The candidates are scheduled to appear in a live television debate within two weeks, and the straw polls predict Martin to be the winner."

Parris nodded and took a sip of her champagne. How could she tell Joshua that she was ambivalent about Martin possibly winning the election? That she loved her husband and wanted him to fulfill his destiny, but not as governor of the state?

Joshua glanced at her unreadable expression. "You don't seem too pleased," he said perceptively. His arm around her waist dropped.

"Does it really matter whether I'm pleased or not?" Her voice was as expressionless as her face. She grimaced, feeling a tightness in her chest. She took another sip of her drink, trying to alleviate the heaviness pressing against her throat and chest.

"Joshua." Her voice was only a whisper and she couldn't control her shaking hands.

"What's wrong?"

Parris couldn't move, her limbs felt as if they were lead. The overhead lights swayed and dimmed. The pressure on her chest increased until she couldn't draw a breath without the pain knifing her heart.

Joshua stared, watching the natural color drain from her face as moisture dotted her forehead. The pulse in her neck throbbed erratically, causing him to feel a rush of fear. Her slight frame swayed weakly against his side, and he knew he had to act and act quickly. He caught her before she fell. Shifting, he grabbed the arm of a man standing nearby. "Get Martin Cole for me! We need to get her to a hospital."

Chapter 32

Jacket and bow tie discarded, Martin paced the confines of the hospital waiting room like a big cat on the prowl.

"Martin, let's go get some coffee."

He ran his hand over his hair for what seemed to be the hundredth time since he raced into the emergency room with Parris.

"I can't, Josh. I can't leave her until I find out if she's going to be all right."

"I'll bring some back for you." Joshua picked up his tuxedo jacket, slipping his arms into it and concealing the firearm secured in a shoulder holster.

Martin couldn't acknowledge Joshua's offer of comfort and friendship because he'd retreated to a place of nothingness where he ceased to think or feel. There was no way he could envision his life without Parris.

I can't lose her. I can't lose her. The litany played over and over in his head. He dropped down heavily to a plush tulip-shaped chair, covering his face with his hands.

What was happening to him, to them? Who was this nameless, faceless person who wanted Parris dead?

Joshua was certain it wasn't Owen Lawson. Or if it was Lawson he had employed experts. Joshua had him under surveillance at his home and had monitored the telephones at Lawson's private security business. There was nothing which indicated he was remotely responsible for the attempts on Parris's life.

A Styrofoam cup, filled with steaming black coffee pulled Martin back to the present. He took the cup, staring down into the muddy depths. "You know I really didn't believe her, Josh. I kept telling myself she was paranoid." Sighing heavily, his shoulders sagged in defeat. "She never fully recovered from Lawson's attack. There were times when she'd wake up in a cold sweat from the nightmares."

Joshua took the seat beside Martin. "Parris is as emotionally stable as you or I. Her fears are very real." His mouth tightened in frustration. "Whoever is behind this is good; very good."

Martin placed the cup on a side table. "If Lawson isn't behind this, then who is?"

"Only Parris knows that."

He picked up the foam cup, taking a long swallow of the black bitter brew. "And I have to get her to tell me what she's afraid of."

Joshua stared at a discarded paper cup under a chair on the other side of the room. "You asked me to protect Parris because she was afraid of something or someone. If you can't get her to tell you who or what it is there are ways to get her to talk."

"What are you saying?" His eyes narrowed suspiciously. "Are you suggesting a truth serum?" His voice was a hoarse whisper.

"That's one possibility," Joshua stated without blinking.

Martin recoiled in shock. "You're asking me to deliberately drug my wife? Don't you think she's been drugged enough?"

"You would have no part in it. I would administer and monitor the drug. Within fifteen to thirty minutes we'll have everything we'll need to find who's behind these very clever attempts on Parris's life. Sodium amytal is quite effective when administered properly."

Martin exploded with a raw curse, startling the nurse entering the waiting room. He ignored her, glaring at Joshua. "You're talking about the woman I love, not some spy who's been passing military secrets, Joshua."

Joshua returned Martin's stare. "How are you going to hide

this from the press? Right now every tongue in West Palm Beach is wagging about how Martin Cole's wife O.D. at his fund-raising. It's all going to come back to haunt you," he predicted.

"Right now I don't give a damn about anything anyone has to say."

"Mr. Cole?"

Martin glanced up at the nurse. His dark eyes mirrored his anxiety. "Yes."

"Come with me, sir. Dr. Austin will see you now."

"Your wife is recovering quickly, considering the amount of Haldol and alcohol mixture found in her blood. The fact that she's young and in excellent health played an important part in our not losing her."

Martin frowned. "What is Haldol?"

The youthful-looking black doctor stared at Martin behind his wire-rimmed glasses. "Haldol is a tranquilizer." He paused as Martin leaned forward on his chair. "Has your wife been under a doctor's care for…"

"No," Martin interrupted, coming to his feet. "She won't even take an aspirin."

Dr. Austin blinked several times, resembling an owl with his heavy-lidded appearance. Lacing his fingers together on the top of his desk, he glanced up. "Mr. Cole, the toxicology report indicates Haldol in your wife's blood. Apparently she's been taking or had taken the drug without your knowledge. It's been known to occur." He managed a comforting smile. "We've counteracted the Haldol with something called Cogentin. We'd like to keep her a few days to monitor her blood pressure and electrolytes. Then you can have her back good as new."

The clear liquid dripped down the tube into Parris's veins, silently signaling the ordeal which had almost cost her her life. The newspaper's headlines glared up at her—GOV HOPEFUL SPOUSE FELLED IN DRUG O.D. She pushed the offending periodical off the bed, scattering the pages to the floor.

"Who is trying to kill you, Parris?"

"I don't know," she answered slowly. Her voice was low and breathless. Sighing heavily, she closed her eyes and pressed deeper against the mound of pillows cradling her sallow face. "I don't know." And she didn't know. She didn't know who the man was who threatened her life; her life and Martin's.

"You don't know who is trying to kill you, and you don't know how that tranquilizer got into your drink. Do you know what I think?"

"What?" She refused to look at him.

"I think you deliberately took those pills to get Martin to drop out of the race," he said, hoping to penetrate her wall of resistance. He wanted and needed a name.

Martin walked into Parris's hospital room, his face contorted in rage. "Get away from her! This is going to be the first and last time that I'll tell you not to interfere with me and my wife. This involves family."

Sudden anger lit Joshua's cold eyes as his body stiffened in shock. For a long moment he stared at Martin. "Then just this once try to think of me as family."

"She's been through enough without you maligning her," Martin said in a softer tone.

Joshua motioned to Martin and both men stepped outside the room. "All I want is answers, Martin."

"I don't have answers, Joshua. How do you explain it? Parris wasn't out of your sight all of last night. When she went into the ladies lounge my mother was with her. We all drink champagne from the same bottle and no one was drugged except for her. Who could've gotten close enough to drop those pills in her glass?"

"The pills were placed in the glass prior to the waiter pouring the champagne."

Martin leaned closer to Joshua. "Why didn't you tell me about this before?"

"I wanted to wait until I gathered something concrete. I've been unable to locate the waiter who served her that drink. The club hired him at the last moment to fill in for a regular who had called in sick. When I find this piece of garbage we'll probably uncover who hired him to do their dirty work."

Martin pushed his hands into the pockets of his slacks, shoulders slumping forward. This feeling of helplessness was foreign and frightening, and at that moment he would willingly give up all he possessed to keep Parris safe.

"Do whatever needs to be done," Martin said quietly.

A slight nod was the only indicator of Joshua's acquiescence. He *had* to find the person or persons responsible for the attempts on Parris's life before they struck again; perhaps achieving success.

Parris lay in bed, staring at the grim expression on Martin's face. He reminded her of Joshua. Both of them had affected silent glares that made her want to hide away in the bedroom.

Her gaze shifted to the greenish-purpling bruises on the back of her left hand from the constant tube feedings. Slender fingers massaged her throat. It was still sore from the tube that had been used to purge her stomach of the powerful tranquilizer.

"I will not become a prisoner in my own home," she croaked ineffectively.

Her impudent response vibrated on Martin's taut nerve endings. He leaned over her prone body. His fingers caught her shoulders in a firm grip.

"I'm giving the orders, Parris, not you. I will tell you when to eat, sleep and when to bathe. You are never to be more than six feet away from me at any time. I have a tap on the phones so every call will be monitored and traced, and no one will be allowed on or off this property without my knowing of it. So you'd better get used to obeying me, *Mrs. Cole*. Cross me once and you'll look for your phantom killer to relieve you of your misery."

"Don't threaten me, Martin."

He loosened his hold. "I'm not threatening you, Parris. I only want to let you know what to expect."

Parris closed her eyes, sighing audibly. "I know what to expect. I'm going to be a prisoner."

"You wouldn't be a prisoner if you told who was trying to kill you."

"I don't know, Martin. How many times do I have to say it." He stared at her unblinking, then released her and stalked out of the bedroom.

She squeezed her eyes tightly to stop the tears from escaping. She'd been back in Florida for six months and she hadn't told Martin about her abduction. But how long much longer would it be before she was forced to tell him?

How many times in ten years hadn't she replayed the words in her head? *"I was paid to get you out of Florida. I'm suppose to kill you once we cross the state line. I don't murder babies. Once you leave you can't ever come back. If you ever tell Martin Cole about our little meeting and chat, I'll cut him up until there's nothing left of him."*

The threat was repeated during the ride from the New York airport to midtown Manhattan. *"If you ever find yourself back in Florida,"* the raspy-voice man said, *"not that you should. But if you do then don't forget what I told you about telling Martin Cole about our little bargain. I'll force you to watch while I gut him."*

The tears flowed and after she was drained she fell asleep; with sleep came the nightmare. Vivid and violent.

True to his word, Parris became a virtual prisoner. If Martin didn't watch her, Joshua did. Joshua rarely spoke and when he did it was as if they were strangers instead of friends. She had no way of knowing Joshua blamed himself for the drugging incident. Both times she'd faced danger it had been his careless-ness that almost cost her her life. He made a solemn vow it would not happen again.

"I need an advance."

"You won't get another dime from me until you do away with Parris Cole."

"Look, I owe some money."

"That's not my problem."

The break in the telephone indicated the call was over. And my life is over, thought the man with the prominent vein. He had to get some money—quick.

Chapter 33

Parris found an empty chair, away from the crush of people where food was served, and flopped wearily onto it, drawing the back of her hand over her moist forehead.

The hot June weather had given way to the oppressive July humidity yet the guests did not seem to be bothered by the sultry air blanketing the Fourth of July celebration. They had been granted a week's reprieve from the fast-paced campaigning they all had been forced to undergo during the past month.

Balloons, ribbons and bunting in red, white and blue festooned tables, chairs, tree trunks, branches and shrubs while a dozen banquet tables groaned with platters filled with dishes as varied as the attendees.

Casual attire was the norm: shorts, swimsuits, sundresses and anything else that allowed for an expanse of flesh to catch whatever cooling breeze deemed to avail itself.

Parris sipped her sparkling water slowly, observing the many people she had come to know well from behind the lenses of a pair of oversized sunglasses. The chilled glass felt refreshing between her palms as she finished the drink. Tilting the glass and grasping an ice cube, she slid it down the length of one bare arm before repeating the action with the other.

"I can think of a better way to cool off."

"Tell me about it and I'll take you up on the offer," Parris replied, staring up at the familiar face looming above her.

"A dip in the ocean," came the reply.

"Even the Atlantic is boiling today."

"You're probably right about that." The dark eyes under bushy white brows swept quickly over Parris's face. "How are you feeling?"

"Well enough, Sammy."

"Are you sure?"

"Of course I'm sure," She removed her sunglasses. "See—no circles and my eyes are clear."

Sammy settled onto a chair beside her, his forehead furrowed. "I worry about you, Parris. You had a close call with that drug overdose, and now Martin tells me that you're imagining that someone is trying to kill you."

She was momentarily stunned. Sammy had never openly expressed any concern about her, and she was certain he had never forgiven Martin for marrying her.

"It's not my imagination," she muttered defensively.

"Don't get upset," he countered. "I'm on your side. I've never liked politics and I don't like Martin dragging you around with him and putting you on display like a museum piece. You need to be in Fort Lauderdale, taking care of your lovely house, giving parties or having babies."

She ignored his remark about babies. "Four more months and it'll be behind all of us." That is if I can survive, she thought.

"But what happens if Martin doesn't win? Is he going to try again?"

Parris gave Samuel a sidelong glance. "Martin has said he'll return to ColeDiz if he loses." Her stomach tightened in apprehension. "Has he told you differently?"

Samuel shifted on the webbed chair. He stared at her before saying quietly, "No."

She stared back at her father-in-law, realizing what should've been apparent the night David revealed Samuel did not approve of Martin going into politics. He didn't want Martin to leave

ColeDiz. Perhaps he was afraid David would not be able to pick up the reins from Martin.

Her gaze swept over a small group, locating Martin. Wearing a blue baseball cap to shield his eyes from the blazing sun, he laughed and gestured with volunteers from his Miami campaign headquarters. His feet and chest were bare although he'd slipped a pair of jeans over his swim trunks. He had opened his parents' home to everyone to take advantage of the swimming pool and tennis courts.

Her clear brown eyes caressed his tall lean form. "I think you've lost him, Sammy," she stated calmly. "If he wins the election, you've lost him. And if he loses, you've still lost him. I don't think Martin will be content to sit in an office and negotiate corporate procedures ever again."

Samuel's bushy silver eyebrows lowered. "And how do you feel about all of this, Parris?"

Her pride would not permit her to reveal her mixed emotions. How could she tell Samuel that she was as unsure of her own future as he was of his son's. "How I feel is irrelevant. Martin is my husband and I must support him. At least publicly." She turned her head, watching Samuel study her. "I love Martin, Sammy. He and I may not agree on everything, but despite our differences we'll survive because of our love for each other."

Samuel sighed, smiling. "That's what I want to hear. You've become a true Cole. We never oppose one another." His face split into a wide grin. "Now, are you going to agree to allow me and M.J. to look after Regina so you and Martin can spend some quality time together?"

"Yes," she replied softly. Her eyes filled with excitement and anticipation.

She had gotten Martin to cancel her personal appearances once again. Once the hubbub concerning her drug overdose faded she was expected to resume traveling with him. The projected date was July seventeen—the day after Regina's tenth birthday.

* * *

A riot of color greeted the dawning day as Parris stood outside of her bedroom, watching the brightening rays of the rising sun kiss the faces of the flowers in the garden.

Sunrise was her favorite time of the day. Everything began clean, new and unique. Each new day would be different from the one before it, never to be duplicated.

Old-fashioned roses mingled comfortably with silvery lamb's-ears, daisies and feverfew. She smiled. Her favorite flowers were spires of foxgloves, snowy phlox and irises. Whenever she had the opportunity to stay home, the rooms were always filled with the fragrance of fresh-cut flowers.

She stared out past the garden and beyond. Somewhere out there was a small private army of men Martin had hired to protect their property. She rarely saw them, but she knew they were there.

She hadn't answered the telephone or the door since her drugging, and she never went out without Martin or Joshua accompanying her. She had become a prisoner in a prison without bars.

Returning to the bedroom, she flexed her bare feet into the deep pile of the pale carpeting, drying her toes of the early morning dew.

"I must be losing my touch if I can't convince my wife to stay in bed with me beyond sunrise," came the silken voice behind her.

Her slender hands covered the dark brown arms circling her waist. She leaned back against the strong body pressed against her back.

"I decided to leave it while I still had the strength."

Martin's nose nuzzled her neck. "You don't need your strength, darling." His voice and warm breath made her shiver. "I'll feed you, bathe you and love you. What else would you need?" He turned her around, smiling down at her. "For the next three days I'm your slave."

Her gaze searched his dark handsome face. Reaching up, she pushed back the gray-streaked hair off his forehead. His black eyes blazed with passion and she felt her pulses racing with desire. His jaw tightened under her fingertips as they inched slowly down his face. She detected the increase in his respiration as he stood rigid, watching her from under lowered lids.

Martin found her a ravishing vision of shimmering ivory lace and silk. A floor-length gown concealed her body from his hungry gaze, but a deep plunging V of lace permitted him to visually feast on her full breasts.

"Why can't I ever tire of you, Parris? Why is it you force me to crave you more and more every time I make love to you? What spell have you cast over me that creates this weakness in my brain and in my loins?"

She lowered her head to his chest. "It's the same with me," she confessed, pressing closer to his naked body and communicating her own need as she rubbed her middle against his groin. "I love you, Martin," she whispered, feeling his sex harden and push against her thigh.

His large hands were gentle as he slipped the narrow straps off her shoulders, the gown sliding down and settling in a pool of silk around her feet.

His fingers grazed her breasts, sending flashes of delight throughout her body with the soft caresses. His fingers tightened with his rising desire and her nipples swelled to a pebbly hardness. A soft whimper, deep within her throat, and the hot touch of her hand on his engorged sex hurled Martin over the edge.

There was no time for preliminaries as he picked her up and joined their bodies, her legs encircling his waist. Moving backwards, Martin fell back to the bed, his body vibrating his uncontrollable urge to possess her totally.

Reversing their positions, he rotated his hips as he thrust deeply into her hot, wet flesh. He slowed, then stopped, pinning her to the bed, unable to continue because he was afraid it would be over too quickly.

Parris's fingertips sank into the hard muscles of his hips. Martin's hardness filled her with a craving she had never experienced before. She also feared moving because she wanted the sweet burning fire to last forever.

"Don't move," she panted against his throat.

"To ask me not to breathe would be a lot easier, darling," he countered between clenched teeth.

Liquid fire swept through her body, bringing tears to her eyes. This new feeling frightened her. In the past she had always assumed control in bed. Now it was Martin and the fear spiraled with the trembling, straining passion.

"Martin," she whispered.

"I know, baby," he gasped. "I feel it, too."

"Martin!" This time she couldn't hide her weakness from him. He moved, his hips rolling and surging heavily against hers and her flesh opened and closed tightly around his hot sex.

Martin strained against her, then his control was shattered with the turbulence of their lovemaking. It swept them away in a fevered mating unmatched by any of their previous encounters.

The pleasure Parris gave him was pure and explosive, and he was drawn into her as she rose to receive his strong driving thrusts. Cradling her face between his hands, he stared down at the waves of excitement tightening her flushed features.

At the moment of her release, her eyes flew open, then closed as deep, gasping shudders ripped through her body. His mouth covered hers and he felt the heat of her breath as she breathed the last of her passion into his mouth.

Parris's last sighing moan signalled the beginning of his own gratification as he surrendered himself to the explosive ecstasy she always aroused in him.

Martin stood in the corner of the game room, watching Parris lean over the pool table as she concentrated on her next move. He thought he had "taught" her to shoot pool, and he was mildly surprised when she beat him after the second game.

"You've done this before, haven't you?"

Parris lined up her cue. "What makes you say that?"

Moving closer, he stared at her as she bit down on her lower lip, his dark hungry eyes drawn to her mouth. Her pursed mouth conjured up what he'd been reduced to when she matched his unbridled passion. He'd become putty in her hands, being shaped and molded into whatever form she desired.

He frowned, thinking about the other women he'd known. Not one of them had ever been able to come close to Parris when he remembered their schemes to get him to marry them.

Even after losing Parris, he found himself comparing every woman he met to her. It took a while to realize that the others tried too hard to please him.

He hadn't known whether it was his name, money or maybe himself, but they constantly tried to impress him with prearranged gimmicks or faked responses; and more than once he'd leave them before they could begin their rehearsed performances.

Parris never hesitated telling him what she wanted or didn't want. It was as if it didn't matter if she angered him, and he often wondered if she inherently knew that he would never give her up or leave her.

His hands tightened possessively around the smooth cue. Parris would be his until he stopped breathing.

Parris missed her shot and swore softly under her breath. "I could hear you praying for me to miss that one."

Martin slowly chalked the tip of his cue, smiling. "Now, why would I want to take advantage of a *novice,* darling?"

She pushed a fringe of bangs off her forehead, flashing a mysterious smile. "I suppose you realize I've played before."

Martin stroked his moustache with a forefinger. "What would ever put that notion into my head, darling," he drawled in feigned surprise.

The soft chiming of the telephone preempted her reply as Martin walked over to answer it. *"¡Dios mio! . . ."* M.J. sobbed in Spanish.

He felt his heart lurch. *"¿Qué pasa?"* he questioned in the same language.

"I can't find her, Martin!"

Trying to slow down his pounding heart, Martin took a deep breath, closing his eyes. "Start from the beginning, Mother. Who can't you find?" he continued in Spanish.

"She was here, and when I went back for her she was gone."

A knot coiled in the pit of his stomach and somehow he knew the answer before asking the question. "Who?"

"Regina," came the dreaded answer through a heartbreaking wave of tears.

He caught a glimpse of Parris's large eyes staring at him. He couldn't mention Regina's name. Not yet.

"Listen to me, Mother. I want you to look again. I'll be there as soon as I can."

Depressing the hook, he turned his back to avoid Parris's questioning eyes. Methodically he dialed seven numbers and waited for a response. The seconds ticked off mercilessly while he waited.

"What's happening Martin?" Parris questioned. He didn't answer her, the telephone receiver pressed to his ear. She caught hold of his arm, her fingernails biting in to the tender flesh on his wrist. "Is something wrong with Regina?"

"Kirkland."

Martin let out his breath when he heard the reply, ignoring the bite of Parris's nails. "Joshua, I need you."

"What's up, buddy."

He closed his eyes before bringing himself to reveal the news he was certain would unhinge Parris. "M.J. just called to tell me that she can't find Regina."

"I'll be in West Palm when you arrive," came the stilted reply before the line went dead.

Chapter 34

If she hadn't held onto Martin she would've collapsed to the floor.

"Let's go," Martin ordered, pulling her along with him as he raced from the room.

Parris did not remember anything until Martin shoved her into the car to begin the wild drive which would take them northward up the coast to West Palm Beach. She was numb—her brain refusing to acknowledge the scene of ten years ago. First her and now Regina. Someone had abducted her baby.

Martin was silent during the trip. His expressionless face led her to believe he thought she was responsible for the child's disappearance. There were so many things she wanted to say, but couldn't. Who would want to harm an innocent little girl? Who hated her so much that they would attack the one closest to her? What had she done to evoke such hatred? What crime had she committed except to fall in love with Martin Cole?

M.J. twisted a square of linen around her delicate fingers as she spoke, her eyes red and swollen from weeping. "She had lunch with me and when Nancy and the girls came over she went swimming with them. I promised her that we would go out for dinner, and that's why she refused Nancy's offer to spend the night." She blotted her moist cheeks. "At first I thought she'd changed her mind when I couldn't find her. But I knew she would never go anywhere without telling me. I...I called Nancy but she didn't have her. Nancy said she left Regina playing with the litter of pups."

"What time did you last see her?"

M.J. looked at Joshua, not displaying any of her usual hostility. "It had to be sometime between one and two."

"What the hell is he doing here?" Everyone turned in the direction of the booming voice.

"Please, Sammy. Not today," came M.J.'s soft plea.

"Just answer my question and there won't be any trouble," Sammy warned.

"There's enough trouble without you adding to it," Martin shouted at his father. "My daughter is missing!"

Samuel ignored Joshua's presence, looking at each of them. "Missing how?"

Joshua stood up. "No one can find her. Your wife fears she's been kidnapped."

Samuel swallowed, sinking down heavily to a chair. "Someone came here—on my property and kidnapped my granddaughter?"

Joshua's cold eyes drilled Samuel. "Yes, old man. Do you want me to say it in another language for you?"

Samuel shook his head. "Who would want to take the child?"

Joshua's eyes and expression mirrored rage when he stared across the room at Parris. "That's what I'm going to find out. I think it's about time Parris, Martin and I had a private talk."

Martin sat in the library in a corner while Joshua took charge. Never did he think he would feel the emptiness, the loss he now felt. The little girl had been a part of his life for little more than six months and suddenly he felt as if someone had cut out a piece of his heart, leaving him to bleed to death—slowly.

Regina, who was so much a part of him and Parris; the tiny being they had created through their very intimate expression of love. Regina, who had been so pleased with finding her father and sharing her love with him. Regina, who discovered the delight of having a grandmother and grandfather spoil her. Regina, whose very smile brightened his day and made him plan for her future. Regina, whom he had grown to love beyond description.

"I want you to tell me everything, Parris," Joshua warned quietly. "And if you attempt to leave anything out *I will* drug you and get what I want without your cooperation."

Parris was numbed and she couldn't think. "I was threatened and paid to leave Florida and Martin," she began slowly.

"Who threatened you?"

She stared down at the blood red and royal blue pattern on the Aubusson rug. "That I don't know. The man who abducted me said someone hired him to get me out of Florida and away from Martin."

"Why did he want you out of Florida?"

She covered her face with her hands. "I don't know. He was supposed to kill me." She uncovered her face, her eyes filled with pain. "He didn't because he knew I was pregnant." She shook her head in disbelief. "I don't know how he knew, but I'd only received the results of the test that night." Tears were now streaming down her cheeks.

Martin crossed the room and stood over her. "Why didn't you tell me?"

"I couldn't…I just couldn't," she sobbed, unable to look at him. "He said if I told you he would kill you. And then he'd wait until my baby was born then kill it too. I would be left alone. I would be left alone," she repeated quietly.

Martin pulled her limp body from the chair. "You couldn't because you didn't love me enough to trust me. Did you really think I wouldn't have been able to protect you if I'd known about this? What the hell do you take me for?"

"Don't," she pleaded, closing her eyes.

Martin shook her. "I kept asking you and you wouldn't tell me."

Joshua caught Martin's arm. "Let her go, buddy. I believe your wife has more to tell me."

Martin rounded on Joshua. "How much more could there

be?" he ranted. "Her playing mute all of these years has kept us apart and has put not only her life but Regina's in jeopardy!"

Joshua stared down at Parris's grief-stricken face. "Is there anything else I should know, Parris?"

She sniffled loudly, wiping away the tears with her fingers. "I was blackmailed. The amount I received was the exact amount I received for my divorce settlement."

Both men stared at each other. Joshua nodded and Martin acknowledged the unspoken gesture as they turned to leave.

Parris saw them leaving and panicked. "Where are you going?" Her eyes were enormous pools in her tawny-brown face.

Joshua turned, giving her a lethal glare. "I'm going to see if I can find your blackmailer before I look for my niece."

She felt as if a hand had closed on her heart. "What are you talking about?"

Martin shot a quick glance at Joshua. "Well, since we're into true confessions I suppose you should know that Joshua Kirkland is my brother."

Her life had come full circle. This time she waited for her heart, instead of her face, to heal. It was the fourth day since Regina's disappearance, and each day found Parris dying, little by little. She ate only enough to keep herself alive and stopped hoping, thinking and looking for the next sunrise.

The humid air, rising above the glassy surface of a nearby lake, cast a gray pall over the lushness of the verdant lawn and gardens of the Cole property. She memorized the intricate geometric designs of the boxwood garden, fascinated by the precision of the meticulously maintained area.

A shadow blocked out the warm rays of the rising sun, and she glanced up quickly to find Joshua staring down at her with a faraway expression on his face. She felt like a dissected specimen on a slide under a microscope as his light green eyes examined her closely.

She hadn't seen him since the day M.J. informed them of Regina's disappearance. The shadows under his eyes accentuated their compelling paleness in a face drawn and lined with exhaustion.

The damp morning air curled her hair tightly around her face and despite her fragile appearance there was a sense of strength in her slim body. "You've heard something." The inquiry came out like a statement.

"Finally," he admitted. He hoped the news, even if it wasn't what she wanted to hear, would lift her from the course of self-condemnation she had initiated.

Her eyes flooded with tears of relief and she held out trembling hands to the one person she entrusted her last hope. His face swam before her teary vision as a heart-rendering sob escaped her constricted throat. She fell against him.

Joshua held her gently, alarmed at the slimness of her body and the starved, haunted look in her clear brown eyes. His arms tightened on her waist as he unselfishly offered his strength. Her tears soaked his shirt. His hands moved up to cradle her face. His thumb moved over her quivering mouth and he lowered his head until his mouth was only inches from hers.

"I can't touch Lawson, Parris," he whispered. "It's too risky. If I do anything to Lawson and someone found out, then my association with Martin would make him suspect."

She stiffened in his embrace. "Owen had Regina kidnapped?"

He led her over to a wrought iron bench, sitting and pulling her down with him. He held her hands firmly within his grip. "I don't believe he was responsible for you being blackmailed, but someone had to get to him to find out all about you. You dated the man, married him and lived with him. He had to let the blackmailer know how much he had given you as a divorce settlement."

Her eyes searched Joshua's face frantically. "Are you saying someone blackmailed Owen?"

Joshua nodded. "I think someone may have put some pressure on him. But we won't know that until a friend of mine arrives tonight."

"Who's this friend?"

Joshua stared over her head. "Someone who's the best when

it comes to interrogation. The only other thing I can say is that he's an expert when it comes to rescue missions. He'll get Regina back," he reassured Parris as she closed her eyes.

She prayed as she had never prayed before. And in her pain she felt a thread of hope. The hope she would get her daughter back—alive.

Parris found Martin in the library with David, pacing the floor. David sat on a chair, his face in his hands.

"What's wrong?" she asked. Had they heard something? Had something happened to Regina and they didn't want her to know? "What the hell is going on, Martin?"

David's head came up. "Tell her, Martin. She has a right to know."

Martin stopped pacing, glaring at David. His face was covered with the growth of a three-day beard. "No!"

"You're a fool!" David spat out. He rose to his feet and stalked out of the room.

Green lights glinted in Parris's eyes. "You'd better tell me what's going on, or so help me I'll…"

"You'll do what?" Martin asked, the veins in his neck bulging. "Haven't you done enough? I've lost Regina. I can't lose you, too."

"What are you saying?" Her voice was barely a whisper.

He turned his back. He didn't want to see her expression when he told her about the telephone call. "Regina is alive." He closed his eyes as he heard her sigh of relief. "But the kidnapper wants an exchange of hostages."

Parris stepped around Martin. "Who?" she asked, knowing, but needing to hear it from him.

"You. They'll release Regina, but only if you take her place."

"When? How much time do we have?"

"You're asking the impossible, Parris."

Her eyes narrowed. "I'm not asking any longer, Martin. I'm telling you…"

Martin gripped her shoulders, pulling her up hard to his chest. "You don't…"

"Don't ask, don't say this, and don't say that," she flung at him, her voice rising to match his runaway temper. "Dress like this, Parris, and don't forget to smile, Mrs. Cole. Please sit this way. Get up, Parris! Go to bed, Parris!" Her voice continued to escalate and the brown color disappeared from her eyes. "Not once since I've become the enviable Mrs. Martin Diaz Cole have I been allowed to be Parris."

She struggled to free herself from his iron grip. "Ever since I've known you I've suffered because of who I am. And because I had the misfortune of falling in love with you I've lived on a tightrope of fear. But do you want to know something, your lordship? I'm no longer the frightened awe-struck little girl of ten years ago. I'm tired of living in fear. This time Regina's involved and in no way will I permit her to experience what I've gone through." She paused to watch disbelief freeze his features. "You better tell whoever has my child that if they want me they can have me."

"You intend to give in to their demands."

"Hell, yeah!" she spat at him, ignoring the pain in his eyes.

"They'll kill you, Parris." Martin's voice was hoarse and shaky.

"Without Regina I am dead."

There was a sharp rap on the door before it swung open. "You'd better get out here, Martin. The news is out and the FBI are swarming all over the place!"

Martin released Parris, spinning around and following David. Someone had leaked the news of Regina's kidnapping.

The air was charged with static as the formal agents concluded their questioning and Vincent Daniels waited for answers. His red eyebrows rose an inch higher as he shook his head.

"The press has been hounding me, Martin. They want to know something. Anything."

Martin bowed his head, unable to face his press secretary. "Do they want the low-down on the madness affecting my private life or do they want the truth. Parris has been threatened with death three times, and now my baby has been kidnapped." He ran a hand over his face. "Tell them Regina Cole is missing."

Vince nodded. "What if the word kidnapping comes up?"

"You know nothing of a kidnapping," Martin insisted. "All you've been told is that the child has been reported missing."

"Then missing it is," Vince repeated. "Again, I'm sorry about the girl, Martin. If anything comes up I can't handle I'll call you on your private line."

Vincent Daniels never heard the low murmur of thanks as he closed the door and was escorted off the Cole property by a stoic agent.

There was a knock on the library door and Joshua opened it. Standing beside David was the person he'd been waiting for.

He extended his hand. "Thanks for coming."

"You owe me," replied the tall man with long black hair. He shook Joshua's hand, his golden eyes sweeping around the room, missing nothing. "Fill me in on everything and we'll see how quickly we can get this wrapped up."

Chapter 35

Only Martin's grip on her hand kept Parris from bolting when Matthew Sterling walked into the room. He was tall, taller than Martin, Joshua or David, and broader. There was something wild, almost savage, in the amber-green eyes under thick black eyebrows. His sun-browned skin was smooth where a short black beard didn't conceal his face. He held his head like a large cat, sniffing the air for the scent of his prey. He didn't sit, preferring to stand in a corner where he blended into the shadows.

"Is there anything about your ex-husband that would make him vulnerable?" Matt asked Parris. "Any bad habits or vices?"

Parris sucked in her breath, staring at Martin's profile. He tightened his grip on her fingers. "Owen was addicted to cocaine." All eyes were trained on her face. "It wasn't until after we were married that I discovered his addiction." Her gaze shifted, focusing on the crystal base of a table lamp. "It was the reason Owen was never able to perform sexually with me."

"You've never told anyone about his addiction?" Matt Sterling questioned.

She shook her head. "No one. I told him I wouldn't if he gave me my freedom."

"When was the last time you saw your ex-husband?" Matt continued with his questioning.

"I saw him once since I've returned to Florida." Parris felt the force of Martin's gaze on her face as she turned away from him. "He didn't see me. I was driving through Palm Beach and I saw him coming out of the condominiums on Bradley Place."

"L'Ermitage," Joshua said softly.

"When do we make the exchange?" Parris asked.

"There won't be an exchange," Martin declared with quiet emphasis.

A lump formed in Parris's chest. "They'll kill her," she cried out.

"They won't kill her," Joshua said. "It's you they want, not Regina."

"I don't believe you. None of you!" Her eyes were wild with fear. "You're playing Russian roulette with my child's life." She lashed out to strike Martin, but he caught her free hand, trapping her. "I hate you!" she screamed at him.

Martin held her effortlessly until she yielded to his superior strength. He buried his face in her hair. "I can't afford to lose you, darling."

A stabbing pain wouldn't permit her to breathe. "They'll kill my baby." She sobbed weakly against his chest.

Martin tightened his grip on her body. "We'll have more children, Parris. I would sacrifice ten Reginas for you." His hand curved under her chin. "I love you more than any baby we could ever have. If I lost Regina I could go on living. If I lost you again I couldn't," he confessed.

Parris saw the pain in his gaze. "You lost me before."

"I had no choice then, darling. Now I do. And if we lose Regina that's beyond the both of us. But as long as I'm alive I'll hold onto you until that is beyond me."

She melted against him, unaware that Joshua and Matt Sterling had slipped quietly from the room.

Only David remained, awed by the depth of his brother's love for his wife. He prayed he would never be tested where he would be faced with the dilemma of choosing between the woman he loved and the seed from his loins.

* * *

Word of Regina's kidnapping flashed across the television screen. Martin clenched his jaw as the news bulletin preempted regular programming. He punched the button on the remote.

Six days; it was now six days since Regina's abduction. Was she frightened? Had she been abused?

He walked out of the family room and made his way up the staircase to the bedroom where Parris lay, hiding herself away from him and the world.

She was right, he thought. She hadn't been allowed to be a wife, a mother or even to manage her own career. She had become a pawn for him in his bid to secure an elected office.

Parris was young, intelligent and beautiful. Women were beginning to emulate her style of dress and graceful gestures. And most of all he had been aware that having Parris as his wife only enhanced his image appreciably when he rethought her virulent tirades.

He slowed his steps, staring at the top of the stairs. What happened to their walks along the beach? The weekend sailing and fishing trips? And the late-night exotic meals over candlelight with soft music? And if he did win the election and embark on a political career would there ever be time for her, Regina and the other children they planned to have?

He had given Parris his name in marriage, his wealth, his child, his love yet not himself. And that was all she'd ever wanted from him. Just Martin Cole and nothing else.

Martin felt as if all of his burdens were lifted when he reached the top of the staircase. He had just made a decision which would change their lives.

"Parris?" He looked around the bedroom. Walking through the bedroom, he opened the door to the bathroom. Where could she have gone? He called out her name, his voice bouncing off the walls.

Martin bounded down the stairs, his heart pumping painfully in his chest. He was breathing heavily when he ran into the dining room. "Where's Parris?"

M.J. stared at him. "She went upstairs to take a nap."

"How long ago?"

M.J. shrugged a delicate shoulder. "Less than an hour ago."

"Where are you going?" Samuel asked.

"To find my wife."

Now Martin knew how his mother felt when she had to search the large house for Regina. Doors were swung open and slammed on their hinges. Silent servants shook their heads and gave him a blank stare when he asked if they saw Parris.

He was mindless with fright as he closed the door to the last room. He had searched the interior and now he headed outside.

Annoyance prickled his nerves as he walked through the darkened shadows of the garden with only a slip of a moon darting behind opaque clouds.

Wending his way through the maze of the boxwood garden, he swore under his breath. The Cole property encompassed twelve acres of land, and nearly one-fourth of it was made up of gardens: tropical, exotic Japanese and boxwood.

His agitation increased the more he searched. The agents were pulled after Joshua made a call to someone in Virigina. His request was confirmed and acknowledged within two hours, leaving the property unguarded.

Martin's cotton shirt was soaked through with moisture and he pulled it away from his chest. Relying totally on his heightened senses, he detected the subtle fragrance of different flowers, the crisp crunch of insects under his feet and the intermittent glow of a firefly. He brushed at the gossamer touch of flying night insects against his exposed face and arms.

The bright glow of the house and floodlights faded the deeper he intruded into the stillness and darkness of the garden.

"Damnit, Parris. Where the hell are you?" he whispered. A flash of light and the soft murmur of voices stopped him.

"You couldn't stay away, could you?" The raspy voice reverberated in the quiet night. "I told you what would happen to you if you told anyone about our little chat. I caught hell for not killing you, but this time I'll do what…"

Martin recoiled when he heard the sharp crack of flesh meeting flesh, then Parris's voice. "You low-life frog. You can't feel like a man until you abduct women and children. I could…" Her words were cut off by the sound of two slaps in rapid succession.

"Don't kill her yet," came another masculine voice, freezing Martin where he stood. There was more than one man in the garden with Parris.

The blood roared in his head. The moon slipped behind a veil of clouds, casting an eerie glow on the network of swirling knots of sculpted greenery.

Crouching lower, Martin moved forward, trying to remember in which direction he'd heard the voices. He was almost certain the two men could hear his heavy breathing as he made his way through the maze. A shadow moved on his left and he dropped lower, ready to spring.

"Careful, buddy. It's me."

"Josh." Relief was evident in his voice.

"Stay put," Joshua ordered in a low tone. "Matt and I will take it from here." Reaching out, he squeezed Martin's shoulder. "Your daughter is safe."

Martin sank down to the ground, pressing his head against a thick wall of shrubbery. His breath was coming so quickly he nearly panicked; he was hyperventilating. Tucking his knees to his chest, he lowered his head, then froze when he heard a blood-curdling scream of terror. There was another scream, then a deadly silence.

He waited and waited. He sat, frozen, until footsteps brought him to his feet. He saw Joshua, the front of his shirt stained with a darker color, leading Parris toward him. She moaned his name once before he gathered her to his chest. She was *safe*. Regina was *safe*.

"Get her up to the house while Matt and I look after our *friends*," Joshua ordered. His voice, though quiet, had an ominous quality. "They're pretty tough when it comes to bullying women and children. We're going to test their courage a little more before turning them over to the police."

Martin tightened his hold on his wife's shoulders. "Don't kill them. I want to make certain they spend the rest of their lives behind the walls of a prison."

"Remember, this is Florida. They may get the death penalty. Kidnapping, blackmail and attempted murder are serious charges. Wait about fifteen minutes before you call the police. Then get your family together. Ten years of blackmail and kidnapping will end tonight."

Parris clung to Martin, unable to believe she was still alive. It was over. No more stalkings, threats or living in fear. She had lived with the fear so long she knew it would take her a while before she could relax completely.

"Regina?"

"She's all right, darling. They found her. Joshua would give up his own life to bring her back to us." Lowering his head, he kissed her deeply. He had to reassure himself that Parris was still alive.

"Why didn't you tell me before that Joshua is your brother?" Her arm went around his waist as he led her toward the house.

Martin frowned in the darkness, staring at the large house ablaze with light and filled with both tender and bitter memories. "Joshua is not very proud of his Cole blood. Aside from my family only a few know his lineage. Maybe one day he'll tell you of his background."

They were silent as they walked arm-in-arm to the house. Parris took a deep breath, then walked through the door. She made her way to the suite of rooms where she'd spent the last six days. She couldn't bring herself to run up the stairs. Too many things had happened to her, to Regina, and she didn't trust her present state of mind. It was as if everything that had happened was a bad dream and she'd wake up to find everything as it was.

She stood in the doorway, watching Juliana as she pulled a lightweight blanket over a sleeping Regina's shoulders. Juliana glanced up, placing a finger over her lips. Parris nodded. She turned to go downstairs. Her baby was safe.

Parris waited with the other Coles. The cool interior of the antique-filled living room set the stage for Joshua when he strode in and closed the sliding double doors.

All conversation ceased as he stood, giving each person a slow examination as his eyes grew colder and forbidding. A handgun hung limply from the fingers of his left hand. Leaning against the door, he brought it up slowly.

"David, take Nancy and Juliana home." His voice was low and demanding.

"Who do you think you are, Joshua?" Juliana questioned.

"Take them out of here!" he ordered again.

David stared at his half-brother, then rose to his feet. Within seconds Joshua Kirkland had established his position as his older brother *and* his equal.

Juliana and Nancy gave Martin looks of desperation, seeking his assistance; however, Martin's expression was closed, and they followed David out of the living room.

All gazes were fixed on Joshua as he slid the doors closed for the second time. There was a chorus of sighs when he concealed the gun in his waistband behind his back.

Parris shivered and averted her gaze from the dark red stains on his shirt. The blood was a reminder of Matthew Sterling's way of dealing with the two men who had attempted to kill her. His razor-sharp knife was lethal and silent.

"It's too bad this family gathering couldn't be for a joyous occasion instead of the sickness and madness which has been allowed to run rampant for more than ten years," Joshua began.

"Get the hell out of my house!" Samuel ordered. He pushed away M.J.'s hand when she tried to keep him from lunging at Joshua.

The gun was back in Joshua's hand in a motion too quick for the human eye to follow. His lips were drawn back over his teeth. "I'd love to blow your sick head off, but I won't because I want you to live and wallow in guilt from the filth you've created." His gaze never wavered from Samuel's face. "Parris, meet my father and your blackmailer."

Chapter 36

Parris sagged limply on her chair, unable to believe what she was witnessing. It was like a scene from a Hollywood melodrama, and she'd laugh hysterically once it ended.

M.J. glared up at her husband. "I told you that you would come to regret your liaison with *that* woman. She was nothing but a tramp and…"

"That's enough about my mother," Joshua cut in.

M.J.'s delicate jaw snapped loudly, and she looked to Martin for support.

He stared at his mother, shaking his head. "Go on, Josh," he urged, closing his eyes.

"Sammy didn't want you to marry Martin," Joshua continued, staring at Parris's stricken face. "So he hired someone to frighten you away from Martin. He made certain to cover himself so nothing would be traced to him, but forgot there is no such thing as a perfect crime.

"It took Matt less than two minutes to get a name from Owen Lawson as to who came to him asking about his ex-wife. Our next informant proved to be a lot more resistant. He nearly drowned in his own blood, but he named Samuel Claridge Cole as the man who'd made him a rich man for doing his dirty work."

Martin's black eyes blazed with a sudden anger. "You're lying, Josh! You hate him so much you'd…"

"I'm not lying," Joshua shot back, his chest rising and falling in rage. "I am not lying," he repeated in a softer tone. "And how I feel about…" His gaze swung back to Samuel, narrowing as he studied the man whom he couldn't openly claim as his father. "How I feel about Samuel has nothing to do with the truth. And I'm telling you the truth when I say that he's responsible for having Parris abducted ten years ago."

Samuel crossed one leg over the other, smiling at Joshua. He patted his wife's hand as she moved closer to him on the love seat. "I'm going to give you an opportunity to leave my home before I call the police and have you forcibly removed."

Joshua replaced the gun behind his back, walking slowly toward Samuel. "You do that, old man. Right now there are three slugs in police custody who are willing to say anything to keep off death row."

Samuel's smile vanished. "You sick bastard. You'd make up any story to discredit me."

Joshua took several more steps toward Samuel. "You only got half of it right because I am your bastard, Samuel. But you're the sick one."

Martin sprang to his feet. "Enough of the name-calling," he warned quietly. His gaze swung to Joshua. "You have five minutes to tell what you've uncovered. And, Dad, you'll keep quiet until Josh is finished. The only thing I want to hear from you is the sound of your breathing."

"Martin, get him out of here," Samuel demanded.

"Father!" The single word exploded from Martin. "Parris, Regina and I have gone through hell for six days and it's going to end now. Tonight," he said slowly. He retook his seat and closed his eyes. "Talk, Joshua."

Joshua sat down on the sofa facing Samuel and M.J., turning slightly toward Parris. "You were right about the landscaper, Parris. He was hired to watch you. But he was only one link in the chain. Samuel managed to keep his hands clean while he hired someone to do his dirty work. The man responsible for hiring the landscaper was the one who contacted Owen Lawson. Your ex-husband never knew that the information he'd offered would be used to blackmail you. And when you were given the same amount of money as your divorce settlement Samuel hoped you'd think it was Lawson who was blackmailing you.

"The chain grew longer when the landscaper hired a hit man who had a pang of conscience when he discovered you were pregnant. He had no compunction about killing adults, but he drew the line when it came to babies."

Parris breathed quickly through parted lips, trying to slow down her runaway pulse. "What about the sniper and the snake?"

"Your stalker was responsible for both. He knew every move you made because Samuel passed along the information about Martin's campaign schedule."

"And the drugging?" she asked breathlessly.

"Samuel's personal flunky took care of that. He was at the fund-raiser. He hired the waiter and when Samuel brought you over to the bar that was the signal to give you a drink in a glass that had been set aside just for you."

"And Regina's kidnapping?" she whispered.

"That was your stalker's idea. His gambling debts were adding up and his bookie was putting pressure on him. Samuel never would've given the order to kidnap his own granddaughter. Correct me if I'm wrong, Samuel."

Martin watched his father's face during the interchange between Joshua and Parris. There was no surprise, no anger, no uneasiness. He sat, holding M.J.'s hand, eyes closed.

"Why, Father?" Martin was surprised at his own lack of emotion. It was as if something wouldn't permit him to feel anger. He hadn't wanted to believe Joshua, but before his father said a word in his own defense he knew Joshua had spoken the truth.

"She was going to take you away from ColeDiz," Samuel said, his eyes still closed. "All of my life I worked to make ColeDiz an empire, and when you met her you wanted to walk away from all of it."

"Parris had nothing to do with my leaving ColeDiz," Martin countered.

Samuel opened his eyes. "She was just like Teresa. She did to you what Teresa did to me. Teresa made me love her. I didn't want to love her, but I couldn't help it."

Martin stared at Joshua, remembering the stories he had heard about his father seducing a young woman who'd worked for him. When Teresa Maldonado discovered she was carrying Samuel Cole's child, he paid her to marry a stranger and sent her away so she wouldn't remind him of his adulterous affair. Seventeen years later she contacted her child's biological father. She needed his influence to help Joshua get into West Point.

"For seventeen years she never came to me to ask for anything," Samuel continued in a singsong tone. "Nothing for herself, but only for her boy." His eyes grew larger, giving him the look of someone crazed. "I hated her because she didn't need me for herself."

Joshua turned away, rather than look at his father. "It galled me that she had to come to you because I knew what it took for her to ask you for a favor."

"I loved her, Joshua," Samuel mumbled. "Believe it or not I loved her. Just like Martin. He told me he loved Parris when he only knew her for two months. But she didn't know I had her followed and knew every place she visited and every person she met. It was so nice with her gone, but then she came back." Lowering his head, he buried his face in his hands. "I would never harm Regina. She was too much like my M.J. My beautiful, beautiful M.J."

Martin studied his mother's face, noting the lack of surprise on her aristocratic features. His eyes widened with realization. "Why didn't you tell me Dad was behind this?"

M.J. raised her chin. "I couldn't. Sammy is my husband, and a wife doesn't betray her husband."

M.J.'s casual rationalization pulled Parris out of her stunned trance. "You sought to absolve him of his guilt by remaining silent while he tried to have me killed?"

The green lights flashed in her eyes. "I should hate you, but I can't because I don't want to end up with hate poisoning me the way it's done to you and Sammy. You don't have to worry about my reminding you of Joshua's mother because I'm leaving this house. Only death will bring me back."

She rose from a tapestry-covered chair in regal elegance and walked to the door. She stared back over her shoulder. "Joshua, I want you to take me to Jamaica in the morning. The sooner Regina and I are away from this place, the better it will be for both of us."

She missed the cold fury on Martin's face when she issued her request. Her hand was steady as she placed it on the door. "Doomed is the man who builds his empire by injustice and enlarges it by dishonesty." The door slid open and she was gone, Joshua following her.

Martin blinked once, then his wife vanished from sight. He sat in shocked silence, unable to believe all that had happened. It pained him to look at his parents.

"You've done to me what my most bitter enemy has been unable to do." His voice was low and deadly. "You've still lost me. With or without Parris." Rising to his feet, he walked out of the living room.

Martin stared at Parris's back. "You're leaving me."

"I'm leaving Florida, Martin." She turned to face him. "There's no way I can stay here. Not now."

"You can't run away."

"I'm not running away. I'm only going away for a while. I have to give myself time to let go of the pain." She sank down to the large bed where she'd shared her first Christmas with Martin. "I don't hate your parents. But if I stay I will. Regina is to never know what they've done to her, to me or to Joshua. The Coles are the only family she has and I know how important it is to have a family."

Martin stared at the woman he loved with all of his being. Her leaving him was killing him. And he was frightened. More frightened than he had ever been in his life, but he knew she was right. She couldn't stay.

"I won't stop you, Parris. But remember that I love you."

She nodded and turned away. Martin stared at her back, then walked out of the bedroom to find a place where he could grieve in private. The tears filling his eyes overflowed as he mourned in silence.

Martin watched Parris as she stood ramrod straight, waiting for the pilot's signal to board. He tightened his grip on his daughter's hand, refusing to look down for fear of losing his composure.

A group of reporters and photographers stood behind a fence, watching his every gesture. They waited for a clue which would reveal why Martin Cole was putting his wife and daughter on a private jet scheduled to land on an island in the Caribbean.

"We're being cleared for takeoff, buddy."

Martin continued to stare at Parris. "Take care of my girls, Josh."

Joshua nodded. "As soon as I see them settled I'll be back."

Martin exhaled, dreading the inevitable. Bending down, he swung Regina up in his arms, flashing a forced smile. "Are you going to live up to your promise to take care of your mother for me?"

Regina's dark eyes crinkled in laughter. "I'm not going to lose this bet, Daddy." She giggled when he rubbed his nose on her smooth cheek.

Martin tightened his grip on her body. "I love you so much, cupcake."

Regina squeezed his neck. "I love you too, Daddy."

He forcibly pried the child's arms from his neck and handed her to Joshua. One, two, three, four, five—he counted the steps that took him to Parris's side.

She was appearing in her last performance as the candidate's wife. Today she wore a white linen and silk blend suit with a single-buttoned hip length jacket over a slim skirt. The sun caught the fiery light of the emerald and diamonds earrings he had given her for Christmas and the matching necklace he had given her for her birthday.

Parris turned, mistaking his closed expression for indifference, and in that instant she would not permit her pain and longing to show. She managed a demure smile, successfully controlling the tremors coursing throughout her body.

"Let's make it look good for the press, Martin. We must not tarnish our image as the perfect…"

The harsh plunder of his mouth stopped her words and her breath. His lips and the bite of his fingers on her shoulders revealed his anger. He'd agreed to let her go because he was powerless to stop her, and not for any other reason.

She pulled out of his punishing grip and walked quickly to the plane. Joshua and anyone close enough to view her face interpreted the tears staining her cheeks as a sign of sorrow, not pain.

Joshua took her arm, helping her up the steps and into the aircraft. Not once did Parris look back—for if she had the expression on Martin's face would have told her what he was unable to verbalize at that moment.

Epilogue

July. August. September. October. November. It had finally come. And it was gone. The election was over and there were no winners. At least not for Parris.

She stood on the beach, facing the clear waters of the Caribbean, arms raised to catch the warm breezes caressing her face. Her unbound hair lifted, brushing her cheeks.

So many things had changed in the short time since she'd come: Regina had turned ten and Joshua felt comfortable enough to reveal his childhood.

Raising her face to the sky, she closed her eyes, reveling in the peace she discovered. She wanted to stay in Jamaica forever.

"But not without Martin," she whispered to the wind.

She continued her stroll down the beach. She wanted to push all thoughts of Martin out of her mind, but she'd been unsuccessful. His calls every morning and every night would not allow her to forget him. However, as the days changed, as did her body, she carried his memory and his life.

The deep violet and navy blues gave way to streaks of lavender, then mauve until the pale pink and light hues of blue brightened the heavens, heralding a new day.

Birds sailed the wind currents, seeking early morning morsels. Parris turned to retrace her soft impressions in the sand, seeking out her own breakfast.

She was so involved in placing her bare feet in the already-made impressions before the incoming tide swept them away, erasing the evidence forever, that she did not see the dark figure looming before her until it was too late.

Their gazes met and locked as her heart turned over in joy. She tried denying that she cared, she loved him, but his very nearness said differently. Not once since she boarded the plane had she stopped loving him.

She tore her stunned gaze away from his graying dark curling hair, lifting gently from broad shoulders. He was so much like the first time they had met she thought her mind had conjured him up. His hair was long, his face clean-shaven and he was dressed entirely in black.

Martin's emotions were spinning out of control. His hungry eyes moved over the straightened hair tossed about her face by the wind, and the amber and green of her large eyes in a delicately sculpted face. His gaze dropped to the fullness of her breasts, and lower still to the swelling against the fabric of her white cotton dress.

He stood poised, hands shoved into the pockets of his slacks, waiting for her to make the first overture. Turning, Parris moved away from him and continued walking.

Martin fell in step beside her. He smiled, acknowledging her challenge. She was not going to make it easy for him. "Good morning, Mrs. Cole."

"Is it really?"

"Of course it is," he replied, stealing a glance at her enchanting profile. "I'm back and we can get on with our lives now."

She stopped, frowning. "Just like that, Martin. You come back when you damn well please and expect me to jump to your command. Sorry, mister. Not this time."

She was unaware of the tempting picture she made as the rising sun bathed her in a glow of pink and gold. Martin reached over and laid his outspread fingers over the slight roundness of her belly. He ignored the rush of breath from her parted lips. His black eyebrows lifted slightly.

"I spoke to you twice every day and you never told me. Were you going to have this one and also not tell me?"

She pushed his hand away. "If you'd been with me I would've told you the day it was confirmed. All I wanted was a word that you cared about me more than the power you've been chasing."

Reaching out, he caught her hand. "Every time I spoke to you I wanted you to tell me that you needed me; you needed me more than I needed the power. All you had to say was *come* and I would've walked away, telling everyone that personal problems wouldn't permit me to continue as a candidate."

Her eyes widened in surprise. "I couldn't do that to you. It had to be your decision, Martin, not mine. We must always allow the other the freedom to be what we want to be. With you it was becoming a politician."

Martin sank down to the soft white sand, pulling her down with him. He settled her on his lap, a hand cradling her belly. Burying his face in her hair, he sighed heavily.

"I lost and Eliot Howard lost," he said quietly. He smiled. "I believe Russell Baker will be a good governor."

Shifting, she stared up at him. New lines were etched around his heavy-lashed black eyes. "What happens now, Martin?"

He placed a gentle kiss on her forehead. "Are you referring to my brief affair with politics?"

"Yes," she sighed softly.

"It's over, my darling." He looked over her head, staring at the calm blue-green waters stretching out and touching the horizon. "Joshua has decided to try his hand in hotel management here in Ocho Rios and has asked me to become a partner. We've talked about putting up a string of lovely little bungalows in tropical colors of pink, yellow and blue with red-tiled roofs. Do you think you'd be interested in decorating the interiors?"

Her pulse raced like the fluttering wings of a delicate butterfly. Her sparkling clear brown eyes searched his familiar features, unable to hide the naked love she felt for him. Lowering her head, she gave him a seductive look through her lashes.

"I think that can be arranged."

A long brown finger tilted her chin. "This time it's for real, darling."

It was later, much later when they finally returned to the house to make plans for their future.

Martin was unable to dispel the urge to celebrate his final victory. He'd accepted the ultimate challenge and won—as a candidate for love.

NATIONAL BESTSELLING AUTHOR

ROCHELLE ALERS

INVITES YOU TO MEET THE BEST MEN...

Close friends Kyle, Duncan and Ivan have become rich,
successful co-owners of a beautiful Harlem brownstone. But
they lack the perfect women to share their lives with—until
true love transforms them into grooms-to-be....

Man of Fate
June 2009

Man of Fortune
July 2009

Man of Fantasy
August 2009

ARABESQUE®

www.kimanipress.com
www.myspace.com/kimanipress

KPRABMSP

A little luck is all it takes....

NATIONAL BESTSELLING AUTHOR

ROCHELLE ALERS

Childhood friends Kyle, Duncan and Ivan have become rich and successful, though they lack the perfect women to share their lives with—until true love transforms them into grooms-to-be!

When Ava Warrick dents Kyle Chatham's vintage Jag, her lack of interest in him only piques his interest. And as friendship gives way to cozy dinners and blissful nights, Kyle's sure Ava's his soul mate. Now he has to convince this love-wary beauty that their passion is anything but an accident!

Every wedding has a bride and groom. Now here come...The Best Men

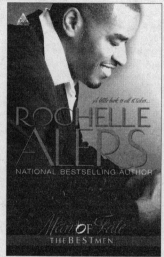

MAN OF FATE

Book #1 in
The Best Men trilogy

*Coming the first week of June 2009
wherever books are sold.*

ARABESQUE®

KPRA1600609

**www.kimanipress.com
www.myspace.com/kimanipress**

For love you have to risk it all....

NATIONAL BESTSELLING AUTHOR

ROCHELLE ALERS

Childhood friends
Kyle, Duncan and Ivan
have become rich and
successful, though they
lack the perfect women to
share their lives with—until
true love transforms them
into grooms-to-be!

Love-wary Tamara Wolcott
has good reason to be
cautious of men—but after
being trapped in an elevator
with sexy financial whiz
Duncan Gilmore, she's
willing to reconsider! But
is Duncan willing to let her
into his life?

**Every wedding has a bride
and groom. Now here
come...The Best Men**

MAN OF FORTUNE
Book #2 in The Best Men trilogy

*Coming the first week of July 2009
wherever books are sold.*

KPRA0500709

www.kimanipress.com
www.myspace.com/kimanipress

The ultimate bachelor just met his match...

NATIONAL BESTSELLING AUTHOR

ROCHELLE
ALERS

Childhood friends
Kyle, Duncan and Ivan
have become rich and
successful, though they
lack the perfect women to
share their lives with—until
true love transforms them
into grooms-to-be!

No woman has ever
gotten past the wall that
Ivan Campbell has built
around himself—until he
meets Nayo Goddard.
Suddenly the love-'em-and-
leave-'em bachelor wants
more. Only problem is...
Nayo doesn't! This time,
Ivan may be the one left
heartbroken.

Every wedding has a bride
and groom. Now here
come...The Best Men

MAN OF FANTASY

Book #3 in The Best Men trilogy

*Coming the first week of August 2009
wherever books are sold.*

www.kimanipress.com
www.myspace.com/kimanipress

KPRA1640809

**The thirteenth novel in
the successful *Hideaway* series...**

NATIONAL BESTSELLING AUTHOR

ROCHELLE ALERS

Secret Agenda

When Vivienne Neal's "perfect life" is turned
upside down, she moves to Florida to take a job
with Diego Cole-Thomas, a powerful CEO with
an intimidating reputation. Vivienne's job skills
prove invaluable to Diego, and on a business trip,
their relationship takes a sensual turn. But when
threatening letters arrive at Diego's office, he
realizes a horrible secret can threaten both of
them—and their future together.

"There's no doubt that Rochelle Alers is a compelling
storyteller who has the ability to weave romance with
the delicate subtlety of Monet."
—*Romantic Times BOOKreviews* on *HIDEAWAY*

*Coming the first week of May 2009
wherever books are sold.*

ARABESQUE®

**www.kimanipress.com
www.myspace.com/kimanipress**   KPRA1350509

National bestselling author

ROCHELLE ALERS

Naughty

Parties, paparazzi, red-carpet catfights...

Wild child Breanna Parker's antics have
always been a ploy to gain attention from
her diva mother and record-producer father.
As her marriage implodes, Bree moves to
Rome. There she meets charismatic Reuben,
who becomes both her romantic and business
partner. But just as she's enjoying her
successful new life, Bree is confronted
with a devastating scandal that threatens
everything she's worked so hard for....

*Coming the first week of March 2009
wherever books are sold.*

KIMANI PRESS™

www.kimanipress.com
www.myspace.com/kimanipress

KPRA1280309